A HEART as RED as PAINT

JENNIFER KROPF

FOR ELLIE LYNN

The one who petitions the One who listens

WINTER

WENTCHESTER COVE

ROOM 406

THE RED KINGDOM

CHOCOLATE

FACTORY

THE GREEN KINGDOM

THE FESTIVAL

POLAR TERRITORY

THE THREE KINGDOMS OF THE EAST

DWARVE'S COZY COTTAGE

MIKAL'S HOME

THE WHITE KINGDOM

THE LIBRARY

THE DUNES

WATERLOO CANADA

NORTH (ISH)

LEFT OTHER LEFT

TRY TURNING AROUND

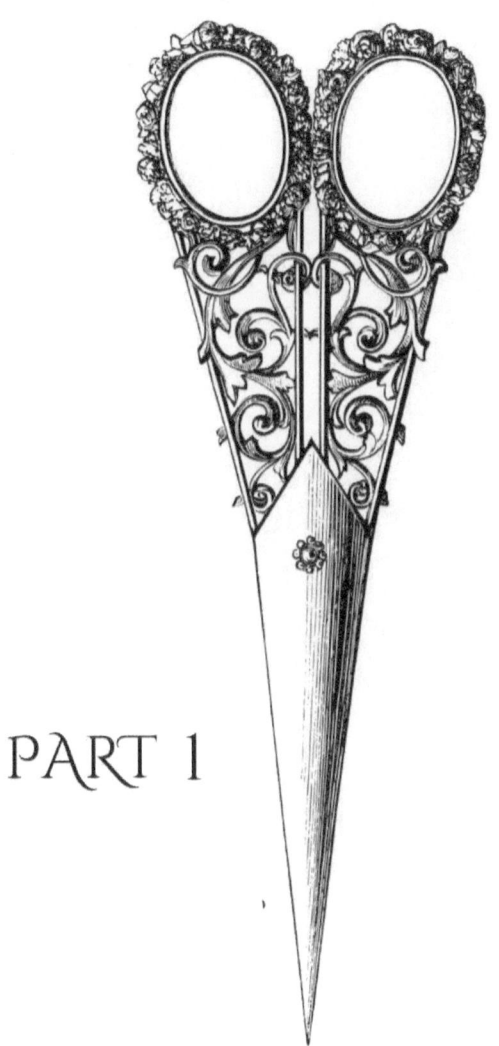

PART 1

THE
STORYTELLER

$\mathcal{A}$ lullaby is how this story begins.

A multihued song of a saint bursting from a heart that had sung once, then twice, then had never truly stopped. 'Twas a hymn saturated with intercession for many seasons and creamed to a milk of revival. As the wise woman was stirred to raise an anthem in the day's hushed middle, she was alert, listening for the signs of the times. Her song sailed the high seas, plunging through ice and snow, tumbling around the walled forces of ignorance and cruelty. It reached out to a young Patrolman on the verge of his death, whom the believers had come to call Zane Cohen; a boy who had found himself pinned beneath a wicked force which had arrived to bring upon his agonizing end.

The sprinting song drove into the boy's chest, a blade of mist and comfort for his last seconds, soothing the ocean of colours collapsing into darkness.

The song still rings.

Quiet, can you hear it?

HMM… IT SEEMS WE'VE LOST OUR SECOND PROLOGUE.

HOW ODD. PERHAPS IT WILL TURN UP SOMEWHERE ELSE.

Chapter,
The First

Over a plain of grass darkened by night skies, Lucas Leutenski raced. Golden eyes wild, and smile nowhere to be found, he stumbled and clutched his staff to himself as he sprinted past the gardens towards the stained-glass domes and copper doors.

He burst through the entrance with a commotion, staggering to the middle of the room to whirl and raise his weapon. His hands trembled as he backed through the unlit lobby and crashed into a table, causing his staff to fly from his grip. When he swiveled to grab it, he sprang back at the sight of a pale-skinned Greed staring in through the window.

Two more Greed seeped from the shadows, already inside. Lucas looked to his weapon on the floor, then to the wall at his right.

He sprang for the wall, thrusting a gold-stamped button hidden amidst the copper details.
Bells erupted through the darkness.

Two things told me that something was wrong in Winter. The first was a dream I had five weeks ago that ended in a clanging symphony of church bells. The second was *this*.

No clatter or announcement warned me he was coming; he was just there—a cold presence outside my window in a robe that fluttered like a curtain and blanketed the moonlight. I shouldn't have recognized him—we had never actually met—but I knew he'd been here before because the storm in the street swept into a tunnel the moment he arrived. The gray clouds breathed toward my window where he waited, and my bedroom filled with still, chilled air as it had only once before.

Whoever this fluttering phantom was, he was the same being who had delivered my summons from the Crimson Court last year, pegged it to my window with a splinter, and then slithered away into the storm before I could get a look at him. There was a crack in the glass still, one that had disappeared for a while after the intersect had closed. It seemed to have found its way back now.

It was clear the ghostly creature wanted to talk. Unfortunately for him, I couldn't get past his wispy body of air, or the mask of shadow hovering where a face was supposed to be.

So, I stood there, in the middle of my bedroom in nothing more than a slinky, silk pajama set, breathing a whisper of thanks that Kaley had fallen asleep on the couch downstairs in front of the TV and had left me to find this other-worldly monster alone.

I rolled a tiny black pearl over my fingers as I stared, where, in return, he stared back at me. Ten other similar gems bowled in the drawer of my nightstand, placed there one by one after an unusual treasure hunt led me to believe they were being left out for me on purpose. There was a red gem too, and a green one, and an octangular black one.

The rest of my family slept in peace, safe as long as I didn't include them in whatever this smoke-creature had come for.

With that in mind, I walked to the window. I failed to unclasp the latch the first time, and I paused to wipe a bead of sweat from my temple.

I'm Helen Bell, the Trite who faced Mara Rouge in Wentchester Cove.

The squeak of the hinges prickled my ears when the window slid open. With a dramatic wave of my arm, I welcomed the presence inside, assuming he was going to come in whether I invited him or not. But the vapour stayed where he was as the wind broke into my room, brushing my hair off my bare shoulders, and tugging my night tank against my body.

"What do you want?" I called, stuffing the pearl into the pocket of my shorts. I folded my arms, bracing against the current as shivers scurried over my skin.

It was a long, bothersome wait before the smoke-being spoke. I shifted my footing, wondering if he was studying me. Wondering if he even realized how inappropriate this late-night visit was.

"With me, comes a sequence of warnings," the vapour's

7

voice was as deep as the thunderous storm, "in the count of three."

It took all my self-control not to react to the vague, weird answer. "Okay," I said. "Who sent you to *warn* me?"

As I trembled in the cold, the vapour-being swept in through the window, filling my room with mist. My nails dug into my arms.

"I've left gifts so you might believe what I can do. Simple black sea stones, all but three. A single ruby, an emerald, and an onyx. The three warnings." He disregarded my question.

"Warnings of what? And who are you?"

Another pause. "I am a Timepiece of Winter future, Winter present, and Winter past. Once, I wandered the Midnight Forest for one thousand seasons. Now, the Forest wants me back." The Timepiece tilted his hood. "I've come because our fates are interwoven."

I really couldn't decide if I should be scared or amused; the storm he conjured was really throwing me off. I eyed the mist quivering at his hem. "That is why I bring the warnings," he said. "In the order of one ruby, one emerald, and one onyx—"

"Yes. You said that part already," I muttered. "Like a hundred times."

I huffed and scrubbed my eyes. "Tell me your warnings then, and if you don't mind, I'd prefer you leave and don't come back to my house. My family is here."

The Timepiece stared. "Very well."

With a sweep over the floor, he returned to the window where the shrills of slapping air strained to plunge in. "It is against the laws of the time overseers to speak of the future precisely as it is; to speak a name, or of a specific occurrence before it comes to pass. Therefore, I shall deliver your warnings in the form of a puzzle. Solve the puzzle and you will see the future in time to change it," he began.

Despite how much this felt like a blatant lure, he had my full attention.

"Listen carefully, as these three hearts will contribute to your destruction when you pass back into the wintersphere." His whisper sailed the room, and I started.

"Wait, what—"

"These are they: a heart as black as a viper, a heart as red as paint, and a heart green with envy. Three beating hearts, inside three beings."

My lashes batted. And then, I laughed.

It was too loud to be polite, but for some reason all I could think about was that moment last year when I'd come out of the key room at Wentchester Cove. Mara Rouge's entire Red Army had been scattered like a bunch of flies and Elowin had barely lifted a finger. Now this Timepiece was trying to put on a verbal juggling act with mysterious riddles to scare me—probably into doing something for him. I wasn't going to fall for that.

"That's it?" I asked. "You must not have heard: Winter doesn't need me back until the Rime Folk start to forget the sacred truths. But thank you for the warnings anyway."

I thought that was the end of our discussion. I was looking forward to sealing the window, drawing the drapes, and dragging Kaley half-asleep up to bed.

But the Timepiece had gone dead-still at my cackling. My smile slipped away as the seconds passed and he didn't speak.

"You will enter the wintersphere, *soon*," he finally said. "Once you do, we shall have this conversation again."

Something pinched my forearm and I jumped. When I looked, I saw a bronze circle take shape over my wrist, a thread-thin hand stretching down the middle, and strokes around the circumference. It looked like a numberless clock.

The Timepiece didn't bid me a good night. He left with a wisp into the moonlit dark, collecting the storm back into himself, turning his back upon where I stood.

"Great," I muttered, scowling down at the new glittering tattoo on my flesh. "I ticked him off."

Chapter,
The Second

It wasn't normal for me to have midnight rendezvous with cloud monsters at my window, but for days there had been signs that something was coming.

The first black pearl I found was waiting for me on a desk in biology class. I nearly threw the gem out, but it looked expensive and I figured the student who sat in the desk before me might come back for it.

But then I found another pearl at my house the next morning while Winston, Kaley and I were scrambling to catch the bus; tucked into my shoe and giving me a *Princess and the Pea* moment when I slid my heel in.

A third pearl was served atop my coffee lid at the drive thru that night. That was the gem that had given the game away—the one that made me realize no one else could see them and someone was leaving me a trail. Grandma had passed the coffee to me in the back seat of her car and hadn't batted an eye at the gemstone rolling around the perimeter of the cap. Kaley's coffee hadn't gotten a pearl on it.

There were eight more after that, waiting for me in all the places I went: one on the cafeteria table at lunch, another on the shelf of the school library in front of the book I went to find, another waiting upon the random seat I chose on the bus. It didn't take a genius to figure out that whoever was leaving me this trail already knew exactly where I'd be before I got there.

It wasn't even December yet—things weren't supposed to get weird so soon. But nothing about Winter had ever happened the way I'd expected, so maybe I shouldn't have been so surprised.

My brain rattled with visions of the night-visitor as I trudged into school the day after his arrival. I melted in my winter coat the moment the heaters blasted over me, tossing a lap of my hair into my mouth. Construction paper pine trees lined the halls above the lockers to remind everyone the holidays were nearly upon us, and tacky Christmas music rang from the static-laden announcement speakers between every class. It was as though everything around me was working together to drive me crazy. Especially the pearls.

In English class, I got stuck in the cursed seat beside the window where it was always cold, but I wouldn't have seen the twinkle in the snowbank at any other desk. My gaze snapped to it, but I found only foggy glass and fresh flakes drifting over the schoolyard.

For the rest of the class, my stare was glued to that spot where I was sure a set of bright blue eyes had peeked from the snow.

By the end of last period, my lips throbbed from biting

them together. The snow rabbits were the scum of the earth, but even so, the thought that I might have seen one ignited a hint of optimism in my chest that I never thought such an irritating creature could muster.

On my way out of school, I passed beneath the old *Hope for Emily Parker* banner whose once vibrant red words had faded to pink. I kept my head down and pulled a piece of lint off my sweater as the banner flapped in my wake. That obnoxious sign had hung limp for well over a year now and I wondered why no one had taken it down.

The next morning, my rabbit-paranoia skyrocketed. My locker was in shambles; my books had been tossed and my pencil case hung open with its contents strewn along the locker floor. There was no way this was chance—now I knew for sure those rabbits were messing with me. But how in the world had they managed to get inside my *locked* locker? Why could they walk through some things, like Trite people, but still tear apart a solid textbook?

I huffed and started piecing my belongings back together, shaking my head as I scolded myself for getting so feverish. I shouldn't have had any "Wintery" feelings coursing through my veins. But since the first fleck of snow had fallen on Waterloo, I hadn't been able to stop asking myself the obvious questions: what if every year when the intersect opened I had to dodge the invisible dwarves, silver birds, and Winterblood elves who filled the streets downtown? And more importantly, what if Zane never came to see me?

He had no reason to come. Zane never said he would visit; he only swore he would return to the Trite world the day Winter started to forget the Truth. And after we'd brought the orb to Wentchester Cove and trumpeted a message of hope across Winter, I guessed it would be a while before that happened.

But the Timepiece of Winter past, present, and future—or whatever that flappy ghost had called himself—said I would go back. I still hadn't decided how to feel about that.

When I was certain no one was behind me, I lifted my sleeve with the eraser end of a pencil to see the world's most sparkly tattoo. The arrow ticked down a notch, reminding me of a time that was coming—soon if I was understanding the clock correctly. I didn't know what was supposed to happen when the time ran out.

I hadn't yet discovered if people from my world could see the tattoo. I'd spent the last eleven months trying to deduce why certain things from Winter were visible to the Trites, and others weren't. When the intersect had closed, my orb and *Shammah* necklace became visible to my family. After scribbling my theories on paper, I'd concluded that it was a matter of possession. Once something belonged to me, it belonged to the Trite world, too. Whatever still belonged to Winter, remained invisible. At least, that was my theory. I'd hoped to run some tests when the intersect opened up again, but I'd gotten preoccupied with the pearls.

Dropping my sleeve, I drew in a long breath and imagined Zane here, explaining to me what the clock tattoo was, and giving me advice on how to deal with the rabbits ransacking my locker. With all these unexplained sightings of the snow-world, I bristled at the thought of becoming the clueless "peg out of its shell" again. I thought I'd buried that nickname in the snow with Mara Rouge.

My locker made a loud *clang* through the hall as I

slammed it.

"*Fight!*" The hitching voice of an adolescent cracked over the people herding past in both directions, but at the announcement everyone seemed to change course all at once—students rushed towards the lifting grunts and loud crashes of bodies hitting metal lockers. I would have slipped away unnoticed, but I caught a glimpse of a fitted olive football jersey with block numbers on the back: *51*. He was pulled into a headlock after jamming his fist into the gut of another boy, and I stopped.

My feet squeaked against the floor as I spun back, trotting towards the smell of sweat and egos where heated threats were being yelled from strained throats. Bodies created a wall of flesh when I reached them, some cheering on the carnage, others angled in laughter.

"Winston!" I yelled, but my call was a drop in a sea of raised voices.

I jammed the corner of my history textbook into the side of the boy in front of me until he sprang out of the way, and I pushed my frame through the fence of howling teenagers. I was a breath away from shouting Winston's name again, but a gasp came out instead.

My brother's nose was a faucet, blood drenching the collar of his jersey. But it was a speckle in comparison to the other boy. Winston's opponent was an artwork of crimson body fluid and pink, swelling flesh.

Winston's fist—a rock hurtling towards his enemy— nearly collided with the other boy who spun out of the way. The boy thrust his own fist back in retaliation, landing his knuckles against Winton's cheekbone.

I couldn't take it; I knew I might take a stray punch, but

I swooped in before Winston could dish out another blow.

His hand was raised, fist gripped and white as bone, and he barely had time to stop before it would have dislocated my jaw, but he lurched to a halt with his fingers hanging inches from my mouth. Winston's chest rose and fell like a pump; he had to blink to register what he was seeing—*me.*

"Get out my way." It wasn't a kind threat.

"*No.*" I shot back, skin warming.

His blond lashes fluttered, but it did nothing to smother the fire behind his eyes.

I folded my shaking arms. What was he going to do? Hit a girl? In front of all these people?

The boy behind me took the opportunity to surrender and stumbled into the chanting crowd. The moment he was gone, I swatted Winston's still-raised hand aside, giving him a look only our mother had ever managed to summon until this moment. "Should I even ask what happened?"

"No." Winston turned to leave before I could scold him further, his olive jersey blending into the dozens of other school sports and music uniforms as students clapped for him like he'd provided some rich entertainment on an otherwise monotonous day.

I let out the breath I was holding as people slid around me to carry on now that the excitement was over.

I hated that I was partially responsible for Winston's behavior. I hated that he hadn't been the same since I'd tried to tell him parts of where I'd disappeared to last year, and it hadn't gone well.

Letting my heavy shoulders drain, I watched the crowd fizzle away, but stayed in the middle of the hall until I no longer felt like a pot boiling on a hot stove.

Why did Winston have to become the exact sort of self-absorbed high school bully I hated? A year ago, he hadn't been stupid enough to throw punches at people to defend his rank at school. Now, he reeked of idiot.

I awoke from a restless sleep to my grandmother's soft rapping on the bedroom door. When I opened my eyes, they shifted to the window first, eyeing the long crack webbing across the glass, and then to Kaley sleeping across the room. But when the old woman poked her head around the door, her gray hair spiralling from where it had escaped her bun, she whispered, "There's something wrong with the toilets!" Her wiry glasses slid down her nose.

I stifled a moan and pulled off my sheets, knowing that if Grandma was coming to wake me, it was because she'd already tried everything she knew and there was no one else to ask. I stuffed my toes into my slippers and shuddered against the chilly morning air as I dragged myself down the hall after her.

Grandma led the way into the bathroom, and only then did I notice that her hands were pink from whatever she'd been doing to try and fix the plumbing.

I glanced down at the porcelain bowl and my eyes narrowed.

Pearls. *Dozens* of them were crammed into the bowl like tiny, black bubbles with the water sitting idly on top. My heart did a twist as frustration worked its way in. It seemed my little problem with the Timepiece was going to affect

Grandma, too. My grandmother would suffer paying for a plumber, who wasn't going to be able to fix the issue because his Trite eyes wouldn't *see* it, and frankly, it was money she couldn't spare.

Maybe I shouldn't have laughed in the Timepiece's face.

"I'll deal with it," I said to Grandma. "Go back to bed. You look exhausted."

"Dear, I grew up on a farm where being tired was considered a laughable excuse." She tossed an old cloth on the vanity countertop. "We're going to have to get someone in here to fix this."

"No, Grandma, I'll fix it," I said again. "Just..." How was I going to haul out all those pearls with her watching? "If you don't mind, maybe you could put on some coffee? I'm barely awake yet."

The old woman sighed. The wrinkles around her eyes had deepened these last months, and it wasn't just the toilet problem that had done it. I'd noticed Grandma finding it more difficult to get up the stairs, to be on her feet all day, and to keep the yard maintained. The weeds had gotten out of control this summer—I'd tried to hassle Winston about dealing with the gardens and cutting the grass, but he was such a hothead about it, I figured it was easier to just do it all myself. I'd been shovelling the driveway since the snow came, too.

"I must be losing my mind," my grandmother's mutter wasn't quiet enough for me to miss. "I used to fix the plumbing all the time."

A new ache found my chest when she shuffled down the hall and descended the creaky stairs to the kitchen. My grandmother had been my advocate. My defender when

18

Winston had been awful about everything all year. And this was what she got for it—toilets plugged by invisible gems and the crippling wrath of age.

"You're not losing your mind," I whispered toward the empty hall.

I grabbed the garbage bin to toss away the wretched black gems.

In my first class, the teacher rambled on about something related to the rooftops of the parliament buildings originally being a copper-red, and *blah, blah, blah*, Canadian history.

My precious double note taking had taken a dive since June, as I no longer knew what classes I shared with Emily Parker in this new school year and the reality had set in that she likely hadn't absorbed a single word I'd read aloud to her anyway. I used to be the one everyone would ask for help when they missed a day of school, but now no one bothered.

I still visited Emily Parker but for entirely different reasons now. Her hospital room had turned into a hideaway to drink my morning coffee in peace on Saturdays, and normally there was at least one monthly therapy session where I plunged into her room, barely wasting a second before spilling my guts about how everything this year had gone for me.

After history class, I opened my locker and three of my books spilled out, tiny shreds of torn-up pages peppering my feet like snow. I released a groan as glossy textbook paper floated down the hall in the wake of people rushing by.

Those dang rabbits. I would eat them.

When I slammed my locker shut, I jumped—electric blue eyes looked at me from where my door had been. I nearly dropped the notebooks in my arms, but his hand swooshed out and caught them.

I gaped. I knew those eyes.

My instincts told me Zane was standing in front of me— the striking blue irises, the raven-black Patrol jacket, the liquor-coloured staff... My heart took off at the sight of a Patrolman standing amidst the lockers and muddy floor slush.

But it wasn't Zane.

"Season's Greetings." The boy's sizeable lips pulled into a smile, putting a soft wrinkle in his cheek. When the strap of my bag began to slide down my shoulder, he reached over to take it from me before it could hit the floor.

The Patrolman's hair was darker than Zane's—a rich coffee colour tousled with curls—and his jaw was different; more rounded. His uniform hung loose in different places, but his eyes...his eyes were the same.

"Sorry if I startled you, Trite, but I didn't want to interrupt your agitated book-tossing." His voice had a naturally low tone, but my knees went weak at the sound of his accent. He was practically glowing in comparison to this dull hallway and the blurs of olive uniforms; the fastened black buttons of his jacket, the hooked Patrol staff, the silken laces on curled-toe boots...But I didn't recognize him from last year.

At my ogling, the Patrolman cracked another smile. "My name is Eliot Gray," he said. "But before I say anything else, I should remind you that no one else can hear or see me." His electric eyes flickered over the reaction paling my face.

I slapped my jaw shut and tilted toward my locker, though there was no hiding how I fumbled to get the lock back open.

"I actually owe you a measure more of an apology than that, Miss Bell. There's been a shift in the Winter winds. I'm here to take you into the care of the Patrol, and away from this…" His finger twirled as he looked around for a moment, eyeing the tacky construction paper trees. "…academy."

The lock slid from my fingers. My pulse magnified in my wrist as it became abundantly clear what the tattoo was counting down to.

"In fact…I'm not really allowed to take *no* for an answer," he said.

"Of course you aren't." I kicked the locker with my toe, officially giving up on it. "Are you here because I'm being *followed*," my whispers weren't concealed enough and someone a few lockers down craned their neck to watch my lunacy, "by that stormy wind-monster?"

But Eliot Gray lifted a dark eyebrow. "The details of your return are complicated. Really, it's better if I just show you."

"Show me—"

He took my hand and a vision filled my head, so vivid I thought we'd teleported to another place.

My surroundings transformed to the inside of a dark house. Familiar copper-threaded tapestries and old books lined the walls; difficult to see in the nighttime. The scent of fresh bread from stone ovens lingered, and I was sure I was there, breathing in the lush fragrance of the flower gardens outside of Mikal's home.

*Wait…I've seen this moment before…*I tried to say it, but

my voice wouldn't work.

"Brace yourself, Miss Bell," the Patrolman warned me from outside the vision, a mere echo in the background.

As he said it, the air turned cold. A perforated metal barrier slid closed in front of me with a rusty screech. Through the decorative slits, I watched someone burst through the front door and whirl around with a Patrol staff in his grip. A slice of silver moonlight bleached his face as he backed up, his topaz gaze fixed on the door. Lucas Leutenski's body was rigid. He collided with a table and his staff tumbled from his hand, rolling across the floor.

Two slender, white-skinned creatures emerged from a dark corner of the room in bare feet, carrying bows mounted with ice-arrows.

I held my breath as Lucas abandoned his weapon and sprang for the wall, striking a gold button camouflaged into the wall-mural, and chimes erupted through Mikal's home like deep cathedral bells over a city.

Scarlet fire burst from the shadows, slamming Lucas against the wall where he collapsed into a heap on the floor. My heart wrenched as I tried to move, to yell, but my limbs weren't my own.

Frost coated the room like veins, burning my nose with the scent of sour cranberries. In the shadow, I could vaguely make out a man with long, diamond-white hair. The darkness hid his face.

The Greed slinked along the floor, tilting their bows down toward Lucas's exposed throat. I wanted to pound against the metal grate before me to wake him up.

"You have no power here, Asteroth." A new voice swept in like music; a strong, warm current. Mikal's buttery eyes stole a look at Lucas's still form as he emerged from the hall into the moonlight. "I'm sure you felt your enchantments weaken as soon as you stepped onto the grass. Perhaps you and I can negotiate a way to release the boy from your sights."

Mikal was answered with silence. As the Patrol Commander stood there, his face changed, his irises sinking to sunset-orange, "I see."

His gaze dropped to where blood from Lucas's face puddled into a blossom on the floor. "I will make it count, then. I'd like a deal; my life spares his. You will be bound to let him live when this is over," he said.

Silence. Then, a voice whispered from the shadows, splitting into two beastly strands. "Deal."

I tried to scream.

"A witness will share what happens here." Mikal paused as he eyed the shadows. "I know who you really are," he added. "And all your ancient knowledge will not save you in the end."

Mikal lowered to his knees.

The Greed to his left barred its teeth. "We have waited many seasons to see you this way, Mikal Migraithe," it whispered. The moon reflected off the creature's fangs.

"Glory to Elowin." The Patrol Commander smiled.

A sharp blast of fire roared over Mikal too fast for me to grasp that this was it, that this was the end. The last thing I saw was Mikal closing his eyes to accept it.

The cyclone left nothing behind—all that remained was a hint of smoke and a flutter of glistening snowflakes.

The vision was torn from me and my voice returned. I clutched my throat, swallowing down the scream that had been trying to escape. Tears heated my cheeks, and I blinked the fog away to see the Patrolman, Eliot Gray, along with the bland tones of my high school hallway.

The dream I'd had five weeks ago came back in a rush. I'd thought it was a random nightmare of Lucas running in the dark. I had no idea it was *real*.

"I was the witness," Eliot said. He folded his arms, seeming uncomfortable with my tears. "That's why I have the vision. I'm sorry you had to see it, but now you know why you can't stay here unprotected with the intersect open. Asteroth Ryuu declared war on the three responsible for the death of the witch. Lucas was just the first. Zane Cohen was the second." The Patrolman shifted his weight and my stare shot up to see what he meant.

I was the third—that's what Eliot Gray was too modest to blurt out. But that wasn't what gutted me right there in the hall.

"He found Zane?"

"It's a rather unmerry story," he said. "But we need to move our scotchers. It took me two days to track you down since I hadn't any idea where to find you. I believe Asteroth is already here."

"You didn't answer my question about Zane."

"Come, Miss Bell. We can speak of it on the train."

"No, I want to know right—" Panic swelled my throat as a pale creature—a *Greed*—drifted around the corner, stopping right where the hallways split to different wings of the school. It was so still; a ghost in a painting as it searched, memorizing the faces in the crowds of students passing by.

Eliot Gray grabbed my arm and veered the other way.

"If we can make it to the train…" he started, but never finished that thought. "We just have to make it to the train." He pulled his staff from the contraption on his back as we passed the cafeteria.

"Don't run off, Miss Bell," he added. "Stay with me, and don't run *no matter what*."

My reputation must have preceded me.

We aimed for the side doors that led to the parking lot, but I barely registered the coldness of the door handles, the sweep of chilly air that brushed in when the doors opened, or the blizzard whisking over the football field.

I was going back to Winter. I was going *back…*

What about Grandma? What about the snow piling up on the driveway? Who was going to shovel it so she could get her car onto the road?

I pulled up my sleeve and blinked at the silent hands of the clock tattoo *spiralling* out of control, telling me I was almost there, almost to my destination.

"Helen?" My sister's voice halted me, and the hem of Eliot's black coat whipped as he spun around.

Kaley's bare arms were already pink from the cold. "Are you crying?" she asked, squinting through the blowing snow.

"No…I mean, *yes…*" How could I tell her this? "Listen, I have to…*go*. You remember those things I told you about where I went last year, right?"

My heart dipped. I'd only revealed a few things, and even though she said she believed me, I knew how it all sounded. I hadn't told anyone else apart from Winston, Grandma, and a girl in a coma who couldn't hear me. Winston had spiralled, calling me delusional, probably terrified his older sister would say something about her "visions" in front of his friends. I hadn't spoken another word about it to either of them after that. Kaley had never asked me about it, but I overheard Grandma talking to her in the kitchen once, telling her that things aren't always what they seem, and maybe she ought to have a little faith.

"I have to go again," I swallowed.

My sister clutched her books. Those big green irises were ones I used to stay up late confessing my secrets to, whispering so we wouldn't wake Grandma and Winston. I'd wanted so badly to tell Kaley everything, to tell her about the Truth I'd found in Winter.

But Kaley surprised me by nodding. "What should I tell Grandma?"

"I don't know," I realized. Eliot appeared beside me and Kaley didn't bat a glance towards him, reminding me she didn't know he was there.

"I'll think of something," she promised. She even cracked a smile, and I might have melted into the snow if I'd had time. I would tell her once I got back, I decided. I had to tell her *everything*.

I backed towards the field and Kaley returned to our brick-and-mortar school with her hair floating in the wind.

"Your sister?" Eliot's guess tore my stare from my sibling, and I found his Patrol jacket extended towards me. His cheeks were rosy, his electric eyes lights against the storm.

"Yeah," I said. But I couldn't talk about her. The thought of leaving her again was too terrible to dwell on.

Eliot flung the jacket over my shoulders and tugged me against his warm body with a gloved hand. It was an all-too-familiar feeling, but with a stranger.

We broke into a glide, tearing over the football field,

kicking up wings of snow, a touch of thrill blooming in my heart. More than once since last year I'd woken from dreams of whipping over the snow at an exhilarating speed.

Downtown, I looked for The Steam Hollow, sure I'd spot it easily even though I'd avoided this street since I realized the intersect had opened. A wide smile spread over my face—I didn't even know why. It was a strange reaction at a time like this.

Creatures that had felt like legend came in and out of alleyways, heading into small shops my regular world didn't see.

And then there it was—Lola's hot chocolate shop.

My face contorted. "*Stop!*" I yelled.

Eliot lurched to a halt, and I scrambled over the sidewalk, gaping up at the brittle wood panels, glistening windows, and the steam pouring out from the chimney up top.

It was *red*.

Crimson paint covered every inch of wood, steel, and stone. Dark metal chains gripped a long sign over the door that read:

RUBY LEGION OUTPOST
ROYAL CHOCOLATE BREWERY

I ran for it, bursting through the door that boasted the same calligraphic "W"—the only thing it seemed that hadn't changed. The scent of hazelnuts and milky chocolate encompassed me as I scanned the tables, the counter, the new menu fastened to the wall with silk bows.

"Miss Bell," Eliot whispered from behind me. "We don't have time."

"Peanut."

At the greeting, I spun to find a tall being in a cloak that shadowed half her face, but the black hair spilling from her hood revealed who she was. She had a broom in her hands.

"Lola," I said, glancing at the heavy cloak, then back to the tables where a pair of finely dressed Red elves sipped from steaming mugs. The hot chocolate shop was otherwise empty. "What happened to The Steam Hollow?"

Lola's hands tightened around the handle of her broom, but she drifted to stand beside me. "It's a different age, Trite. Many have been forced to choose a side." The joy was gone from her voice. She stared at the pair of elves who ignored us and chatted in cheerful tones. "Out here it's no different."

With that, she wandered away to continue her sweeping.

My eyes were glued to her back until the silence-shattering *Tooot!* of the train whistle filled the shop.

"Miss. *Bell*." Eliot said again.

I didn't object this time. I left The Steam Hollow and waited on the sidewalk until the sound of the door clicking shut behind us filled the air.

A sparkling cloud of train-smoke mixed with the blizzard past the buildings. My hand slid to the pocket of my pants, misshapen by eleven black pearls.

What exactly had the Timepiece said? Something about three hearts who would contribute to my destruction when I pass back into the wintersphere?

My mind began to compartmentalize what I could remember. Up until this point, I'd thought the Timepiece was on a personal mission to evade his "Midnight Forest." But what if he really had ventured across the realms to warn me about something?

I had nothing to go on but a riddle. Though, after I'd seen Eliot's vision, I knew of one person associated with the colour *red*—the man who was coming for revenge. Did his association to Mara Rouge make him a Red-Kingdom-dweller, too? His blast of fire had been *red*. He'd even smelled of cranberries.

Maybe that was it. Maybe the Timepiece was warning me to stay away from Asteroth Ryuu. He must have known Eliot would show me the vision, and that I'd solve one of the three hearts right away.

"Miss Bell, we're in a *hurry*—"

"Shh. I'm thinking," I cut Eliot off. But I couldn't talk to him right now, rude as it might be. I'd wasted too much time ignoring these warnings and now that Winter was approaching, I wasn't ready.

"Sorry," I added when Eliot made a face. "I just…need a moment."

Eliot shut his mouth, but still reached and tugged me to him to skate over the snow. We sailed down the sidewalk and ducked into an alley where he set me on my feet again to walk.

If Asteroth Ryuu *was* the red heart, then I still had two hearts to solve. The *heart green with envy*…I didn't know anyone from the Green Kingdom, *yet*, but maybe it wouldn't be difficult to figure out. I just had to keep my eyes open for a Green who crossed my path.

But the part of the puzzle that stumped me was the *heart as black as a viper*.

Another blast of the train whistle shook me from my daze. The echoing chugs of the cars' spinning iron wheels filled the air as Eliot came to a stop at the platform.

The shiny navy train carriages and bronze hitches, the arched windows and golden doors, the smell of freshly ground cinnamon sticks, the cacophony of steel grinding against steel, and the promise of magic swept me away from my inner turmoil.

The doors brushed open, and Eliot wasted no time trotting up the steps to board. But I glanced back at Waterloo. It wasn't December yet, so the streets weren't as packed as the last time I'd stood at this platform, but they bustled with the usual midday rush.

Somewhere past this busy street, my grandmother's house was nestled in a small community by the park. Grandma was probably sipping her decaf coffee and reading the paper at this time of day.

"Last call!" A voice enveloped the sounds of the street, and I turned to follow Eliot aboard.

The fragrance of warm lemon wafted over me as the new doorwoman blinked. "Name?" she asked in a high voice.

"Peg!" A young gentleman in a turquoise coat approached, a top hat balanced upon his cinder-black hair. Cornelius Britley swung his pocket watch chain around his finger. "Well...maybe not anymore," he said in his strikingly thick accent as he looked me over. "My, you've changed a measure, Miss Bell."

A blush hit my cheeks. Cornelius Britley wasn't making an advance, it was merely an observation, but I felt Eliot's gaze sweep over me too. Eliot wrapped an arm around my shoulders to usher me inside.

"Don't worry about her name, she's with me," Eliot informed the doorwoman loud enough for Cornelius to hear. Cornelius paused his sauntering, and a funny smile cracked his small mouth. I looked back and forth between the two young men who briefly locked eyes, my cheeks as hot as furnaces.

Cornelius stepped to the side and removed his hat to let us pass to the community seating. "You can have a cabin if you'd like, Miss Bell. I know you have a ticket for one," he added as Eliot tugged me down the narrow aisle. I caught the fragrance of tealeaves as I brushed past Cornelius's chest.

"Um, this is fine. Thank you." I barely got the words out before Eliot was sliding into an unreserved row at the back. Cornelius watched for a moment with that same twinkle of mischief, then continued his stroll through the train carriage. He disappeared through the door at the front and into the carriage ahead.

"We're here," I turned to Eliot. "So, tell me what happened to Zane."

A streak of annoyance muddied Eliot's boyish features, and his dark curls bounced as he slumped back in the seat.

The golden doors swooshed shut, hissing as they sealed. The doorwoman moved to put logs on the fireplace in the corner, and vibrations lifted into my feet as everything began to move. I wanted to take in the brass candlestick holders with dripping wax, and the constellations across the navy ceiling, and the pointed crystal windows…but my attention hovered on Eliot Gray, who had specifically *not* confirmed what had happened to Zane.

The Patrolman brushed his fingers through his hair, making it stand on end.

"You'll see when we get to the library," he tried, but I shook my head.

"You said you would tell me."

"I needed you to get on the frostbitten *train*," he said, shooting me a look and pushing his sleeves up to his elbows. And that was all he said about that.

"What happened to Zane, *Patrolman?* Tell me or I'll jump out of this train car!" I shifted in my seat to face him, tempted to actually run for the doors and try it.

Eliot's jaw slid back and forth. "Your sister is pretty," he said, stomping slush off his boots. "I always heard Trite women were rather boring-featured, but neither of you are that."

I ignored the compliment to myself, not sure I could trust it anyway, and let warning spill into my eyes. I had the sudden tremendous urge to punch him, and I had no idea why. Maybe it was the comment about him noticing my sister like *that*. Maybe it was because he wouldn't confirm or deny if Zane was in trouble. Maybe it was the fact that Lola's hot chocolate shop was different.

My fingers flexed but I huffed and dropped my hands to my lap, doing nothing but sliding my back against the seat and looking straight ahead.

"You're not her type," I promised.

Eliot snorted. "I wasn't asking your permission to *marry* her."

I rolled my eyes and took in a slow breath, glancing to my arm where the hand of the clock was nearly invisible from the speed at which it spun: *tick, tick, tick—*

The hand stopped.

I blinked in surprise. It halted flat against where the midnight twelve would be if there were numbers.

Suddenly the train lurched to a halt and my hair whipped into my eyes. "What in the *world…*" My mutter fizzled out with the other sounds that ceased: the chugging of the train, the crackling of the fireplace, the chatter of the passengers, the wind against the windows—everything was as silent as death. I scrubbed my bangs away. "Eliot, what—" I shrieked when I looked over and found him perfectly still, like a marble cut-out, along with every other living being on the train.

Frozen.

"No..." I sprang from my seat. "No, no, no..." I spun and nearly stumbled over the end of the row, taking in the horrific sight of everything stuck in place—something I'd only ever seen happen at the hands of the witch who'd nearly killed me. I looked around for somewhere to hide.

The sky outside collapsed into darkness and the train doors hissed open. The carriage filled with shadows and wind that smothered the candles' flames overhead and tore my hair away from my face.

Black ribbons of fabric reached through the door, and all my terrors of the resurrected Mara Rouge uncoiled as the Timepiece swept in. His rolling mist filled the carriage-front all the way to the ceiling.

"You," I said, stealing another look at the passengers. "Have you frozen them?" I swallowed halfway through the question.

"No. I do not freeze the living. I am a mechanic of time. I have stopped it now."

Okay. "Why?"

"Because now you have seen that I speak the truth," he said. "And now you are paying attention. So, I've come to offer an extra measure of knowledge." The Timepiece advanced beyond the front row and I folded my arms over my chest, tight enough to hurt.

"At what cost?" I knew better; I knew of Winter deals, and what they could do. I had just watched Mikal be killed because of one in Eliot's vision.

But the Timepiece tilted his head, a breath of steam escaping his hood. "I don't wish for a deal. Just a simple trade will do. Information requires a tax, according to the laws of the time overseers."

"I didn't pay you for the first warnings you gave," I pointed out. "Are you telling me I'm in your debt?"

"By the laws, yes."

"I don't have anything to pay you with."

"You do." He waited.

My hand dropped back to the pearls in my pocket. I fished them out and held them up in disbelief. "I threw out the ones you left in the toilet." I chucked them at him all at once, and with an easy sweep of his sleeve, they vanished, cleansing me of whatever imaginary debts I owed.

"I'll need another payment for the extra measure of information I bring."

I grunted and went to dig out the ruby, emerald, and onyx from my other pocket, but his hand raised to stop me. "Not those," he said. My jaw shifted back and forth, and I stole a glance at the lifeless forms of the passengers.

"What do you want to trade for your *extra measure* of knowledge then? I probably won't give it to you."

"The only thing important to a Timepiece," he said in his voice of drafts and ash. "Time."

I raised a brow at that.

With a sigh, I looked at the dark windows. I was back in Winter, like the Timepiece said I would be. The last time I'd been tossed into Winter there were no warnings, no written guide or even a confusing puzzle to help me survive. I'd almost been a victim of Mara Rouge because I had no idea what I was facing. I almost didn't get back to my family.

Kaley's big green eyes blinked in my mind's eye. Grandma's slow climb of the stairs every night to get to bed. Winston's preposterous fist-fights.

"How much of my time do you want?" My nails dug into my arms again.

"Just a pinch will do. In exchange, I will grant you knowledge pertaining to one heart of your choosing."

I imagined having to spend time with this creature, even if it was just for a bit. "You'll tell me the name of the person one of the hearts belongs to?"

"A name, I cannot say."

Red heart. Green heart. Black heart. A dangerous Red Kingdom dweller, and a dangerous Green Kingdom dweller, my unsupported theory so far had pinned. They were shallow guesses, but it might just be that easy.

The black heart still had me stumped.

"Tell me about *the heart as black as a viper*," I decided.

His vapour darkened as pure as ink, and frost crisped the window edges. I drew Eliot's jacket tighter around my throat.

"The onyx," the Timepiece whispered his agreement. "The heart as black as a viper covets the Red Kingdom throne. He watches from the shadows, with blood that runs as black as the night sky and as venomous as poison. He manipulates the royal family, placing them all in danger and the Red Kingdom along with them. The viper will be a worse king than the Crimson King if he steals the throne. Of these things, I can speak no more. But do with it what you will."

I blinked. "That's it?"

"It's enough."

"No, it's not! You must be out of your *mind*—"

The floor of the train carriage shook as the Timepiece rose to his full height, towering with a crack of thunder. I stumbled back with rounding eyes.

The carriage door at the front opened with a leisurely squeak, stealing my gaze. The Timepiece whirled as Cornelius Britley strolled through, his pocket-watch tucked safely away now, his top hat gone.

The Timepiece's smoke stilled. "Trainsmith...how have you entered my time pocket?"

"Well, I'm a master of time too, you see. And I've come to ask that you leave my train. You've broken rule number seven." Cornelius's pleasant voice remained calm, but the look on his face was uncompromising iron. "That's just naughty."

The Timepiece stared at Cornelius Britley, who appeared entirely content to stare back.

Finally, the Timepiece nodded. "Very well." But the wispy being turned to me again before he left, "Do not forget to guard your own heart, common-blood. Or this will all be wasted."

With that, the Timepiece swept out the doors.

I expected time to return to itself when the doors closed, and for the peppery blizzard to return to the windows, but everything remained still. I found Cornelius eyeing me with his inset turquoise eyes.

"Are you keeping everything like this?" I waved at the still-frozen train. "And what exactly do you know about that

Timepiece, and time pockets? And the laws of the time over-seers?"

Cornelius's nose twitched. "It's not my place to meddle, Peg," he said. "I was instructed to never get involved. Unless a rule is broken, of course." A touch of humour lit his face, but I couldn't believe that was all he would say.

With an odd look, Cornelius turned to head back to the front. I stepped to follow him, but the flames flickered back over the candles and the passengers all began to move. The chatter lifted, the fire crackled, and Cornelius Britley disap-peared while I took a sweep of everything that had come back to life.

WELCOME BACK

PART 2

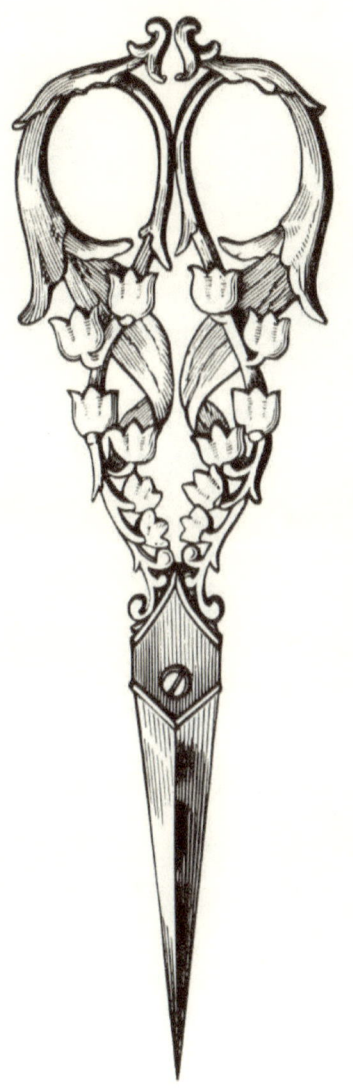

Chapter,
The Third

My fingers traced my bare wrist where the clock tattoo had dissolved, leaving a phantom prickle on my flesh.

Quiet laughter and conversations had warmed the air since the locomotive had resumed its journey, and though I'd considered banging on the doors between the train carriages to find Cornelius Britley, I'd returned quietly to my seat to think instead.

"Eliot…" I finally spoke, once I was sure he had no idea what had transpired. "Do you know what a Timepiece is?"

Eliot made a face but shrugged. "Sure. They're the overseers of time. Some people who've never been to the Red Kingdom would say they don't still exist, but I know some do. I've met one."

"You have?" I sat straighter.

"It's not that exciting. They whisk around making deliveries for the Crimson Court. Keeping things organized and on schedule."

"Can we trust them?" I asked. "Has one ever tried to do good?"

Eliot blinked. "The Timepieces that still exist traded their free will to the court. Doing good, or doing *anything* outside of following orders, isn't really their specialty."

I sat back and processed this new information.

A puzzle that might save me from something I couldn't see coming. Mikal sacrificing himself for Lucas. Asteroth declaring war on me.

Zane...I still didn't know what to think about Eliot's evasiveness. What if Zane was already a victim of Asteroth's wrath and Eliot was keeping it to himself to get me to the library, the way he'd kept things to himself just to get me on the train?

I should have asked the Timepiece about Zane. It seemed the Timepiece was the only one giving me real answers, even if they were weird ones. Either way, I couldn't help but think that if Zane was fine, he would have come to get me himself if I was in danger. And he hadn't.

Eliot swatted my thigh as the train rolled to a stop, startling me out of a fitful sleep. "We're here!" The Patrolman sprang over me to rush down the aisle. I scrambled to follow, rubbing my eyes.

"Be careful out there, Peg." Cornelius's voice caught me on my way out. With a tip of his hat, he gave his lovely customer service smile, but it didn't quite reach his eyes.

I nodded as I fastened the buttons of Eliot's Patrol jacket.

We trotted out into the blizzard and surveyed the rolls of white-icing hills. The train began pulling away—I watched the links of surging cars and spinning golden wheels plunge through a snowdrift until Eliot pulled me to him and skated into the snowy sea.

A silly smile cracked my cheeks as we launched up a hill, and my eyes feasted upon the millions of sparkling white flowers clapping together in the gales. Their shimmering vapour turned the sky to milk in the wind, and the intoxicating scent of syrup and sour rhubarb made me laugh.

Eliot dropped me onto my feet and began running through the blossoms. I realized I was supposed to follow when he didn't come back, but through the haze, the outlines of a building came into view and I staggered to a halt.

The pale stone castle that had once been invisible to me was so much bigger, and so much shinier than I had imagined. And I knew, without a shadow of a doubt, that *this* was the library.

White rock pillars formed steeples that pierced the pewter sky, and balconies wrapped the building like ribbon embellishments, sloping in and out of tunnels and knotting at the front like bows. Stained-glass arches rose two stories high—a mosaic of colours depicting gardens and flowers mirroring the lush flora at Mikal's home. Domed rooms were hoisted upon golden perches, dark blue with crystal gems like a curved glass sky.

It was a castle of colour, glistening even in the overcast.

I threw my head back and laughed again as I kicked through sage stems.

Eliot glanced back, stained from head to toe in blossom dust. He gave me an odd look but cracked a smile and held out his hand for me to take. "Come on, Trite. We're late."

We ran hand-in-hand to the maple door, newly carved and polished. The inscription was different than before. Now it read:

ELOWIN IS KING OF ALL WINTER KINGS AND LORD OF ALL WINTER LORDS

Eliot yanked one of the metal handles and a beam of bright light spilled over the field, a chorus of voices along with it. We jumped in, and the roar of the wind finally ceased.

I gaped. The scene before me was everything the opposite of the dark, empty building that I had seen with Zane—speckled in debris and abandoned. Had I not just trekked through the White Blossom Fields to get here, I would have sworn I was in the wrong place.

The scent of sweet sauces drizzled over warm baking brought back memories of the dwarves' cabin, and fresh pine garland and mint tickled my senses. Warmth from a towering stone fireplace enveloped my chilled skin. Wooden staffs leaned against every available surface, and *hundreds* of candles flickered across shelf tops. A magnificent chandelier lit entirely by candles hung above with ivory wax steeples. Everything was so *bright*.

But the best part was the slew of boys in raven-black, drifting past each other in a rippling current, busy and deep in conversations. Books laid open over tables, the sound of old pages being flipped rustled through the space. Some Volumes were being read aloud in groups.

I was at a loss for words.

"You did this, you know," Eliot said. "You brought us back."

"No. You all did this when you came for me in Wentchester Cove."

Eliot didn't respond, but a gasp escaped me—I spotted dwarves I recognized scurrying to perform important duties: checking off lists with feather pens, stacking books in categories, rolling up maps; old Delma balanced carefully atop a ladder overhead.

I searched for Theresa or Annabelle, but Eliot's hand found my arm.

"Come, Miss Bell. The Elders need to know you're here." He veered us towards the staircase where white and gold ribbons wrapped the rail in a multipart pattern, tiny bells tucked into every crevice.

This space was familiar in a thousand little ways, but different in its wild transformation from dark to light. For a moment, I mourned the realization that I'd been away while it had happened.

The balcony atop the stairs overlooked the wide room. I watched the bustling raven jackets until Eliot tugged my sleeve to a door and let himself through without knocking.

A heated discussion washed out, and I faltered in the doorway as my courteous Canadian temperament warned me not to barge in unannounced. But when I saw snow hovering in the middle of the crowd to form some sort of three-dimensional map, I realized it was holding the focus of everyone inside. I snuck in and eyed the purplish hue of the centre-piece that reminded me of the dancing smoke inside my glass orb.

My orb. *My orb!*

I'd left it at home in my nightstand where the Greed could find it and smash it over my bedroom floor.

I moved to raise this vital concern to Eliot when I spotted a face through the map that made my words drop dead.

Lucas Leutenski talked to the boys across the table with a theatrical wave of his hands. His dark hair was tossed to the side, his topaz eyes as wild as a fox. The sight of him living and breathing made me nearly call out to him in the middle of the discussion. But when he turned his head, I flinched at the long scar running down his face by his ear.

Frustration dampened Lucas's tone: his naturally infectious smile had been abandoned. But Eliot cleared his throat, and Lucas's edge dissolved when his caramel eyes found us—he stood up straight.

"Trite!" It shot from his mouth as he pushed through the boys between us. In a heartbeat Lucas was in front of me.

I wasn't an affectionate person, but I grappled my arms around his midsection and squeezed, not caring if it was considered appropriate to the other Patrols watching.

His beautifully wide smile returned. "Ragnashuck, I was worried the Greed would find you before us." He didn't hesitate before wrapping his arms around my shoulders to trap me against him. He'd grown taller, I realized; I could barely see the rest of the room over his shoulder.

"The Greed did find her," Eliot interjected. "We got away with a mere pinch to spare."

Lucas didn't acknowledge Eliot, but the rest of the room

did. "By the sharpest wind," one of the older men muttered.

Lucas grabbed a towel off the shelf in the corner and handed it to me so I could deal with my blossom dust. I smiled, and Lucas bit his bottom lip through his grin as he poked a finger into my cheek to steal a swipe of silver. The scar by his ear pulled just a touch, but it didn't take away from his adorable smile. I had a feeling that would be impossible.

A girl in the corner chewed on her sleeve at the wrist like she was bored, her large eyes bulging like a fish's as she watched us. I tried not to make a face when I noticed.

"I'm so glad you're okay after what happened," I said, and Lucas's honey gaze flickered in surprise. "I'm sorry about Mikal," I added. Those same tears that had melted out at school threatened to come back.

There was a subtle flex in Lucas's jaw, but he nodded and patted the top of my head, puffing out dust. "I'm going to fix it," he swore.

A Patrolman with auburn stubble coating his chin raised his arm to take back everyone's focus. He wore a snowflake brooch over his heart, as did several other middle-aged men in the room. "Welcome, Miss Bell," he said. "I'm Trevor South. We're glad to see Eliot made it on time. *Some of us* were worried Gray might not be up for the job," his sapphire gaze shot to Lucas, who stifled an eye roll. "But you're here. And that's all that matters. As for the rest of you, Patrolmen," Trevor shifted his stance to face the others. "Let's start over. Maybe we can stop muddling each others' buttons now that we have a lady in our presence."

"Hey!" the girl in the corner spat out the mouthful of her sleeve.

"Really, Wanda?" one of the boys snorted.

"Why don't I stick an ashworm in your bed, Mirkra, and we'll see who turns into a screaming little girl then?" she threatened.

Trevor leaned against the table with his hip and rubbed his eyes. "Let's all relax."

"I'm relaxed. But I'm not changing my mind," Lucas said as he drifted toward the centre table.

"Lucas, you don't know what you're suggesting. The last time someone talked about *changing our ways*, we created Jolly Cheat!" Trevor flapped a hand through the air. "I know you're disappointed, but—"

Lucas slammed his fist on the table and bystanders jumped. A beat of silence passed through the room and he shook his head in apology as he leaned against his palms.

"I'm a great measure more than *disappointed*. Please, just let me get justice for the man who raised me in his own home and gave his life for mine." His voice cracked, and the sound of it burrowed into my chest.

Trevor's wide torso rose with a deep, slow breath. There was complete silence in the room now.

Wanda gagged on the fabric as it hit the back of her throat and spit it out, a mouthful of her demented sleeve falling into her palm for all to see. A horrified look crossed her face as she looked up and realized everyone had watched her do it.

Everyone except Lucas and Trevor.

"I loved Mikal too. But it's not our way, Lucas. We're *guards*, not attackers. We serve Elowin, and he knows what Asteroth did to Mikal," Trevor's eye colour sank to gray.

"Then why hasn't he *done* something about it?" Lucas

50

rasped.

Trevor stared at Lucas for a moment before dropping his gaze to the floor. "Let's call this meeting. We all need rest." He swatted the suspended map and the snow floated to the table.

"Actually..." Eliot cut into the silence with a raised finger to halt those turning to leave. "I have a proposal to make." He took a step into the room but stopped as a door at the back flung open, hitting the opposite wall with a clatter.

Twelve Patrolmen marched in with torn clothes and muddy gloves, snow still clinging to their hoods. Their hair was tangled, their cheeks rosy, and every exposed inch of them sparkled with blossom dust.

The electric-eyed one in the front pulled down his scarf and a well sprang up inside of me.

Zane.

Chapter,
The Fourth

"Sorry to muddle up the meeting." The tone of Zane's voice made it clear he wasn't actually apologizing. But, moody or not, I bit down on a treacherous smile at the sight of him.

His mess of creamy pecan hair was shorter at the sides than before, but his eyes burned as blue as ever, plagued with dark rings of exhaustion beneath. I didn't mean to notice it all—I felt like I needed to stop staring, but I *couldn't*. It wasn't until this very moment I realized I'd completely convinced myself something terrible had happened to him.

At first I wasn't sure if he knew I was there, but then his dazzling, starlight gaze found me. Against the tension in the room, I let my smile show. So did he, just a small one.

"Cohen, I trust the snowsquatch you boys were hunting has been snuffed out." Trevor cracked his thick fingers.

The Patrolmen behind Zane began taking off their destroyed garments, their boots clanking against the wood floors where they dropped them into heaps. They all exchanged subtle glances.

"Fortunately, yes. Even though it turned out to be a goliath and split into two entities we had to fight instead of one," Zane said. "Which brings me to the reason we came straight here instead of going to the steam showers. We were led into a trap."

Murmurs rumbled through the room.

"It almost killed Cohen," a younger boy with bright red cheeks spoke up. "I'm still not sure how he survived..." He stole a glance at Zane.

"Doesn't matter." Zane's fingers brushed over his chest, but his eyes remained hard. "We were sent there on scotchy information and got stuck in the plains for *days*. Someone led us into a *trap*," he repeated, ripping off his gloves and tossing them onto the table.

"How? I got the information on the squatch myself." Trevor's brows tilted.

"I don't care how. And since I'm getting into things that burn my whittles, I'd also like to know why I wasn't summoned back here when the situation in the common world..." Zane glanced back at me. "...*changed*."

"Eliot insisted he could take care of things himself." Trevor folded his arms.

"I bet he did." Zane's attention fired over to Eliot now, who grunted.

"It was a good thing Gray went, Zane. The Greed were looking for Miss Bell across the intersect and you were...*delayed*, apparently," Trever said right back.

"And there was no one better to send?" Zane asked the room. I made a face, wondering how Zane could be so rude after Eliot had rescued me at my school.

"I was the fastest Patrolman here," Eliot articulated through his teeth. "I'm probably faster than *you* now."

"So you keep telling me." Zane tugged off his scarf and added it to the pile on the floor. He stripped his jacket, shaking dust onto the boots of everyone standing nearby, and took a towel from the shelf to scrub his hair as he walked. Sparkles trickled onto his shoulders as he rounded the table toward us.

But Eliot pushed further, "You're going to have to get used to me breaking your records, Cohen. I'm sure once I scrub your name off the banners, no one will remember you broke them in the first place."

And just like that, I got it. Lucas's eye-rolling. Zane's rudeness.

"I've been *hunting*," Zane enunciated.

"Perhaps. But I'm unmerrily ubbersnugged you feel you have the right to be our *last Carrier's* Patrolman when you're not the best of us. And you're being hunted yourself, like her," Eliot nodded in my direction like I was an object in the room. "You two should be split up and taken to opposite ends of the snow globe. And the Patrolman best suited for the Trite should be her guard."

I became aware that my teeth were clenched. "My *name* is Helen." I balled my fists, feeling that same urge to thrust my knuckles against his nose that I'd felt on the train. "And how dare you?" I added, at Zane's defense.

"Sorry, Trite, but Mikal assigned the Patrolmen to their

charges. The Carriers weren't involved in these kinds of decisions," Eliot stated, bringing fire to my cheeks as he turned back to the rest of the room. "Which is why I wish to remind everyone how things are traditionally done here. According to our own regulations, if there's a good reason to challenge a Patrolman's position, it must be allowed. Mikal often brought things down to a competition when there was something to be settled—"

"For *fun*," Lucas interrupted from across the room. "Not for what we all know you're suggesting."

"Mikal would have wanted the last Carrier of Truth to be under the guardianship of the most qualified Patrolman," Eliot restated his case. "That's what I was going to propose at this frostbitten meeting before we were interrupted. That we settle this Mikal's way. That we make the brightest decision moving forward, rather than just appeasing a common folk who doesn't have the same wits of Winter as we do."

My fists tightened at my sides, solid bones bracing.

"Are you actually proposing a *competition* for the last charge?" Trevor's question silenced all the astonished chatter.

"Yes."

"Seems like you've thought about this a measure while I was stuck across the mountains," Zane remarked, his dust-speckled brows tugging together.

"You weren't there when she needed a Patrolman, Cohen. I was the one who crossed the intersect and fetched her before anything else from Winter found her. I was there when you *weren't*—"

I did it. I hit him.

My fist was crunching against Eliot's jaw before I knew

I'd thrown it. Tingles fired up my wrist and Eliot launched backwards into the shelf of towels. Zane appeared before me, wrapping his arms around my waist and hoisting me off the ground to carry me out like a child before I could strike again.

"You don't want to be my Patrolman, Eliot Gray! I'll wake up and do that *first thing every morning the moment I see your face!*" My words were cut off as the door swung shut behind us.

Zane carted me to the nearest empty hallway and dropped me to my feet. My body was a vessel of heat—I was sure I looked as ridiculous as Winston throwing punches at school. I braced for Zane's righteous lecture, but he was biting back a smile, his subtle dimples giving him away.

"Ragnashuck, I've missed you," was what he said instead.

I blinked as he enveloped me into a hug that cooled my temper. He brushed the hair from my eyes, and the fury I'd built up towards Eliot drained into an invisible pool on the floor.

"I missed you, too," I said. He had no idea just how much.

"Your hair is longer. And, ragnashuck Trite, you're as sturdy as a spuddlepun. It's like you learned how to use your legs!" Zane's hand swept down to tilt my chin up for an assessment.

I obediently held still and stared at his quirked mouth and dirt-smeared jaw. His freckles had disappeared, in fact, most of his childish features had morphed into something more grown up. This close I could see the rings of purpling shadows below his eyes and an ice burn scathing his cheek.

I wondered what kind of snowquatch he'd faced, if it had claws…

"How is your grandmother? And your other beloveds?" he asked. "Did you tell them about Winter when you got home? Did you tell them about the stories with the dwarves? And the sacred truths?"

Grandma. I had no idea how she was right now, or how she would be when she discovered I was gone, again. I didn't trust Winston to stay out of trouble and I had a feeling Kaley wouldn't know what to do with him.

"I told them a little. But…I have things to tell *you*."

"Me too." Zane's almost-dimples returned, but I swallowed.

The Timepiece. The puzzle. Asteroth's hunt. Mikal's death. There were too many things to pick one to start with. And then there was the most recent nonsense, "Eliot isn't really going to try and take me from you, is he?"

Zane's face fell from its magical height. "Unfortunately, I don't think there's much Eliot *wouldn't* do to get what he wants."

"I'm sure I can make him hate me enough to change his mind." I was only half joking. Tears inched into the corners of my eyes as pain spread up my knuckles from my punch. "Ow," I added, stretching my fingers out.

Zane grinned and took my hand to see. "You can't do that, you know. Not here. The library has rules."

"I'm not a Patrolman," I said.

"But you're a Carrier. Same rules." He dropped my hand and folded his arms. "And I'm not worried about Eliot. I suppose I'm glad he was there to stop the Greed from snatching you, vexatious as he is."

I grunted. "Yes, I guess I'm relieved that pompous dummy showed up too." A pair of Patrolmen moseyed down the hall eating pretzelled pastries and my stomach growled.

"But there are protocols," Zane said. "I'm your Patrolman, so Eliot should have contacted me. If I hadn't gotten so delayed in the mountains, I would have come to get you myself."

I huffed in response. No wonder Eliot had been in such a rush to get me here, to turn himself into the hero before Zane got back. "Well, two can play that game. I'll put every one of my annoying habits on display, and I'll force him to change his mind."

Zane laughed in his high tenor, "I can't decide if I'm excited or terrified to watch that. Either way, I'm dying to see what he thinks of you after you've walked for days and barely eaten."

At that, I suppressed an eye roll. "Anyway," I cleared my throat. "Regardless of how I got here, there *is* something I need to tell you." I dug into the pocket of my jeans and pulled out the onyx, ruby, and emerald. I dropped them into Zane's hand.

He raised a brow and blinked. "Helen, what are you doing with a bunch of pirate loot?"

"Despite what Eliot said in that room, he wasn't the first being from Winter to find me. I was visited by a creature who called himself a *Timepiece*. He warned me about three hearts."

Zane's expression changed, his hand turning into a fist around the gems. "Tell me," he said.

The empty room Zane ushered me to was an auditorium of multicoloured glass with an arched ceiling. A swimming pool of rainbows lit the walls, prismed through the space and transforming our bodies into collages of flowery violets, sweet oranges, and ocean greens. The first thing I'd done was pitch Eliot's Patrol jacket toward the hall and wave my arms to watch the hues dance over my skin.

"Don't show anyone those gems," Zane decided after hours of me explaining—and then re-explaining—my encounters with the Timepiece. There wasn't much to tell since I'd only seen the Timepiece twice, but it was the little treasure hunt of pearls in the Trite world that seemed to bother Zane the most. We talked of other things too; I told him about my dream of Lucas, and then seeing it unfold in Eliot's vision. He talked about Asteroth's declaration of war sent via Red Kingdom papers, and Mikal's funeral in Winter, which had been magnificent and attended by many. But we kept coming back to the time overseer.

Zane rolled his Patrol staff between his palms as he paced. "Keep them in your pockets until I can get a meeting with the Elders. I don't know what to make of them yet and I don't want the whole library nattering about it. Trust me, there's enough tension between the Patrols right now as it is."

"Didn't you say your mother spoke prophecies?" I asked, hoping he'd have some insight about the future-seer. But Zane shot me a look that made me close my mouth and forget I asked.

"I've heard rumours about Timepieces, but nothing to

explain why one stepped out of order and sought you out."

Zane tossed his staff over his head and did a fancy spin before catching it again, performing tricks like we weren't talking about a future-heralding ghost.

"Should we tell Lucas?" I asked, but Zane shook his head.

"Lucas...isn't himself." He bit the edge of his lip and tucked his staff beneath his bicep to fold his arms. "He thought Asteroth and the Greed came to the gardens to hunt down Mikal, you know. That's why he was scared that night. He wasn't afraid for himself—I don't think Lucas even knows *how* to be afraid for himself."

"That's why he was running to the house?" My dream and Eliot's vision came back in pieces.

Zane nodded. "He was trying to warn Mikal that Asteroth was coming. But Asteroth was really hunting Lucas the whole time, and Lucas led them right into Mikal's house."

Then Mikal had sacrificed himself to save Lucas.

I shook my head in disbelief and stared at the glass above, trying to imagine how Lucas must have felt after that.

Zane wandered to where I stood in the middle of the room. He studied me. "Were you well these last quarters?"

My gaze found his and I realized he was serious, possibly even worried.

"I was fine."

It wasn't really a lie. In some ways I was no different than before I met him. I hadn't mastered the art of making a thousand friends, I hadn't moved on from my obsession of reading, I took advantage of Emily Parker's quiet hospital room even more than I had before. And I still lived in my grandmother's house with my siblings, though the dynamic had changed a little. Truly, I hadn't done anything noteworthy this past year.

Except that I'd spent eleven months missing Winter until it was painful.

And wondering if I would ever be allowed back.

And feeling hollow without Zane at my side, like a piece of me had been torn away and left across the intersect when it closed. I couldn't tell him that now, though. Frankly, I probably wouldn't ever tell him.

"Did you...um..." Zane scratched the back of his head. "Did you meet anyone new?" he asked, bright eyes flickering drab.

I blinked. "Anyone new?" It took me a moment. "Good grief, Zane, are you asking me if I got a boyfriend?"

He bit his lips together and pink touched his cheeks. "I suppose I am. I'm your Patrolman, I'm supposed to know everything about your life. Especially if you found something to keep you in the common world."

My face broke and I smiled. "You want me to stay this time?" I realized, and he huffed.

"I wanted you to stay *last* time. I'll want you to stay *every* time." He pulled his Patrol staff out again and proceeded with his walk. "You're going to have to get used to that," he added with a mutter.

I almost laughed, probably a little *too* flattered, but the humour of it fled when I remembered the Timepiece's advice on the train to guard my own heart.

"How am I supposed to defend myself against three mysterious hearts?" I asked.

Zane grinned back at me with a devilish shrug of his brows. "Do you think I'm one of those hearts?"

I rolled my eyes. "No." I sighed.

Scents of sweet mint and evergreen sap drifted from his clothes as he passed close behind me. Those lovely aromas brought back memories from our trek across Winter...But there was something else too; a tune moved with him, almost too quiet to hear. It faded as he drifted away and I studied his back, wondering if I'd imagined it.

I sank to the floor to give my winded legs a rest, and Zane appeared in front of me, the foot of his staff brushing my knee. "I don't understand why a Timepiece would warn you," he admitted, "unless he saw something in your future that he's trying to change."

When I looked up, two geometrical shapes of light patched Zane's face, giving him a purple and salty green mask. "Do you think there's any chance he's actually trying to help? Do you think we should trust him?" I asked.

"I don't trust anyone these days. Except the Patrol and the dwarves." He extended a hand to help me back up. I took it even though I'd barely rested. "I bet you're hungry," he changed the subject as he hoisted me to my feet.

I was. But I had a feeling admitting it would draw up another snarky reminisce about how grumpy I got when I didn't eat.

"It's nearly evening-banquet. I can smell the cinnamon apples and peppered meat." The rippling hues on his face made him look like a handsome clown. "Give me some time to think about the warnings. Maybe I can ask around to find out if anyone has ever encountered a Timepiece before."

"Well..." I glanced off. "I know someone who has, but you're not going to like it."

Zane grimaced. "Please don't say—"

"Eliot."

We looked at each other. Zane sighed. "Of course it's bloody Eliot."

"I don't want to ask him," I admitted.

"Neither do I."

We both smirked.

THE FIRST INTERRUPTION

Wendy Wilthsmurther knew a thing or three of the Truth. Perhaps not in the same way her granddaughter, Helen, had come to know of it. But she knew things—things like the forces behind whispered intercession, and psalms that could bring a lost soul back from the folds of a dark shifting warren when they could not find their way.

Lost, as her soul had once been. The day her second oldest child had slipped away and left Wendy with three new children.

"Grandma?" It was Kaley Bell; a lovely girl as sweet as honey dips and sharp as glass, pretty as silk and never missing a thing. Wendy noticed the girl seemed to have grown an inch or three in recent months.

"Dear?" Wendy beckoned her granddaughter into the living room where the fire had gone out, leaving a breezy chill behind. Kaley eyed the lifeless cinders scattered in the mouth of stone and got to work on it right away, disappearing to pull a log off the withering pile in the kitchen. Wendy remained seated in the same rocking chair she had once used to nurse the children she bore, scratched over the armrests from years of cuff-buttons doing their worst.

When Kaley returned with a flush in her cheeks, she gripped the wood with bent fingers bleached white at the joints, speaking in her silent way that told Wendy to take note.

"What is it, dear? Is something bothering you?" The old woman paused the rocking of her chair, her slippers holding her in place on the cool floor.

"Grandma, it's Helen. She's gone again."

"Gone…" This put a new stir inside Wendy's chest, for the last time Helen had left she had come back with quite a story.

"Yeah. And I don't know what to think of it. You told me to believe her once, and I really tried, even when she talked about that boy, *Zane,* with those *special blue eyes.* I tried to imagine she wasn't crazy, naming an invisible friend like that. But now I know."

"You know what, exactly?" Wendy blinked through her spectacles at her granddaughter, who had the strangest look upon her Wendy had ever witnessed.

"There was a boy with her today," Kaley said. "I don't think I was supposed to be able to see him, but I did."

Chapter,
The Fifth

The air was filled with scents of juicy meat, sweet apples, and nutty sauces. Zane trotted down the staircase to the main room and waited at the bottom while I descended. He huffed and moved to hang his Patrol staff on one of the many iron hooks sprouting from the wall.

"You still walk like you're about to trip on everything," he called up. "I kind of hoped all that walking we did last season would have made you better on your feet."

I hustled faster, blushing at all the attention his shouting brought, but stopped when I noticed Eliot appear at the bottom of the stairs; a swollen patch blotting his cheek where I'd smacked him. Trevor was there, too.

When Zane turned, he came face-to-face with Eliot. If

he was angry about Eliot's plotting, he was holding it back better than I was; he smiled.

"The Elders have agreed to host a competition to settle our *matter*," Eliot began.

"On the condition, *that Zane agrees*," Trevor said, rubbing his bloodshot eyes. "It's up to Zane what we do next."

The blue of Eliot's irises looked treacherous to me now. When I first met him, I'd thought his eyes were the same as Zane's, but they weren't.

Zane folded his arms. The two boys were nearly the same height: Eliot a thinner build, but his confidence giving him a certain dominance. Across the room, Patrolmen hushed themselves to lean in closer and watch, but it didn't look like Zane was preparing to toss Eliot out into the snow.

"You're up to something, Gray," was all he said.

Eliot's cheeks blossomed pink. "I'm up to something *noble*."

"Okay, this competition is getting thrown to the snowseas if the two of you can't be civilized," Trevor cut in.

"We can be civilized," Eliot swore, his stare hovering on Zane for an answer. "Can't we, Cohen? Tomorrow? For a competition?"

Zane didn't glance back to see what I thought. He didn't look to his fellow Patrolmen either, who waited on the edge of their seats. "Fine," he said.

My jaw dropped. "What?" My word was a lonely protest in a near-silent room. But how could Zane agree to this? How could he risk letting someone else take me against my will?

The corner of Eliot's mouth lifted. "We'll settle this in the tower, then."

"And I expect everyone to show up with a pinch of cheer. Let's eat." Trevor waved everyone away and Patrolmen began to disperse, staffs clinking as they were dropped on various surfaces and dragged across the floor.

Chatter washed back over the space as Eliot disappeared into the crowded locker room. I thought my theatrical seething was for myself only, but when my blazing eyes drew back, I realized half the room was staring at me. Some were smiling, too wide, and others just studied me with minimal curiosity; the Trite spectacle who was the cause of all the drama. Two Patrols even waved flirtatiously from where they were seated. No one seemed rattled by this upcoming competition—not even Zane. No one except me.

Realizing I was going to be the centre of attention during my stay, I clambered down the last steps and tucked myself into Zane's shadow.

An array of mismatched cutlery adorned the long dining table; twisted forks and embellished spoons sat alongside tin and china plates, all resting atop twig placemats. It was a chaotic sight but also warm and homely.

It wasn't until we were seated in front of a tree-like candlestick that I finally let my words fly, "Why in the world did you agree to compete with him?"

"Because he's right." Zane's answer was all wrong. We had *just* talked about this in the rainbow room. "I think Eliot is a conniving ashworm, but you're the last Carrier we have. I can't let my own feelings muddle everything up." His jaw shifted back and forth. "And anyway, you're in *all* of our care now. So, it doesn't really matter who wins."

"The Elders have to see that this is madness. The Carrier having no say in who gets to be her Patrolman is a stupid rule."

Zane's mouth twitched into a smirk. "It *was* Mikal's way though. To delegate and assign without the influence of our personal aspirations. We learned the hard way a time or three that he knew best. It was also his way to put petty disputes to a competition to sort a matter out—Eliot wasn't lying about that," he said. "But that's why it won't just be me and Eliot competing. Plenty of Patrols will take part. It's supposed to be fun."

"Wait..." I rubbed my temples. "So, you're not just going to have to beat Eliot, you're going to have to beat *everyone?*"

"Don't worry," Zane laughed, "most of them will let me win."

"*Most* of them. That's reassuring."

He attempted to smooth his wild hair. "Trust me, it's not a big deal. I've beaten them all plenty of times."

"Except Eliot," I concluded. "You aren't sure you can beat him."

Zane lifted his plate and began spinning it on his hand. "Do you want me to convince one of the dwarves to tell us a story later?" he asked, then dropped the plate and chose a spoon instead.

"Don't change the subject."

He made a face, but his attention slid to something past me, and his fingers stopped their cutlery-baton-twirling. "Ragnashuck," he muttered. "I've got a spinbug to squash. I'll be right back. Don't wander off, Trite." The spoon clattered back onto the table as he lifted and brushed by me.

I sighed. *Typical.*

I closed my eyes, baffled that Zane was still a master at

avoiding difficult conversations even after a year had passed—apparently that habit hadn't left with his freckles.

"Has Zane abandoned you already?" Eliot's voice, and his odd fragrance of lavender and roses, overwhelmed my senses before I even took a breath. The curly-haired Patrol-man slid into the open chair beside me, and I scowled.

"This might all seem harsh, Trite—"

"My name is Helen," I told him for the second time, be-cause when he called me *Trite*, it felt like an insult.

"Right." He bit his large bottom lip. "I just came over to offer some good tidings after you seemed rattled by...*that*," he nodded back to the staircase.

"Yes. I'm rattled. How am I supposed to feel about you, Eliot Gray? You snuck across the intersect to get me—"

"I didn't *sneak*—"

"Then you hit on my sister—"

"What? I didn't—"

"Now you're trying to *steal* me from my Patrolman like I'm a bag of goods to be traded!" I finished.

He'd pinched his big lips shut with his teeth.

A beat passed, and I stole a quick glance in the direction Zane had gone.

"Do you want to know why I need to do this?" Eliot said. I didn't humour him with inviting an explanation, but he gave it anyway. "My parents and I were flower farmers in the early seasons of my timestring. I lost both my parents to the Winter snow because of a pointless war they shouldn't have been forced to fight in. I was only six seasons old and the whole matter was entirely out of my control. So, I might be a little fanatical about controlling situations now, but it's because I care the most about keeping the people who matter alive."

My fingers stopped their agitated tapping.

A not-so-polite Trite word popped into my head at the frustration it brought me to know that he had lost both his parents, and now I couldn't hate him anymore. Eliot dropped his gaze to his jacket cuff, unable to make eye contact. It was worse that his curls made it easy to picture a six-year-old him having lost something so important—something I had also lost.

"So, because of that, you can't accept the last Carrier's fate being in anyone else's control?" I said. "That doesn't seem fair to anyone."

Eliot ran his finger along the rim of the nearest water glass on the table, coaxing a subtle hum from it. "They want to go after him, you know." He nodded to where Zane had stopped by Lucas and another boy.

Despite how much it bugged me that everyone kept changing the subject without warning, I glanced to where Zane was leaning in to speak with the two boys. The strawberry-blond Patrolman beside Lucas was folding his arms, and I realized he'd been standing by Lucas in the meeting room when I'd first arrived.

"After Asteroth? For killing Mikal?" It was an easy guess. "To do what?" My hand shot out to my own water glass and I took a long, uneasy drink.

"Provoke him? Make him pay? Kill him?" Eliot pulled a shoulder up to shrug. "They're crazy if they think it's a good idea. I've met Asteroth. The man is a monster," he said.

"If Zane thinks it's a good idea to go after him, then I think so too." I decided to leave my uneducated opinion at that.

But Eliot chuckled. "Oh, Zane doesn't think it's a good idea. He'll try to talk Lucas out of it if he isn't already."

My eyes shot back to the three Patrolmen. Zane's brows were pulled together, and Lucas's tilted stance was defensive. It seemed Eliot might have been right.

"I'm not a bad person, Tri—*Helen*. I'm just an excellent guard, and most of the Patrols here know it. It seems like your two friends over there are the only ones who refuse to see it." Eliot brushed a finger over the swelling skin on his face. "I'll prove it to you."

Eliot was a coin, I decided. He had two sides.

"Prove it to me by telling me about the Timepiece you once saw."

It was a cheap test, one that only benefitted me and Zane.

But Eliot paused, unblinking, and an amused smile found him. "How about if I win the competition and become your Patrolman, I'll tell you everything I know about Timepieces?"

"*Do* you know things about Timepieces?" I shifted.

He flashed a smile. "More than anyone else here."

Dwarves began carrying trays to the dining table; shaved meat bordered with fruit garnishes, all gooey with syrups and speckled with flakes of herbs. Steam billowed up from the platters set equally spaced down the table, soaking the air with the scents of hickory and sweet spices.

Hoots and hollers of praise erupted from the Patrolmen who scrambled to find a chair—some grabbing their cutlery and tapping it together to make a ruckus of tinkling metal I guessed was a salute to the dwarves who'd prepared the feast.

Bowls of toppings came next: a thick cream spread that

reminded me of cream cheese, sprinkles of crimson berry seeds, walnut shavings, finely chopped leaves, and a whiskey-coloured molasses. Patrolmen began hauling forkfuls of meat onto their plates and decorating their steamy food with everything in sight.

I realized Eliot had disappeared when I heard the feet of Zane's chair slide out. Zane shot me an apologetic smile as he took his seat.

I was about to ask about his conversation with Lucas when someone down the table broke out in a song. A dozen more voices joined, drowning out the first, and just as quickly as he'd sat down, Zane sent his chair screeching back to stand with Patrolmen all around the table who raised their cutlery and sang:

"We eat to keep strong and witty!
We're thankful for what we can eat!
All good things, they come from Him,
All the bread and milk and meat! *Hoorah!*"

Patrol staffs banged against the floor in rhythm and the dwarves began dancing around the chairs.

"Love!" Theresa's familiar voice made me jump from my chair to embrace her—not realizing she meant to drag me into the dance with the other dwarves in full view of everyone at the table. My horrified stare shot up to Zane who snorted a laugh through the words of the song.

Theresa passed me off to Old-Jymm and then all the dwarves I remembered flocked me for hugs. I was adorned with a freshly knitted blanket around my shoulders like a cape, and a wreath of branches upon my head.

I was out of breath and beaming when I finally made it back to my seat.

"You look…" Zane pressed a fist over his mouth to suffocate his laugh.

"Oh, shut up. I look adorable." I patted my wreath.

Around the table, every feud from moments ago seemed to have dissolved. Patrolmen bantered and laughed, and Lucas stole a mountain of berry sauce off Wanda's plate while she was twisted in her seat to talk to someone else.

"Some of the Patrolmen here seem really young," I called to Zane over the noise.

"We're training again. In these last quarters we've gathered a measure of sprightly recruits," he said.

"Where'd they all come from?

"Oh, you know. The streets. The orphan villages. Some escaped the Polar caves, others just volunteered," he rattled off. "Most of the seasoned Patrols have taken on apprentices to mentor the young ones."

I arched an eyebrow at that. "Who's your apprentice?"

"Active Patrolmen don't take on apprentices." He ran a hand over his shoulders to pat off the dirt and I wondered if I'd kept him away from the showers all afternoon. "Which is just as well. I couldn't handle two of you stubborn, lazy spuddlepuns to drag around."

I moved to shove him, but he caught my hand and held it too tight for me to tear away.

When I managed to untangle my fingers from Zane's, I paused before asking the next question, "Are you training new Carriers, too?"

Zane halted with his fork stabbed into a meat slice, his electric eyes hovering on his plate. "No."

I wasn't sure what to feel about that. Should I have felt relieved? With other Carriers trained, Winter might no longer need me. Zane would no longer need me. But *without* them...

"Maybe you should be," I said.

He sighed. "That's a long story, Trite. And I'm too hungry to tell it." He shoved the largest mouthful of meat I'd ever seen into his mouth, forbidding him from answering any more questions.

When plates became empty around the table, Patrolmen dragged wood sleds from angled cupboards beneath the staircase. Zane seemed plagued with exhaustion, but he grinned.

"Sledding. Steam-shower. Evening snack. Bed," he dictated the agenda for the remainder of the day.

THE
STORYTELLER

ANOTHER TIMELY INTERRUPTION

A sweet song of revival hummed in the Patrolman's mind; a tune that had plunged into his body and fastened itself to his very being. Zane Cohen could feel it tickling his feet, seeping through the ground, and drifting with the subtle current in the floors below. He hummed along with it.

'Twas a song Zane was certain had rescued him whilst he was pinned beneath a snowsquatch's palm. The storm had been so sharp, the air had disappeared. Zane had never felt such confusion about which way was up or down or right or left.

A spec ruined the mirror's misty perfection in the shared

lavatory that stretched the measure of eight mirrors above a row of identical sinks. Zane stopped his tune and reached to flick it off, far too rattled to be soothed by anything now, even an ancient hymn of Winter.

What a wonder this all was. Helen Bell had returned to him, and he had not even been forced to create an excuse to go to the Trite world and bring her back on his own.

A touch of pink had brushed Helen's cheeks after their dash of evening sledding. He could not seem to shake the colour from his mind now. The way she had laughed, high and right from her gut, had melted his colours to liquid. But Zane pushed the thoughts away before they took root.

His chest was warmer than usual—he could not stop rubbing it.

When the intersect had closed a full season ago, he realized after an excruciating thud that he could no longer *feel* his Carrier's presence anymore, that his chest dipped cold when the doors between their worlds were closed. A pinched bond.

He did not ever want to feel that again.

If only he could make her stay.

Chapter,
The Sixth

During the hours we'd spent in the fields after supper, I realized the Patrolmens' way of "sledding" was really just to beat the snot out of each other and see who could throw everyone else down the hill first. Lucas kept trying to sneak up and drag me down the slope until I miraculously tripped him. I got to watch him tumble all the way down on his own.

After several sessions of scrubbing off blossom dust in the shower, I was swimming in a spare Patrol top too large for my shoulders, and a pair of tights Wanda had donated that held an unusual smell.

I took a handful of fabric at my neckline and sniffed as I

made my way down to the main room, finding it sparsely scattered with dwarves tidying up, and Patrolmen tucked into various corners, reading.

It seemed almost everyone had already gone to bed. I was headed there too, to bunk with googly-eyed Wanda, but all through my shower I'd been aching to know if the words in the Volumes of Wisdom had become visible to me. And since I'd come out of the girls' lavatory to find Zane snoring on one of the couches in a study room, I figured now was the perfect time to find out.

I studied the winding bookshelves filling half the great room and anticipated getting lost in the rows of aged spines and old paper, brushing my fingers along the ribbed covers and cracking open the stiff leathery backbones. Truly, I couldn't imagine anything more wonderful than a booklover wandering through a secret library at night.

I tugged the closest book from the shelf and laughed when I flipped it open and found gold columns of text. "*Yes!*" I punched the air, forgetting the main room wasn't empty.

The second book I chose lit the aisle around me like a lamp—I gasped as the silvery words twirled into spirals and leaked onto the next pages as I flipped them.

I ended up with three books, and that was only because they were so thick, my lanky arms couldn't carry more than that up the stairs.

In Wanda's room, I tossed my loot onto my cot and crawled into the bed, eyeing a velvet navy cover titled, *Days of Creation*. I'd barely cracked it open before slapping it shut again when a choir of voices burst through Wanda's room in pitch-perfect falsetto.

Wanda's snoring hitched and she grunted.

Abandoning the carolling book, I grabbed a violet tome, peeking into its pages to make sure it wouldn't sing before I flipped it open. I nestled into the knits to read the collection of short stories in plain black text, finding a tale about a thousand believers from the ancient seasons who escaped slavery when the snowseas were miraculously parted to form a dry path.

In the next tale, one name began to glow, and another faded into dark, twisted letters. I sat up straighter in my bed as I read about two great forces named *Day* and *Night*. Every time my eyes landed on the word *Day*, the page would brighten. But when I stared at *Night*, the book's page melted to near black with swirling stars like a whirlpool. Its hollow centre beckoned me to peer in. A whisper lifted from the pages—

I slapped the book shut. The glow ceased; the darkness dissipated.

Wanda's snoring was steady in the room.

There was no title on the violet book. I stared at it for a moment before sliding it onto the bedside table to read later, preferably during the daytime.

Stifling a yawn, I flipped open the last book to find a nearly blank page with a short poem in the centre:

The stars can't wait, it's well past eight!
Go to bed, the hour is late!

I made a face as I flipped the page and found the *same* poem. I tipped the book onto its side to let the pages roll, but all were the same—just the poem, telling me to go to bed.

On the last page, the poem changed:

By the moon's shine, it's well past nine!
Get your rest and you'll be fine.

(But perhaps put me away first,
If you don't mind.)

I snorted and slapped the book shut. I'd never met a book that told me to stop reading and go to bed.

I sighed and dragged the tomes to myself to return down-stairs, sure the old book was right, and I should be sleeping like everyone else. But I eyed the violet book on my beside table, deciding to keep that one.

The main room was nearly deserted by this hour. Old-Jymm shot me a toothy grin as he hoisted fresh logs onto the fire at the far end.

I ducked into the shelves to slide away the first Volume when I felt it—a dull tug. It was like a string was tethered to the organs in my chest. I peered through the shelf, but no one was around except a Patrolman asleep with his face pressed against a table, and Old-Jymm whistling to himself by the fire.

I slid the last book away before I felt it again, and this time it wasn't subtle. I whirled around, eyes scanning the bookshelves. The main room. The staircase. The...

A set of wooden doors sat tucked into the foot of the staircase, overshadowed by the glamorous décor of the rail above. There was no explanation for why it caught my eye except that I *felt* the doors inviting me.

For a moment I had the most absurd thought that maybe the book had sent me back down here so that the door could get my attention.

I moved for it, sweeping across the main room and reaching to take the lever, but the doors unlatched with a soft *click* and cracked open on their own. I let out a comical snort and went in.

Copper bowls spat fires to life in the heights, warming the stone tunnel with gold. On each bowl, words were etched:

A lamp unto your feet, and a light unto your path.

Vines dangled down the walls, dewy and moist. I followed, bowl after bowl, and blinked when the fires ended. There was still plenty of hallway to go, but the rest remained unlit.

"What...in...all...of...*Winter*?"

I was turning to leave when the lights glimmered off a carving in the rock, half hidden by overgrowth. I brushed the vines aside, wondering if Zane even knew this stone hall existed, if *anyone* had ever bothered to set foot in it.

The inscription was chipped and damaged, but it read:

Knock, and the door shall be opened unto you.

"Okay, then." I rapped a few times on the wall.

After a beat of silence, puffs of dust coiled into the hallway as a section of stone slid backward, the murmurs of grinding gears echoing as loose pebbles and debris tumbled to the floor. It slid to the side to reveal a dusty room.

Glass lanterns came to life, illuminating cobwebs and walls of shelves full of... *orbs*.

My mouth parted as I stepped in. The orbs were pale and lifeless, drained of their gold and ivory, and in need of a good cleaning. My gaze travelled from shelf to shelf as it dawned on me what these were: fallen Carrier orbs. Relics of a dead generation. A hidden storage room meant to seal away the past.

I was positive now that I should never have left my orb behind in the Trite world, never left it somewhere there was even a *chance* it could end up like this. I was standing in a graveyard for martyrs with glassy tombstones.

I turned and came face-to-face with a dusty, faded mirror where a blurry version of myself looked back, though I was barely comprehensible through the filth on the glass. Something moved and I realized someone was standing behind me...

My heart went still in my chest at the sight of the woman with long, dark hair, and a familiar height. The realization sailed in, and I almost cried out her name as all the prayers I'd sent this year came rushing back.

My mother.

Chapter,
The Seventh

After my mother had passed away, Christmases for the Bell-Wilthsmurther family had brought a different set of feelings than tidings of comfort and joy.

Every Christmas Aunt Sylvia's parties got bigger, the conversations got louder, the laughter came easier, and my cousins grew older. They all lived on when I couldn't, because I was still stuck in time as that little girl with sticky chocolate fingers staring up at the marvelous Christmas tree my mother had dragged in that last Christmas before she died, and told me I could help decorate. Winston was too busy in the kitchen licking cocoa from the spoon we'd used to stir the cake batter earlier, so it was just me and my mother who wrapped the chubby pine in ribbons and tossed on silver tinsel that day.

Grandma couldn't really afford presents, and Sylvia's charity had run out as soon as my mother's funeral was over, but it wasn't the lack of presents or the loss of having a spectacular tree to decorate that made Christmases so hollow for me. Truly, it wasn't even that my mother had died that gutted me the most.

It was that everyone had been so content to move on without her.

I would have given anything to see my mother once more at Christmas, to decorate that tree with her again. And that was why I'd found myself whispering quiet prayers with the first snowfall this past November. Because Christmas was coming again. And call me crazy, but this year I had something I hadn't had in all the years since my mother left.

I had the Truth. I had Elowin.

And if the Truth himself could reverse the effects of Mara Rouge's poison in my blood and bring *me* back from the dead, couldn't he bring back my mother, too?

The mirror was painfully faded, but I stared at the blurred sweep of dark hair around her face and swallowed with my expanding throat. I had to turn around. I had to see...

"Season's greetings, Carrier," the delicate voice washed over me, and the battling tempo of my pulse died away. That voice wasn't my mother's.

I turned and gazed at a collection of purple markings on

tanned skin that curled right down to the woman's fingertips. Those weren't my mother's, either.

My heart sank back to where it belonged. "Oh…" I tried to be polite and hide my disappointment. "I thought you were…someone else."

The woman's eyes glowed a soft mauve to match her markings. A thin, gold band of nobility rested around her forehead. She was stunning, but not just because of her features. The blurry mirror had concealed that she had *wings*; thin, gentle, and periwinkle.

"Your mother?" she guessed, and warmth struck me as I wondered how in the world she knew. I tried to swallow my shame for thinking such a thing was possible in the first place. It's not like I just *forgot* that my mother was dead.

"Who…" For some moderately embarrassing reason, I couldn't ask the woman her name.

"I've been called a measure of titles. Mostly I'm called Porethius Plum. Also announced as Porethian, Prunella, Purple Sweet, or Sugar Plum in ages past. But my names are not meant to be repeated for now, beyond your own Patrolman from whom you should not keep secrets."

"Wait…I can't tell anyone about you?"

"No. Otherwise ignorant minds will beg for, or even demand, my help. And I'm not able to join your war." It wasn't an apology; it was a fact.

My stare grazed over her from top to bottom, then back up. I felt I needed to convince her otherwise. This woman, whoever she was, was *built*. A sword was strapped to her back with blades out both ends of the hilt.

"Well, that's not ideal, is it?" I said after my assessment.

"My assignment is elsewhere." When she folded her

arms, her tattoos glowed and moved with her body. "I am a messenger of Elowin." My gaze snapped up. "I chose this room to meet you in because there are some places in this library only Carriers can find."

She unfolded herself and reached into a satchel at her hip.

"Well maybe the Patrols should start training new Carriers then," I said, still puzzled by Zane's evasive response at dinner, "so these secret rooms don't get left unattended for so long—"

A thread of rose-gold unravelled from Porethius's fingers with a nickel-sized glass ball on the end, ivory and gold dancing within. The colours seemed to launch towards me, rattling the chain in her grip.

"Is that..." My eyes widened.

"I retrieved your Revelation Orb from your quarters in the dead world and reduced its size." She extended the necklace to me. "You should know that I was *not* the only one after it."

Instead of gaping like an idiot, I took the gift. A thin clasp wrapped the orb like metal fingers to keep it in place. I added it to the snowflake necklace already around my neck, relieved to have it back.

Two chains—that was more jewelry than I'd ever worn at the same time.

"About your mother," her eyes sank to eggplant-purple, and I felt a twinge of embarrassment again for thinking she'd been my mother in that mirror. "You should know that Elowin has heard your cries. Some people don't have it easy, Carrier. But some things are meant to stay the way they are for a purpose."

The words were numbing. "I know. Obviously. It was a fool's hope..."

"Carrier," she said, and I glanced up. She put a warm hand on my shoulder. "Elowin cannot show himself in Winter. Not before the end time. But he has heard you. He knows."

With that, she smiled and moved for the stone door as though the conversation was over in the heartbeat it had taken her to deliver my orb.

"Wait..." I called, baffled by her quick departure. "What about Asteroth? What about the heart riddles from the Timepiece? Can't you tell me what terrible thing the Timepiece saw in my future? Or how I'm supposed to overcome Asteroth?"

Porethius shook her head. "I'm just a messenger. It's not my place to alter your course." But she paused and turned to face me again. "You're not alone, Carrier. You *must* remember that when it's dark."

She came back and took both my hands. I wasn't sure what she was doing until she remarked, "Didn't that book tell you to go to bed? Tomorrow will bring its own troubles. Sleep now."

And like a log falling into a river, I fell asleep.

Chapter,
The Eighth

I rolled onto my side, getting the first whiff of baking bread and cinnamon in melted butter. My fingers were poking through the holes of a thick knit blanket like bear claws when I opened my eyes. I wiggled them free as nearby chatter made me realize I wasn't in my cot in Wanda's room, but on one of the couches in front of the grand fireplace in the main room.

I rose to sit, hoping no one had seen me sleeping there.

"I found you here this morning. Had to smack away ten plus three of those pesky youngsters set on pulling pranks on you while you slept." Theresa was snuggled into a chair beside the couch, knitting. "I couldn't keep them all back though, love. It is what it is now."

She paused her work to slide a mirror over the coffee table between us. I dragged it up and let out an outrageously unfeminine sound at the sight of the *mustache* drawn across my upper lip.

"It'll take a while to get it off," Theresa sighed.

A choking noise brought my eyes up to find Zane diving face-first into the couch before he managed to say hello, shaking with poorly suppressed laughter.

"It's not funny," I tried, brushing my fingers across my lip. Black smeared my fingertips, and I knew I'd only made it worse.

"I know, I know, I know…" Zane waved in apology, but the moment he stood to face me, he snorted again.

Across the room, I noticed several Patrolmen cloaking grins.

"Who did this?" I asked when Zane finally bit his lips together hard enough to keep his sentiments to himself.

"I don't know. Probably Lucas. Maybe Timblewon or Mirkra. Or Wanda and Kilen—"

I rubbed my forehead in disbelief. I couldn't hunt down and accuse a prankster I didn't know. But Zane snatched a cloth napkin off the dinner table and dipped it in a waterglass. He was still grinning ear-to-ear when he came back, but he dabbed my mouth to clean it while I sat there pathetically.

I scratched at my collar, unearthing my gold snowflake necklace. Zane's gaze dropped to it, and I realized he didn't know about my orb. So, I dug that up, too.

"I'm only allowed to tell *my Patrolman* about who I crossed last night. And that's you, at least until the competition."

He flinched at the mention of this morning's big event.

"I'm guessing you were visited by a messenger, if you have *that* now," he nodded to my orb.

"I was," I said, and he paused his scrubbing. "Porethius Plum."

"Ragnashuck," he muttered as though he recognized the name.

His stare lingered on my mouth when he finished washing the ink off my face, and a bead of warmth settled in my stomach.

"Don't you dare let Eliot win," I whispered. Zane's eyes shot back up to mine. "I need you to fight to keep us together."

The electricity in Zane's gaze flickered, but he nodded. "I'll keep us together," he swore. "Regardless of who wins the competition, Helen, I'll *always* keep you and me together."

My fingers tingled with the impulse to take his hands. My Patrolman stared at me; I stared at him.

"Anyway," Zane cleared his throat and tossed the cloth onto the coffee table where I noticed Theresa was watching us with an uncharacteristically broad grin, "I convinced Scorfal to tell us a story this morning in honour of you being back. But you slept so long, and everyone couldn't wait, so he told it without you. It was great," he informed me, and I grunted.

"All this kindness. I'm overwhelmed."

He smiled and glanced over at Theresa. "Make sure she finds the tower before the competition, will you? I'd hate for my Carrier to miss watching me mop the floor with Eliot Gray."

Theresa guided me to breakfast where I ate a gooey cinnamon spread on hot bread slices with the rest of the dwarves. I spent all morning answering questions:

91

"Did you miss us?"

"How many seasons old are you now?"

"Have you and little Cohen kissed yet?" I might have blushed at that one.

"What's a hamburger?"

It kept me occupied but still, the competition came too soon.

I was led to a cylindrical tower with a gaping hole at the top that was open to the sky above. Plush seats wound half-way up the tower's perimeter, coliseum style. The winding rows were *packed* with Patrolmen and dwarves, all seem-ingly much happier about being here than I was.

Foil-wrapped candies were passed around, black and gold ribbons were waved through the air, and a chorus of voices cheered in anticipation of what was to come.

Theresa chatted as we squeezed through the rows to find two seats open together. She snatched a handful of candies from a basket on her way and handed me one.

"Welcome, seasoned scotchers and spuddlepuns alike!" A voice boomed through the tower and the audience cheered—some of the older Patrolmen rolled their eyes from their seats. The announcer was on a podium jutting out half-way up the wall; his hair was bright fuchsia like it was made of candy.

"Let's hear it for our competing Patrolmen!" he hollered with a dramatic wave. "And *woman*..." he added too late, and a few chuckles lifted from the crowd.

Tuneful bells chimed over the tower, and an all-male choir began to bellow at the side of the stage in the centre. It wasn't a sweet tune; more like a call to war as they grunted and stomped their staffs to welcome the competitors sliding out from the stage entrance and kicking up snow.

Eliot swept out first, raising a fist into the air. The boy with the strawberry-blond hair I'd seen with Lucas earlier followed. Then a much younger, light-featured boy, and then Wanda who rushed out fast enough to jam the foot of her staff into the snow and lift herself to run on air. A boy with a blond bun slid out with a twirl, and *Lucas* appeared a second behind him.

When Zane came out, the crowd erupted. He couldn't help himself; he was too much of a show-off to let it go to waste and he jumped onto the hook of his staff, balancing himself atop it while he bowed. I rolled my eyes as Theresa giggled, but the energy in the tower became infectious and I smiled.

"Eliot, Dentone, Kilen, Wanda, Mirkra, Lucas, annnnnd…. *Zane!*" Another roar from the tower.

"Reveal the records!" When the pink-haired host lifted an arm, thirty black banners unravelled around the tower's rim to reveal lists of names and dates in gold script. The loud flaps of fabric added to the buzz in the room and I found myself clapping.

Even though I'd heard of these records, their influence had never sunk in until I saw Zane's name stitched at the top of two records in a row: *Most Wicked Avalanche*, and *Swiftest Patrolman in Existence*. Zane was in second place on two other records too, ones where Eliot had taken the lead.

I spotted the name *Nicholas Saint* and wondered why they hadn't scratched the madman's name off. He still held the record for *Trixen Moon Champion*, whatever that was.

"For our first competition," the host waved his palms like a magician, and thick ropes burst from ports around the tower that fell into gaps between the seating. *"Battle of the Climb*! Patrolmen, find your rope!"

All at once, the Patrolmen below rushed for the ropes. The young, fair boy—Kilen—and Wanda both aimed for the same one until Wanda tripped him with the hook of her staff.

The crowd bellowed with laughter as snow-covered Kilen sprang up and raced back toward the last remaining rope. All the Patrolmen snapped their staffs into the contraptions on their backs and got ready. Zane stole a glace at me. He smiled devilishly, and I wondered what was so funny.

"Watch carefully, love, they won't make this easy on the competitors!" Theresa said.

"Who won't make it easy?" My words were lost to a bell ringing over the tower.

The Patrolmen climbed, and suddenly a hundred Patrol staffs reached from the audience and poked at them, tickling under their armpits, and trying to hook around their waists to pull them off. Kilen erupted in giggles and slid back down the rope.

Wanda unclasped her Patrol staff and started fighting back. It was chaos, and comedic, until I realized Zane and Eliot were both already at the top, sitting on the ledge above their ropes. I didn't see who'd made it up first.

Lucas was about halfway up the wall when he abandoned the rope and leapt into the crowd to swat back, bringing squeals from his section. Dozens of hands caught him, and he surfed his way back down to the snowy floor, disqualified.

Theresa laughed so hard; tears escaped with her snorts. "By the sharpest wind, Kilen, *climb!*"

The burly, blond boy with the bun finally made it to the

top and stuck his tongue out at his aggressors as he flopped down on the resting perch—his section erupted in a fit of booing in response.

"Third place goes to Mirkra!" The announcement brought fresh cheers. "Release the ropes, Patrolmen, and return to the centre of..." The fuchsia-haired boy's voice trailed off as his gaze travelled up the tower. He had a higher vantage point than most; all I could see was snow blowing into the ceiling's opening. I wondered if the rest of the competition would be cancelled because of the weather—maybe Zane would get to stay my Patrolman after all.

The competing Patrolmen scurried back down their ropes, Kilen kicking up a generous wave of snow to sprinkle over his section.

An irritating scent brushed into my nose and I rubbed it.

"The dwarves must be burning the lunch bread," Theresa scowled, glancing back toward the kitchen.

Someone up by the hall doors began coughing, and I glanced back to see a Patrolman bent over, two others shaking his shoulder. I stood, turning my back to the competition as the smoky air rippled over my skin. The hairs on the back of my neck stood on end.

Theresa was assuring me there would be plenty of other options at lunch, and no one would be forced to eat the bread, but I barely heard. As the crowd shouted, I realized almost every library dweller was here, in this tower.

My breath hitched as the sour scent hit me, warning me of a presence that didn't belong, from a memory that wasn't mine.

I smelled cranberries.

Chapter,
The Ninth

It was Eliot's screaming that quieted the crowd and halted everyone's hearts, *"He's here!"* he cried. *"Asteroth is here!"*

Everyone looked around in confusion.

Chaos erupted. Chairs were kicked, voices raised. The fuchsia-haired announcer grabbed his staff from behind the podium and jumped to a bridge of ice spiralling up from the floor. The dwarves split like a nest of ants, disappearing into whatever holes they could find, gathering loose rocks and ribbon poles.

The tower sank into shadow, drawing all eyes up to something creeping over the opening and swallowing the sun like a deep, red curtain. Bells rang in an eerie, off-beat shrill of clanking metal, and antlered beasts galloped into view, ushering along a crimson sleigh, their deafening screeches echoing through the tower.

"Defend the library!" Trevor's command rose over the panic from somewhere in the mass of raven-black. I watched every Patrolman scramble for his weapon.

Zane's eyes found me through the chaos. I tried to hold his gaze, but black uniforms rushed between us as Patrols jumped into the centre to create a formation.

My stomach dropped as white-skinned beings crept over the tower's brim like pale spiders and slid down the walls. Greed icicles speared into the horde of Patrolmen, and boys began rolling onto the snow. I found Zane when he sprang from the mob, pinning a Greed into the wall and ripping the white ghost down into a freefall.

"Stay behind me, love!" Theresa gripped her knitting needles with rosy cheeks. But my feet were frozen in place. These monsters were here to find *me* and...

"Zane!" I shouted in a fit of panic. "Where did Zane go?" My eyes darted back to where I'd seen him, but there were too many moving bodies.

A Greed fell beside me and I screamed, too panicked to realize it was tumbling down the stairs. It plummeted into the mouth of the raven-black crowd and I spun to find Lucas stomping after the creature, eyes torches of gold.

A hand took my wrist. I almost tore myself back, but when I saw Zane's electric irises, I reached for him. He lifted me by my waist and danced us over the chairs, kicking a pole of ribbons out of his way to reach the doors. I clutched him so tight, I thought I'd crush his bones. I could feel his heart pounding against my own.

Zane slashed backward at a Greed, and I was speckled

with violet blood.

"Cohen, get her out of here before they take you *both*!" Trevor kicked back a pale attacker. Past him, the older Patrolmen were mounting a strong defense while pulling the youngest boys out of the swarm and tossing them toward the exit tunnels below.

"Lucas!" Zane called, setting me on my feet.

Lucas's stare found us. But he shook his head from where he stood on the stairs. "I'm staying to face him," he shot back. "Move your scotchers!"

"Ragnashuck, Leutenski," Zane swore under his breath and ushered me towards the upper hallway.

"Cohen!" Eliot appeared ahead, kicking open the hall doors where a sea of smoke spilled into the tower. "The underground!" he called over the noise, and Zane nodded as he pulled me through. Eliot swept in to seal the doors behind us.

I coughed as Eliot kept moving, bashing through another set of doors, clearing us a path through the smoke into the main room.

"How did they find the library?" he shot at Zane, blinking his reddening eyes.

"I don't bloody know." Zane marched into the main room first, but we all came to a halt when we saw what waited there—crisping pages and *flaming* shelves.

Eliot tried to grab me, but he wasn't fast enough as I bolted through the coils of smoke and slid around the staircase to see what had become of the books. My croak was lost to the roar of flames.

The dining room table was one giant bonfire—the cutlery was melting. Flames crawled over the walls, licking up the curtains and devouring every garland, ribbon, and Volume of Wisdom in sight. My eyes felt like they were frying in their sockets. My wheezing halted when someone turned around by the sizzling shelves.

Asteroth Ryuu's long, diamond-white hair glowed in the flames, and my stomach dropped.

He devoured me through hollow, silver eyes without moving a muscle. A beam broke from the ceiling and plummeted to the floor at my back, putting a wall of fire between me and my Patrolmen, but I couldn't look away, even as portions of the floor caved in.

"Found you." The two-tone whisper plunged into my soul. I buckled, barely catching myself on the floor as he sped forwards like an apparition. The hem of his red velvet coat brushed my fingertips and I screeched, launching myself backwards.

A river of snow spiralled in through the crumbling ceiling, blanketing patches of fire. Somewhere outside a Patrolman was fighting back, trying to put out the flames.

Asteroth's eyes dropped to my skin where I realized columns of glowing, silver words rippled over my flesh. True, sacred words.

I didn't give Asteroth time to conjure his scarlet flames; I lashed out my hand and tore the stream of snow down across his face like a whip, just as the floor cracked open and my body tumbled backwards into nothingness.

I dropped too fast to scream. I was clawing at blackness when hands captured my limbs, and two sets of electric blue eyes tugged my sanity from its coffin of hysteria. I didn't know how Zane and Eliot had gotten to the library's basement, or how they'd torn the floor out from under me.

Zane swept me off my feet, wasting no time telling me to run. Eliot's body folded with choked coughing as he shoved furniture out of our way. I saw him glance back to the hole where I'd left Asteroth—his expression transforming him into a child running from the monsters under his bed.

Dark tunnels and staircases took us deep below ground where the sting in my eyes did little to help my vision. Zane dropped me on my feet again once we reached a wooden bridge.

My senses were clouded by the roar of rushing water. I made out glacier walls surrounding a river gushing below us, and carved out shelves on the clifftops that hosted *thousands* of books.

"Come on, Helen!" Zane barked and I snapped out of my daze. I stumbled after them until Eliot snatched me from the lowest step and tossed me into the boat like a sack. Zane was already holding an oar; Eliot scooped up the other one.

The boat rocked with the current and I moaned as nausea rushed in. All the smoke inhalation, the spiralling thoughts, the teetering boat...

Icy water sloshed over the edge, prickling my hot skin like needles as the canoe slammed a stone ledge. Eliot grunted and stabbed the cliff wall to shove us away, but I could already feel the water trickling over my fingertips, soaking my knees from a leak.

"Here it comes! Ready your scotcher, Gray!" Zane shouted, gritting his teeth as he steered the wobbling vessel toward a half-oval of light approaching at full speed.

It was blinding when we burst out into the sunlight; the white riverbanks glowed as sharply as the sun against our eyes.

Zane wrapped an arm around my hips and launched from the boat, sending the world tilting. My back hit snow and I shrieked as Eliot landed beside me, curls bouncing.

For a moment, our heavy breathing was the only sound left to accompany the river's roar—no more blazing fires, no more screaming Patrolmen, no more whisking of Greed arrows...

The canoe banged off the snowy walls down river until it caught a rock and tipped right over.

"Frostbite..." Eliot's breaths were strained.

Zane struggled to his feet. His eyes were pink, his skin sticky with bits of ash. Violet blood wrapped his shoulder from the Greed he'd slashed in the tower.

I stood, too.

"Bloody frostbite," Zane agreed, but he went still.

I pulled my stinging eyes from the river's edge to find somebody waiting by the treeline; a hauntingly familiar face filled with tricks and false promises, staring at me with devilish half-curled lips, and liquor-brown hair peeking from beneath an absurd, crooked hat. A face I'd seen only in nightmares over the past months, even with the intersect sealed.

Jolly Cheat smiled.

The Patrolmen unlatched their staffs, panting and trembling, glistening with sweat and denial. A wall of snow erupted, hitting us like an avalanche and pushing us onto our backs.

Zane and Eliot rolled to their feet, and I bit my teeth to follow, searching my hands for any trace of glowing, moving words. But a crinkling sound like the crushing of candy wrappers made me glance back at the blossom fields, and I gasped.

The fields were *engulfed* in flames. Burning flower petals floated through the air like the pages of the Volumes of Wisdom had, the buds folding into themselves and crisping to midnight black.

The library was a torch in the distance. The flames reached for the sky, folding over the building and smothering the beautiful structure to death like a fiery spider sucking its lifeblood.

When I turned, Zane and Eliot were tumbling onto their backs again, half blanketed in snow. I braced for the blow that would throw me down next, but it never came.

Jolly Cheat had the nerve to look bored as he studied the hook of his staff. I wanted to scream.

"I'm going to throw you off that cliff." Zane dragged himself back up, eyeing a glassy canyon past the trees.

"You wouldn't *dare*," Jolly tested, eyes twinkling.

Zane looked more like a lunatic than Jolly in this moment—swollen red eyes and a soot mask.

But Jolly's gaze flickered to me. "I've dreamt about meeting you again, sweetheart. My, my, you've turned to sugar and roses. I'd make a generous deal to kiss that pretty little mouth." He had the audacity to bite his bottom lip.

"Gray," Zane's words were level. Smooth. Like he was a breath away from snapping. "Take Helen to the Patrols' meeting place."

"Not so fast. I come with a tasty deal." The ice slithered from Jolly's staff like cold, glass worms. "You're both delicious targets, but I'll be a darling and settle for just one of you." The madman's nickel irises flickered between me and Zane. "If one of you becomes my prisoner, I'll steer Asteroth clear of the other. Fairly generous, wouldn't you say?"

"We don't accept," Zane said, panting. "You're outnumbered anyway."

Jolly sneered, but a rustle in the spruce trees at his back made him go still.

In a flash of metallic feathers, the branches above where he stood shifted as dozens, then *hundreds*, of silver-winged birds emerged from the shadows. Their beady eyes tilted towards Jolly, whose own eyes widened a fraction at the sight of them. "Well played…" He whispered like he was trying not to disturb the winged legion.

Zane whistled a sharp three-note tune, and the entire flock burst into flight.

Jolly barely had time to thrust a shield of snow over himself before the flock would have pecked him to ribbons. The jester growled, holding his stance as one bird broke through and scathed his jaw with a talon.

"Forget him. Help the Patrols in the tower!" Zane stomped his staff against the snow and sprouts of ice fingered out.

The flock arched off Jolly and tore through the smoke lifting off the blossom fields, heading for the tower of the library where flames reached from the main building to swallow anyone still inside.

Jolly flashed his teeth. "Any time you want to surrender, Cohen, I'll be waiting," he slapped snow off his shoulders. "I have other fun things to tell you, too. You might enjoy being in my company."

"Take her, Gray!" Zane spoke like he hadn't heard, but I knew he had.

Eliot didn't give me time to object before kicking himself up the drift and grabbing me on his way.

"Wait! What if Zane takes that deal?!" I smacked Eliot's chest. "Go back and help him!"

"I hope he *does take it*! It would solve our problems, Trite!" Eliot didn't stop.

I watched Zane and Jolly swing their staffs until Eliot tipped off the deep slope into the icy canyon, and everything was torn away.

AN INTERRUPTION

"'Twas a true seasons' miracle the Crimson King was still awake. One after another, nobles sneaked to whisper a thing or three into his ear, hoping to sway his opinions before the meeting would begin. The king rested on his throne, his wife's chair cold and empty at his side ever since the gruelling illness had swept over him and she could no longer bear to be in his presence, or with the court, or at the palace at all.

As castle attendants carried in trays of cake for the forth-coming meeting of the Crimson Court, the king closed his eyes to block the light streaming in through the stained-glass windows, bleaching the red carpet that spilled over the floor of his throne room like a river of blood.

It was as though iron nails pressed into the four corners of his head, tugging him in every direction. He could hardly concentrate—

"Father." His son's voice brought him back, the pain vanishing like scattered snow.

Quinten Barsavian Crimson-Choal stood on the bottom step of the platform where a long line of thrones rested, one of which was his. But his son did not dare come near his royal chair anymore. His foot was perched as though he might rise to the second step, but that was all.

"What it is, Quinten?" The king rubbed his temples in circles as the healers had taught him.

"You don't look well," Quinten's voice was hushed, his black hair against his fiery purple eyes making him look the striking prince the ladies in the palace gossiped about.

But being pretty was not enough, the king knew that. He had possessed another handsome son once—one who had brought dishonour upon the Crimson dynasty.

No, beauty should never be mistaken for greatness.

"The irons are pressing in again, Son," the king admitted, "but you shouldn't muddle your buttons over it. Where is Tegan?"

If Quinten was disappointed the king had asked for the heir, he didn't show it. Instead, the prince slid his foot back down to the floor, his sweet, candied eyes sinking to droplets of deep violet. "I'll fetch him for you, Father."

Quinten was too clean, the king noticed as the boy

walked away. Too pretty and too clean. Not the fixings necessary to slay kings and queens and conquer the Winter globe. Quinten seemed the sort to scribe poetry like his old mentors, rather than ride a beast into battle. But Quinten Crimson-Choal had a greater awareness than his brothers. The third prince was the king's only son who had noticed the effects of the illness, who had concerned himself with the king's feelings and health.

Feelings. The king grunted as his crow-haired son disappeared through the staggered archways of the throne room.

If only Quinten could grow into a ruthless thing. If only the boy could take up a weapon and thrust it without conviction. Perhaps Quinten would have made a good Crimson King if he could rid himself of that horridly soft heart of his.

Chapter,
The Tenth

I refused to look at Eliot during the race across the crystal-topped canyon, or through the thorny evergreen forest. I refused to hold him tight over the uneven field of salty snow blowing in whirlwinds. His coat smelled of lingering smoke from the fire instead of the peppermint and pine fragrance Zane left on everything.

My lip quivered as I re-watched the flames consuming the library in my mind—that beautiful building of balconies and stained-glass I'd barely spent any time in before it was ripped away. Eliot's grip tightened but I had no way of knowing if it was because he saw the tears in my eyes.

It was afternoon when we arrived at the meeting place—a monumental building big enough to host a small village. It was boarded with coppery metal, and tin lanterns hung across the front with flickering gas-like flames. Surrounding it were plain fields of rolling snow. Perfect for sledding.

I swallowed.

"This is our meeting place, but it's not the only one. Hopefully some of our friends show up here," Eliot said as he set me on my feet. But by the look on his face, I wondered if he was afraid to get his hopes up about who'd made it out of the tower.

I nodded and reached to catch his hand before he went up the front stairs of the building. He blinked as I swallowed my pride.

"Thank you for getting me out of the library."

Eliot forced a smile and dropped his eyes to the snow as his only response.

Pictures were etched into the brilliant cathedral-like doors before us, telling stories over the entrance with faded paint. The innermost picture depicted a boy, a lion, and a bird. A large star glistened above them—an inset gemstone.

Suddenly the doors swung open and I nearly tripped. Eliot caught my wrist as a white-haired man with a book tucked beneath his arm blinked at us through copper-rimmed spectacles. His glasses hung off his nose the way my grandmother's did.

He did a brief sweep of Eliot's raven-black uniform and grinned. "Excellent. Come in!" The old man stepped aside.

Eliot tugged me through the entrance when I didn't move, and I was taken off guard by the immaculate detail of what could only be described as a factory.

Everywhere I looked, I saw *chocolate.* Milky streams billowed from holes in the wall, stacked bricks with fruit pieces formed a mountain to the left, and a sugary brown river wound around the enormous room in a raised moat. Only the fresh memory of the devastated library kept my enthusiasm in check as I revelled at this russet museum.

Hundreds of bronze gears rolled together high overhead like the innerworkings of a clock, with metal bridges weaving around them, crossing and sloping to connect different balconies. An umber waterfall spilled down the great height of the room into the moat.

From one of the balconies, a girl descended a spiral staircase. Her large gold earrings looked like upside-down trees, and a congested collection of metal bracelets clapped together at her wrists as she reached the bottom. Her dark lipstick made me think she'd dipped her finger into a vat of chocolate and smeared it over her mouth.

"I'm Apple Dough," the girl said with her brown lips as she approached. Her eyes were brown too, which struck me as odd since I didn't think any of the human-shaped Rime Folk had brown eyes. "This is my father, Fred Dough," she nodded to the man who had let us in.

They both stared at us like they were waiting for something. I took my first look at Eliot, but he seemed just as confused as me.

The girl, Apple, sighed. "We're the official Chocolatiers of the Red Kingdom. We're *legends*." She put her hands on her hips.

"Oh, I knew that," Eliot realized, seeming to finally grasp what Apple wanted. "Yes, your reputation is impressive, Miss Dough. I've heard your chocolate sweetroot tarts are to die for."

Apple's face smoothed into a smile. "Thank you." She glanced at her father. "Father, may I let them taste our new juniper truffles?"

"Perhaps we should find out why they're here first." Fred Dough drifted to a shelf to slide his book away and poked his glasses up higher on his nose.

Grandma did that, too.

"Right. We'll discuss it over juniper truffles," Apple said.

A spread of treats was before us a moment later; smooth round chocolates stacked on pedestals, pale cream ovals stamped with flowery patterns, smoking scotch-coloured squares whose steam drifted over the table and made my mouth water, and cool minty twists with a green hue.

"So, tell us, friends, what have you come for?" Fred asked when we were seated at a long table.

I glanced at Eliot. Zane had told us to come here, but it hadn't gotten past me that Apple said they served the Red Kingdom; Asteroth Ryuu's kingdom. Mara Rouge's kingdom.

"The library was attacked," Eliot explained.

Fred and Apple were quiet for a beat until Apple peeped, "How is this possible when those who don't believe in the Truth can't see it?"

"They burned the whole blossom field. I think Jolly Cheat led them to it."

I clasped my fingers beneath the table, feeling cold.

"Jolly Cheat," Fred grunted. "That traitor has caused nothing but problems. We cross him once a quarter, at least. We've walked right past him a time or three bringing our chocolates to the palace parties."

"He doesn't know we serve Elowin," Apple said. "Only the dwarves knew we joined Cora Thimble's underground

111

cathedral. Which is why we promised them a full season ago that we'd help any believer of the Truth, any follower of King Elowin, as long as they kept our secret."

"We just need a place to hide until we can regroup with the Patrol." Eliot gripped his hands. He'd been staring at them since we sat down.

"Of course," Apple placed a dramatic hand over her heart. "May I be so bold as to ask your names? No, wait, let me guess! You're Miss Helen Bell. Am I right?"

I knew my eyes had probably given me away, but I nodded and forced my face to look impressed.

Apple laughed. "You look exactly like Scarlet Strange!" Her bracelets made music as she rose from the table and disappeared into the next room without an explanation. Eliot's wide eyes drifted over to me. It seemed we could agree that Apple was a different sort of weird.

"She draws people," Fred explained. "She's been doing it since childhood. She catches one glimpse of someone, and she can sketch them for seasons to come."

Apple rushed back in with a leathery paper in her hand. A detailed charcoal drawing of a face took up the page.

"See?" She shook it to catch our attention as though we weren't already looking at it. "When the dwarves described you, Miss Bell, I couldn't help but think of the infamous vanished noblewoman. Every detail they gave made me remember young Scarlet from when I knew her. Only, you don't have the scars, of course."

"Ragnashuck, that does look like you," Eliot muttered.

The drawing was complete with shading and feathery lashes, but the girl in the picture had spots across her cheekbones on both sides. "I do hope she's grown out of those scars. Poor girl," Apple said.

I tried not to make a face and moved on. "Well. I guess she's lucky to have a friend like you."

"Oh, not anymore, Miss Bell. Scarlet left the Red Kingdom. You see, a certain *prince*," she left a dramatic pause without saying his name, "mocked her rather cruelly for her scars. Drove her right into insanity, some say. She left the kingdom, promising to mark her revenge by returning one day with magic to turn him into a wood puppet. Can you imagine?"

This was a touching story, but my thoughts were still back at the riverbank where Eliot and I had left Zane to face Jolly Cheat alone. I rubbed my forehead, wishing I had a way of knowing what had happened after we left. All this talk of Scarlet Strange's insanity was making me think I was going to be the next madwoman of their stories.

A loud bang rattled the factory door and Eliot sprang from his seat, but Fred was faster—the old man scurried to open the door, revealing a triad of panting Patrolmen. They stumbled in, coated in ash, one boy with a burn up his cheek that ran into his sepia hair.

"Gray!" one of the Patrolmen called when they saw us. He was half-carrying the burned boy.

"What happened to Uriah?" Eliot jumped to help the boy to a chair. Fred was already racing back to us with a pitcher of water.

"The walls caved in," the third Patrolman said, scrubbing cinders from his orange beard.

"Did anyone else make it?" Eliot shrank to a knee to study the burned Patrolman who slumped into the chair, coughing.

"I saw Mirkra and Calmer jump off the north balcony, and Trevor pushed Felix into the tunnels. Wanda went back in for Kilen."

Eliot looked stricken as the burned boy hitched into another fit of phlegmy coughs—he sounded like a barking animal.

"We tried to save it," the orange-bearded Patrolman stared off. "But the fire in the fields melted the snow and there was nothing to draw from to put out the flames. The birds flooded the tower and peeled the Greed off our backs, but there wasn't time to save the library."

"Mirkra!" someone shouted as two more raven-cloaked boys trotted in through the open door—one of them was the blond boy with the bun who'd competed in the competition this morning. He marched right to the sepia-haired boy to see his burns.

"Ragnashuck," he mumbled, glancing over at Eliot with tugged brows. He noticed me standing there. "Where's Cohen?"

"We crossed Jolly Cheat during our escape." It was the only explanation Eliot gave as he strutted to the table where Apple handed him a damp cloth. He took it to the sepia-haired boy and held it against the burn marks.

Time seemed to stand still as I watched them.

Apple swept through, administering words of encouragement and passing out chocolate truffles. Fred wheeled out cots from a storage room. It seemed the Chocolatiers had been preparing for this day. Even the Patrol had been prepared for it—designating a meeting spot in case anything went wrong. It seemed I was the only one who wasn't prepared for this.

Moments later, a new knock sent Eliot racing for the door and another duo of Patrolmen jogged in, drenched in sweat—neither of them was Zane. Fred and Apple left the factory door open after that.

My legs jerked; I spun to grab the pitcher of water and filled the cups on the table. My hands shook as I carried drinks two at a time to the injured boys. They continued trickling in one by one, each newcomer bringing my eyes up to see who it was.

When I'd used up the cups, Apple appeared with more so I could keep going. The Patrolmen mumbled gratitude and the optimistic ones winked their thanks.

I stared at the white flurries roaring over the hills outside. The afternoon had turned to a dim evening with soggy clouds, mirroring the fog seeping into the hope I had left.

"Miss Bell...you look exhausted." Apple's tone dipped when she found me hours later, still by the table.

"Just...waiting for someone."

She didn't pry or ask me to explain. She nodded, gold earrings bobbing. "Come, friend. I'll find you a bed."

But outside, a shrill female scream halted us. "*Help!*"

Wanda dragged someone over the snow by their hands. Mirkra bolted out to help, and when he carried the limp body inside, I recognized young Kilen's light features, patched with burns.

He seemed so much younger to me now. I just wanted to curl up and cry.

"Come, Miss Helen. There's not much more we can do at present." Apple took my elbow and led me to a staircase in the wall. A candle flickered from a holder in her opposite hand, lighting a path through the darkness encompassing the factory from the evening storm.

I numbly followed the sound of Apple's clinking brace-lets as she led me up the brass stairs to a hall with metal lan-terns turning the space yellow. We arrived at a quaint gues-troom with a quilt bedspread and an antique nightstand.

I was asleep, with tear-stained cheeks, moments after I fell on the quilt.

Chapter,
The Eleventh

The Timepiece stood at the end of a long hall, waiting. His tendrils whisked silently, mist seeping from his cloak. He was waiting for me to remember something. Waiting for me to see what I was missing, to figure out what he was trying to tell me. Waiting for me to solve the warnings before it was too late—

A hand flattened against my back and I flipped around, tangled in Apple's quilt.

My fingers were out like talons until Zane's sooty, half-smeared face appeared over me. His gaze flickered to my pouncing-cat stance, then back up to my face. "Ragnashuck, are you going to claw my eyes out?"

"Thank goodness," I croaked, melting against the bed. I bottled the explosion of emotions that would have driven me to drag him into a hug and never let go. "You made it," I said.

He cracked a smile, illuminated by the glowing sun coming through the window that told me last night's storm had passed.

Morning had rolled in; it had taken Zane that long to arrive.

I grabbed a flap of raven fabric hanging from his wrist, brow arched. I dropped it to sit up and wrung my fingers together to keep myself from shouting at him for staying behind, and for taking so long to follow. But mostly, I wanted to shout for joy that he was here.

"I haven't had a chance to change," he said. "I guess I wanted to find you first to make sure you were…" He waved a hand over me to finish the sentence.

"Eliot wanted you to take Cheat's deal," I ratted, feeling a smidgen guilty for selling Eliot out so fast.

"Yes. Well. Eliot can get frostbite." Zane stood from the bed and pulled the strap of his staff contraption over his head. It left a fresh smear along the armrest of the chair he tossed it onto. "I was furious the whole skate here. It's probably just as well I was alone, especially when I arrived and saw what had become of everyone. But it was hard to stay mad when I remembered what this place was," he said. "Helen, did you know that this is a *chocolate* factory?" His eyes rounded as he said it.

Good grief. I bit my lips over a smile. "Yes, Zane."

"They invited us for breakfast." He pulled off his Patrol jacket, revealing more shredded fabric and a rosy scrape that stretched down his chest—half his shirt hung open. I wondered how long he and Cheat had fired ice daggers at each other before they'd finally called a truce, or Zane had run. He was faster than Jolly Cheat; he'd proven it more than once.

Zane looked himself over, twisting to see his sides and scanning the backs of his arms for cuts. "I suppose we should give Gray a break," he then said. "I know he's an ashworm, but he brought you here when we needed him to."

"Yeah…" Particles of dirt fell from his hair. "Shower. Breakfast. Nap." I mimicked him with the agenda for the morning.

Zane smirked and tugged my fingers to pull me from the bed. "I don't want to think about what happened back there," he nodded in the theoretical direction of the library, and a spark of gray dimmed his eyes, "or the condition of everyone downstairs. You're my distraction now."

He chuckled when I raised an eyebrow. "Trust me, Trite, you've been my distraction for a merry measure."

The last comment flitted in my stomach and I wondered if he was still joking. But he swept his coat, staff, and contraption off the chair and went to leave.

When I was alone again, I remembered my dream.

A handful of Patrolmen sipped thick, hot liquid chocolate in glasses around the table at breakfast—it reminded me of The Steam Hollow.

More Patrolmen must have arrived throughout the night;

they were camped around the room in clusters, leaning against walls and sprawled over cots as they nibbled on chocolate-covered pretzels or dipped their fingers into the chocolate river.

Zane and Eliot both made faces when I arrived.

Apple had dressed me up. She beamed as she escorted me in my high-collared blouse and voluminous pink skirt with pleats. I felt like an old French woman, but I lowered into a chair with all the dignity I had left.

Zane sat up straight and set his gaze on Apple. "*You* look lovely," he told her, and I knew full well it was his way of letting me know I looked ridiculous without openly insulting Apple's handiwork.

I might have grunted, but I watched Apple strike a sweet smile and realized she did look lovely. Apple was pretty— prettier than me.

Her gaze locked with Zane's and lingered there just a little longer than it should have. Her dark-lipstick smile curved up. Even her eyes were a more appealing brown than mine.

Zane's gaze dropped to his plate and he scratched his temple. "So, you're going to let us hide here a day or three?" he changed the subject and glanced at Fred.

"As long as we can," Apple poured juice into her glass, then offered the jug to the Patrolman beside her.

Half-moons of chocolate sweets surrounded each of our place settings, along with fluffy white cake squares, whipped cocoa cream, and flaky tarts with orange filling. The Chocolatiers knew how to present a feast, even amidst chaos.

"But the Ruby Legion comes here to collect dessert orders for the palace," Fred told them. "They come every quarter. They'll be here in ten plus two days."

"Does the Ruby Legion have a quarrel with us?" Eliot interjected from down the table. "Only Asteroth has declared war on our Carrier and Cohen. I'm sure not all the Red Kingdom will be looking for a flock of Patrols."

"That's true, Mr. Gray. But there must be a better place to hide where you won't constantly find yourselves before eyes pledged to the Red Kingdom. Word spreads there faster than you can imagine." Fred peeled apart some mocha-black bread and dipped it in an oily sauce speckled with tea leaves.

The discussion drifted to other things; simple things shallow enough to avoid stirring delicate emotions. One by one Patrolmen left, retiring to a cot, or venturing up to the wiry bridges by the skylights to explore, until only the Chocolatiers, Zane, Eliot, and me were left.

I ignored most of the conversation, staring off at the bright spaces of the factory where all was still, and the dream I'd had last night crept back into my thoughts.

The Timepiece. The hearts. I was missing something. Something that was quite possibly right in front of me.

Do not forget to guard your own heart. That was what the Timepiece had said before he left the train.

My stare flickered to Zane, who was indulging in a citrusy, mango-pink pudding. Was it obvious to everyone, even Jolly Cheat, that there was something more between Zane and me than friendship? Was it obvious to everyone except for me? I couldn't think of a girl who wouldn't be swept away by Zane—he was a boy of extraordinary talents, beautiful eyes, and heart-melting dimples. Even Apple had done a double take of him.

I shook the idiocy from my mind, wondering why I was even thinking about it. Zane would never cross that line with his Carrier, and he'd never seen me as anything more than a friend and his charge anyway. I was losing my wits after the trauma of yesterday.

I rubbed my eyes. I thought my long sleep would have made me wide awake this morning, but I was starting to think another nap would do wonders for my mental state. Clearly my judgement was still all burned up with the library fire.

Three hearts.

Why couldn't it have just been one heart to figure out?

I picked up a teardrop chocolate and stared at it. When I squeezed, marshmallow dripped out, plummeting onto my plate in a glob.

Solve the puzzle and you will see the future in time to change it.

I hadn't been in a rush before, even after Porethius Plum had avoided giving me answers at the library. It occurred to me that she'd abandoned the library hours before it burned to dust. I wondered if she'd known Asteroth was coming; if that was one of the things she decided not to tell me to keep from "altering my course."

The Timepiece had urged me to hurry, and I'd decided to go sledding instead of rolling out a sheet of paper and hunkering down to figure this out. And now I couldn't stop myself from asking the horrid, obvious question—Would the library still be standing if I'd just solved the riddle like the Timepiece told me to?

The only theory I had was that Asteroth was the red heart, and even that I didn't know for sure. But suddenly it didn't matter. Asteroth would get me and Zane if things went on this way. The Timepiece had given me a way out. I needed to take it.

During my conversations with the Timepiece, I had been given *one* clue.

The heart as black as a viper covets the Red Kingdom throne. He watches from the shadows, with blood that runs as black as the night sky and as venomous as poison. He manipulates the royal family, placing them all in danger.

I balled my sticky hand into a fist and pressed it against my mouth.

"Well, if that's the case, why don't Helen and I just hide in the Green Kingdom? Asteroth wouldn't *dare* go there."

Now that it was just the five of us, the conversation had gone back to the matters at hand. Zane's sarcasm made it clear he did *not* want to go to the Green Kingdom at all.

The heart as black as a viper covets the Red Kingdom throne...He manipulates the royal family...

The person with the black heart was in the Red Kingdom. If I wanted to figure out who the black heart was, I had to go there.

"Maybe the Red Kingdom is exactly where we should hide," Eliot echoed my thoughts and my eyes shot up. Though, I hadn't missed how he'd said '*we*'.

"Yes, I think we should." My response shot out before Zane had a chance to shut the idea down.

"What?" Zane and Fred both said at once. Eliot looked just as surprised.

"The Red Kingdom. That's the last place Asteroth would look for us." My argument was weak, but how was I supposed to explain that I wanted to solve a riddle from a

Timepiece to stop Asteroth before he found us again?

I glanced at Eliot to see if he had anything else to sway the others with. He caught my look, though, he seemed perplexed by it.

"I think we'd be fools to take one step past the iron gate. But that's exactly why Asteroth wouldn't find us there. It's just so foolish it might throw him off our trail and give us a measure to sort things out," Eliot pitched.

Zane's jaw hung open.

"Do I ever have a *crazy* idea." Apple's eyes swam like the brown river at her back. She slipped the drawing from her dress pocket which she'd kept there for a reason I couldn't guess. When she held it up, Zane's response was exactly what sealed the deal.

"Why do you have a drawing of Helen?" he asked, and Apple's mouth twitched into a smile.

"I think it's time Scarlet Strange returned to the Red Kingdom to tie up her loose ends." The young Chocolatier laid the picture on the tabletop and we all stared at it.

"Trite!" Zane snapped. "When I said to give Gray a break, I didn't mean you should agree with him when he comes up with an idea that's bloody mad!"

He paced inside a curved mechanical room with loud, grinding gears overhead, and gold fluid pumping through a network of clear tubes. Zane had ushered me here with a set jaw the moment breakfast was over. A host of white butterflies watched us from the cracks in the walls.

"The black heart is in the Red Kingdom," I said. "If we can figure out who it is—"

"What? Helen, this is about that heart-puzzle rubbish? Forget the Timepiece! We just lost the library! I may have just lost some of my *brothers*..." His hand was outstretched to the doorway, but he inhaled sharply, and I was sure this was the first time he'd actually admitted to himself that either of those things had happened.

"Ragnashuck..." He balled a fist and pressed it hard against his mouth as moisture filmed his eyes, sinking them to navy. "What if everyone didn't get out before the fire took the library? What if Lucas did something reckless?" He covered his face, digging his fingers into his hair. "What are we going to do?"

Neither of us had to point out that the Greed had destroyed the library on their hunt for *us*.

When I stepped close enough, he reached to take me the rest of the way in, tugging me against his chest where his forest and mint scent enveloped the ever-present cocoa smell of the factory. I dropped my head along his neck and his hand drifted idly into my hair. I was surprised, but I didn't fight it.

I *swore* a tune was seeping from him; the same one I'd heard at the library.

"You need to get some sleep," I said, recognizing that his travels through the night weren't helping his spiralling mental state.

"Maybe I should take Jolly's deal," he whispered.

"That's a terrible idea," I scolded, driving back to look at his face. But he held me to him by my waist, eyes shining with a seriousness I wanted to slap away. "Zane, are you out of your mind?"

He was though—I could tell he was losing it as everything settled in. "The Timepiece said if we can solve the heart puzzles, we'll be safe. What if that's all there is to it? What if it stops Asteroth?" I tried.

A heavy breath slid from him. "I don't believe in prophecies, especially from strangers." He released my waist to resume his pacing.

I couldn't blame him for having that opinion, but I knew Zane didn't have any other ideas. And after Asteroth had *stolen* the library, and Zane had seen the state the Patrols were in, I knew he needed a way to fix this as much as I did.

"The Timepiece wasn't trying to sell himself as a prophet when he came to me. I think he warned me about what he saw coming to try and spare me from it," I said. "Zane, I think this might be the single key to stopping Asteroth. I think it's why the Timepiece risked stepping out of order."

A chug of bubbles rattled a pipe, drowning out the peaceful rhythm of the gears. Zane turned to me, arms folded.

"Fine. We'll do this your way. But something about all of this doesn't feel right. And I'll be dead before I'm caught parading around the Red Kingdom like a pompous Red noble, so I'm going as your guard and nothing more. Apple Dough had better know what she's doing."

THE STORYTELLER

THE FOURTH INTERRUPTION

The ground rumbled in anger where youthful Lucas Leutenski raged a howling gale of splintered ice into the heavens. He gritted his teeth to hold the whirlwind of Winter-cursed snow, all twisting and churning by the guttural grunts of his flesh where he aimed to consume the man levitating above. The liquid red of the man's cloak had already dissolved into the mass.

But the ice winds parted, and that once-prophet of twisted verses descended, a flaming torch in his hands. He struck back at the youthful foe who had followed him through sweat and snow to this end. Upon Asteroth Ryuu's head, a crown of diamond hair whisked out like silver wings.

Lucas's staff rose to block, but the flames thrust him into a drift. He rolled back to his feet, pins piercing into the shades within his chest like dark venom strangling his rainbows. It beckoned him, like it had so many others before.

One strike more from Asteroth, and the youthful Patrolman knew he would be forced to bow.

The bitter hand of Asteroth Ryuu—*murderer* of Mikal Migraithe—came down to crush him into the snow. The Patrolman pulled all he could into himself, rumbling the frost up to his staff's blades. One last thrust, he had. One last season's greeting for the executioner in velvet red.

Chapter,
The Twelfth

The night of the Halloween dance in October of this year, I had left the bathroom door open while I washed my face to get ready for bed. I'd stared at myself in the mirror, listening to Winston's dress shoes clunking over the kitchen floor downstairs as he got ready to leave. I'd never met the girl Winston was going to the dance with, but I'd seen her in the hall at school a few times whispering in his ear.

Even though Kaley was in grade nine, she'd been asked by Skylar Hans—a boy in *my* grade—to go as his date. She'd declined with all the humble politeness of a low-income Canadian freshman. She didn't even tell me about it; I'd learned about Skylar's advance from eavesdropping on Mia Fillard in French class as she trash-talked the "grade nine *child*" that

Skylar was after, who apparently "everyone was talking about."

Kaley was confident, and stronger than most, but I'd still felt a beat of terror that these senior high school hyenas would gang up on her and drag her name through the mud.

My sister didn't often wear makeup, but she kept a bag on the bathroom counter with a few tubes of lipstick, some concealer, and a wand for mascara. It sat open at the foot of the mirror and I dragged it to myself as I thought about how relieved I was that she hadn't said yes to Skylar Hans.

Downstairs, the front door opened and shut again, ending Winston's loud stomping.

The lipstick I dug out of Kaley's bag looked like it had never been used; a light matte-violet colour that I'd noticed other girls at school wearing. Though my face was splotchy from just being washed, I smeared the colour over my lips to see what it would look like on me.

I didn't have a chance to decide if I liked it before Winston appeared in the bathroom doorway. I slammed the lid back on and threw the lipstick into Kaley's bag, but Winston grunted.

"Since you're clearly not doing anything important, how about you let me use the bathroom?"

I rolled my eyes and grabbed a tissue, but he went on, "Please tell me you're not planning on coming to the dance."

I stopped. When I glanced up at my brother, he looked annoyed.

"Would that really be so bad?" I wiped the tissue over my lips, regretting ever touching Kaley's makeup.

"Yes." He didn't waver. "I don't want you there. Your lipstick looks disgusting, and you're *not* pretty. If you were, someone would have asked you to go to the dance. Now get out of the bathroom. I'm already late."

Winston pushed his way around me when I didn't move, as though threatening to use the bathroom with me still in it if I didn't leave.

I had to remember how to walk. My hand shook while I tucked the tissue into my palm, sure I wasn't done with it. Sure I never wanted to get dressed up for anything for the rest of my life.

Trunks of billowing fabric, glittering jewels, feathers, and lace covered half the main floor when I came down for lunch. The dining table was stacked high with old ledgers and scrolls of scribbled notes and pictures. There was nowhere to eat.

Eliot appeared from a hallway with a trunk and placed it with the others. Two other Patrolmen were helping, too.

Eliot had that same odd look, like he was wondering why I'd ever agreed to this. I had a feeling he'd have questions for me later, but I could also ask why *he* was so willing to go to the Red Kingdom.

A shiny pair of scissors wound around the stacked rings on Apple's fingers. "Too bad the masquerade festival is at the palace tomorrow night," she said. "The festival is glorious—it's to mark the approaching season of the Silver Jubilee Renewal. Oh, I wish I could have had you ready in time to see it! Everything, even the food and drink and chocolates, will be *silver!*" She dragged a pallet of claret fabric from a dusty trunk.

"Unfortunately, it would be impossible to train and dress you in such little time. I think I'll make you ready for the Alabaster Ball instead, hosted by Holly Kissing at her chateau. That would mark an excellent return."

Stage-fright rose to the surface as she spoke, and I worried Apple might go to all this trouble to try and make me lovely, and I'd still end up looking ridiculous instead. Some people couldn't be pretty, even with makeup and a nice dress.

Apple draped a strip of fabric around my body to take measurements, the embellished scissors balancing between her teeth. Her dark lips curled up at the corners when she saw my expression. "Don't worry, friend. I'm an expert in Red Kingdom fashion." The words had to work their way through her teeth.

Zane hopped over the staircase rail, not bothering with the last half-dozen steps. He stifled an eyeroll at the piles of red fabric and continued to the lunch spread Fred was setting atop Apple's notes. Several other Patrolmen were already heading that way.

"I'll enjoy working on your wardrobe. Scarlet Strange was a bit of an odd girl, but no one understood her fashion sense like I did," Apple went on, finally pulling the scissors out of her mouth and snipping the end of the fabric ribbon to mark my size.

"Great." I imagined I would be quite the spectacle. And I wasn't surprised at all that Apple had bonded with the "odd girl."

"Let's go taste the milk biscuits, Miss Helen, and I can

teach you of the royals while we sip our cocoa."

Moments later I was in the seat beside Zane. He passed me a biscuit and said nothing of our plan; he didn't object, or make comments, or try and talk us out of it. He just ate and stole a swipe of frosting off my plate when he thought I wasn't looking.

"We'll start with the Red Princes. Scarlet was rather close to the Red Princes, before a certain prince chased her off across the globe." Once again, Apple neglected to say the *certain prince's* name.

"Prince Tegan is the oldest, and heir to the Red Throne. He's somewhat of a brute, truly. The stories of him would make you shiver." Apple shuddered, and a few grunts rose around the table from the eavesdropping Patrolmen. "Next is pale-featured Prince Forrester, an equally horrific prince on the battlefield."

Someone down the table actually *booed*, and Zane snorted a laugh.

"And then Prince Quinten," Apple continued, holding up pictures of faces I'd have to pretend I knew from my childhood. More booing erupted.

"Prince Quinten is loved the most by the Red Kingdom," Apple said.

"Why?" I interrupted. "Why do the people love him?"

"Well…" Apple fought a smile. "He's beautiful, Miss Helen. Sweeping charcoal locks and eyes of a velvet sunset. You'll see."

I wished I hadn't asked. Everyone got to watch my neck warm.

When Apple introduced the next prince, the table exploded with noise and inappropriate gestures. Zane cackled, whipping a chocolate at Mirkra who'd flipped over a tray of chocolates in feigned outrage and shaken his fist.

But even with all the energy, the information made my head spin. I rubbed my eyes and stopped listening as Apple described the next few princes' looks and habits. Instead, I stole a glance at Zane and Eliot, who'd paused their laughing to exchange a look that told me they didn't think I could pull this off.

Apple held the last two drawings up, side-by-side. "These are the youngest of the nine Red Princes. Sputtlepun troublemakers. I would avoid them." She laid all the pictures out in a row. "Shall we move on to Red Kingdom celebrities now?"

"No!" I halted her. I couldn't take any more. I couldn't even remember which name went with which Red Prince, or what the names were to begin with. "I think this was a mistake."

"Let's find another way," Zane agreed.

"No," Eliot spoke at the same time, standing from his chair. "You can do this, Helen. You went to Wentchester Cove to face the witch. You can face these people, who are far less dangerous than she was."

"That's debatable." Zane flicked a nut off his plate.

I ran my fingers through my hair. The Patrolmen around the table had gone quiet and were looking off in a hundred different directions to pretend they weren't listening.

Apple settled her stare on my tangled hair. "I ought to do something about that, too," she said, quieter now. "If you're still willing to give this a shot, Miss Helen."

I looked between Apple, Eliot, and Zane—who only shrugged, leaving it up to me.

"What are you going to do to my hair?"

Apple's dark lips curled up at the corners and she pulled a fresh set of scissors from her pockets.

Chapter,
The Thirteenth

The Trite world would be the ideal hiding place if things didn't go well. I could pack my things and move to Toronto before the intersects opened again and hide among the large crowds until it closed. I couldn't stop thinking about home.

Apple had run over the princes' names with me again as she untangled my hair, snipped the ends, and pressed my hair between curved pallets to give it waves. She'd smoothed a thick mahogany paste through the strands to change the colour, too. "Satin rose," she called it.

Apple was unusual, but I couldn't deny that she had an eye for transforming something mundane into something remarkable. Her embossed scissors hung on the wall in a row—some for cutting hair, some for cutting fabric, some for cutting paper, and some for snipping jewelry into pieces that she used to make new jewelry.

When I finally stood before the mirror, I blinked at the bright golden eyes in the reflection—the result of a trick with special eyedrops Apple had invented to change her own eye colour to chocolate.

"It won't last forever. Maybe just a day or three," she said. "Same with your hair. You'll be looking yourself again in a pinch. I'm going to have to come with you to keep this look up."

Relief welled up in me. I wouldn't survive in the Red Kingdom without her to remind me who was who.

My gown brushed the floor, a collection of toffee gems and red feathers from some rare bird Apple had mentioned. "It was my mother's favourite bird. That's why I kept the feathers," she added when she caught me staring, and I glanced down to watch her reshape my hem.

I knew that tone, that specific pit one's voice dipped into when they spoke of someone they'd lost.

"What happened to her?"

Apple's dark-chocolate smile was sweet. "Captured and martyred during the collapse. She was part of the underground cathedral's operation into Polar Territory. There are souls to be saved there still, Miss Helen. My mother believed in bringing them the Truth."

Wow.

I stared back at myself in the mirror where I no longer resembled a Trite, but a convincing Rime-blood. As I studied my eyes, I imagined Apple's mother being killed just for trying to bring the Truth to people who were without it.

"I lost my mother, too," I told her.

Apple's movements were slow now, melancholy. She folded a piece of the fabric by my ankle and pushed a pin through, then began threading a needle.

"I'm sorry, Miss Helen," she said.

"You can just call me Helen."

"Well, I'm so very sorry, Helen. It's a great hardship to lose a mother." Her cocoa eyes flickered up to mine.

We were an unlikely pair—a Trite with Rime-coloured eyes and a Rime Folk with Trite-brown eyes. But for the first time since meeting Apple, I wondered if this strange girl could understand me better than any of the girls I'd had fleeting relationships with in high school. She didn't seem so odd all of a sudden.

It was difficult not to react when Apple and I emerged from the lantern-lit hall. I never thought I'd see the day Zane Cohen wore red.

"We *must* practice the dances. Father, will you play your violetta-lin?" Apple took Eliot's hands in the main room, and Fred lifted an ivory instrument with strings. "Pay attention, Helen!" Apple snapped her fingers and my focus darted over.

Zane's crimson guard uniform didn't suit him. His curled-toe boots had been replaced with delicate palace slippers, but he didn't complain. He finished buttoning his cuff and tugged me to him. "I can't wait to watch you try this," he said. I almost shoved him right back off, but he gripped my waist and began half-forcing me through the steps Apple demonstrated until I gave in.

When Zane couldn't contain himself anymore, the grin broke out and I smacked his chest.

"Stop it!" Humiliation washed through me.

"It's like trying to dance with an infant!" he complained.

As the day passed, Patrolmen drifted off to different parts of the factory. Apple and Fred retired to bed at twilight, and Zane and I were left alone in the large room.

Zane, despite all his mocking, stayed with me until I had the three most common dances figured out. But when the sunset dimmed to gray-blue skies and the stars peeked through the skylights, our commitment to learning the steps disappeared. Before I knew it, I was slung over Zane's shoulder like I was being kidnapped, stifling my laughter so I wouldn't wake the others as he trotted around the room, imitating a spoiled Red Prince in a ridiculous voice.

"More snacks!" he commanded invisible servants. He picked up a bead of chocolate and tossed it in the air, then swung me over to his other shoulder, and still caught the thing in his mouth when it came down.

In the dusk, Zane's eyes glowed as he slid me back to my feet. "Red Kingdom dances are dreadfully boring," he said.

I yawned, feeling the first of my adrenaline drain away. "For you, maybe. It took you three seconds to figure them out."

"Sometime, I'll take you ice dancing. Then you'll see." He gazed up at the skylights. Whatever style Zane's pecan hair had been in before was destroyed; it looked like he'd battled a snowsquatch.

But his glow melted away with his dimples, and his gaze drifted back down. "Helen, there's something I haven't been honest about," he said out of nowhere.

My brows burrowed as the deal Jolly had offered by the river came back full swing. Zane had never actually told me what had happened at the river. I knew it shouldn't have taken him so long to get to the factory.

"What did you do?"

But Zane looked surprised. "Wait..." He drew back. "What do you *think* I did?"

A crashing knock against the factory doors froze us both. We exchanged a look as the pounding sounded again, and Patrolmen began spilling out of the places they'd disappeared to, wondering what the ruckus was.

Apple rushed down the stairs in her nightgown, a long white cape fluttering behind her like a bride, a lantern glowing in her grip.

"It's the Ruby Legion," she said as she slipped past us— the first time I'd seen her without dark lipstick or dangling earrings. "I'll deal with this."

Fred half-tumbled down the stairs, grabbing his glasses before they slid off his nose, and Zane's hand found my arm. He pulled me into the dark hall as Patrolmen all over the main space slinked into shadows and cracks until their raven-black uniforms could no longer be seen.

Chapter,
The Fourteenth

G usts of cold rushed through the factory when the doors swung open. The pair of Ruby Legionnaires wore long crimson coats and bronze helmets, their pointed spears glowing in the moonlight.

Zane's quiet breathing was the only sound I heard until Apple raised her voice. "Our order isn't ready yet, friends. We weren't expecting you for a measure."

Low words were exchanged, pleasant enough. Zane leaned to the hall's edge to try and listen.

Across the long room, Patrols were tucked into cupboards, dangling in rafters, ducking behind the moat...dozens of eyes peeked out of the shadows.

"Well, *we* will deliver them to *you* then. Tomorrow! I

apologize for the trouble, but we've had company the last day or three." Apple glanced in our direction and I wasn't sure if she wanted me to show myself and prove she wasn't lying. Zane made a face, too.

Without discussion, I emerged from the hallway. The Ruby Legion soldiers glanced over as I stepped into the moonlight, and to my continued bafflement, they didn't scowl, or even look doubtful. I felt the heat of their eyes travelling over my new dress and hair, which was reasonably tousled from riding over Zane's shoulder.

"Lady Strange! I didn't realize you were still awake," Apple bluffed. "Legionnaires, this is Lady Scarlet Strange. We are accompanying her to the Red Kingdom. I'm sure you remember her from many seasons past?"

Recognition flickered between the soldiers, and I hoped they couldn't tell I was shaking beneath my dress. A frozen smile was plastered over Fred's wrinkled face.

"My lady," both the men muttered at once, bowing slightly.

"Anyway, inform the Crimson Court that we'll be there tomorrow for the Silver Masquerade Festival. And please ensure this news makes it into their Pebble Paper in the morning—that Lady Scarlet Strange is returning, at last! Have a pleasant ride back, friends." Apple shut the door on them, and I let out the breath I was holding. Fred's smile vanished; Apple put a hand against her forehead.

"Oh, sweet grace of Elowin, what have I done?" she tugged her brunette hair. "I panicked, Father!"

"It's alright. We'll figure it out," Fred said.

"Didn't I fool them?" I asked.

I realized Zane was beside me again, and Eliot, who

must have heard the noise. Wanda rolled out of a cupboard and landed at my feet.

"Well, they've seen you in our home now, Helen. As *Scarlet*. So, if you go into the Red Kingdom and are *caught* impersonating Scarlet Strange…they'll know we were involved and they'll come for us," she said. Apple stopped fussing with her hair. "So, you cannot be caught—even after you leave the Red Kingdom, we must keep up this charade and hope the real Scarlet Strange never plans to return. This *must* work now, for all of us, and there's no changing our minds about it."

Zane cast me a dark look. That black heart had better be where I thought it was.

"And on top of all that, we're expected at the palace by tomorrow night for the Silver Masquerade Festival. You are barely trained, and now I have to make you a silver dress before we can leave!" she said to me, eyes wild.

"I'll load the chocolates at dawn, Apple. You spend the morning working with Miss Helen," Fred offered.

"We'll all help you load the sleigh," Zane offered. Eliot nodded, along with the other Patrolmen trickling into the half-circle around us.

"To bed then, everyone!" Fred clapped.

A MEDDLING MIDDLE INTERRUPTION

*D*eep in the belly of an ancient ice cave, a youthful once-prince with burgundy eyes and mahogany locks paused his walk, and his reading.

'Twas a particular sound Porethius Plum made as she approached, always quiet as night, eager as day, and faithful as the rising sun. A fairy who had once stood atop the abandoned gravestone of Elowin himself to inform the next to arrive that the King of Truth had already risen and a new age had dawned.

The burgundy-eyed once-prince had a name. One that used to be lengthy and noble but was now simply: *Cane*. And that was all.

He slapped the book shut to end the silence.

"Plum," he greeted. "Do you have a thing to say?"

"No." The fairy glanced at the icy walls. Then, "Well. Perhaps." And finally, "I visited our Carrier. And I sense she feels a pinch...*lonely*."

Cane tapped his forefinger against the Volume he held. He watched as the fairy unhooked the ancient, double-bladed sword from her back and studied it for dirt, though there was not a spec to be found.

"And this worries you?" Cane guessed, because a fairy's emotions were often riddlesome.

"I'm worried the Beast will feast upon her spirit if she thinks she is alone."

"Surely your visit must have proved she's got a friend or three she hasn't yet met. Why would she feel lonely?"

"Because she misses her mother," the fairy said. "More than she'll admit, I think."

Porethius finally met his gaze, and Cane saw a thing. For fairies were, and always had been, the motherly, caretaker sort. A factor that drew them to watch over little ones from the shadows, with a special devotion to babies and infants, and most especially, the orphaned.

Orphaned—as Helen Bell was. As Cane himself had become the eve his father had blotted his name from the family documents and renounced him for his choice to leave the Crimson Court.

"Also, a little bird whispered a thing in my ear on the way in. You may wish to know that the Carrier means to sneak into the Red Kingdom by impersonating an old friend of yours," the fairy added.

Cane sighed and flipped his book open to continue his reading. "Oh? And who might that be?" he asked. But the once-prince cared not for his old life or the folk he might have once called *friends*.

Porethius shoved the book back down. "She is pretending to be Scarlet Strange."

145

At that, the book slipped from the once-prince's hand, caught quickly by the fairy before it might have clattered on the floor. Without another word, Porethius sealed it shut and pressed the cover against Cane's chest as she passed.

His fingers barely came up in time to catch it when she let it go.

Chapter,
The Fifteenth

The last time I had set foot in the Red Kingdom, I'd gotten Wren Stallone killed and I'd gotten trapped in the dark tunnels of Mara Rouge's underground fortress.

My sleep had been restless. Every time I woke, the moon looked like it hadn't moved in the sky.

When the creamy, yellow morning light finally came in through the window, I sat up and let Apple's quilt warm my legs. I tugged the orb necklace from beneath my shirt and reached for the ruby, emerald, and onyx on my nightstand, threading them onto the chain with my orb. My orb clouded silently, like a greeting.

A quiet rap sounded on my door and I sat up as Eliot poked his head in. "Apple wants you to try on your dress for the Silver Masquerade Festival," he said.

I nodded. "Any news of the dwarves?" I asked. "Or the Elders?"

Eliot's face fell and I knew the answer before he shook his head.

Apple was a basket case when I arrived at her room. Not a single pair of scissors remained on their hooks—heaps of crinoline and satin buttons spilled from trunks, sparkling gems were sorted into categories on the floor, and thread and needles were strewn everywhere. It was hard not to step on anything when I came in.

"Excellent!" she said when she looked up, and I cringed at the dark bags beneath her eyes.

"Apple...did you sleep at all last night?"

She ignored the question and tugged me toward a dress lying on the bed. I gaped at the bodice and skirt covered entirely with white gems like a shapely diamond rug.

"You're going to glow like the silver stars, friend," she breathed. "Try it on!"

I fumbled out of my nightclothes, strangely nervous. Apple laced up the pewter ribbons at the back and beamed when she came around. But her focus fell to the necklaces at my throat. "I think those may give you away."

I clutched the snowflake pendant and orb. I'd only taken off the snowflake necklace a few times all year.

"Does this dress have a pocket?" I tried, but her eyes drifted past me to the clock on the wall and widened.

"By the sharpest wind, it's time to go! It's half a day's journey to the Red Kingdom. We'll be late for the festival if we don't move our scotchers!"

My heart sank into my stomach. I couldn't remember the

names of the royal family, or the map of the palace. Or anything else, frankly.

"I'll be right there with you," Apple promised. "We will
do this, friend. We must."

"Trite, there's no way I'm letting you waltz through the
palace in *that*..." Zane's steady voice came from the doorway. He was already strapped into his red uniform, his hair
stained with black ink and combed to the side. His blue eyes
had been bleached to gold from Apple's drops—they were
as round as coins when they flickered to Apple. "She can't
wear that!"

I hugged my arms to myself, certain I looked absurd.

"Do you want everyone to believe she's Scarlet or not?"
Apple said, snatching all her scissors off the floor, the
dresser, the bed, and going to the wall to hang them. But she
paused with the metal tools overwhelming her hands. "On
second thought, I'd better take these." All the scissors went
into a satchel.

"Helen...this isn't what you signed up for!" Zane said.
"You look..." He stepped into the room without finishing
his sentence, and I braced myself for the worst.

"Beautiful? Magnificent?" Apple offered. "She needs to
draw attention—that's the point of this costume. Scarlet
Strange wouldn't return without vengeful beauty to bite
those who once only saw her for her hideous red spots. You
didn't know Scarlet, Patrolman, I did."

Zane answered through his teeth, "Fine." He forced an
utterly phony smile and scuffed his neat hair—Apple
winced. "Helen, I might be posing as your guardsman, but I
can't protect you from the royal princes if they get any
ideas."

"Ideas?" My gaze fell to the dress. He couldn't be serious.

"I know the servants' tunnels like the back of my hand. If Helen needs to slip away, I'll get her out." Apple tossed everything in sight into her satchel.

"That won't work," Zane said. "She's *too* beautiful. It's dangerous—"

"Zane," I stopped him. "I can handle myself." I wasn't sure it was true. I was uncomfortable when boys merely *glanced* at me, and unfortunately Zane had picked up on that from all the times I'd blushed like a tulip.

"Time to get on the snow," Fred appeared from the hall. "We can eat breakfast in the sleigh."

Apple gave the remaining Patrolmen a lecture about staying quiet, not answering the door while we were gone, and keeping their dirty fingers out of the chocolate river, but I watched Zane as she spoke, thinking about what he'd said.

Finally, we set out in Fred' sleigh, while a hundred or so boys in raven-black shouted farewells and other mildly-inappropriate dismissals at Zane and Eliot.

Chapter,
The Sixteenth

The Red Kingdom's iron gate glimmered in the mist. Messy warnings were scribbled across the stone base, breathing their cautions over my skin as we drew close.

"It would have been faster if we'd skated," Eliot muttered after making faces at the horses' rears the whole ride. His hair was slick like Zane's; they looked sharp enough to pass for a noblewoman's personal guards. But even though Apple had changed their colours—turned Eliot's eyes dark purple and pulled his curls into a bun behind his head—I had a feeling we would still be noticed by anyone who'd crossed us before.

"And then what? Scarlet Strange would show up to the Red Kingdom with wild, tangled hair and a red nose from wind burn?" Apple snorted at Eliot—the first sign her long night was taking its toll. She'd spent our time in the sleigh coaching me on my Winter accent.

Nausea touched my stomach when I saw the obsidian roads of the Scarlet City, the daunting ruby statues poking up through the mist, and the gold sleighs navigating the streets.

My eyes dropped to my crystal heels as we passed through the gate, beneath the watchful glare of those horrific guardian statues facing outward that seemed ready to pounce. An enormous flag lapped overhead against a breeze I could barely feel, one proud ring of stars encircling the royal family's symbol. A star for each Red Prince I would have to face and deceive, and a burn hole to delete the third star from the top.

Then *her*.

I gasped—Zane's hand flew out to press over mine on the bench. There *she* was, in a statue of solid, sparkling white. The witch who'd nearly killed us both.

Mara Rouge's alabaster monument was erected over the Scarlet City, with blank, pale eyes cast down on the road as though she watched all who passed. My blood froze in my veins while we inched under her stare. She was dressed exactly as she'd been at the Quarrel of Sword and Bone—right down to her scaled armour and her wild, loose hair.

The statue they'd raised in her honour was a monstrous act of worship to a self-proclaimed queen who'd been a celebrity but never truly royal blooded. Someone who had earned her title by the lives she'd taken and the souls she'd crushed.

People paused in reverence as they passed by it—some stopping to lay flowers and berry bouquets on the pedestal by her sabatons. Even in death, she had admirers under her spell.

Apple smiled up at the statue as we sailed by. "It's alright, friend. I've been coming here since I could speak," she whispered, and I realized I was trembling when Zane's hand swivelled beneath mine to interlock our fingers. "It's just a lot of show to entertain a bunch of little minds. Before you arrived at the factory, I heard that Asteroth Ryuu officially left his post as the Red Kingdom prophet. I don't think he'll come back any time soon now that they've replaced him with that fearsome blind woman they keep in their basement," Apple said. "Apparently, she has the most frightful ashworm tattoo, right up her spine and into her hair!"

"Gross," Eliot remarked.

Zane was absent from the conversation. His eyes had remained closed since the moment Mara Rouge's statue had come into view. I didn't know if he was thinking about the Quarrel of Sword and Bone, or about how *she* had killed Thomas—his first Carrier—and undid his spirit before he'd met me.

I took in a deep breath and let it out slowly. I hated this place.

"You are Scarlet Strange. You belong among these people. You're as arrogant and entitled as any Red Prince. Don't forget that," Apple coached, and Zane's freshly bronzed eyes finally opened to glance at me as I nodded. "Feel free to boss them around in public." Apple's mouth curled up as she nodded toward Zane and Eliot.

Eliot grunted, but Zane's foot drifted to the middle of the sleigh where his and Eliot's Patrol staffs were tucked away beneath the floorboards.

On a stone as black as ash,
appearing on the coldest day,
One can read a scribble
on an iron gate that would say:

THERE'S A KINGDOM
THROUGH THIS GATE
COME INSIDE, DON'T HESITATE
PRESENTS FALL FROM THE SKY
REACH OUT AND TAKE WHAT
YOU DELIGHT
YOU'LL FEEL ALIVE
SO VERY ALIVE

PART 3

OH, FANCY THAT! IT SEEMS WE'VE FOUND
OUR SECOND PROLOGUE!

READ ON, THEN…

THE
STORYTELLER

PROLOGUE, THE SECOND

*F*urthermore, folly is how this story begins.

Many seasons ago, a young prince in a crimson cape spied upon a girl of the court with a word of malice on his tongue, a fruit of jest in his mind, and a spool of darkness in his heart.

The scars that speckled the girl's face shone in the candlelight of the meeting room as she tilted her head and found the boy watching her. He mused at her observation of his pretty mahogany locks—the deepest red of anyone he had crossed in his seasons. Lovely, the prince was, on the outside. A thing he knew.

But a bitter heart beat within his chest. A thing he refused to know.

As the prince studied the girl with scars, he batted his lashes over his burgundy eyes, drawing her cheeks to flush as he considered how he might unravel her next; wondered what cruel thing he might do to unleash her tears.

How glorious it was, each time he did.

And so, he walked into the meeting, eyeing her among the nobles and esteemed members of the Crimson Court, and pulled out a handful of hard-shelled nuts. Between his teeth, he cracked them with a ruckus that pulled the girl's attention back. He winked to make her blush a time again. The girl certainly despised when he did that, which was precisely the reason he did it.

'Twas the young boy's routine to bring torment to her doorstep, quarter after entertaining quarter. A game that went on until the morning the scar-faced girl disappeared from the palace and the young prince could not find her anymore—in her chambers, in the ice gardens, in the courtyards, in the cities.

By a riddlesome turn, it seemed the girl with the scars had vanished.

And to the young prince—Cane Endovan Crimson-Augustus—it was all not so very funny anymore.

Chapter,
The Seventeenth

Lights twinkled in the marble pillars like fiery glitter, countering the navy evening sky. Glass-bead curtains clattered like stones in the night breeze, lining the gaping entranceway of the Red Kingdom palace.

As Apple had forewarned, everything was silver; the gleaming moons dangling from the ceiling by shimmering threads, the twisted fountain of ice sprouting from the lobby's centre, the harps and flutes being played by a small band in the corner—even the floor had been dusted over with a sheen of glitter. For the first time since sliding into the dress Apple had made for me, I didn't feel overdressed.

The black-lace mask I wore around my eyes did nothing to hide my nerves, though.

Crowds swept past us in sheer gowns and fitted silvery suits, starlight hats and crystal-toe shoes. Wreaths of opals crowned the heads of twin girls who scurried past.

But I faltered at the sight of the *cages*. Bars of steel trapped in elves and humans like pathetic animals, lining the walls like a twisted zoo. Bored eyes stared out at the crowds rippling through the lobby, and one or two of the prisoners hollered at guests who passed, but no one paid them any attention.

The prisoners all had something in common: green coats, heavy olive boots, and wooden armour. They looked well enough fed, but they were splattered in bright red liquid that soaked their once-green clothes. It looked like blood, or...*paint*.

Apple huffed. "Prisoners of the wars," she explained. "The Crimsons put the Greens on display so they can gloat. Frankly, I think we're safer with some of these Green brutes contained."

Three decorative cages hung over the entrance into the wide hall I gathered would take us to the ballroom. A pair of legs dangled out of one, swinging in boredom. My mouth parted as I stared up at them: stranded, spectacles.

Zane might have become one of these decorations if I'd never found him in Mara Rouge's underground fortress. I glanced over at my Patrolman to find him already looking at me. He hadn't looked so wrong in red until this moment.

"Keep moving, Trite. There's no going back now," he gave me a knowing look. His hand found my arm to usher me, forcing me to keep moving even though my knees felt weak.

"Lady Strange." A voice cooled the air.

I whipped around sharply, tearing out of Zane's grip.

A young man leaned against the inside of the entrance in a taffeta coat the colour of blueish nighttime snow, a porcelain mask concealing the top half of his face—but not his eyes.

Good grief, his *eyes*...

He was wearing a silver crown.

"Your Highness!" Babbling, fearless Apple went as red as the fruit of her own name. She dropped into a curtsey.

"Miss Dough, I thought the help was supposed to come through the servants' passages," the young man said. But a smile broke his face, and Apple burst into a laugh when she realized he was joking.

"Yes...I was just heading that way," she promised, casting me one last look, to my horror, before readjusting the satchel on her arm and aiming toward a hall in the other direction. "I look forward to being your personal stylist for your stay, Lady Strange. Thank you for the opportunity," she called back, no doubt so she could come find me later without raising suspicion.

I didn't have a chance to ask Apple which prince this was, but it seemed everyone else in sight knew. Across the hall, a pair of slender girls in quartz masks glanced my way. One of them had honey-gold hair to match her bright eyes that held me captive through the peep holes of her mask.

My face must have been pale when I finally turned back to the boy-prince with the richest black hair I'd ever seen. He still leaned casually, his crown gleaming beneath the pillar-lights. "I heard a rumour you were coming. I've been waiting for you."

I could *not* do this.

The prince lifted from the stone frame and drifted over, the crowd spreading like a river around a rock to give him all the space he wanted. "Keep moving, guardsmen." Even though he said it to Zane and Eliot behind me, his amethyst eyes remained settled on mine.

All too quickly, the cool scents of pine sap and peppermint vanished.

My back felt cold as I stood alone with this Red Prince. Feminine stares flitted over my gown and shoes, sizing me up as I stood before one of their beloved stars. Zane had warned me this would happen if I wore this dress, but I hadn't realized how fast it would all come sweeping in. I hadn't even made it into the ballroom yet and I was sure my cheeks were already pink.

"Come inside with me." The prince extended the arm of his ice-blue coat. I tried to steady the shaking of my fingers as I took it.

When we turned for the ballroom, I scanned the crowd for Zane or Eliot, but all the frosty colours bled together like a silver lake. I knew I had to speak, I had to say *something*, but my nerves had stapled my mouth shut.

"Would you care for a dance, Lady Strange?" the prince invited, guiding me into a massive pear-shaped room with a cathedral ceiling—a brilliant chandelier made of tiles and mirrors hung from the centre, casting marbled reflections over the floor. One brushed over the prince's face as he turned to me.

"Scarlet?" he asked again, dropping the formalities.

"I'm..." I swallowed. "I'm worried my seasons away

have made me forget the steps," I said in my best Winter accent. "But I'm happy to try."

"Then I'll merrily remind you." His gold-ring-stacked fingers came out to accept me. "But Scarlet, I just…I need to *see…*"

Heat burned through my veins as he reached up instead. I stood frozen in place as the Red Prince took off my mask.

He stared at me with his jewel-toned eyes, absorbing my face, my lipstick, my topaz irises embellished by the black wings of liner on my lids, and my skin Apple had gone to great lengths to smooth with cream. "Kingsblood," he whispered, close enough that I could feel the word on my skin. "You sure know how to make us pay." He smiled.

This was what Apple had wanted. But the prince's opinion still surprised me.

"Thank you…I owe it to my dressmaker, Apple Dough. We're old friends, if you remember." I sealed the job for Apple, wishing she was with me now. Wishing we had never come here in the first place and tried to pull this off.

In a heartbeat, the prince's mask was off, too. And upon seeing his striking, husky, long-lashed features, I realized exactly which prince this was. This was Prince Quinten. *Beautiful*, was how Apple had described him. And she was not wrong.

No wonder all the women had been casting me daggered stares. But that wasn't the only revelation that struck me; I realized I'd seen him before. Last year, during the Peppermint Carnival, he'd been part of the parade. I could have sworn those amethyst eyes had looked right at me at the time.

Prince Quinten tucked both our masks into his jacket and took my sides. He whisked me toward the middle of the moon-bleached tile floor.

"I can't believe you came back. I'm merrily ub-bersnugged." There was real shock in his eyes. He pulled me along, ignoring the true steps of the dance, to my relief, and made his own path through the couples who parted for him without a flinch. "I'm sure my brothers are dying to steal you away and see you for themselves. But I needed to catch you first." He lowered his voice, "I want to know if you found him."

I blinked and tried to stay composed. But there was no way the prince missed my confusion. "Found who?" I finally just asked.

"It's alright," he whispered. "I'm not trying to get you in trouble, but I know you were looking for that *nutcracker*. Your old maidservant told my butler a season or three ago."

The colour in Quinten's eyes drained to glass when I didn't reply. His smile fell and he stopped dancing; there was no mistaking the flash of fear that followed. "Kingsblood, Scarlet, don't tell my father," he begged. "I'm not trying to cause a muddle in the Crimson Court, I just wanted to know if you found my brother."

I *had* to say something now. The way the prince was looking at me, like I was suddenly the most dangerous person in the palace, made me blink. "I won't speak a word of it, Your Highness," I managed to get out.

Quinten stared at me for a second too long, but nodded. "Scarlet, you know full well you can call me *Quinten*," he said, pulling my mask back out and uncurling it.

He placed the lace back where it belonged around my eyes and fastened it. His fingers knotted with quick precision, even though he looked visibly rattled by all the things it seemed he'd hoped I would say and didn't. I wondered if he and Scarlet Strange were friends as children, or at least, had something in common they didn't tell others about.

An old connection like that would make things considerably more difficult for me in this role. I couldn't fake a real bond.

His amethyst eyes darted down to mine as he finished the tie. "You seem different," he said, and by some miracle, I didn't flinch. But a smile tugged at the edge of his mouth. "I like it."

Quinten swept us back into the dance, shoulders more rigid than before. His stare darted to a couple floating by. Then another. "Forrester has found you," he said. "Don't let him bull you around—they'll all try and see if they can. Welcome home, Scarlet." He dropped my hands.

"May I steal you away, Lady Strange?" A deep voice came from behind me.

When I glanced back, I found another silver crown nestled into a head of pure ivory hair. His brows were still as dark as soil, and his eyes shone with the same lustrous purple as Prince Quinten's.

"Um," but when I looked back, Quinten was gone. "Of course."

Prince Forrester—my mind raced with everything I could remember Apple saying about him. I tried to tell myself that this was like a test at school, and I just needed to remember the answers.

Prince Forrester sauntered around, purple eyes sharp. He moved like a hunting animal; slow, creeping, stalking. With his bone-coloured hair, he reminded me of the Greed, and I fought a shudder. "You've grown up, Lady Strange." His

169

JENNIFER KROPF

voice was raspy and sweet, too unnatural. But he extended a gloved hand, kindly enough.

I took it. And there wasn't much talking after that.

Prince Forrester put the wind to shame, brushing through the dancers faultlessly and silent as a graveyard, aware of every crack in the crowd, every space on the floor. His grip was firm, and I recalled Apple telling me that he was known for his blood-spilling war hands. My fingers grew hot in his glove.

"My turn, brother." A boy who couldn't be more than fourteen or fifteen arrived. I could only guess at this point which of the nine Red Princes this was.

A navy jacket covered his thin torso; a silver wreath hugged his chestnut hair. He held out a white-gloved hand for me to come to him, and Prince Forrester glided me into the younger boy's arms.

"I don't remember much about you, Lady Strange. But I've heard the stories." The smile that flashed over the boy's mouth when we started to dance was cruel. But for all his arrogance, the boy could dance just as well as his brothers. "I don't imagine you'll find yourself very comfortable here. Not with all the people *staring*. I heard you hated how everyone stared at you." He stole a look around, seeming to revel in it.

Scarlet Strange's despicable scars…I held my breath so I wouldn't bite at him with nasty Trite language.

"Lady Strange," the prince bid me farewell when the music ended. It seemed he'd seen all he needed to.

I wiped my warm palms over my diamond skirt. Before anything else could find me, I scoured the crowd for Zane, or Eliot, or Apple, or Fred, or *anyone*.

170

But who I found, passing by an open door of the silver-ornamented ballroom, filling the narrow hallway with his smoke and black-cloaked tentacles, was the Timepiece.

The Timepiece glanced at me as he passed—as though he knew *exactly* where I was—and then he was gone, past the archway and down the hall. Behind him, another smoky being travelled by, and then another. They all looked slightly different; lighter smoke, different robes, longer hoods, but I knew the one at the front was *him*; the Timepiece who had visited me at my bedroom window, marked my arm with a countdown clock, and then frozen everyone in the train until Cornelius Britley had shewed him away.

Eliot's words about Timepieces being messengers for the Crimson Court fired back, and I stuffed my questions down into the pits they belonged in. He wasn't the only

Timepiece here, so maybe his reasons for being at the palace had nothing to do with me.

I saw an attendant slip past a slitted door off the ballroom where I was sure servants watched the fluttering nobles on nights like this. I made for it, determined to avoid being caught by another Red Prince.

Scatters of chandelier reflections hit my eyes and I swatted at them like bugs, my rising panic birthing irrational paranoia. So, when a red coat rushed from my left and grabbed my arms to pull me through the slit-door, I almost screamed.

The door slammed shut and I was pressed against the wall of the dark hallway, a hand coming over my mouth. My golden-eyed captor's black hair blended into the darkness, and my pulse lifted until the familiar curve of Zane's jaw reminded me he was wearing a disguise. A moan of relief came from my throat, muffled by his hand.

I wondered if he'd ever even taken his eyes off me.

"Do you still want to do this?" Zane whispered as his pine scent soothed my senses in the dark. "We can leave. Just say the word and I'll have you out of this bloody palace before the Reds can blink." He dropped his hand from my mouth and unpinned me from the wall.

Beyond the slits of the door, the ballroom roared with noise. Shrill laughter erupted from somewhere nearby.

"The Timepiece is here," I whispered to his half-lit face. "I just saw him."

Zane tilted his head with a skeptical look. He'd been so adamant that we needed to forget about the Timepiece, but I had a feeling he didn't really want to abandon a chance at stopping Asteroth. "Ragnashuck, Helen, you're shaking. This is mad; we shouldn't be doing this," he said.

"We can't change our minds now. Apple and Fred are depending on us." I teetered off the wall and looked into the gloom of the servants' tunnel. Further down, soft lights flickered along the bend. "But I've shown myself enough. Maybe I can be done for tonight."

I wanted to find Apple and ask her about what Prince Quinten had said. I had a feeling it wouldn't be the last time the pretty Red Prince would bring it up.

"Eliot and I agreed to meet in your rooms. Apple requested chambers in the palace for your stay." Zane turned me away from the ballroom, not needing any more convincing. "This is madness, Trite," he added again, not releasing my arm. "I'm going to turn into a nattering spinbug in this worm-nest."

Apple paced, twirling a pair of gunmetal scissors over her rings. Everyone seemed to silently agree it wasn't safe to be within five feet of her—she wasn't watching where she was going. So, we all spread out over the living area of the chambers the Crimson Court had kindly bestowed upon their returned Lady Strange.

Zane was perched atop the dining table, legs crossed, his chin resting on his closed fist. He'd already abandoned his red coat.

Eliot had an elbow leaned up on the fire mantle where he watched the flames dance. I wondered if he was regretting everything he'd done to get here—insisting that he be my Patrolman, rushing to aid my escape from the library, and then getting stuck with us on this absurd mission. Though, in a way, he'd been the one to suggest it. And he'd practically forced us to bring him along.

Fred stood by the door in a cocoa-stained apron, ear against the wood to listen for anyone who might pass by and overhear.

"It doesn't make any sense," Apple stopped her swinging and gripped the scissors. "I suppose I didn't know much about Scarlet if she kept secrets with Prince *Quinten*. I didn't know they'd ever had a civilized conversation in their early seasons."

"I don't know that she kept secrets with him." I tugged at my neckline, itching to get out of the heavy, bejeweled dress, beautiful as it was. "I think he thought I knew something about his brother. But what brother is he talking about?"

"He's talking about the disgraced prince, Prince Cane. The one who left." Apple tapped her chin with the point of her scissors. "Cane is considered a deserter to the Crimson royals—his name isn't even allowed to be spoken in this kingdom anymore. He chose to leave and abdicate his position as a Red Prince, so his father cut him off from the royal family." Apple slammed her scissors down on the tabletop, making Zane jump.

"How could I have predicted *this*?" Apple asked. "Everything I know about Cane is just rumours. The nobles say he lost his mind before he left, tossing away his devotion to the Red Kingdom traditions and cursing his own brothers and parents for their cruelty. I didn't believe the rumours, of course, after I had watched him spend *seasons* mocking and tormenting Scarlet. But if it's true how he left, I would think it was Scarlet running away that tipped him over the edge.

He did love to torment her. It was a rather obsessive game of his."

Apple tapped her ringed fingers on the tabletop. Zane made a face at them, then slid himself to the opposite side of the table.

"Cane was like a snow pup with a bone," Apple said. "But why would Prince Quinten want to find him?" That was the question of the night.

I was already lost on these royals and their drama. Whatever family secrets they had didn't concern me, and wouldn't affect me, if I could just find the black heart and take off before I had to get involved.

"Helen could just keep denying she was ever searching for Cane. Prince Quinten clearly thinks any association to his disgraced brother will only bring trouble," Eliot piped up after minutes of silent staring at the fire. "He would stop asking, eventually."

"No. You need to ask him, Helen," Apple's brown eyes found mine. "He seems to think you and he are on the same side about something. You need to ask him why he wants to know about Cane."

"Couldn't that get *me* into trouble?"

"Maybe. But if you're going to convince the Crimson Court that you're their long-lost Scarlet, you're going to need to know what Prince Quinten is talking about. What if Scarlet *did* begin a search for Cane after she learned he'd left the Red Kingdom? What if members of the Court heard the same rumours Prince Quinten did? This could put you in a great deal of danger if we don't get to the bottom of it. If you're suspected of aiding Cane, you won't last long here. None of us will."

I let that settle. How was I supposed to ask a Red Prince for his secrets? Secrets that had already scared him enough to beg me not to repeat what he said?

"Just so we're clear," Zane spoke, raising a flat hand. "I don't think Helen should be alone with *any* of those princes. I think being here is dangerous enough as it is. If the Patrol Elders had any idea we were here—"

"If you want to hide here from Asteroth Ryuu, Mr. Zane, and spare me and my father from a measure of bad tidings, then you're going to need to let Helen convince these princes like we planned." Apple cracked a sweet smile, not hiding that it was forced.

"And we don't know what's happened to the Elders," Eliot muttered. "They could be spread thin across the globe by now or taken by the Greed. Our only job now is to keep Helen from Asteroth."

Zane's gaze flickered to mine. We both knew us being here had nothing to do with hiding from Asteroth, but I wasn't sure we could tell that to Apple and Fred just yet. Eliot though, probably deserved to know.

I wondered if I should take the Timepiece's arrival as an opportunity to find him and beg him for help. He'd traded me information about the black heart on the train. If he wanted me to solve his puzzle, I'd need more clues. This was the one thing Zane and I risked coming here for—and if we couldn't figure out these hearts, we were going to be embracing that future the Timepiece saw soon enough.

The night came with a wild windstorm. Pellets of snow

whipped against the rose-petal glass windows of our chambers; low roars breathing against the panes, trying to get in. The fire had gone out, but we didn't need it as we took turns telling stories to pass the time.

Zane started with a stirring tale of two believers of the Truth who had been placed in a public cage like the ones we saw when we first arrived, left there to die for their beliefs, until they began singing old hymns from the ancient days. Their songs rattled the sticks until the cages all down the square split apart, and all the prisoners were set free. The cage guards were so bewildered by the power of the believers' worship, that they chose to believe in the Truth themselves and joined the movement of sacred truths, living words, and magic hymns.

Apple lit a candle and dove into a performance that rivalled the dwarves' with actions and different voices; at one point even using her scissors collection as puppets which she held up from behind the sofa.

Even though worry weighed on my soul, I found myself grinning at Zane who had squeezed his eyes shut to stop watching Apple's show when he couldn't take it anymore. At first, I thought it was from sheer annoyance, but I realized he was trying desperately not to laugh and ruin her show.

Apple told the tale of a beautiful girl who lived with her uncle by unfortunate circumstance, until one day, she was recruited to enter into a competition to steal a historic Winter king's heart. By the whispers of the Truth feeding her soul and equipping her with strength, the woman became Queen and saved her people—the believers—from a wicked plot against them to turn them all back into snow. *Esther* was her name. The Star Queen. A nothing, who became everything.

Chapter,
The Nineteenth

We spent the next two days in my chambers, stealing back the time we lost to learn about the royal family, the Red Princes, and common celebrities. On the second day, Apple arrived with a leaflet of articles titled: THE PEBBLE PAPER. Within the columns issued by the Crimson Court was an announcement of the return of Lady Scarlet Strange. Immediately afterward, the news had gone into rumoured details regarding Lady Holly Kissing's upcoming Alabaster Ball.

Zane and Eliot cured their boredom with mindless games and got on each other's nerves when they ran out of things to do. The only ones who left the chambers were Apple and Fred, and that was to fetch carts of food, or to go on chocolate deliveries in the Scarlet City.

On the third morning, Zane strutted down the hall beside me in his red attendants' coat; the fabric warping pink beneath the direct sunlight from the windows. I glanced over at him twice before he shot me a look to tell me to stop—that my not-so-subtle glances at him were going to give us away.

"I'll be watching you all through breakfast," he said. "Just don't wander off alone with anyone."

The Crimson King had extended an invitation for Scarlet to dine at his breakfast table with his family and closest allies of the Court. I hoped none of those *closest allies* were people who'd recognize the Carrier and her Patrolman who had faced off with Mara Rouge before one thousand witnesses.

Apple's notes littered my brain in no logical sequence as we came to the massive walnut doors of the dining room. I was trying to focus on the task at hand, but this morning I realized that Zane was being forced to stand among the very people of the colour he hated most, and he wasn't complaining about it. I'd expected him to make a comment around every corner since we arrived, to point out every wicked thing that bothered him, and to try and get us to leave. But apart from the one instance in the servants' tunnel at the Silver Masquerade Festival, he hadn't said a word about rushing out of here.

I eyed him again as he stretched his neck, likely sore from sleeping on the floor in the living area of my chambers alongside Eliot, rather than in the attendants' villa where the rest of the guardsmen slept.

Zane's falsely golden eyes darted over to me, catching me staring *again*. He held my gaze this time as we passed through the walnut doors, and only put his sights where they belonged once we were in the dining room. Like the other attendants and guards, he veered to the right to stand in line, and I was left to navigate the dining room by myself.

Cooked eggs and sizzling meat wafted delicious scents into the air. I eyed the wreaths of silver bells hanging from ribbons above, left over from the festival's revelries, and the bubbling burgundy liquid filling the tall juice pitchers on the table. Steaming pots of tea rested between them.

Prince Quinten's head lifted from where he sipped tea across the room. He raised his cup in casual greeting like he *hadn't* spoken to me at the festival, *hadn't* asked me to keep quiet about what he'd said, and *hadn't* looked at me in terror afterwards.

The gaze of the girl with him flickered in my direction, and I recognized her from the masquerade ball. She'd been staring at me through a quartz mask. I wondered if it was jealousy that rose behind her beautiful toffee stare, or something else.

"Lady Strange," a broad chest with a crimson cape cut off my line of sight, and I stilled. "I never got a chance to say *welcome back* at the festival."

The Crimson King, in the flesh.

His voice was scratchy, mostly air. Instead of the sweet, purplish jewels I'd found in Prince Quinten's irises, the king's eyes were hard stone, almost black, with a glimmer of purple at the corners like a rotted plum. He smiled, and frost crawled through my gut. Wren Stallone had told me such gruesome stories about this man, I'd felt nauseous every time I'd thought of him since.

I couldn't help it—I stole a look at Zane. His face was unreadable, as it should be, and I dropped my eyes to the floor before the king read into my sideways glance.

"It's good to see you again, Your Majesty. Thank you for inviting me to breakfast." It was a miracle I got the words out, and with a moderately convincing accent.

But the king tilted his head, cold eyes hollowing as he studied me. Without a response, he left to stand behind the glorious seat at the head of the table where the ivory leaflet of The Pebble Paper rested by his place setting. I tried not to be nervous that the king would be reading about me this morning.

I found a spot behind a seat I hoped wasn't meant for someone else, and the princes and nobles flitted to their spots, too. Prince Quinten wandered to the seat at my side; something the honey-blonde girl noticed from across the table. When the king sat, everyone else followed.

"This morning we welcome Lady Holly Kissing, and the returned Lady Scarlet Strange to dine with us," the king nodded to the honey-blonde girl, then to me.

Holly Kissing. So that was why I didn't recognize her— half her face had been erased in Apple's sketch, as though Apple couldn't seem to get her features quite right. It also explained why the girl felt threatened by my presence; a returned noblewoman who might steal the attention of the royal family, who it seemed *she* had an eye for.

"Let us chant our faiths," the king said.

All at once, the nobles began to recite a prayer, "May the Red paint spread..." *May the Red... what?* "...and bring the snow globe to order, as our prophets lead the way with visions and treasured script."

My mouth might have moved once or twice to try and

catch up, but no sound came out. Prince Quinten was smirking at me.

When everyone began reaching for their tea and juice, I shifted in my chair and reached for a jug of liquid to try and blend in.

"Bold choice," Quinten remarked, and I paused with my hand on the jug.

"I'm feeling bold this morning," I decided, pulling the jug towards me so he wouldn't realize I had no idea what it was. With a wobbly hand, I poured it into my goblet, splashing droplets on the tablecloth and sprinkling the bust of my dress. I gaped at my own idiocy as attendants rushed in to take over.

Quinten snorted a laugh. "Kingsblood, where were you staying all this time that made you forget how to call on a servant, Scarlet?"

I had no idea. I didn't even know where in Winter someone like Scarlet Strange *could* stay. "I think I'll keep that to myself." I winked like it was a funny secret.

Winked. Because it seemed like something *he* might do. But as soon as my awkward eyelid flapped, I knew it was a mistake and that I looked like a ridiculous child trying to be a grownup.

From the back of the room, Zane was biting his smiling lips together. And, frankly, that made it more embarrassing.

Quinten smiled too but not quite in the same way. He looked like the king, I realized, but twenty years younger. Same dark hair and light skin, though, they *all* had light skin.

I skimmed the rest of the Red Princes and tried to match them with their names. Each of them had stacked rings on their fingers; a combination of gold and copper, studded with jewels.

Some of them stole glances at me as they ate sliced pink meat and baseball-sized hardboiled eggs that definitely weren't from chickens. Most of them didn't care that I was there and chatted amongst themselves.

A cloth napkin slid toward me. Quinten's fingers drifted back to his spoon.

"The captured Evergreen Host soldiers wish to be released in honour of the season of the Silver Jubilee Renewal." The prince who spoke sat at the king's right hand. He had to be the oldest, Prince Tegan. Scars lined his bare shoulders where his leather chest covering didn't reach. The comment he'd made about the Evergreen Host stirred chuckles across the table, and I was glad for the distraction as I snatched Quinten's napkin and dabbed the juice off the bust of my dress.

"Would they like some mint pies and iceberry pudding too?" Prince Forrester's violet eyes glowed.

"It seems they think begging might save them from our Directors of Tournaments," Prince Tegan muttered. "I think it only makes the Directors want to terrorize them more."

"Have they tried to make any deals?" a noble asked from down the table.

"Deals?" Prince Tegan leaned back and folded his bulking arms. "We don't need to bind any more spies to us. Once my father kills the Queen of the Pines at the Silver Jubilee Renewal in the new season, the rest of the Green Kingdom will fall apart. We can spend the next seasons conquering right to the ends of their borders."

"But putting them in the arena..." Quinten ran his finger along the brim of his goblet, "surely we can use them for something other than sending the poor fools to that fate."

Tegan glared across the table at Quinten, who only returned a taunting smirk. I wondered if Quinten actually cared about this conversation or if he was just trying to push Tegan's buttons.

"Lady Strange," the king said, and my head shot up. "You've been away long enough to have an opinion unbiased by your favouritism of any of my sons. What do you think we ought to do with the Green prisoners?"

All the heads in the room turned—I could even feel the servants' stares on my back. Was that a sliver of worry tucked into the corner of Holly Kissing's face?

"Um…" Shockingly, Red Kingdom punishments were one topic I knew a few things about, thanks to Wren Stallone's rambling. But how was I to sentence a punishment to another human being? "I think my time away should make my opinion worthless."

Still, they waited—one of the younger princes slouched forwards and dropped his chin on his palm in boredom. So, I cleared my throat and thought about how the Patrols handled disagreements. "What if you let them compete in a special tribute to the Silver…*season*…? The big prize can be their freedom?"

There was a beat of silence, during which Prince Quinten stared at me in surprise.

Prince Tegan raised his large arms to clasp his hands behind his head. "I say we let the Directors of Tournaments do their worst to them in the arena."

"Actually, I think having a special competition outside of our traditions would bring good tidings," the king said,

and I breathed a sigh of relief. "We can disqualify partici-
pants when they leak blood. Shall we pit them against each
other and let the one who survives the longest without their
blood dripping on the floor go free?"

My stomach contorted.

"I suppose that's an option." But Tegan took a long drink
from his goblet, eyeing me as he did.

My gaze shot to my own goblet. I took it and began to
drink. There was no way I could eat now; this drink was the
best I was going to get until lunch.

Prince Tegan and Quinten still watched, so I drank and
drank until the goblet was empty, praying they'd find something else to look at by the time I was finished.

"Would you like to take a walk through the palace museum after breakfast, Scarlet?" Quinten asked. I returned the
empty glass to the table and wiped my mouth on my
sleeve—realizing a second too late how barbaric the gesture
was.

"The Hall of Paintings is the same as before, I'm afraid.
Stale and unremarkable. But art always interested you more
than the rest of us."

Zane had warned me not to be alone with any of the Red
Princes. But...

"I'd love to."

I was looking for a chance to ask Prince Quinten about
what he'd said, and now I had it.

When I glanced back at Zane, I found my Patrolman's
face blanched, his eyes wide, and his shoulders tight beneath
his red coat like he was struggling to stay put.

My eyes fired back to Quinten to see if I'd missed something, but Quinten stabbed a slice of meat, nothing unusual

about it. Zane couldn't have heard Quinten's invitation from where he was. I blinked against the tiredness that crept into my thoughts.

"Sons, drink your truthspire. I'll not have you all spitting falsehoods at our meeting this afternoon," the king waved a thick hand towards the bubbling jugs. "And I don't want any of you to be late this time," he added, glancing at one of the younger princes in particular.

I counted down the seconds until breakfast was over.

There wasn't a chance to talk to Zane, or to even make a show of dismissing my guardsman after breakfast.

Quinten escorted me out a different door and we entered a hallway of mirrors. I saw so many versions of myself—my freshly trimmed hair, Apple's miracle-working makeup, and the cherry, lace dress she'd fitted me into.

"I looked for you yesterday. But the Chocolatiers said you were resting in your chambers," Quinten ushered me through the hall of glass and caught my hand to help me descend the stairs.

"I've been pretty tired with everything going on," I admitted, which was true. When a beat of silence passed between us, I blurted, "The decorations at the festival were stunning."

But Quinten patted the top of my hand with a laugh, "It's alright, Scarlet. You don't have to pretend to like us."

I wasn't sure what to say to that, so I said nothing. Was it obvious that I was uncomfortable here?

"I wish *he* could see you now, though. I wish that nut-cracking whipsteamer could see the star you've become."

I stole another look in the mirrors. Despite my initial doubts, I realized I was pretty—prettier than I'd ever been in my life. And with my gold-red hair and topaz eyes, I started to feel a little courageous.

"I wanted to ask you…now that we're alone," Quinten's grip on my fingers tightened as he continued, "if you told anyone what I asked you at the ball?" He stopped me on the stairs, amethyst eyes flickering back and forth between mine.

I opened my mouth to deny it, but my tongue struggled to make noise. "I…" My thoughts tumbled. "I haven't spoken of it to a single member of the court," I *finally* said. "I told you I wouldn't."

He relaxed and smiled. "Of course," he shook his head like he shouldn't have asked.

"Speaking of which…" I wouldn't find a better opportunity. My tongue still felt odd, but I spit out the words with as much grace as I could, "Why *were* you asking me about your brother?"

"Why? Do you know where Cane is? Have you seen him?"

I blinked. "No."

Quinten's jaw slid to the side; he glanced off.

A splinter of light from the windows touched his silver crown as he drew in a step. He lowered his voice, "Scarlet, you and I both know the consequences of me asking such a thing. I don't know what you were up to while you were gone, or why you came back. I don't know that I can trust you."

I tried to tell him he could, that his secrets were safe with me, even though I knew full well I'd tell Zane, Eliot, and the Chocolatiers whatever he said. But again…my tongue.

"Have I given you any reason not to?" I asked instead.

"No," he realized. "No, you were always good at keeping secrets. But I don't know why you would protect me after what we did to you." Quinten fiddled with the rings on his fingers. "After you left, a cold wind moved through this place and some of us faced our actions towards you better than others."

"I don't hold it against you." For some reason that was easy to say, even though the thought of these princes' bullying bit at my nerves on Scarlet's behalf. I understood the sting of cutting words and cruel laughter, but I had no personal memories of being mocked by the Red Princes.

My words seemed to shift something in him. "You don't?"

"No."

Quinten blinked for a moment. "Kingsblood, I assumed the reason you came back was to make us pay for what we did. Scarlet, I know the things Cane said to you. I know you liked him, and he found out and tormented you for it. I thought it was funny in my young seasons but I look back and judge myself for it now."

"I'm not here to get revenge upon you, or your brothers," I repeated.

Quinten stood straight, his red jacket flattening out over his chest. "Kingsblood," he swore again. "You're telling the truth."

"Of course I'm telling the truth."

When I said it, he laughed like I'd made a joke. I didn't get it, but his laughter tugged a smile across my face. He might have been beautiful, but he laughed like a horse. It was unappealing, and frankly, a smidgen endearing.

He extended an arm to guide me down the stairs. "Yes, I'm sure our truthspire started working before we even left the table." He scuffed his crow-black hair with his free hand.

Right...

"Quinten," I began again. "Why are you looking for your brother?" My lips and jaw felt warm.

"Because something is wrong with my father," he said. "He's not himself. He's been having scotchy headaches, and saying the most absurd things..." It seemed like Quinten's secrets came out easy. I wondered what sort of wall had come down since we left breakfast.

"You think Prince Cane can help treat your father? Is that why you want to find him?" I tried.

"Prince..." Quinten flexed his jaw. "Of *course* you would still think to call him that, Scarlet. You left right before he did. I suppose you missed the seasons where the Red Kingdom stopped referring to him as a prince." It was a cold and detached statement in comparison to how our conversation had been thus far.

I clamped my mouth shut and faced the curved entrance that led to high walls of brass-framed oil paintings. I wanted to smack my face. Apple would scold me for slipping up so bad.

"Yes, it's a hard habit to break," I back-pedalled.

"I won't hold it against you," the Red Prince said. "And I'm not looking for Cane, *specifically*. I just thought maybe if you had found him, I might ask him if he knows what's happened to our father."

"I see," was all I could rasp out.

"Cane saw things differently here in the end. He spoke of a blackness. He claimed he could hear it seeping up from the ground." He shook his head. "Nutty boy."

"You think your father is going nutty, too?"

"No, Scarlet, I think the same blackness Cane tried to warn us about has found my father."

My heart skipped a beat, and I stared at him.

Blackness...*found* the Crimson King?

The heart as black as a viper covets the Red Kingdom throne.

I swallowed a gasp, but Quinten caught my flush and his brows pulled together. "Scarlet, if you know something about what's happening to my father, please tell me."

I couldn't say, *"It's nothing."* The words wouldn't leave my mouth. My tongue burned when I tried to speak, and my mind began to bubble with things I'd been keeping quiet about. I was overcome with an unexplainable desire to run into sparkling rain, to smell the steam off warm butter, and to build floating paper lanterns...I scratched my hairline, trying to shake the absurd dips interrupting my train of thought.

I needed to talk to Apple and get my head straight, and figure out why only half my words were coming out. And I needed to tell Zane...

Good grief, there were so many things I wanted to tell Zane. All sorts of feelings twisted at my heart when I thought of him.

"Scarlet, are you alright?" Quinten's question snapped me from my thoughts. "You look flushed."

"Show me the museum." Somehow, that suggestion came out as fluid as water.

Quinten nodded. "I need to be back up for the court

191

meeting in a pinch." He tugged me toward the heart of the museum where painted canvases and scrolls patched the walls in colour.

Monarchs in crimson robes stared down at me, seeing through my shield of disguise, knowing that I wasn't who I was claiming to be.

The artists in the Red Kingdom were clever—adding special details into the pictures that you had to search to be able to find. I spotted a few hidden symbols in shirt collars, on eyelids, and engraved on buttons. I wondered what sorts of secret messages they contained.

"I haven't told anyone else about my father," Quinten said. "I'm sorry I brought you into this. I'll be cut off if my father finds out I'm whispering of his illness and mentioning my abdicated brother. He'll go after you too for even speaking to me of it."

"Why *did* you tell me?" I brushed a finger along a frame. The woman in the picture had long ivory hair like Prince Forrester's, and I wondered if it was the queen.

Then I wondered why she wasn't at breakfast.

"I guess I'm tired of being alone here. I'm a pinch different than my family, so I've gotten used to being forgotten by them over the seasons. But after the way they renounced Cane, I've worried a time or three they'll disown me, too. Cane and I were quite the naughty pair as boys, I'm sure you remember."

I smiled, because my pesky tongue wouldn't allow me to tell him that I remembered.

But looking at Quinten, I saw something I didn't expect to find among the golden Red Kingdom stars that proudly marked the flag at the kingdom's gate.

For a moment I wondered if Apple had been wrong about the most beloved Red Prince. I wondered if *everyone* was wrong about him, and I only got to see it because he thought I was someone else. Because he thought I was his childhood friend, and I wasn't.

Chapter,
The Twentieth

The job I'd picked up this past summer was only part-time, but it suited me well—a barista in a small independently owned coffee shop just outside Waterloo where customers were few and far between. Unfortunately, I understood why customers didn't flock to the shop. It was painfully bland—the brown floors and walls, the small windows and outdated register. I found myself thinking of how different I could make it with a few coats of paint, a few shifted tables to steal the light by the windows, and large mugs that made a *thunk* on the tabletops when they were set down. I envisioned making it like The Steam Hollow, with melted chocolate and a drop of freshly squeezed orange, or ground up cinnamon sticks, or pure-pressed vanilla...I'd make sure the shop billowed with warm steam and the scent of pine.

So, on that first day when Eliot had whipped through downtown Waterloo and I'd seen that the Steam Hollow was *red*, it had been a punch to my dreams.

My memories were light, dancing through my brain like fireflies as I waved goodbye to Quinten, who slipped into a meeting room.

I imagined scribbling down drink recipes, tasting citrusy hot chocolate until I got the measurements just right, surrounded by warm steam. My thoughts got away from me after that, slipping off to where I couldn't catch them. They lifted right off my brain, swirling around like a halo as a joyful current ran through my chest. Even when I passed Red elves gliding by in their attendants' slippers, I smiled, finding no reason not to.

And then Zane was there. *Zane.*

He strode down the hall in his pristine red coat, as handsome as I'd ever seen him. "Lady Strange," he greeted, glancing at passing servants. But as soon as the servants rounded the corner, Zane grabbed my shoulders and drove me backwards toward my chambers. The door slammed shut behind him.

I looked around at the unlit fireplace, the quiet living area, and the six empty chairs at the dining table.

"They're not here," he answered my unspoken question. "I sent them off."

"Why?" I had so much to tell them.

"Because you drank a full glass of truthspire!" Zane scuffed his blackish hair as he strutted over. "And I had no idea what sorts of things you'd natter to them, or if you'd spill about the Timepiece—which I'm certain Eliot would be furious to find out about at this point."

I made a face. But before I could object, my tongue warmed, and I realized maybe he was right. The king had told everyone to drink the bubbling liquid at breakfast before the meeting to keep them honest. "Oh."

"*Yes*, it makes you tell your truths, and makes it almost impossible to lie," Zane answered another question I hadn't asked. "And *yes*, I went crazy after you wandered off with a Red Prince moments after you drank it." His gold eyes narrowed, reminding me of a look he'd given me many times before.

"I miss your blue eyes," I confessed, and he shut his mouth. "I missed them all year, too."

Zane let out a breath and dropped his head, rubbing his eyes like he wanted to scrub them away.

"I missed you so much," I added, a fountain sprouting within me of everything I'd held back. I didn't want to keep it down anymore. More than anything, I just wanted him to *know* how hard it had been to be apart from him.

"Helen," he shook his head. "Go to bed and nap this off."

"I missed you until it physically hurt. My chest felt hollow, like someone had taken a shovel and dug out a chunk of me." It all came back in a wave, too real—the tossing and turning when I couldn't fall asleep because a part of me felt absent, the drifts of Winter wind I swore had brushed over my face, pulling me back out of sleep after I finally drifted off.

"*Helen...*" Zane took my shoulders, golden irises urgent. "Stop talking."

"Why?" I pushed his hands off, flexing my tongue behind me teeth. It was getting hotter.

"Because you wouldn't tell me these things in your right mind," he waltzed past me and yanked the bedroom door open, "and it's just going to make everything more difficult if you do."

I huffed in disbelief. "There you go again, always evading every real conversation. Always avoiding the hard truth so you don't have to deal with it," I rattled off as I brushed past, noticing his chest go tight. Feeling the air escape his lungs.

He snatched a hold of my arm and I stopped in the doorway. I went too far—why did I say that? My eyes took their time travelling back up to his.

His eye colour had turned from gold to rust. Yes, I had poked the bear.

"Is that what you really think?" he asked, abusing the state I was in.

"Yes." I bit my tongue after I said it, furious with my own stupid mouth. I would never sip truthspire again.

Zane's fingers uncurled from my arm one by one. He stared at me for several seconds.

"Sleep well, Trite." He shut the door to my sleeping quarters and trapped me inside.

Chapter,
The Twenty-First

A heart as black as a viper.
A heart as red as paint.
A heart green with envy.
I couldn't believe what I had said to Zane.
A heart as black as a viper.
A heart as red paint.
A heart green with envy.

The fireplace made a crackling sound in the living area of my chambers. My feet were still cold.

The door groaned on its hinges and I closed my eyes, dreading seeing my Patrolman already. But it was Apple who floated around the sofa, twirling a pair of gunmetal scissors. She had a grin on her dark-chocolate lips. "You're going to love what I've made you, friend."

Fred came in rolling a copper rack of gowns, and I jumped off the couch to ogle at the feather bodices and lace hems, scalloped necklines and sweeping chiffon, lush rosettes and glittering sheer skirts...

"I know, I've outdone myself," Apple twirled her hair around her finger and slid her scissors away. She bit her russet lips, tone flickering. "I hear you had an incident with truthspire."

I groaned and dug my fingers into my hairline, tearing apart my braid.

"Hmm," Apple mused. "Yes. Truthspire tends to muddle a thing or three." She sauntered over to the rack and took off a dress for me to wear. "Did you ask Prince Quinten about Cane?" she changed the subject, as she carried it over.

"I did. And it was a pretty interesting conversation when I couldn't lie."

I watched her fiddle with the cerise feathers at the dress's shoulder and wondered if I was making a mistake keeping the Timepiece's puzzle from her.

But Eliot was the one who'd told me he'd met a Timepiece before. He'd sworn to tell me about it if he became my Patrolman. It was information, I now realized, he'd never actually handed over.

As though my mind had beckoned him, Eliot hustled in carrying what could only be a set of Patrol staffs cloaked with a black sheet. I'd wondered when those were going to make their way into our chambers. "I'll be right back," I said to Apple, and swooshed around the sofa as Eliot was tearing the black sheet away.

"We need to talk," I said to him.

Eliot nodded. He led the way out to the hall and reached past me to shut the door so Apple and Fred couldn't hear.

"Are you going to start, Helen, or should I?" he whispered, crossing his arms.

I blinked. "Wait...what?"

"Isn't our common goal what you came to talk about? You *wanted* to come to the Red Kingdom. We backed each other up at the factory. I have my own reasons for wanting to hide in this frostbitten kingdom, but I want to know yours."

His dishonestly purple eyes were no match for Prince Quinten's. One of the downsides to Apple's drops—the colour was never quite natural-looking.

"That's not what I was going to...oh, whatever. Fine. I'm here because I have to do something for a Timepiece. And *that's* what I pulled you out here to talk about."

He blinked. Then he huffed and tore the bun out of his hair, unleashing his wild curls. "Ragnashuck, you brought me out here to ask about frostbit Timepieces?"

"You said you met one," I reminded him.

"I did. A good measure ago. But in case you haven't noticed, this place is crawling with them. If you want to know more about the time overseers, why don't you go ask one of them yourself?" He unbuttoned his coat and I stole a look over my shoulder to make sure he wasn't revealing us to the whole kingdom.

"You said *you* would tell me."

"I said I would tell you everything I knew *if I became your Patrolman*. But the competition was cut short." Eliot folded his arms again, fidgeting with the hair tie in his fingers.

I couldn't believe my ears.

"Wait...you don't *want* to tell me what you know, do you?" I realized. "Seriously, Eliot, I thought we'd decided to be allies by this point."

"We are allies as far as I'm concerned. But you haven't been telling me what you're doing, so why would I tell you what I know? The only reason you sided with me about coming here was *apparently* because you were on a secret assignment for a Timepiece, like a little ashworm."

My jaw dropped. I figured he'd be annoyed we didn't tell him, but I didn't expect him to turn the tables on me. "You're really going to keep being the pompous boy who's upset about not being the last Carrier's Patrolman? You're not going to let that go?"

"Why would I?"

"Because of what happened!" My eyes burned with visions of the library fire all over again.

"Why did you even care about winning that competition so much?" I snatched the hair tie from his restless fingers. "Was it so you could gain back the respect of the Patrol after you *failed* to stop Asteroth from killing Mikal?" It came out before I could stop it, and I didn't even have truthspire to blame this time.

I slapped my mouth shut and drew back, surprised at myself. I took in a breath to voice an instant apology, but I didn't know what to say after I'd just spewed such a thing. "I shouldn't have...I mean I don't blame you for...Eliot..."

Eliot's stare absorbed me in a way it hadn't since he met me at my school. Like he was seeing me for the first time.

"I know it might be *hard for you to understand*, Trite, but I'm the best chance you have at making it out of this muddle alive. Not Cohen, *me*," he articulated. "Asteroth craves Cohen's blood as much as he craves yours. So as long as Asteroth is following Zane's scent across the globe, *I'm* your best option."

His condescending tone riled my muscles to flex. He made it so easy to want to hit him; I could feel the pull in my knuckles, still yellowed with old bruises from the last time they'd taken a swing.

"You might not *like* it," he went on, "but it's time for you to shake off your blinders and realize that if something bad happens to Cohen, we'll all still have hope, because we'll still have you. And there are a thousand other Patrolmen who can take his place. But if something happens to *you...*"

"I don't know if I should be furious or admit that you're right, Gray." Zane's voice broke our loathing stares.

Zane had shed his red coat, too—it was balled in his grip where he stood down the hall. Soon we were going to look like a bunch of stowaways. "Can we please talk about this inside?" I nodded to the chambers' door.

Eliot shot me one last look and shoved his way in. But I paused before I followed.

Zane didn't look mad or hurt. But still. "Zane, I didn't mean what I said before—"

"It's alright, Helen. I know what truthspire can do." He pulled an envelope out of his pocket and brought it over. "I was told to deliver this to you. It's an invitation to an evening-banquet in the orchard tonight for Prince Ember's seasonal birth celebration."

The envelope felt heavier than it should have. "I'm surprised you even delivered it."

"I almost didn't." A dull half-smile found his face. "But it'll give you something to do while I'm gone."

My face fell. "Gone? You can't be serious."

"Not *forever*, Helen," he rolled his eyes. "Just for tonight. I need to go...deal with something."

I swallowed. "Okay."

As Zane brushed by to slip into the chambers, I wondered what he could possibly have to deal with here that didn't involve me?

Apple's eyes kept flickering to my face as she fitted me in the white evening gown. She glanced over at Zane and Eliot at the table, then back to me—her fingers tugging at loose threads and snipping them with her scissors.

Finally, I couldn't take it anymore. "What?" I asked.

"Something's different." She spoke too quietly for the boys to hear. "It's you and your Patrolmen. None of you are talking."

"We all have our own things to think about." It wasn't an explanation, but it was enough.

Apple nodded and pulled a small pouch of diamond earrings from her pocket.

"You'd better figure it out, friend. Our enemies love to drive wedges between us when we need to be united," she said, and her dark mouth quirked. "My mother used to say that."

"Really?" I stole a look at the metal wreath on the wall where I could vaguely make out Zane and Eliot in the reflection.

Apple fitted the first earring onto my lobe. "She said a thing or three of that sort during her seasons. She also said, *'Should someone be kind enough to gift you a prayer, you ought to then pass a prayer on to someone else. The prayer you send might be precisely what that person needs at that exact time.'*" Apple mimicked another voice when she said it—deep and certainly not a woman's voice. But the message was clear enough.

I said nothing else as she finished getting me ready.

Chapter,
The Twenty-Second

The sky was as clear as still water, the glassy stars twinkling against the navy ocean. Around the orchard, crisp pure-white apples clung to snow-dusted trees, their bark lightly frosted by the chilly night.

The long table in the middle was sprinkled with red butterflies like drops of blood, spreading out from the king's seat that was warmed with a lush ivory fur as though he'd ended a polar bear's life in that very spot.

I walked below the lanterns wrapping the party area, where white flames cast pools of light over the snow-bedded floor. I wasn't trying to *hide* at the crease of the clearing, I just wanted to watch them—the kingdom's highest-ranking nobles.

The king arrived, introducing a white-masked magician he'd hired for the party. The magician flicked his fingers and a pearl-coloured apple appeared in his palm, nearly blending into the suit he wore—also white from head to toe. The magician bowed to the applauding group, while I watched the palace's back entrance for the princes.

The mouth of the doorway glowed a warm yellow, inviting me to return to the palace and leave this birthday party I was pretending to belong to. It was too cold to be outside anyway.

I nearly jumped to find the magician standing directly in front of me—arm outstretched, pallid apple resting on his palm. "A gift," he said through his mask. We were both in the shadows, but most guests watched the magician, and his choice of whom to bestow his gift upon.

Blinking, I took the apple just to make him go away. But he lingered, a slow tilt of his head telling me he was studying me from behind that all-concealing white mask.

I shifted and glanced at the darkness of the orchard behind me. The trees formed a twisted labyrinth, not grown in structured rows. I'd get lost if I tried to sneak away into it.

But the magician turned with no gesture of goodbye and sprang upon the opulent table. He snapped his fingers and apples fell from the sky into his hands. He wound them into a juggle as he danced between plates and platters, never touching a single item on display.

I huffed as the princes began emerging from the palace—all coronets, jeweled buttons, and rich coats.

Prince Forrester came out first, moving like the cold breeze, barely making footprints as he swept to take the arm of a beautiful, dark-skinned girl off the path.

Prince Tegan emerged; a bulking frame of uncovered muscle even though it was freezing. His purplish stare travelled over the group, and he made a face into the trees at where the two youngest Red Princes crept through the shadows, one stopping to push the other up onto a branch before anyone would notice. Prince Tegan rolled his eyes and ignored them.

A flicker of red in the darkness revealed that someone else was slipping past the party towards the young princes. Suddenly, a guttural growl tore through the night, and both young princes screamed like girls. The one in the tree lost his balance and slid off the branch, but two hands snatched him out of the air before he hit the ground.

Quinten stepped into the light and I chuckled as he carried the youngest prince into the clearing, his horse-like laugh filling the space as he tossed the boy into the snow.

My attention was stolen by another prince as he entered the orchard. Our gazes locked and he puckered his mouth to blow me a kiss. My eyes widened when I realized he was trying to make me flush. He sneered as he passed.

"Just ignore Hamsa," Quinten's voice came from beside me. "The rest of us do." He brushed the snow off his shoulders.

"He's not ruffling my feathers," I promised.

But Quinten made a face. "Ruffling your what?"

"Never mind."

"You know," Quinten changed the subject, "being outdoors isn't nearly as exciting as the coordinators claimed it would be. It's starting to feel a little stuffy out here."

My mouth spread against my will. "You don't say."

JENNIFER KROPF

"You know this celebration isn't mandatory, right? Ember isn't even going to notice who's here and who's not."

"Are you encouraging me to leave?"

"Maybe I'm hoping you'll invite me to leave with you."

My smile dissolved and I looked over at him. His sweet mouth was full of mischief; amethyst eyes set on the crowd before us. His crown was slick with water, a result of his scuttle with the younger princes.

"Maybe I *want* to be at the party," I bluffed. But he turned slowly, his hands in his royal pockets, and dropped his eyes down with a dramatic thud.

"I don't think that's true, my lady. Should we sip some more truthspire and sort this out?" I felt the blood drain from my face, and he suddenly laughed—that comically horrendous sound. "It's a jest, Scarlet. I know you won't go anywhere near that stuff after the measure you had this morning." He flicked my hair away from my face—such an easy gesture, but I felt it all the way down in my chest.

I wasn't an expert with boys, but I knew toying when I saw it. "You're a flirt."

His jaw twitched, but he didn't lose his composure; in fact, he dragged in another step, hovering over me until his coat was nearly a blanket I wore. "So what if I am?" It was quiet.

"I'm not looking for...*that*." I felt heat rising through my abdomen, whether from speaking so brazenly, or because of how close he stood, I wasn't sure.

The lavender in Quinten's eyes blossomed. "Maybe I'm not either. Maybe I'm just looking for a trusted friend."

A trusted friend.

I needed him to lead me to the black heart, and he believed I could help him with his father's illness, or he wouldn't have told me about it.

Maybe we could be friends.

"I think that would be nice," I whispered, my breath steaming up in the cold.

The corner of his mouth lifted; his husky features set on me as he ignored the cheers that erupted from the party at the arrival of the guest of honour.

My gaze flickered to the youthful prince arriving in a pure-gold cape and a wildly braided wreath upon his head. But as I did, I spotted someone else standing in the palace entrance, out of sight to everyone but me—because I could never miss noticing him.

Zane was back in his red attendants' coat, dark-washed hair neat, boots shining from polish under the entrance torches. A bothered look was stamped over his face.

He'd said he was busy tonight, but it seemed he'd come to check on me anyway.

I realized he didn't know that I saw him when he glanced back into the hallway and tipped inside to disappear.

I studied the empty archway, going back to the moment Zane had chosen to stay behind with Jolly Cheat at the escape tunnels and told Eliot to take me to the factory instead. It was the second time Eliot had been forced to act as my Patrolman instead of Zane.

Those moments weren't what wormed their way through my resilience though. Most of all, it bothered me that Zane never told me what had happened by the river, and now he had something to *deal* with tonight.

"I have to go," I turned to apologize, but Quinten had

already flitted back into the mix of guests clapping at the magician who juggled a dozen apples at once.

I spotted Holly Kissing with a glass in her thin fingers. She'd been looking my way, so our gazes locked: gold and honey. She didn't glare or spin to give me a cold shoulder like most of the pretty girls at home might have done. She lifted her drink in salute. I didn't know if she was simply saying hello or acknowledging that I was her official competition for Quinten. I had a sinking feeling it was the latter.

Yes, it was time to leave this party.

I ducked into the shadows and scurried back toward the palace entrance, using the magician's theatrics as a distraction for my escape.

Zane was *not* an easy person to follow. His feet were as light as feathers; he made no sound as he moved. I finally took off my heels when keeping quiet became impossible and left them at the edge of the hall to trot after my Patrolman barefoot. I ripped the laces of my coat open too and left the overgarment in a heap on an end table, hoping Apple would forgive me.

The route Zane took had so many turns and sets of stairs, my head spun trying to keep track of where I was. He flitted over carpets and through doorways, keeping to unlit hallways until the glossy tile floor turned into the solid stone of servants' tunnels. I'd never find my way back through this palace on my own, and I wondered if I was going to be forced to reveal myself before the journey back so he didn't leave me behind.

Cobwebs clung to the ceiling as we went further down, down, down, until every noise and sign of nobility and wealth disappeared. What was left was cool rock walls— damp like a basement—and the horrid smells of rotted fruit and sprouting fungus.

A tune drifted from the innermost parts of the tunnel, *not* a lovely one. More like the careless hollering of someone who'd been left alone for too long and thought no one was listening. It was a female, chanting. I lost Zane's red coat around a bend but followed the squawking music until I spotted him again, standing in the hazy light of a doorway.

He waited there, fingers moving slowly over the buttons of his guardsman jacket as though he contemplated taking it off. His chest rose and fell, his jaw was flexed, but he finally stepped inside, and the manic song went quiet.

My bare feet were glued to the floor where I stood. Following Zane suddenly felt like a terrible idea. If he'd wanted me here, he would have told me to come.

I scuffled back, stuffing down my worries of never finding my way out of this dark basement, when I heard a voice. "Come in. Welcome."

It was too calm—the opposite of the off-pitch singing that had just flooded the passageway a moment ago.

I couldn't help it; I snuck to the doorway and glanced in to see him. To make sure he was alright, because I'd be ruined if something happened to Zane after the last real talk we'd had was me babbling about how he avoided tough conversations. But what I saw made my insides nearly spring from my skin.

Across a clean maple-purple carpet, a woman sat at a

desk. A globe sparkled before her on a bronze pedestal, rich and striking in comparison to the rest of the dreary basement. Her eyes were pure white—*no irises*—and I put a hand over my mouth to keep myself from yelling for Zane who stood in the middle of the room, a safe distance from the desk.

Waves of long pecan-brown hair tumbled over the woman's shoulder when she slanted her head, revealing the edge of a long, black, serpentine tattoo that disappeared into her hair. "Welcome," she said again. Her red lipstick was as smooth as cherries when she smiled.

Zane was silent for a heartbeat. "Do you know who I am?" he finally asked, and with the way he said it, I wondered if he was about to turn and leave again.

The woman lifted a hand over the glass ball and tapped long, wine-red nails against it. A metal cuff bound her wrist, attached to a chain that slid over her lap like a metal snake.

She spoke with monotone dryness, "Did you think that just because my vision has slipped away, I wouldn't recognize my only son?"

The skin on my arms tightened, and I backed away. No, I should *not* have come here. But I couldn't get away before her words curled into the hallway. "Bring *her* in."

"Bring…" Zane paused. When he spun back to the hall, there wasn't enough time for the hallway's shadow to swallow me. My Patrolman grabbed my arms and yanked me into the light. For a beat, he stared at my face, unblinking.

Behind him, the woman smiled again.

"I shouldn't be here," I apologized. "I'll go."

But Zane didn't release my arms; his hands steamed against the sleeves of my dress.

"Trite..." he said quietly through his teeth. Anger flickered across his eyes, but his grip loosened. "You're staying." The words were tight. He dropped one of my arms but held the other as he turned to face the woman. "This is Scarlet Strange."

"Lady Strange," the woman greeted, resting her hand on the glass ball. "Have you come to see the future?"

"No," Zane growled. "She's here to watch and listen and be quiet." He paused. And then, "Did my father ever return?"

"Did you bring payment? Only the highest members of the Crimson Court get insights for free," the woman purred.

"I'm not asking for your bloody insight, sea witch, I'm asking because you're here alone. I'm guessing that means the rest of the Kelidestone's insufferable crew was over-tossed." There was no feeling in Zane's tone; he'd turned stone-cold.

"You already know how I got here." A flit of amusement.

Zane glared at the white-eyed woman. His fingers around my arm started to feel less like containment, and more like he was using me to stay balanced so he didn't lash out.

"Did Cheat offer a deal to my father, too?" he asked, but she remained quiet, plain-faced. She wouldn't tell him anything without payment.

I dug my orb necklace from beneath my dress. Zane glanced at it with a flit of surprise but didn't object when I unclasped it and shook the ruby stone from the chain. "Will one ruby give us answers?"

A gift from the Timepiece; one I'd gladly regift to Zane. The woman showed teeth when she smiled this time.

"What a generous gift. And an interesting choice, coming from *you*."

I didn't know what she meant by that, but Zane rolled his eyes and snatched the ruby to toss onto her tabletop. The woman didn't pick it up when it stopped bouncing. Instead, she raised a hand over her globe and smoke billowed into the glass like an awakened fog-creature.

"Don't go all pale-eyed and mystical," Zane said. "Just tell me why Cheat wanted you here."

"Nicolas Saint has a lovely sense of humour. I can't read into his well-guarded heart. But he kept it no secret that he wanted you to find me."

"So, this is about me? Jolly dragged you from the ships to try and *agitate* me?"

The woman's face dropped its charm; a glare took its place. "I haven't been on those ships for five full seasons. But you wouldn't know that, would you? Not since you left with that man of *irritating* verses."

Mikal.

The woman's menacing smile returned. "How is he, by the way?"

"Zane—" My hand flew against his chest, my fingers splayed over the red coat he hated. But he wasn't moving to barrel forwards; he wasn't even posing to yell at her.

"Yes, *Zane*," the woman mimicked me as she rose from her seat, rattling the chains at her wrists. "Zane. Cohen. Margus. *Bowswither*."

I ignored her and leveled my gaze on my friend, who I worried had been driven to come down here because I'd been careless with my words after I drank truthspire.

"Son. Abandoner of his crew. Steelheart." The woman's

cherry lips kept moving. "*Pirate*."

Beneath my palm, I could feel Zane's heart thunder. I had no idea what sort of creature I'd unleashed by driving him down to this basement to face this demon of his past.

Zane's eyes slid closed. "We need to go," he whispered to me. His mouth began to move with no sound—like he was silently reciting a speech from memory.

"Jolly Cheat knows I'm here, in the Red Kingdom. In this palace." When his eyes flashed open, they were on me. "I've been foolish. I didn't think this through." He took my hand from his chest and laced his fingers through mine, gripping them as we spun for the door.

I glanced back at the woman one last time. She smiled with her pallid stare like she knew I was looking. "See you soon," her sultry whisper crawled into my ears.

Zane shook his head with a spiteful laugh. "I won't be back here again. If you could really see the future, you'd bloody know that."

But his mother was still smiling, cherry red lips against sun-kissed skin, black ink vining up her neck. I had the strangest inkling that she hadn't been talking to Zane.

We didn't go back to my chambers. My heart sank deeper and deeper as Zane guided me from the basement, not rushing or pulling me along when I lagged. We just walked—hand-clasped-tightly-in-hand—until we stopped in a servant's tunnel where half a dozen sets of grated doors hid us from the rest of the palace.

"So now you know," his words filled the silence.

"I already knew you were a snow pirate. And that your mother saw the future."

But he shook his head. "No, now you know why I agreed to let us come to this kingdom."

The insubordinate son that had just argued with his estranged mother was gone now; this was the Patrolman looking back at me. I felt a small hole open in my soul at how easily he'd left his own blood relation behind, how easily he'd sworn he would never go back and see her again.

"I don't blame you for wanting to see if she was here. She's your mother."

But Zane made a face. "No, she's not. And I should have never cared what Cheat told me by the river, but he was up to something. I could tell then, and I can tell now. I just can't figure out what it is." He glanced off, the light through the grates showing that his golden irises had faded to a muted green as Apple's drops were wearing off. "And *she* didn't give me any answers," he nodded back toward the basement.

My heart sank. "Zane...She's your *mother*," I said again.

He blinked, and at first it looked like he might form another callous retort, but his gaze travelled over my face. He held his tongue as he no doubt tried to imagine how I saw this—watching someone who still had a living mother and chose to be separated from her, when mine was taken away and all I wanted was to have her back.

"That sea witch wasn't a mother," he said. "Forgive them, forget them, and get back up. That was what Mikal taught me after I left the snowseas. If I give that woman a single shred of my heart, she'll reach in and squash my colours. I've already learned that lesson."

I couldn't be upset about that—I'd followed him down here. I was the one who hadn't trusted him when he told me he had something to deal with.

"At least everything's out in the open now," he chewed his lower lip. "No more secrets though, Helen. I can't handle any more secrets between us."

I nodded.

"Also, I don't like how Prince Quinten has been looking at you. I think you need to be careful."

A smile peeled over my face. "Jealous?"

He cast me a look and took my elbow to lead me out of the servants' tunnels. "Ready to bite his head off is more like it."

"Definitely jealous, then." I didn't mean to taunt him, but when he glanced at me again, he wasn't laughing the same way I was. I decided to leave it alone.

"Jolly Cheat must have a spy or three here waiting to tell him if I show up, and I don't think this costume is going to fool anyone. Cheat might already know I'm here, and I'll bet he knows you're here too," he said. "It's only a measure of time before Asteroth shows up or sends word to the Crimson King about the band of fibbers in his Court. I don't want to think about what scotchy things the Reds will do to us if they catch us before we escape."

This had gotten out of hand so fast. Quinten had *just* decided to trust me. If I could get him to tell me who the black heart was before we left...

"What if we just stayed *two* more days?" I said. "I can do this, Zane. I'm sure Quinten knows something *big*. I just need to find out what it is. Then we only have one heart puzzle left to solve and we can figure it out once we've left. We could stop Asteroth from showing up for more of our friends."

Zane huffed and I could see he wasn't going to hang in there much longer if we didn't figure this out.

"Fine, Helen," but he shook his head as he said it, unsettling his hair. "Ragnashuck. Fine. But Eliot and I are coming up with an escape plan for when things turn backwards. Because something about this still feels muddled to me. My colours have been all over the place since we got here."

It was September of this year, the first week of school, when Winston had stumbled through the front door of Grandma's house and filled the entryway with the horrid, sour smell of substance abuse and late-night idiocy. He'd been louder than a bull thundering through a fence, even snorting like an animal at the obstacles on the floor that got in his way—Kaley's flats, Grandma's purse, the kitchen stool.

I'd half-fallen out of bed and trotted down the squeaky stairs to put an end to his clamouring.

He didn't try to explain himself when he saw me standing on the stairs, or even apologize for the noise. He just looked up with blank eyes; the eyes of someone who no longer cared about much.

We stood there, at that impasse—the high school athlete and his delusional sister—until he finally dropped his gaze to the fresh muffins on the table Grandma had made after we'd eaten supper without him.

He took one, seeming to already forget I was there, peeled off the cup, and stuffed the entire thing into his mouth all at once.

It was the first time I'd been angry at Winston. Not just annoyed, but *angry*; the first time I realized it wasn't entirely my fault he was acting out. Or my father's. Or my mother's.

I would have gone to bed at that point, but I noticed the blush of freshly tattooed skin up the middle of his neck: a set of crossed black pistols making an "X" that reached around his throat. It was the stupidest thing I'd ever seen. And unfortunately, soap couldn't clean away stupid. Not in this instance.

"Keep it down, or I'm kicking you out and locking the doors," I said.

And that was how I left him—his head seeming too heavy for his body, a partially eaten muffin hanging from his fingertips.

It was the moment I realized that holding a family together was sometimes impossible. And that family members were the ones who had the power to hurt us the most.

Chapter,
The Twenty-Third

I was mid-yawn the next morning when I came out of my chambers and saw Quinten leaning against the wall outside the door. Apple bumped into my back when I halted.

"Hi—I'm mean, *season's greetings*," I said to Quinten, questioning what in all of Winter he was doing outside my room.

He lifted from the wall and drifted over, mouth quirking into a smile. "I've brought you breakfast."

A plum appeared before me—the sweet and tart smell filling the pocket of air he'd left between us. Apple's cocoa eyes widened, but she kept her mouth shut.

"Thank you." I reached to take it from his hand, but he didn't let it go.

"It's a bargain, my lady," he said. "You can feast on all

the plums you like in my sleigh this morning, and I'll rescue you from breakfast with the king where you'll feel obligated to drink his truthspire. In return, I want you to tell *me* your truths."

I thought about that, then plucked the plum from his fingers. "To the sleigh, then."

Quinten's sleigh was frilled with bouquets of clapping silver bells, alerting everyone in the Scarlet City that we were coming. The crowds and golden sleighs moved out of the way so we could glide over the obsidian streets without hindrance.

My fur-lined collar did little to hide my face, so when I spotted a slender Greed drifting from a building like a pale shadow, I looked the other way to hide. The last time I'd been here, the Greed had followed me simply because I looked guilty. They'd almost caught me too, before Wren Stallone had shown up.

Oh, Wren. It was difficult not to think of him while I rode these streets. I wondered how differently things might have been if he'd survived that day in Mara Rouge's underground fortress, instead of slapping his medallions together to turn himself to snow. He would've fought alongside Zane and Lucas when it came down to it, I was sure of that. He would have helped the Patrols rebuild the library, too.

"What are you thinking about?" Quinten asked. "You seem troubled."

"I was just thinking about the last time I was here." The

response was fitting.

The prince nodded, his amethyst eyes clouding pewter. He reached for the bowl of plums on the ledge before us. "As promised," he smiled.

I put on a smile of my own and took a fruit. "Thank you."

When I glanced back, the Greed was drifting across the street. It didn't look my way.

"Do the Greed make you queasy?" Up until now, Quinten had been fiddling with a gold ring that kept sliding off his finger. "You wouldn't be the first. They used to scare the snow out of me in my early seasons. Tegan used to tell me stories at dusk, dreadful enough to keep me awake until sunrise," he said, twisting his rebellious ring. "The Greed used to be Red elves, you know. Few people remember that."

I made a face. That was something I wouldn't have guessed. "How did they come to look like *that*?"

He shrugged, finally dismissing his hand to his lap. "They sold their colours for swiftness and intuition. That's why they're bone-white."

I tried not to shudder. "Lovely."

But Quinten smirked. "For a while, my brother Driar was interested in how the creatures had changed, even though their ancestry dates back at least a hundred plus fifty seasons. He tends to waste away in the palace studies when he's supposed to be attending public functions. Can't say I blame him, though I'm not sure how he keeps getting away with it," he said.

"Huh," I feigned interest, but I had no idea which Red Prince *Driar* was. I stole another look at the streets, realizing I hadn't seen a single gnome since I'd arrived. I wondered if they'd slinked into hiding after their great witch had fallen, or if they were still lurking below the kingdom in their fallen queen's haunted fortress.

"Anyway, let's skip the pebble talk," Quinten took a plum but didn't eat it. "If we're going to be allies, Scarlet, you need to tell me what you know of my father's illness. I know you've learned a thing or three. No one reacts the way you did if they don't know a thing."

His father's illness...I took a bite of the plum to kill time.

Savoury juices spilled into my mouth and a drop hit my chin. Apparently, I was still no better at eating fruit even when I was pretending to be a noblewoman. "What do *you* know of it?" I diverted, brushing my jaw to try and locate the spill.

But Quinten twisted, cloth handkerchief in hand, and touched it lightly against my face as he held my gaze. His eyes were fairylike; fields of icy purple flowers and burning violet planets.

"Tell me what you know first. And then I'll tell you what I know."

I swallowed, melting below his blackbird lashes. My stare flickered down, and he released my chin, waiting.

"I do know of something. I was warned about someone in the Red Kingdom who has a black heart. Someone whose blood runs as black as the night sky and is as venomous as poison." I glanced back up to find him perfectly still, and I knew I'd struck a chord. "Do you know of someone like that?"

"Who warned you?" he asked. "Where did this come from?"

"I can't tell you that." I brushed my hands over my dress.

"But I think someone is after your father's throne."

A breath escaped Quinten as he slumped back against his seat. He remained quiet as we slid beneath a stone bridge. Dangling claret ribbons licked the sleigh's edges as we passed through.

"Kingsblood," he cursed. "No wonder you were unmerrily ubbersnugged when I mentioned it. No one else has noticed my father's illness. No one else sees what I see." He tossed his plum back into the bowl. The subtle dimple in his chin shifted.

"What's happening to the king?" I tossed my plum, too.

"He admitted he's been getting headaches. Like iron nails digging into his head." He turned to me, "Do you think it's possible for him to be mindswept? For someone else to be moving him, like in a game of crest? Is that as spinbug-crazy as it sounds?"

The heart as black as a viper covets the Red Kingdom throne... Or, maybe the viper had already made his move to steal the throne by stealing the Crimson King's mind. Quinten did say his father was *different.*

"I don't think it's crazy."

Quinten faced forward again, fidgeting with that same ring. "My father knows I've seen what's happening to him. He's been punishing me for it, discreetly."

I made a face. "*Punishing* you?"

"It started with him separating me from my brothers at court meetings to sit alone, to make my opinions appear less supported. But now he's forcing me to get married off, of all things." Sunlight sparkled over his silver crown as unanticipated heat rose in my stomach. "Not Tegan or Forrester, even though they're seasons older. Just me. He claims it's to save my frivolous reputation, but I know he, or whoever's got him mindswept, is using this to threaten me to stop probing into his illness."

"How do you know that?" I brushed my fingers over my warm cheeks.

"Because my father knows I'm not near ready for such a thing," he said. "Even the Crimson Court was ubbersnugged when he told them I'd be married off before the Silver Jubilee Renewal, whether I liked it or not." He tapped his fingers on his knee. "I fear the day my father realizes the measure I already know. I don't think it'll make a difference that I'm his son. I've seen what he's willing to do to his own beloveds."

"You think he'd disown you like Cane?"

A spiteful smile warped Quinten's face. "I'd be merry by such a good tiding as that. Cane left before the king *could* do anything. If my brother ever returns here, I'm sure my father will ruin him, publicly and horribly. I gather it will be the same for me soon, too. I've suspected my father of being mindswept for a measure, I just haven't known what to do about it. It's why I wanted to find Cane."

I couldn't even speak. What sort of a father would be so cruel to his own children? Though, after meeting Zane's mother, maybe it shouldn't have surprised me.

Quinten's hand slid over to take mine, our chilly fingers coming together to bind our secrets. But my mind still lingered on Zane as I glanced at my hand interlocked with Quinten's.

"Scarlet, are you sure you don't know where Cane is? Or even have a way to contact him, to ask for help? My family is going to turn on me. I'm alone in this."

Alone.

I wished I did know where the former Prince Cane was hiding. That I could give Quinten the help he needed; a brother who understood the dangers of what he was up against. But I didn't know who or where Cane was, and all I could give Quinten was me—and a *false* me, at that.

"Will you have to run away like Cane when the king figures you out?"

"Scarlet, if my father ever learns the sorts of questions I've been asking the mediciniers, I don't think I'll make it past the iron gate. If I want out of this muddle, I need to sort out how someone is making him ill, and if I can't muster a cure, there's no easy end for me."

I blinked. "So...find the person manipulating your father, or...you die? That's your only option?"

The Red Prince's chest inflated, but he shook his head and chuckled. "You know, Scarlet, sometimes you sound a lot like a Trite when you speak."

I swallowed and fought to keep the red out of my cheeks. "I..." My stupid mouth couldn't find a better answer than that. For all my days of dancing through the Red Kingdom palace in stunning gowns, and walking with my chin high for once, I was suddenly transformed right back into the peg out of its shell.

But Quinten stared. "Kingsblood," he mused, more to himself. "I knew something was different about you. You've lost your arrogance, Lady Strange. And there's something not quite right with your eyes. It's as though your Rime blood has started to slip away," he said, looking me over right down to the hem of my coat. "You've been hiding in the dead world with the Trites, haven't you? That's where you went!"

My heart plunged. Quinten was crawling dangerously close to the truth.

"You think...I was..." For a moment I didn't know whether I should deny or confirm it. "When I left..." I raised a finger, but it hung there stupidly; I couldn't think.

"Kingsblood, you did slip over an intersect!" He slapped a hand over his mouth in amazement. "You know the Crimson Court will put you in the arena for that if they find out," he added, purple eyes flashing. "What was it like? I can't imagine being somewhere so plain where the ground stays quiet and no one eats cake!"

"We eat cake," I objected, and then clamped my mouth shut, my pulse pounding in my neck. He stood and the sleigh driver halted the reindeer.

"You've half-transformed into a sputtering Trite!" He whispered loudly, and my horror flared. I hoped the driver hadn't heard. Quinten gawked at me until I got to my feet, levelling us so I didn't feel on display.

"Will you ever go back?" he changed course, face sparkling.

Of course.

I had to.

I would go back. No matter what. I would...

"Scarlet," Quinten's voice came out soft when I didn't reply. "I won't tell a soul. We know too much of each other now. You and I are bound in confidence until the end of our timestrings."

Bound for life in a kingdom I'd soon run from and he'd get killed in by his own father.

Unless...

I had the craziest idea—one that might be stupid to even suggest but might solve two problems at once. Quinten and I would only be in trouble if we stayed *here*.

The Crimson King would never follow us into the Trite world, and if Asteroth and the Greed tried to find us, we could be long gone before the intersect opened again in a year's time.

And Quinten...he was alone.

But could I trust him with the truth of what I was? That was the looming question. I didn't know Quinten apart from the few secrets we'd shared. And he might consider my lie a betrayal after the things he'd told me.

"I wasn't trying to upset you," Quinten apologized again when I still didn't speak.

"Quinten, if this all goes wrong..." I took his hands and gripped them. This Red Prince was supposed to be all the worst things, but he'd turned out to be just a boy afraid of his family turning on him as easily as changing their minds about a pudding flavour. "What if you went back there with me?"

Quinten's face changed. "To the dead world?

"It's not that bad," I swore. "There's no court to impress." Just high school kids and bullies like Emily Parker and Mia Fillard, both of whom I was sure would swoon at the sight of Quinten.

But he still looked like I'd suggested he eat his own feet. "I'm not sure I *could*," he blinked. "Scarlet, I truly can't tell if you're speaking in jest—"

"I could teach you about the Trite world." I lifted my hand back toward the palace, "It's better than meeting your end here."

Quinten stared at me, hard-jawed and reeking of nobility.

"Kingsblood, Scarlet." He dropped my hand and disappointment plummeted through my stomach. "With the way you bargain, I'd be better off to just make *you* my wife," there was sarcasm in his tone. "You're noble, after all. You're a lady of the court. I think you could make them see a thing or three."

My huff was visible in the cold. "Don't use your coy charm on me," I said. "I'm being serious."

But he leaned in closer, a blend of bothered purple eyes and a steady tone, "So am I."

Chapter,
The Twenty-Fourth

B lood, sweat, and tears trickled down a boy's neck, soaking his shirt. His head hung forwards, moisture dripping off the ends of his dark hair and puddling on the floor. The boy wore all black—threads the colour of raven feathers.

The sight turned my stomach.

The air was still and quiet; I could only hear his heaving breaths. When he looked up, his caramel eyes were blood-shot with veins. But they were alive. They were wild. They were Lucas Leutenski's.

Lucas set his jaw and braced himself before he was swallowed by a blanket of flaming red.

A body hovered over me when my eyes flew open, and I thrashed my arms until Zane pinned them down. *"Helen!"* he yelled like it wasn't the first time. The sight of him undid me and I relaxed against the bed with a sob.

Zane's chest constricted as he stared, his wide eyes blue enough now that I forgot he was pretending to be someone else, that any of us were pretending, and where we even were.

My lungs felt like they'd shrivelled to prunes; I let out a croak, barely registering Eliot at the door with a stricken face and curls standing on end. Apple was there too in her glorious white nightgown, peeking in and gripping her gunmetal scissors like she'd prepared to stab a monster.

"It's…" My throat was swollen. A hot tear ran down the side of my face, staining the pillow where Zane's hand trapped my wrist.

I didn't care that he was on top of me, that he was holding me still, that Eliot turned Apple toward the door, and they left us alone like that.

I inhaled, filling myself with the room, the memories of where I was, and the smooth peppermint scent above me, muddied by the stench of roses and power that plagued the Red Kingdom hallways.

"Ragnashuck, Trite," Zane looked stricken. "I thought you were being tortured in here." He rolled off and flopped onto his back. I clung to the hand he left between us.

Zane would lose it if I told him Asteroth had Lucas. But I knew the dream was real; the last time I'd dreamt about Lucas running in the dark and setting off church bells, I'd learned it had really happened.

"Was the dream that bad?" Zane whispered.

I swiped my hand across my forehead, wondering just how much of a ruckus I'd made that had brought everyone running. I should have been embarrassed, but I wasn't.

"It was Lucas," I finally said. "And...Asteroth."

A few beats of silence passed; Zane stared at the ceiling. "Asteroth won't kill Lucas," he said. "He can't. Mikal's deal won't let him."

"But Asteroth can hurt him."

"Lucas has been through worse," but Zane sounded unconvinced by his own claim. "And he knew this would happen if he chased Asteroth. I told him not to be reckless—the bloody spuddlepun didn't listen."

The storm outside shuddered the window's glass panes. "But it's *Lucas*..."

"I know, Trite." Zane sat up and scuffed his hair. His voice dipped low, "Maybe I've been selfish, trying to stay with you all this time. Ragnashuck, I think Cheat has been calling my name for a measure anyway. Maybe it's time I go sort it out."

But I had a feeling what he was really saying was that he was going to go get Lucas, and lead Asteroth away from me. That he was finished messing around with vague warnings from an unfamiliar entity.

"Zane, you can't leave me alone—"

"I don't want to. But you have Eliot. Maybe there's a reason the Patrol's greatest guardsman has been with us this whole time, and I've just been too blind to see it."

Even his hair had paled back to its natural nut-brown—there was barely any of Apple's disguise left. We were changing back into ourselves. This idea of ours to trick the

Reds was slipping away, and my confidence along with it.

"Eliot *isn't* the Patrol's greatest—"

"You can't stay here either, Helen. I'll tell Eliot to give you the *one more day* I promised you. But I'm instructing him to take you back to the factory at sunset tonight, no matter what."

I couldn't find it within myself to argue, so I nodded. But there was no way I would let Zane leave. I would stop him in the morning.

The image of Lucas held my mind hostage. I rubbed my forehead and imagined scrubbing the dream away.

"Zane," I whispered.

"Yeah?"

"Can you tell me a story?"

The hourglass-shaped clock across the room ticked several times before he responded. "Have you heard the one about the rebellious Rime who was swallowed by a Great White Frost-Whale?"

A smile touched the corner of my mouth. "No, I haven't. Did he survive?"

"He did. The whale got sick and spat him up on shore," he said. "It was the first account from the Volumes I had to memorize when I joined the Patrol. Try to fall asleep, and I'll recite it."

I let my eyes slide closed and listened to the story about a man destined for incredible encounters, but who ran from the Truth instead of embracing his calling and found himself swallowed by a great creature of the snowseas. The story, along with the tranquil, sweet hymn drifting from Zane's soul, carried me back to sleep.

Chapter,
The Twenty-Fifth

Zane was gone before sunrise. He had slipped out like a thief in the night, a thief who had quite possibly stolen a crucial part of me on his way out the door.

Not knowing what he was doing was worse than him leaving in the first place. I wouldn't forgive him for it.

Apple's dark lipstick was mostly bitten off by the time she finished dying my hair, putting new drops in my eyes, smoothing my skin with butters, and tucking me into a dress. I barely saw her do it, barely felt myself change back into Scarlet Strange.

Past her cocoa curls, I watched two dozen birds flutter by my bedroom window, their silver wings blinding mirrors beneath the bright morning sun. Two of them had been bold enough to come into my room—I'd awakened to find them perched on the windowsill.

As soon as I had realized Zane was gone, I'd charged back into my bedroom, shewed the feathery critters back out, and slammed the window shut. But it didn't stop them from harassing me with their incessant staring through the glass.

"These are difficult times, friend," Apple finally spoke. "But Zane didn't leave you without help." A pair of gold scissors slid from her pocket; the metal covered with tiny block letters.

She studied the pair for a moment, then handed them to me. "You're not alone, Helen Bell."

I blinked down at the scissors, realizing they were a gift. "You want me to have these?" It was the first I'd spoken all morning.

"I want you to have hope. And a friend in these troubling quarters." She put them into my palm. "I want you to remember that you're never alone, even when you don't see us with you." With her forefinger, she tapped the snowflake pendant at my chest that I'd returned to my throat last night before falling asleep.

Staring at the scissors, I thought about what Porethius Plum had said in the secret room of the library. How she'd spoken almost those same words.

The library had been burned to the ground right after, and Elowin's messenger had been nowhere in sight.

My fingers brushed over the orb and Shammah necklace. I considered taking them off and leaving them somewhere, instead of dutifully clasping them back on each night. It seemed pointless to keep wearing them.

I studied Apple's effortless beauty as she pinned back

my hair, and I slid the scissors into my dress pocket where my necklaces would go.

Apple should have been the one pretending to be a noble. With her fluttering laugh and effortless charm, she wouldn't have had to try so hard to fool everyone.

"Come on, Scarlet," she said, pulling me from my daydream, reminding me of the role I had to play. "You're going to be late for breakfast."

I was Scarlet Strange. Noble. Afraid of no one. For some reason, reminding myself of that over and over seemed to make me forget that my Patrolman had left me.

Apple had delicately braided my hair and clasped gold chandelier earrings to my lobes. After all the work she'd done this morning to revive my Rime colours, I'd felt a smidgen relieved to see my Trite tones wiped away when I looked in the mirror.

Eliot dipped to the right to stand with the other guardsmen when I arrived at the dining room. I noticed how easily he fit into the line of red-cloaked guards and attendants. His solemn face held no hint of a smile; I wondered if Zane disappearing was bugging him, too.

I wasn't paying attention to the seat I chose, going straight for the same one as last time. I realized Quinten was sitting further down the table when he began shuffling around, disturbing the peace with his muttering, "*Move, Driar, I think I dropped my ring.*"

I hadn't even thought to try and sit by Quinten, but

maybe I didn't care this morning. It wasn't like we could chat about our troubles at the breakfast table.

The Crimson King's airy voice ushered the room into their unusual chant after we took our seats. I didn't try to speak through it or pretend I knew how it went.

"Ah, magician. Entertain me and my family," the king ordered, and I sharpened my distant stare to the masked juggler slinking around the backs of everyone's chairs. He moved in a way that demanded everyone be curious of what he was up to. It would have been tantalizing, delightful even, if I wasn't already so put off by how he'd handed me that white apple in front of everyone in the orchard.

Snickers emerged from the adolescent nobles down the table as the magician walked with his hands folded behind his back, deciding who he might hassle to perform a trick, no doubt. I noticed Holly Kissing stiffen as he passed behind her chair and wondered just how humiliating it was going to be for whoever he picked.

"I'll do it!" one of the young princes volunteered.

A lord sprang from his seat. "No, pick me!"

I ignored them and took a jug to pour myself something I hoped beyond all measure was just water. I'd only gotten half my goblet filled when a servant rushed to help, plucking the jug from my fingers. I nearly threw up my hands in surrender until I realized Prince Forrester was studying me from across the table. His gaze was so cold, I felt like I'd turned to glass and the second-oldest prince could see right through me.

"You." A voice came from behind my chair, and I barely turned before realizing every other set of purplish eyes around the table was on me, too.

"Lucky," the young Red Prince who'd tried to volunteer slumped back in his seat.

My eyes travelled to a white-gloved hand waiting beside me. Attached was a white sleeve, and at the top of the sleeve, a white collar, and above that, a pure white mask.

Prince Forrester's stare hadn't faltered, so, I reluctantly took the magician's hand, swallowing my reservations.

Instantly, I was whisked from my seat and away from the table where the magician paused and patted his coat as though searching for something. He held up a finger apologetically like he needed a minute to find it.

I tried not to make a face as princes and lords chuckled from their seats. Finally, the magician stopped like he'd figured something out. He pointed at me, and I raised an eyebrow.

Quinten's smile vanished when the magician poked that same finger at him and curled it to summon him to join us. The prince's gaze flickered up to mine, but he obediently rose while the younger princes hooted at this change of events.

I didn't dare steal a look at Eliot by the wall.

The magician raised a finger as if to instruct me not to move while Quinten took his time. I went still as his gloved hand drifted to my neck, my pulse lifting where his thumb grazed.

When the magician snapped his fingers, I felt something fall from behind my ear. He caught it and pulled it out to study it—something gold. And just as suddenly as the trinket had appeared, he turned and kicked the back of Quinten's leg, drawing a startled growl from Prince Forrester and Prince Tegan at the table, and a gasp from Quinten as he dropped to one knee and raised a hand to keep his balance.

The magician grabbed Quinten's suspended hand and shoved the gold item into it.

With a swift brush backwards, the magician left us there like that and silently clapped against his own palm in some sort of bizarre congratulatory praise.

My eyes fired back to Quinten, who was equally as struck. Only the young princes continued to clap at the performance. The king, Prince Tegan, and Prince Forrester stared at where Quinten was bent on one knee, hand raised, with his gold ring hovering in front of me, and my heart stopped.

Quinten's face paled.

Our eyes met.

The magician knew of mine and Quinten's conversation in the sleigh. At least the part about Quinten saying I should marry him—the *theoretical* proposal. If the magician knew about that small part of the conversation, he must have known about the rest.

Quinten was back on his feet in a heartbeat, his amethyst eyes lacking their usual lustre. He avoided the gazes of everyone at the table, cheeks pale. But I watched the magician.

I had no doubt that the magician had just sent a message. But to who? To the king, to reveal that his son had made an alliance with me in secret?

To Quinten, to tell him to back off his investigation into the king's illness?

Or to me…?

My eyes travelled past Quinten, past Eliot's hard expression, to where the magician drifted past in all innocence and stopped behind *my* chair. He pulled it out, inviting me to sit back down. His work was finished.

The silent threat pumped through my ears. There was no mistaking it now.

For all my time trying to locate the black heart, I had never had a reason to consider the magician. But now it was all I could see: that this magician was a snake hiding in plain sight.

Eliot's fists were clenched at his sides the whole walk back to my chambers.

"What exactly are you doing for that Timepiece, Helen?" he demanded the moment the door was shut.

"I would have told you if you'd been willing to help me *before*." I tried to shove him out of the way to go hide in my bedroom, but he reached back and slammed the door—the sound of a dozen startled birds springing from the window-sill followed.

"You've got some frostbit explaining to do," he snapped.

"Fine," I unwound, defeat rushing over me. "I'll tell you. But I want to make a deal first."

"What?" Eliot's face fell. "No way. I'll never make another deal in my whole timestring."

"Just…" I rubbed my face, ruining the makeup. "Just disobey Zane's order to leave tonight. Don't take me away yet."

Eliot's eyes flickered, but he didn't object. "You *want*

me to disobey Cohen? Ragnashuck, I'm merrily ubbersnugged." Pure sarcasm.

"I just came one step closer to stopping Asteroth. If you
let me stay until the Alabaster Ball, I'll tell you everything,"
I promised.

Now that Zane could be knocking at Asteroth's door at
any moment, I had more of a reason than ever to try and end
this war. At this point, I was racing Zane to the enemy's front
gate.

Eliot grunted but again, didn't object, and I wondered if
it bothered him that Zane had given him instructions in the
first place, instead of trusting him to do his job. "It burns my
scotcher that you've kept a thing from me. But if you really
have a way to stop Asteroth, I want in. You're going to tell
me *everything* though, understand? No more leaving me in
the dark with the Chocolatiers. I'm Patrol, not an outsider."

"I'm sorry I didn't tell you," I sighed. "Obviously the
reason I wanted to come here wasn't to hide from Asteroth.
I have a way to stop him, but I need time." I paused, scratch-
ing at my hairline. Finally I asked, "How are you with puzzles?"

Eliot didn't seem as struck as I'd feared. He didn't dish
out mean comments or tell me I was crazy, either. Maybe
learning I had a way to solve our problems was a relief after
he'd stared at the fireplace for so many hours this week.

"Help me finish this," I begged. I extended my hand,
even though no official deal had been made.

To my surprise, Eliot took it, eyes softening. We
shook—Patrolman and Carrier—and I breathed a sigh of relief.

"Lucky for you, Helen, I'm excellent at solving puzzles," he said.

It was barely an hour before Quinten was knocking on my door. He didn't wait for anyone to answer; he barged in, making Eliot spring from the couch where we'd been sitting with our feet up, going over the Timepiece's heart puzzles. Eliot and I exchanged a look, and my Patrolman disappeared from the chambers without a word.

Quinten stopped in front of me, nostrils flared. "Did you tell someone about our sleigh natter, Scarlet?"

I blinked. "Of course not!" I hadn't even told Zane, or Apple. I hadn't told a soul that Quinten had joked about me being his wife. It was such a crazy suggestion; I didn't think it would be worth saying aloud.

Quinten huffed. "Then how did that fool know?" He balled his hands and turned toward the crackling fire in the living area. "Kingsblood, it's like he was listening through the reindeers' ears. No one was around when we talked."

"The carriage driver was," I tried, but Quinten shook his head.

"My driver has served me for ten seasons, since I was nine seasons aged and was gifted that sleigh. He would never repeat my words."

"It wasn't an official proposal anyway. Why did the magician try to make it seem like it was?" I imagined Quinten getting punished by the Crimson King for not discussing his

intentions with his father first. Quinten wasn't going to survive much longer if the king thought his son was keeping
secrets from him.

Quinten doubled back and cupped my face with his
hands. I blinked. "Because we're dabbling in a dangerous
thing. Because he *can*…" When he looked me over, his gaze
hovered on my mouth. "I'll fire that magician for kicking my
leg like that. For making a merry show of us," he whispered.

The prince's hands slid off my warm cheeks and he went
to pace in the living area. I didn't mean to reach up and touch
my face but it's where my fingers ended up. I took a deep
breath.

"It's riddlesome, Scarlet," Quinten muttered.

It *was* riddlesome. How did someone learn insights like
that when they weren't around to hear them?

A white-eyed woman with a winding neck tattoo filled
my mind and I closed my mouth.

See you soon.

The flutters in my abdomen returned.

"My father has no reason to disapprove of a courtship,
or even a *marriage* between us," Quinten appeared before
me again. "But he'll be furious if he thinks I proposed and
didn't tell him. Or *ask* him first."

He chewed on his lip as I reeled in my thoughts about
the woman in the basement.

"So, tell him the truth. Tell him we're not engaged, and
that the idea is ridiculous." I moved to start pacing too, but
Quinten caught my arm and turned me back, ringed fingers
gripping my plain ones. His amethyst gaze swam too much
for me to think his next words were going to be good.

"What if I don't tell him that?" An unlevel whisper.

"What?" I was sure I hadn't heard him correctly; my accent didn't even hold. "You're not actually suggesting—"

"I'm *suggesting* that we do become betrothed. Or at least, pretend to be for a measure. If I ask my father for permission to marry you, he'll say yes. He wants to smooth things over with the Strange family fortunes—he's wanted to ever since Cane became that nutcracker and made such a disgraceful scene," he said. "I'll be put back in my father's good graces for making it seem like I planned to involve him all along, and we'll have time to figure out what's muddling him."

Apple had never coached me on the great *Strange family fortunes*, but that was the least of my worries now.

"You don't even know me."

"Scarlet, I'm going to be forced to marry in a quarter or three anyway. Perhaps we can create some good tidings of it—give my father the impression I'm bending to his will. We don't truly have to become beloveds in the end. We can call it off as soon as I've handled the ashworm responsible for mindsweeping my father." He restlessly flicked the hair away from my eyes—my *deceiving* eyes that weren't really gold beneath Apple's drops. "If the Crimson King makes me marry someone I can't trust, I'll get betrayed by my own wife, vows or not. You remember what happened to the Sneppletons."

No, I didn't remember the *Sneppletons*.

This act of mine was getting out of hand. There was no way I would, or even *could* pretend to be engaged to this Red Prince for any *upcoming quarters,* whether it was for a good reason or not. He had no idea who he was really asking, or what he was asking of me. I had a family in the Trite world.

I would be returning to them before the intersect closed.

I rubbed my temples. Helping this way was out of the question, but...maybe finding another way to help Quinten wasn't.

It felt as crazy as the first time I'd considered it, but I imagined taking Quinten into Toronto's beating heart, where people packed into malls and onto city busses by the dozens. I still didn't fully understand how the intersects worked, but I knew that a Rime Folk could get stuck on the Trite side once it sealed, if they crossed and journeyed deep enough into the Trite lands. My own theories on the matter convinced me that if visibility was based on possession, Quinten would become visible to the Trites once he decided to give himself to the Trite world.

The fact that Quinten felt like he had to stage a fake betrothal to save himself was a good enough argument for me to suggest we run from this place. And for the first time, I wondered if he would agree to come with me, once I admitted who I was. I wondered if he was desperate enough to survive that he might forgive me for fooling him into thinking I was Scarlet Strange.

But I couldn't suggest an escape to the Trite world again when there was a prophetess in the basement of the palace who might expose me and the Chocolatiers at any moment.

Quinten closed his eyes and sighed, brushing through his crow-black hair and nudging the silver coronet off tilt. "Just think about it, Scarlet. Things are about to get unmerrily muddled for us if we don't do something now. And leave that magician to me. I'll take care of him." He dropped my hand and turned to leave.

The chamber doors slammed shut on his way out. Only

the rough sound of logs crisping on the fire remained.

I should have yelled at Quinten to stop; to tell him what I suspected the magician was. That the king's performer may have been the black-hearted monster controlling the throne. But my lips never moved.

I was in way over my head, and the gravity that no one was left to help me weighed on my chest like an anvil.

Last year, my Patrolman had stayed faithfully by my side, right up until the end. Prepared to die beside me at the hands of Mara Rouge. Now, Zane had deserted me to face this task alone.

Even Elowin's messenger had abandoned me at the library the night before it was torched. Elowin had *let* it happen. Why didn't Elowin save the library?

No wonder the Timepiece had stepped out of order to warn me. The blackness controlling the Red Kingdom was spreading. And I was completely abandoned, standing right in the middle of it.

My palms found my forehead as a headache began to pulse against my temples; sharp and aggravating, like needles pushing in.

I didn't feel myself sink to my knees. I barely noticed when Eliot returned and grabbed my arms. I only vaguely heard him ask if I was alright.

Chapter,
The Twenty-Sixth

usk was a gloomy painting of gray and purple over the palace, but in the basement, the shadows were sizably worse. Every turn had me holding my breath, and I ate two cobwebs because of how close I'd been keeping to the walls.

Trying to remember the way through the servants' tunnels was a challenge. There was no whining song haunting the tunnels this time. There was nothing to indicate the prophetess was even there until I rounded the last bend and saw the soggy, pale light spreading over the dirt floor from her doorway. The faint sound of sliding chains echoed down the hall.

I moved like a cat, creeping through the dark with my

fingers brushing the walls. I paused outside her door, taking in a breath. I took in one more for good measure.

"Come in." Her voice leaked from the room and I faltered. I hadn't shown myself yet.

Another deep breath.

"Your son is in danger," I forced the words out as I came from the shadows and entered the room.

No one else was present, thankfully, but the woman's cherry lips were already curved into a smile.

"I *said*, your *son* is in *danger*—"

"I don't have a son," she droned. "I once tried to create a loyal captain with my blood. But my young Steelheart turned out to be neither a son nor loyal. I am curious as to why you'd concern yourself with such a nattery thing though, Lady Strange?" Her iron cuffs clanged over the table as she folded her hands before her globe. "He's only your lowly guardsman, is he not?"

My heart shouldn't have thundered the way it did. Could she see into my thoughts? Could she smell my frayed nerves and sense the beating of my heart?

"If you have any care left for your son, you'll help me save him, and tell me what I need to know." I folded my arms over my chest as though that might hide the noise it made. Scientifically it was impossible, but I was sure she could hear it.

"Scarlet Strange. You don't listen well, do you?" She settled her pale eyes on me with a tilt of her head and I fought a shiver. "I don't have a son."

In the same moment, she lifted her clawed hand above her globe and the mist inside seeped up from the bottom. "I do wonder what your true reason is for coming though," she went on.

What did you tell that magician?

I wanted to ask it, but I was so unnerved by the feelings that spilled in at watching her globe dance. The last fortune teller I'd approached for insight had brought a flock of angry birds roaring over me. Zane had pulled me down into the snow before I was turned to streamers.

"Very well, Lady Strange. If you cannot ask a question, I will see what I can come up with. Do you have payment?" Her pecan hair slid over her shoulder, revealing the black worm creeping down her neck.

Payment. I hadn't even thought of that.

Without debating, I tugged my orb necklace from my pocket and slid the emerald off. The one heart I hadn't even thought of yet.

I tossed it at the woman and blinked in alarm when her hand came up and caught it. The rest of her body hadn't moved a muscle. Slowly, she set it on the corner of her table where I noticed the ruby I'd given her the last time rested.

Instead of wondering about the red gem, I fastened my orb around my neck, feeling like I needed it there, and tucked it away beneath my collar. "You'll tell me what you told the palace magician," I said, harnessing my inner noblewoman. I wasn't afraid of a mere prophetess in chains.

"The green heart," the woman whispered, tapping the end of her finger against the emerald, and I halted my thoughts. "The most deceiving one."

"Wait—"

"You asked what I told the palace magician, but that's not the true answer you seek, is it?" The mist in her globe swirled, and my eyes fired down to it, glued there even as my own orb began to heat against my chest. "I haven't told the palace magician a thing."

I gasped as my Revelation Orb singed my skin.

Scrambling to unearth it from my dress, I tore the necklace from my throat, snapping the chain. My orb glowed—a fierce cotton-white dissolving the speckles of gold. Past the burning glass ornament, the prophetess twitched like she could sense it was there.

"Put that thing away," she growled. "Or we're bloody finished."

My hands shook, but I reluctantly slid it into the pocket of my dress, aware it might burn right through the fabric. This was wrong; even my orb knew it.

I changed my mind about being here—I didn't want this woman telling me anything. I turned to leave, muttering back at her, "This was a mistake—"

"I see your future, noblewoman. In the future, you are wedded to the third Red Prince."

My feet stopped moving.

"But you don't stay in this kingdom. The Red Kingdom becomes too unsafe for you both." Her cherry mouth pulled into a thin line, a wrinkle creasing between her eyebrows. "Furthermore, Zane Cohen-Margus-Bowswither has no part in your future. If that's what you were about to ask next."

Time stilled. My orb sizzled through the threads of my skirts and landed on the stone floor with a thud as I turned back, but I kept my stare on the woman at the table, and her melon-sized glass ball.

Silence hung in the damp room. The prophetess didn't seem to be in any sort of hurry to usher me to leave. She kept as quiet and still as a bird of prey, waiting for me to collect myself as she'd likely done many times after revealing shocking things of someone's future.

Finally, I closed my mouth and swallowed. "If you can really see the future, how was someone able to sneak up and capture you to bring you here in the first place?" The question was strained; my throat was thick.

This time when the woman smiled, it was so wide I could see a chip on one of her canines.

"It's an honour to serve as the Crimson Court's prophetess; a sacred glory bestowed upon few." Her chair made a squeal against the floor when she stood and lifted her hands to reveal the length of her chains, and I paled.

The chains from her wrists connected to nothing; they were just dangling, loose hoops. "Only a fool would believe I didn't see this coming."

THE
STORYTELLER

ANOTHER MEDDLESOME INTERRUPTION IN THE MIDDLESOME

I n a box of iron bars and withered hopes, nestled into the height of a tower, youthful Lucas Leutenski could hardly keep his head up. Sleep bid him welcome—other things too.

But a voice brought Lucas from his drowse, "Do forgive me for my delay."

When he peeled his bruised eyelids open, Lucas spotted a foe he had not crossed in many seasons. Once, he had looked up to Nicholas Saint; Mikal Migraithe's first apprentice.

Jolly Cheat did not pay Lucas a pinch of attention as he strode to where Asteroth waited in stillness.

"You are unworthy of forgiveness." Asteroth's words brushed frost o'er the small room outside Lucas's already frigid cell. The statement only came from himself this time, Lucas noticed. Not spoken by the other thing.

"Ragnashuck, what is so *vital* that you needed me here in a pinch?" The madman lifted a bell-laden hat from the nearby shelf and plunked it onto his head.

"The Carrier's beloveds. I wish for you to fetch them for me."

Though he was so very tired, Lucas's eyes peeled back open at that. He fought a wheezing cough, tasting of bile, blood, sweat, and tears. When he collected himself, he spotted a silver feather drift into the room from the balcony.

"Regrettably, I'm not able to accept such an undertaking."

All the bells on the madman's lavish hat remained quiet as Asteroth turned to face him, the frost in the once-prophet's gaze not warmed by his velvet cape.

"Explain." Asteroth's *other* voice appeared this time, and Lucas stifled the quiver in his spine.

Jolly twiddled his weapon, frustration leaking in at the tight corners of his face. "I'm constrained by a deal I made with the Trite during the season past. I'm not permitted to seek out her beloveds in the dead world. It was the price I paid in exchange for her facing your cousin in the Quarrel."

Asteroth's silver eyes pooled with charcoal, and Lucas, for all his exhaustion, bit back a terrible laugh.

Had the old prophet of *infinite* knowledge not known how Jolly Cheat had gotten Helen Bell to Wentchester

Cove? Lucas could hardly keep quiet, his smile slipped out.

Lucas's cage was forged of iron, but he had grown curious about a pair of bent spokes, wondering if the gap they left might be his size. A measure had passed since he had thought of it, but now it tempted him rather incessantly—beyond the gap was the yawning balcony, and beyond that, a deadly drop the full height of the tower.

"Oh, stop looking at me like that," he thought aloud toward the irresistible gap, only to remember that when one thinks a thing out loud, others can hear it.

Jolly glanced at the youthful Patrolman for the first time since his arrival. And, at the thrill of having an attentive audience, Lucas felt it was the proper time to upstage the visiting madman with a plunge only a lunatic might try.

Lucas Leutenski sprang, tearing across his cage on wobbling feet, and shoved himself through the gap he had spent such a measure thinking of. Jolly Cheat's swiftness failed him as Lucas slid o'er the balcony on unbalanced heels, and plunged off the end into a perilous fall, clinging only to the raging wind.

Chapter,
The Twenty-Seventh

I avoided breakfast, lunch, and dinner for two days straight in case the magician showed up again. Apple brought me snacks from the attendants' villa. I barely nibbled on them, but on the second day, I grabbed a handful of mini cakes and wrenched the window open to toss them at the birds.

Quinten hadn't come to find me, and Zane never returned. Even Eliot was absent in his own way—lingering by the fireplace and keeping to himself while his mind worked tirelessly on solving the heart puzzles. He'd managed to slink into the records room and gather dozens of old ledgers of family histories. He'd gone over them with a fine-tooth comb to find clues about the black heart. Every once in a while, he showed me notes on family illnesses similar to the king's, or family lines who were recorded to have meddled in dark sorts of magic. Occasionally he returned to the room with gossip from the other guardsmen about who they guessed the magician might be.

He asked me if I was alright, if I wanted to talk, and tried to force me to eat. For all his pushing to become my Patrolman, Eliot didn't seem to know what to do with me now that he had the job. I still hadn't told him about Zane's mother, but apart from that, I'd trusted Eliot with everything. Frankly, it was a relief to have someone else working so hard to untangle the Timepiece's riddle.

We didn't bother with novels or games to pass the time, just Fred and Apple's stories. But even those I could hardly pay attention to. Eliot just watched *me* while I watched Apple act out old tales. He made faces whenever her back was turned—justifiably so—and I found myself cracking real smiles after a while.

On the third evening of Zane's absence, Apple fitted me into a button-up bodice of silk rosettes. "Perfect for dancing," she sighed. "I wish I could go with you. All the twirling and music and treats… For all their follies, the Red Kingdom does love the arts in a way that's unmatched by anyplace else in Winter."

"It's just a candlelight celebration." My words were quiet. I hadn't spoken much to Apple, despite finding comfort in her constant presence. I still didn't know how to tell her everything that had happened.

I looked at my friend as she puttered along, stitching a spot here, tucking in a piece there.

I'd gone over the prophetess's words a thousand times.

I couldn't tell Eliot. He just wouldn't get it. "Apple, I didn't just come to the Red Kingdom to hide," I blurted.

Apple slipped a pin between her lips and glanced up with her sugar-brown eyes. "Of course not, friend. You and your Patrolmen have been nattering on to each other since you arrived at the factory when you thought we weren't listening."

"Oh…"

I rubbed my eyes and Apple slapped my hand away from my powdered face.

"We had a reason to keep you in the dark," I said.

"It's alright, Miss Helen. I don't care what other plans you have."

Apple was too trusting. I watched her fiddle with a rosette at my bust, and wished she realized just how dangerous Asteroth was. I wished she had seen for herself what Asteroth had done to Mikal, and then the library, and I wished she would consider what might happen to her if the man hunting for me and Zane showed up here for us.

I found myself shutting my mouth instead of telling her anything else.

"You look beautiful, friend," she said when she was finished. "I wonder how you'll ever go back to wearing hideous green sweaters like the one you showed up to my home in."

Disappointment weighed on my glossed shoulders at the thought of giving up the gowns, the rose-gold hair, the bright golden eyes…The mask made it possible to forget the current hardships of Helen Bell. Apple had painted my lips a deep red for the candlelight celebration, and I didn't even feel an ounce worried about it making me stand out as Scarlet Strange.

*In the future, you are wedded to the third Red Prince.
But you don't stay in this kingdom.*

How was I supposed to get through the candlelight evening with that ridiculous prophecy hanging over my head?

"Time to go, Helen." Eliot appeared and tugged my arm to steal me from Apple who would have kept finding things to fix if we didn't cut her off.

"Have fun!" the Chocolatier twirled her scissors.

Once in the hallway, Eliot looked me over, his rounded jaw shifting. "Don't you think you have enough of Prince Quinten's attention?" he said the moment the door was shut.

"Seriously?" I rolled my eyes, already feeling an ache in my feet from the glass-toed shoes Apple made me wear.

"So, you're just scuttling around this palace, looking like *that*, for a reason other than to make him want you more?"

A flush burned over my cheeks and I halted.

"Oh, come on, Helen. You love all this merry primping," he nodded down to my gown. "I'm not a spinbug."

A clang sounded from somewhere down the hall as I gaped. "Go back to the room, Eliot. I'm going alone tonight," I said when I found my voice. I was too tired for this judgmental nonsense.

I turned to leave him, but Eliot snatched my wrist. "You're frostbit joking, right?"

"No!" I tore my arm away. I shoved him in the chest—a childish move but frankly, it felt good.

Eliot's purple eyes glowered. "Let's get one thing clear; if *I'm* not going, *you're* not going, Trite." He had my arm again before I could escape and began dragging me back toward the chambers.

"Eliot...get your big, *annoying* hand off of me!" I

slapped at his arm, no longer caring about being seen by palace dwellers. I'd publicly fire him as my guardsman.

"Gray," a stern voice came from behind Eliot, and we both stopped.

When Eliot tilted to look back, I saw dishevelled pecan hair, and undisguised electric blue eyes. Zane was back in a red coat. Back in the palace.

Eliot's grip slipped off my wrist. It was the moment in the library all over again—stares level and pressure filling the air—only there wasn't a band of Patrolmen standing by to witness what might happen.

"You left," Eliot reminded him.

"I'm back."

Eliot glanced at me again, eyeing my outfit. "Suit yourself, Cohen. But you should know she's pining after someone else now." He shoved past Zane into the chambers, and my neck roared with heat.

Zane turned, shoulders tight. "Should I even ask what he's talking about?"

I shook my head in disbelief. "Zane, a lot has happened—"

"Apparently." His eyes flickered down to my dress, my heels, back up to my hair, my red mouth.

But I had a bigger problem than Eliot's preposterous comments. How was I going to tell Zane that I'd visited his mother again? I could already see the betrayal that would flicker over his face, the turn of his attitude.

No more secrets though, Helen. His words in the servants' tunnel.

But then he'd left. Without saying goodbye. Without telling me where he was going, like he did the night he went to see his mother in the first place.

I closed my eyes. "I'm going to be late," I whispered.

"Late for what?" Zane's voice in the darkness.

"The candlelight celebration. Apple will tell you about it." I turned to go, expecting him to halt me. Expecting his hand to find mine, or his words to pull me back.

When he let me go without a fight, my heart sank a little deeper into my chest.

The celebration hall wasn't large; less than three hundred people crowded the space. As to be expected, groupings of candles flickered around the room as the only source of light, turning the deep red walls to liquid bronze.

A narrow table stretched the length of the wall with living drinks; wings fluttered in goblets, bubbles danced in others, and some steamed from the top. Everything smelled of sour fruit and flaky tarts. Even the air was thick and oversaturated with the breath of the wicked.

"Kingsblood, there you are. I was getting worried you weren't coming." Quinten appeared with a goblet in his grip, but it didn't look like he'd sipped any.

A pale blue jacket covered his torso, reminding me of the one he'd worn to the Silver Masquerade Festival. With his silver coronet, he looked like a king.

"I got held up." I swallowed, then reached for his drink to blend into the crowd.

But he tugged it away. "Don't drink it," he warned.

When I nodded obediently, he passed it back. I stared at

the phantom butterfly in the goblet's pool, wondering what sorts of things it made the drinker do.

"I couldn't find that magician," Quinten said below the chatter of the room. "I looked everywhere. I questioned Legionnaires and servants, but it seems he can vanish *himself* just as easily as a *ring*," he said. "But I'd bet my princeship he'll show up tonight."

My eyes travelled the room, searching for an all-white outfit complete with a mask. I didn't find a magician, but I found the ever watchful Holly Kissing glance my way. She was stunning in her pink dress and honey-gold hair. A collection of nobles surrounded her.

Tonight, her attention annoyed me, and I dropped my gaze back to my fluttering drink.

"I haven't seen you at breakfast. I thought maybe you were upset about what I had suggested." Quinten reached for a new drink from a passing attendant—the steam from it coiled up to his chin. "I was just trying to get out of this muddle, Scarlet. I would never *make* you participate in a betrothal, false or not. It was a scotchy idea," he shook his head, glancing down at the blueish liquid. He reluctantly took a sip.

I eyed him as he winced from the beverage's heat. "Kingsblood. That's bitter," he muttered.

"Not a scotchy idea." I bit my lips together and Quinten's amethyst eyes darted over. They flickered down to my mouth where they hung on the red lipstick a moment longer than they should have. "Just an idea that's difficult to get my mind around," I finished.

In the future, you are wedded to the third Red Prince.

As we looked at each other in that candle-dotted room, I

wondered if running back home had ever been the right answer. I wondered if this was all meant to set me up to stay with Quinten instead, to help him fight the blackness in the palace.

What were the odds that someone who looked like me would be missing from the Red Kingdom and I'd be able to step into her shoes and take her place? Someone had to be setting this up, pulling the strings. And for the first time, I asked myself if there was something bigger going on.

Was I *meant* to come here and squash the blackness? Maybe only I could. After all, only the Carriers of Truth were able to resist Mara Rouge's freezing spells. Maybe I was the only one able to resist the blackness, too.

I'd never considered that Elowin might have drawn me here for a greater purpose. The quiet Truth that had looked out for me last year when I'd come to Winter hadn't been speaking to me the same way this time. Maybe because I hadn't been speaking to him, either.

Apart from the brief flash of silver words lighting my skin when I crossed Asteroth in the library, and the perplexing visit from Porethius Plum, I didn't have a shred of evidence to support the idea that Elowin might still be listening. Maybe I'd slipped through the cracks while he'd been focused on other things.

Cold memories of lonely sunsets back home haunted my mind; being certain there was a hollowness growing in me, a part of me left somewhere I couldn't reach. I thought I was going insane at the time, but now that I was back, I was sure something had been calling me from Winter.

Maybe this was it. Maybe Quinten was my future. Maybe he and I were meant to find each other and save the

Red Kingdom.

Though it would torment Apple, I dug my fingers into my hair. I couldn't tell what was right anymore. A noisy pressure pushed in at the sides of my brain, the commotion drowning me in its hiss. All I heard here among the Reds was *noise*.

"Scarlet."

When my eyes flashed open, Quinten was pulling the drink from my hand and setting it on a passing tray. He tugged me into the crowded dancing space, silver crown casting a speckled reflection of the lit candles. I went without a fuss when I realized he was trying to lure me away from such a visible place while I unravelled.

"I'm losing my mind," I said, hot tears touching the corners of my eyes. "I have no idea what I'm supposed to do."

The prince let out a slow breath as we stopped in the mass of bunched couples. "What are you talking about?"

But I shook my head, "I think I've messed everything up and I don't know how to fix it."

I'd dragged Apple and Fred into this deathtrap. I'd snapped at Eliot after we'd finally become friends, and then I'd left Zane in the hall without an explanation. I went to see Zane's *mother*.

"Are you thinking of running away again?" Quinten's eye tones flickered to dread and dust. "I can't do this without you, Scarlet. Please don't leave me alone here. Kingsblood, you don't have to do *anything* absurd with the betrothal, but don't run away. I haven't had a friend in a long measure, and it's been even longer since I've found someone I can trust."

His speech moved through me, stirring the guilt I deserved for having tricked him for this long. He didn't want me to abandon him—the way Zane had left me. The way even the Truth seemed to have gone silent, leaving me here to face these demons alone.

In fact, the only one who hadn't abandoned me so far was this Red Prince before me, begging me not to leave him alone.

Quinten needed to know what was really going on. Every dull, Trite part of it. And then *he* could decide if he still wanted me to stay.

"Scarlet..." Quinten pleaded.

Across the candlelit space, the Crimson King's black-plum eyes found me through the crowd as though the room was empty apart from us. The man's hollow gaze drilled Quinten's back.

"Later, we'll talk."

Thankfully, Quinten didn't try and poach my thoughts or beg me to explain my brief meltdown. He pursed his lips and danced slow.

I escaped the celebration as soon as the song ended.

Chapter,
The Twenty-Eighth

My thoughts were clouded as I drifted through the dark palace hallways, getting lost once or twice. I found quiet halls, storage towers, archive rooms, a theatre, and glittering unused party spaces.

I had no idea what time it was, if it was halfway through the night, or if Eliot would still be awake, waiting in my rooms to chat about our incident in the hall before I could go to bed.

My toils all came to a halt when I entered my chambers and found only the fireplace giving light to the room. Everyone was gone, except for Zane.

The fire turned half his body copper where he sat atop the dining table, his legs dangling over the side, dressed in raven-black that blended into the shadows. His Patrol staff rested over his lap.

He hadn't re-dyed his hair dark since he returned, hadn't bothered to re-stain his eyes to gold like mine. Hadn't kept his red coat on.

Though the fire flickered, the silence in the air was cold.

Zane slid his weapon onto to the table behind him. "Someone tried to kill me on the Eastern Plains before you came back to Winter," he said.

When he looked up, his eyes lacked their usual joy. "It's why there's music in my chest. Because a hymn dove in and brought me back from where I'd slipped away to die."

I remembered how he'd arrived at the library in shredded clothes.

"After Asteroth's declaration of war on you and me, I would have thought it was him who spellbound the squatch to kill me. But Asteroth isn't the sort to let another thing do his work," he said. His words were short. Cold. Clipped. "Or he would have just sent snowsquatches after Lucas and Mikal too."

I only stared at him.

"So," he said, fingers tapping the tabletop. "Either Asteroth doesn't care as much about personally hunting us down as he's made us believe, or someone else is out to get me," he paused, and I knew he'd already come to his own conclusion. "I don't think Asteroth Ryuu is behind all of this."

The blackness. The magician. The *other thing* inhabiting Asteroth.

My mind crawled with unconfirmed theories I'd already made in his absence.

"Then who do you think spellbound the snowsquatch?" I finally spoke.

"I'd hoped to find out while I was gone. Cheat has something to do with all this, I can feel it. But that's the thing, Helen. None of this makes sense to me. Not Mikal's death, not the snowsquatch trap, not my mother being here. Something about all of this feels *orchestrated*."

His hand dug against his chest as he rubbed it.

"Where did you go when you left?" I changed the subject. All I wanted now was the answer he never gave before he'd disappeared. I wanted to hear it before I scolded him for how he'd abandoned me in the *Red Kingdom*, of all places.

"To find Cheat, like I *said* I would. To get him to reveal what in all of Winter is going on. But a bird in the sky led me to Lucas instead," he said. "And imagine my surprise when the birds I left to watch over you found us and told me you were still here." His shoulders tightened and he blinked slowly, and intentionally.

"So instead of bringing Leutenski back to the *factory*, I had to bring him to this bloody kingdom and stuff him in a tavern in the Scarlet City to recover, because I couldn't bring the injured sputtlepun into the palace looking the way he did."

My exhale came out heavy. I refused to think about what sort of condition Lucas must have been in if he wasn't able to get to the factory on his own two legs.

Zane slid off the table and walked over, coming close enough to engulf me in his mint-pine scent as he reached past and closed the door at my back. It clicked shut, but his electric blue eyes stayed on me.

He kept his hand flat on the door, arm hovering by my

neck. "You're making this extremely difficult for me, Trite." His breath warmed my mouth and my heartbeat faltered.

"Zane, I don't know what Eliot told you—"

"Eliot was supposed to have you out of here a good measure ago."

"I told him we needed to stay. Not for the reason he said—that I was...*pining* after..." I couldn't even spit the horrible words out.

But Zane's eyes flared brighter. "Tell that to your sweet red lips, and your *painfully* attractive dress." My pulse hammered as he tilted in further like he might bite my red lips right off. "I think you like being here, dressed like this."

I huffed, "*Apple* turned me into this! I couldn't have put this look together if my life depended on it."

"Was Apple also the one who convinced Eliot to stay?" he challenged. "Was it *Apple* who went to visit my mother below the palace?"

My lips parted. How did he know?

"Helen," he growled. "I don't know why a rubbish puzzle is keeping you here. But if me confronting my truths is what you want, then I'll *tell* you them!" His jaw flexed as he spoke, "First, I'm furious about how you've made yourself into a thing no one can keep their eyes off of, including *me*."

I tried to lift my hands in protest, but he snatched my fingers with his free hand. "*Second*..." his mouth twitched, like it was rebelling against saying the words. "If you want honesty...fine. It was excruciating for me too when we were split apart this season past. The moment the intersect closed, I felt a rush of cold I never want to feel again. The *truth* is, I spent that first quarter anxious, hardly bloody sleeping over you." His hand slid off the door to tilt my chin up; meant to keep my eyes on his for this.

I couldn't breathe. "*Zane*—"

"Ragnashuck, my truth is that I'm bloody *desperate* to keep you here with me in Winter. And I've been trying to find a way to convince you to stay."

He swallowed and dropped his fingers to my waist. My whole abdomen swam with warmth, but my waist smouldered where his hands held onto me.

"Helen, my boundaries with you began wearing thin a good measure ago," he leaned to whisper into my ear, and I could feel the hammering of his heart beneath my palm. His cheek drifted against mine until the corners of our lips brushed.

"Zane…"

"If you want to know the truth," he spoke against my cheek, his fingers drifting up into my hair. "The truth is that you've tangled into my chest in ways a Carrier should never mix up with a Patrolman."

His mouth came over mine, and my heart thundered.

It was barely a shadow of a kiss, but it unravelled my thoughts, all but one: *Zane Cohen-Margus-Bowswither has no part in your future.*

Beguiled, I pushed him back before the kiss could grow wings and become something that would shatter me in the next moments. My lips hung parted in astonishment. I wanted to cry. But mostly, I wanted to scream.

Zane was telling me this *now*. He'd never looked my way once last year when I looked like a Trite. And he'd left me alone in this palace and everything had been ruined while he was gone.

But mostly, I despised that I couldn't think straight, because in twenty seconds my Patrolman had unspooled my logic and turned my heart to a kickdrum.

"Helen," he rasped, body rigid. "Ragnashuck, Helen, let's just go." His hands found me again even though I'd pushed him away. "We shouldn't be here. You, especially, should not *be* here."

Go. Stay. Go. Stay.

"Zane, if you want to go, just go." I hated the words as they came out. I hated looking up to find the look on his face. I hated that Zane Cohen was the one thing that might have the power to keep me in Winter for the rest of my days, even when I had a family I loved back home.

"I'm not leaving without you," he said, brows tilting in.

"Well, I can't leave. Not yet." I backed against the door, wanting to run back into the dark halls and avoid seeing him this way. He was my weak point in Winter, and I knew it—I'd known it even before I came back here. Good grief, Zane might very well have been one of the hearts the Timepiece had warned me about after all.

But Zane stood straight, mouth shut, and stared, transformed back into everything as solid and devoted as a Patrolman should be. "You want to stay." A question.

"Zane, you never acted like this when I looked like a Trite," I said, and confusion flickered over his blue gaze. "It's not fair that you suddenly feel this way when I'm in a *painfully attractive* dress, and in a disguise that's hidden my *dull eyes.*"

My hand found the doorknob and it squeaked when I turned it, giving me away.

But his jaw set, and his hand flashed out to halt the knob.

"Don't accuse me of being shallow when I just told you I've been tormented for four bloody quarters because we were apart." His hands swept back to my waist and he *lifted* me.

I gasped, thrashing like a child as I was carried far away from the door. "I told you one day I would explain the bond between a Patrol and a Carrier, but our entanglement has become a great measure more complex than that."

When he set me down by my bedroom door, I swatted at his chest, fuming. "Zane!"

"You wanted me to face the truth," he reminded me. "That's my bloody truth." He extended both arms wide as he backed away, to present himself and all the truths he'd unloaded into the air between us.

He was a solid gate between me and escaping the chambers. We were facing this. There was no getting out of it now.

"Fine. Here's *my* truth." I shot back, "You're right. I *like* being Scarlet Strange. I *like* to be colourful. I never thought I would like being a Red, but I do," I said. "And I'm more than just a useless peg out of its shell, Zane. I'm not that same ridiculous, clumsy person you met last year that needed saving. I can't believe what we accomplished, but what changed me the most was the year I spent *afterward*, away from this place. I've become much more capable since battling...*her*." Even after all this time, it still felt wrong to say her name out loud, to admit that the monster of my past had a name. "I've managed to keep Apple and Fred safe by fooling everyone in this palace. I even figured out who the black heart is, *without* you."

His jaw twitched, but I had to say the worst of it. "And I *am* close to Quinten. I've been helping him learn who's messing with the Crimson King's mind. Quinten isn't as terrible as you all think, he's only trying to save himself from his father."

Zane was silent. Waiting for me to finish. Possibly waiting for a clumsy, pathetic girl to show herself; the same girl he'd dragged over the snow last year. But the peg was gone. Even Cornelius Britley had noticed.

"The rest is a long story, but I can't leave him. We have a plan. Sort of," I said.

"Anything else, Trite?" Zane folded his arms. "Or should I just stay out of your way while you singlehandedly save Winter?"

My mouth slammed shut.

"We've all changed since *her*. The difference between your change and mine, Helen, is that I don't feel like I have to prove something now. Your colours are changing, so stop running like a spinbug to try and prove that you're still worthy of being the last Carrier of Truth!"

My stomach sank, my gusto along with it. The weight of his words slammed into me, magnified by the fact that he'd never had to try hard to do anything well, and I did. All this time, I'd been putting everything I had into trying to protect us *both*, and I hadn't realized he and I were on such different sides. Or that he thought I was running into things recklessly.

"I *did* go visit your mother," I told him, steeling myself and waiting for him to flinch. But he didn't; he just raised an eyebrow.

My fingers locked and I shoved the words out, "She told me that in the future, Quinten and I are...*together*."

It sounded so outrageous, it stung. My cheeks warmed.

But the heat of everything Zane had said up to this point out-weighed any embarrassment I had left.

But Zane didn't look struck by the news. I would have preferred he looked angry or hurt. Looking like *nothing* was worse. "What did she say?" He was too quiet. The shame of the insight started to trickle in.

"That I'm going to end up with—"

"No...what were her exact words?" he asked.

I let out a long breath, "In the future, you are wedded to the third Red Prince. But you don't stay in this kingdom. The Red Kingdom becomes too unsafe for you both." It had been running through my head all day. "And...she also said," I swallowed, losing my edge. "Zane Cohen-Margus-Bow-swither has no part in your future."

There was a subtle tightening of his mouth—a *smirk*, I realized. Almost. Barely a show of dimples. "And do you believe that?" he asked.

"You tell me. Would your mother lie?"

"She can't lie."

She can't...lie.

I felt my last drop of hope drain away.

But Zane drifted back to me, tall and slow, until I could see the pulls of his rigid muscles beneath his Patrol jacket. His smile faded. "I don't believe that," he said, as though I was foolish for believing the woman he'd so carefully avoided for so many years of his life.

"I don't know what to believe anymore." A confession of multiple meanings.

All I was sure of were the chiming gongs and rattling bells in my head that echoed long into the night.

"You're not alone, Helen. Not yet. Don't push me out."

His fingers grazed mine, though he didn't take my hand.

But a quiet huff slipped out. "Actually, for the first time, it's abundantly clear that I *am* on my own with this one."

Zane's electric blue eyes hollowed to slate, and I knew this conversation was over. I'd found a way to end it after all.

His fingers drifted back to his side, the silence between us filling with a chill. It took a while for him to speak, but when he did, all he said was, "Goodnight, Trite."

The worst part was that deep down I didn't really want him to go. I wanted him to wait, to talk me off the ledge and tell me he was going to help me fight the blackness and change the Timepiece's vision of the future. To tell me his mother *was* a liar and lying was something she did all the time.

But Zane made his way across the chambers and out into the dark hall, and he didn't come back.

I waited. And waited.

The fire hissed from the living area.

Chapter,
The Twenty-Ninth

The morning sunlight prismed through the crystal window in my bedroom, where not a single bird remained. It had been a chore to peel off my sheets and make my way out to the living area to meet the Chocolatiers, who it seemed had started sleeping on the sofa and plush chairs. It was like they were too afraid to leave me alone.

Zane was gone again. He hadn't said a word to Apple or Fred before he disappeared, and since Eliot was nowhere to be found either, I strutted to breakfast by myself. It shouldn't have surprised me that the Patrolmen had abandoned me at this point—I was on a roll with hurling people's feelings into the fire. It was a wonder Apple and Fred had stayed around as long as they did.

It was the same at lunch, and then dinner. Zane and Eliot were still cooling off in some mysterious corner of Winter, but Apple stayed close and chatted as she fitted me into a slender black gown with a lace-up back that Zane would have hated.

But after the third round of stories about Red nobles Apple had collected from the attendants, I couldn't take it anymore. It felt like trumpets were being blared against both sides of my head, and raw pain rippled through like a bleeding headache.

"Apple, I'll be right back."

The fashionista had barely finished lacing me up before I whisked for the door. But Zane didn't get to just disappear. *Again.*

I strutted through the hallways and clamoured down the stairs toward the servants' tunnels.

The walk took me long enough that I should have been able to reel my emotions back in, but I didn't—I blinked against the pulsing in by brain, making the dark, damp stones of the tunnel walls a flickering vision.

I rounded into the prophetess's room without looking to see if anyone was with her.

"What did you mean, in my future I'd be married to the third Red Prince?" I demanded. "You can't lie."

The woman was slouched back in her chair, bored. With her red-painted nails, she brushed a long tendril of her pecan hair. "Are you troubled by my insight?" she asked. "Was there someone else you hoped you would end up with?"

I shut my mouth and ground my molars.

She drew forwards and laced her fingers together to rest her chin on them, her marbly, white eyes steady on me. "You should know by now that I don't hand out insight without payment," she said.

Bottling a slew of nasty words, I reached into my pocket for the destroyed orb necklace and pulled the last gem off the chain. I stared at the onyx for a moment—the heart I'd come here to crack open that had only raised more questions. The last of three gems I'd been given by the Timepiece. Almost as though he knew I'd need three payments.

I tossed the onyx onto her table.

"What do you wish to know?" She scooped up the onyx and stashed it to the side in a neat row along with the other two gems: green and red. I wondered if she ever had any other customers, or if she was just making a good living off me.

"I want to know where Zane is," I fired.

The woman paused. And then she laughed; a high, curvy, true laugh that rang into every corner of the room and echoed down the halls behind me. "I have not been able to see into that boy's heart since the day he was born," she said.

"Unbelievable." I put a hand over my eyes and shook my head.

"It's why I called him *Steelheart*."

Suddenly it wasn't a mystery why Zane had a habit of keeping his true feelings to himself. As if I needed something else to feel bad about.

"Don't be unmerried by him running off, Lady Strange. *Abandoning* is in his nature," she said. "He abandoned me first. Then he abandoned Mikal Migraithe seasons later after he suffered his first great loss. Now, it seems, he's abandoned you as well." She crooked her head. "It's foolish to put your hope in someone who acts in a pattern. That is the greatest insight I can give you now."

The prophetess picked up the onyx to study it like she could see it, which was irritating and unnerving when I knew she couldn't. Then she tossed it back to me. "Keep it." I barely had time to catch the black stone; it was a fumble I was glad she couldn't witness. "We have a thing or three in common, you and I. We've both felt the sting of that boy's choices. So, it's bloody simple—skin for skin. Leave him to the Winter winds. Shouldn't he too feel what it is to be abandoned?"

For the next minute, I stared at the woman in silence, until I wondered if she thought I'd left.

Skin for skin.

Abandoning is in his nature.

Shouldn't he too feel what it is to be abandoned?

Despite my bottled feelings and blinding frustrations, I finally saw something clearly for the first time in days. I realized how little this woman knew Zane. Zane was loyal and funny and incredible at everything. This woman was *crazy*.

The tension in my shoulders drained as I grasped how much it bothered me to listen to her. I regretted coming down here again. I regretted chasing Zane off.

I turned from the prophetess's room.

"Season's greetings." Her goodbye echoed against the damp walls as I travelled back through the basement, knowing my way well enough now that I barely had to look.

Zane was right—I could never trust the word of a woman who hated Zane that much, even if she couldn't lie.

I didn't want to abandon Quinten to his fate. But I needed to leave with Zane—it had taken me way too long to realize it. So, I'd give Quinten a choice; he could come to the Trite world with me if he wanted to escape. But I couldn't stay. I *had* to get out of this kingdom. I had to—

A presence emerged at my back. I was slapping my gold-rimmed shoes against the tile stairs when I felt it. I slowed, but I kept moving like I hadn't noticed. The staircase was quiet except for an echo of footsteps slightly off sync with mine. My skin tightened.

I spun around, bracing. But the wide staircase was empty, just still air and polished steps.

"Good grief," I muttered, pressing my palms against my throbbing temples again.

I turned back and jumped in surprise at the pure-white mask waiting for me.

Chapter,
The Thirtieth

I almost careened backwards down the stairs, but my heel caught the step below and I balanced. I tried not to panic at the sight of the all-white outfit, posed like a vanilla sculpture in the dark room of pillars. Far beyond him, the next staircase would take me to a main hall of the palace where witnesses might save me.

The magician waited. I chanced a step to go around, but he raised a hand to halt me in silence. I wondered if I'd make it to the stairs if I ran.

"What do you want?" My voice trembled—I knew full well I wouldn't make it in my heels.

The magician tilted his head. His hand came up to remove his mask. "Ragnashuck, sweetheart," he said.

His daunting face emerged with a gleaming, mad smile, and I backed toward the stairs behind me. Jolly Cheat's coin-flat eyes glimmered.

I tried to run.

He snapped his fingers and his staff appeared out of no-where. "Not so fast, Trite."

The weapon hooked around my waist and lurched me back, fitting me right against a pillar. Jolly's kohl-lined eyes took me in, and he smelled me—*smelled* me—before letting out a long, dramatic sigh.

"Zane is going to find me," I promised. "Wherever you take me..." Jolly shook a finger to hitch my threat—a threat I wasn't sure I could believe anyway.

"What a performance, *Helen Bell!*" he congratulated. "Does your prince know what you are, yet?" His eyes flashed. "I do."

I plunged my fist into his shoulder and twisted to escape, but something tugged me to a halt. I looked back in horror to see the unravelled lace-up strap of my dress in his hand. He twirled it around his fingers like a leash, smiling as he pulled me back.

I felt his chest barely touching my shoulder blades when he leaned forward to whisper, "I won't tell your prince what you are, Trite, because I'm rather smitten with this tasty show of yours," he said. "Shall we make a deal though before you go?"

I swallowed. "No."

"Hmm. How about I threaten you then?" he decided. "If you set one pretty little foot outside the Scarlet City, I'll whisper into the king's ear the names of your Chocolatiers. He does love to do a cruel thing or three to fibbers. Their

281

sweet factory will be gobbled by a *savage* flame. It will be marvelous," he paused. "Perhaps I'll tell the king to torch it either way…"

I stifled a croak.

"Oh, come now, sweetheart. It's only a game." Suddenly he pushed me away, toward the stairs to freedom. "Play it right, and perhaps we all can win a little."

I spun back to make sure he wasn't lashing out to snatch me again, but he just stood there, idly tipping his staff back and forth.

Jolly Cheat looked different without his clown coat and spirally hat. If it weren't for the black rings around his eyes, he might have blended into a normal Trite crowd.

"Of course, my initial deal still stands true. Zane for you. Or you for Zane. I'd prefer to have him, but I'd settle for you." Another flash of his nickel eyes. "Though I desperately hope it's him."

"You're letting me go?" I whispered.

"It would seem so. And you'd better scuttle off. You're late for the Alabaster Ball, I'm afraid." He flicked a loose thread from his shoulder. "Perhaps I'll race you there." He returned the white mask to his face, transforming back into that creature that had been toying with me since the orchard.

I blinked as that settled in. I had to go over the moments I'd encountered the magician and reimagine them. I'd been positive the magician was the heart as black as a viper…*He watches from the shadows, with blood that runs as black as the night sky and as venomous as poison.*

Suddenly it struck me what he'd said about the Alabaster Ball.

As if he'd read my mind, Jolly's voice came from behind

the mask as he sauntered the other way, "Tick, tock."

I spun on my heels and high tailed it up the stairs towards my chambers.

The ball…was I still going? Moments ago, I'd decided I was leaving the Red Kingdom for good. But Jolly had threatened Apple and Fred; I needed to warn them.

When I barged into my rooms, I found them empty, but Apple's scissors were strewn over the table in a metallic collage. The hourglass clock in my bedroom told me I was, in fact, going to be exceptionally late for the ball, and I wanted to smack myself for not leaving clearer instructions with Apple. Everyone must have thought I had already left for Holly Kissing's chateau when I never came back here. And considering the last conversations I'd had with Zane, and Eliot for that matter, they'd probably assumed I had gone with Quinten.

I groaned and trotted back out of my rooms.

"You're late." A pensive voice halted me in the hallway.

A boy stood in the gloom of the evening, studying me from where he leaned by a rose petal window. He twirled a narrow card in his hand with a gold tassel, and I realized it was a bookmark. It was dark, but I could see he wasn't much younger than me.

"Unfortunately, my sleigh left without me." I realized I recognized him from the breakfast table—he was one of the Red Princes.

The prince untucked a book from beneath his arm and opened it to a page he'd been holding with his thumb. "You can take mine," he didn't even look at me when he spoke. "I'm not going anyway."

An attendant appeared from around the corner as though

she'd been eavesdropping. "Cortia, send Lady Strange in my sleigh. Position it in plain sight after she's dropped off so everyone thinks I'm there," the boy rattled as he walked away, already lost to his reading.

"Yes, Prince Driar."

I huffed my relief and followed the attendant. Apple and Fred would be serving a gourmet white-chocolate spread as a feature of the Alabaster Ball. I had to get to the dessert tables before anyone else and warn them.

Chapter,
The Thirty-First

The Alabaster Ball was an ocean of white pearls and
iridescent mosaic tiles. When the sleigh pulled up to
Holly Kissing's chateau, I could hardly look away.
Though my dress had a spectacular rippling black skirt and
metallic beaded shoulders, I felt underdressed. My makeup
was done to match—black and dramatic over my eyelids,
making my freshly gilded eyes burn bright.

The driver had an odd look as I climbed from Prince
Driar's sleigh, likely wondering why I didn't have a single
escort to the ball. I ignored him and trotted up the glassy
stairs to the chateau. It was a long climb, and I was out of
breath by the time I reached the top—something I was sure
the Patrolmen would have had no trouble with if either of

them had decided to come.

No matter how many times I tried to think of something else, Jolly Cheat's wild eyes against the white suit kept coming back. My gaze flickered around the guests to try and spot him, worried he was here, waiting.

A bouquet of brilliant lights thawed my skin as I stepped into the mountainous entrance of the chateau. Full-sized cream trees lined the walls—glowing and wrapped with pearly ribbons. But I didn't feel like ogling at the spectacular presentation, even if it was marvelous.

My eyes danced from person to person. For the life of me, I couldn't find anyone I knew.

"Season's greetings, Lady Strange," a feminine voice ended my spinning.

Pale puffs of organza sprouted from Holly Kissing's waistline. Her honey hair was bound to the side with spilling curls. "Welcome to my chateau," she said.

It was the first time she'd ever spoken to me. So, I replied with something modestly stupid, "Thank you."

But an unusual crease lingered between the glittering hostess's brows. "I'm not sure you should go inside," she admitted at last. "Perhaps you're best off to sleigh home, Scarlet."

Even though the threat was subtle, it tasted bitter. It was every high school social event I dreaded.

"Are you going to drag me out?" I tested. I even took a dramatic gander at the crowds trickling through the lobby to remind her of the scene she'd make if she tried.

Holly Kissing didn't react like I'd hoped. She pursed her lips and stared like an empty-headed marionette. So, I mustered my inner noblewoman and rolled my eyes while I turned to leave her there. If she wanted me to stay away from Quinten, she should have tried harder.

Everyone drew into a cathedral-like room. Sheer, glittering fabric pulled from the ceiling's creases and bunched together into a cloth chandelier, its tendrils dangling over the cluster of couples swaying to the music.

Upon sleek, marbled stages, performers juggled and balanced atop boulder-sized diamonds. I scanned the entertainers for a white mask, but it seemed I'd beaten Jolly Cheat to the ball.

From a distant stage, stringed harps and flutes began to smother the clamour of rattling bells and clinking glasses.

There was so much *noise*. I shook my head, not caring who saw my manic inward torment. My hand drifted down to my dress pocket where my Revelation Orb was quiet.

Once, iridescent black pearls had filled my pockets; pearls that had led me to this very moment. My fingers brushed over Zane's snowflake pendant, stirring an ache in my chest, then finally wrapped around the pair of scissors Apple Dough had gifted me. I pulled the cutters out and looked at the shiny, gold tool of the girl who'd called herself my friend—who was maybe my *last* friend after how I'd acted with Zane and Eliot.

The block letters shimmered beneath the glow of the cloth chandelier. I tilted my hands until I could read what they said:

GLORY AND HONOUR AND POWER
TO HIM WHO SITS ON
THE TRUE THRONE OF WINTER

Apple hadn't chosen this pair of her infamous scissors

to gift me by accident. This inscription was what she hoped I would see—a similar message to what had been boldly written across the doors of the library before it was turned to ash. The hope of the believers.

Warmth bled into my heart, and my eyes slid shut. Apple had been trying to send me a message. My own stupidity shone like a light through the black fog in my brain; I'd been so convinced that I was deserted, but Apple had been here all along, watching over me. Trying to tug me back to myself when she saw me unspooling.

My shoes felt too tight. I wanted to race back out of the chateau. I should have waited in my chambers until the Chocolatiers came back and we could have made a plan for us all to escape together—

"You must find cheer in being late for special evenings," Quinten's voice came from behind me. I'd barely opened my eyes before he was tugging me into the ballroom, snorting a laugh when I was too rigid to glide.

I slid the scissors back into my dress with my other treasures.

A sour, sweet fragrance leaked from him when he brushed against my back to tilt us through the dancing couples. I studied him, all my recent thoughts laying a bridge back to logic.

"Don't fret, Scarlet. We have a merry night ahead!"

I knew I had to tell him about Jolly Cheat, about who I was, about everything, but Quinten seemed so happy in this moment.

My focus narrowed.

Too happy.

"Did you find the magician?" I asked, searching his face,

even though I knew he hadn't found him since *I'd* just been with the magician.

"The magician?" Quinten raised a dark brow and grunted. "I thought the reason you were so worried was because your guardsmen were apprehended by the Ruby Legion."

My feet came together. We became the stillest pair on the dance floor as that casual comment burned over my skin. "What…?"

"Your guardsmen. You know, the handsome spuddlepuns you came here with," he told me again.

Zane's and Eliot's absence the past day swept in like a cold rainstorm. Quinten squeezed my hands and his gaze paused on my mouth.

"Why wouldn't you tell me that?" I imagined Zane and Eliot getting thrown to the palace floor and dragged away by Ruby Legionnaires without their staffs to aid them.

"Probably for the same reason you've kept a thing or three from me." His glowing eyes narrowed on my mouth. He bit his bottom lip *hard*, until his tooth pricked the skin and a dot of blood burst out like berry juice.

"Wicked Trite, I knew you weren't Scarlet Strange from the first moment you walked into the palace lobby. But what fun we've both had pretending."

My stomach dropped as Quinten's mouth slammed into mine, his grip iron around my neck. Heat arched over my tongue past my throbbing lips, and I let out a panicked cry.

I tore myself back and slapped him, the sound of palm-meeting-cheek startling the nearest couples. Quinten's face recoiled, his crow-black hair scuffed, the silver crown nearly tipping off his head.

When he dragged his amethyst eyes back to me, he didn't look like a man with regrets. His tongue slid out to lick the blood off his teeth from the puncture he'd made, and nausea sprang into my stomach. The blood on his mouth...It was *black*.

No...

Quinten's fingers coiled around my arms like chains. Warmth slithered down my throat from the blood he'd pushed onto my tongue, and I fought the urge to vomit in the middle of the chateau ballroom. I knew this feeling. I knew I'd been fooled, but even more assuredly, I knew I'd been *poisoned*.

"You were warned about me," he grinned.

Chapter,
The Thirty-Second

My tongue prickled with the embers of venom. Black fluid dripped down Quinten's chin where he hadn't bothered to wipe it away.

"Where are my Patrolmen?" I whispered.

"You'll see them."

"When?"

"When they entertain us in the arena."

I blinked as that settled. "I'll do anything you want, Quinten. Just let them go... *Anything*," I swore.

But his nostrils flared. "You will address me as *Your Highness*, you common-blooded saltslug! Not even a drop of noble blood in you, yet you walked into my house and tried to fool the Crimson dynasty."

JENNIFER KROPF

But his mouth quirked, black blood pooling in the corner. His grip on my arms was so tight, my muscles groaned. "The true marvel of it is that you didn't suspect any of us, *my love*."

As he said it, everyone in the ballroom froze—a chess board of porcelain pieces stationed over the tiled floor.

Tentacles of smoke caressed the ground, turning the air to chalk as the scent of cinders and burning dreams reached in. The Timepiece's arrival was patient, his current of wind whipping my hair.

My fingers curled into fists as I stared at his hollow face.

But when a new door opened across the room, my fury liquified to horror. I tried to pull away, but Quinten held me tight.

Asteroth's long, white hair floated around his velvet cape in the windstorm. His potent cranberry aroma crept below the Timepiece's ash and turned my stomach. But the worst part was his *eyes*, silver and bright as moonstones, through which the creature watched. I prayed it wouldn't speak; my legs quaked at the thought of hearing that terrible voice.

Quinten brushed the lapping hair from my eyes, pretending to still be that innocent boy concerned for his father. "The Beast of Nightflesh has a reservation for you."

The Beast of Nightflesh.

It had a *name*?

I was numb: my heart, my spirit. I looked back to the Timepiece. "You were against me?" I hated myself with such vigor, I wanted to scream. Zane had never trusted him, and I did.

"Ebenezer was his name, a time overseer of Winter past,

present, and future, until he broke his oath and became a scrooge in chains." The dimple in Quinten's chin creased when he smiled. "One thousand full seasons he was shackled to the Midnight Forest. To us on this side of time, it was only a quarter or three. But he was more than eager to find a way to never go back."

The Timepiece was silent—nothing but a black cloak binding a hollow body of dusty rivers.

Quinten laughed, a deep vicious caw that sounded nothing like the charming horse laugh he'd used in the orchard. "The Timepiece's job was to make you follow a trail to *me*, which must have been a merry challenge, since he's not sanctioned to utter falsehoods."

I couldn't pull my stare from the cloaked shadow, even as Quinten talked. "Asteroth acted to isolate you. His hunt for revenge across the Winter winds was a ruse. His true purpose was to purge the snow globe of that infuriating Patrol Commander. And your Patrolman. And your prized library." Quinten slid the silver crown off his head and studied his beautiful reflection.

"Of course, your Patrolman somehow *lived*. An error my court magician eagerly volunteered to correct. I'm certain Jolly would have finished the job with a flourish too, but I grew impatient and had your Patrolmen arrested before breakfast. Jolly takes so long when he plays." He made a face.

I hitched a sob.

"But my job was my favourite." His flaming amethyst eyes raged. "My job, Trite, was to *keep* you here."

If the couples around us hadn't been stuck in time, they would have seen his hate, and the dribble of black staining his chin.

I almost laughed through the tears—I'd been so swept up in the charade of Scarlet Strange that I hadn't listened to Zane when he said something wasn't right. "You could have killed me the moment I walked into the palace. But you didn't."

Quinten blinked. "You think…" black blood discoloured his teeth when he grinned, "You think all of this is about *you*?" His laugh roared this time, and heat touched my cheeks.

Finally, Quinten wiped the poison from his mouth with his sleeve. "Oh, Trite. The Timepiece warned you a heart as black as a viper was coming for you, and you still ran merrily into my arms. You've done this to yourself. But I wonder why you didn't consider the red heart more warily?"

"Asteroth," I stole a look at the man in the velvet cape but didn't meet his eyes. "He's the heart as red as paint…" I swallowed.

"No, you despicable little common-blood. You traded yourself for the lavish life of a Red. You all but forgot your real name, your virtuous purpose, and painted yourself thrice over. The heart as red as paint…that's *you*."

Me.

Quinten licked his lips. Bile rushed up my throat, mixing with the poison slowly going to work.

"Kingsblood," Quinten grinned, a feral, mean thing, and I could have sworn the blacks of his eyes reshaped to slits. "I'm going to be the new Crimson King. And I'll wed you publicly as Scarlet Strange," he said. "You should be merry about that since you love pretending so much. I cannot *wait* for the believers to witness their beloved Carrier being pulled along by Red puppet strings," he paused. "Unfortunately, our wedding will have to wait until after you've paid your dues to the Midnight Forest. I hear you made a trade for your time with Ebenezer."

"You can't *force* me to do anything. I didn't make a deal with the Timepiece; we didn't shake on it." I had Apple's scissors to thank for reminding me how to think straight. Scissors, I realized, that were still in my pocket now.

My hand slid toward the folds of my dress, but Quinten's gaze shot down and my fingers went still. He shook his head slowly.

"I don't need a deal to keep you bound. I've already sprinkled you with my venom, *my love*. You can't leave my side—even ten plus two steps away—or the poison will spread. If you leave me now, you'll be on the floor with a still heart before sunrise tomorrow." He dragged himself closer, leering down with those twinkling purple eyes I'd nearly agreed to stay in the Red Kingdom to fight for. "Only residing in my presence will keep you alive now."

Asteroth and the Timepiece were both cold, still forms behind him. I couldn't bring myself to look at them.

"And about the *other* thing," Quinten said. The Red Prince bit his lips together and brushed the hair from my face. I fought the impulse to slap him again. Fresh tears stung the corners of my golden eyes—eyes I now hated so much more than my ordinary, dull, brown ones.

His mouth quirked. "This was never about you. What would we want with a dim Trite, or with a Carrier of those old, obsolete truths? You're just bait. This was always about destroying *him*."

I closed my eyes, not ready to face what I'd really done.

"I shan't utter *his* name. He has not shown himself in the flesh yet, but I think you know as well as I that the dead king is *back*."

The dead king.

Elowin.

His name is Elowin.

PART 4

THE STORYTELLER

THE SEVENTH INTERRUPTION

I n a gap between storms and seasons, where time is a fragrance rather than a thing come and gone, a young man's eyes were sealed to silence the emerald, bronzed amber, glistening lilac, and sugar pearls in his irises. A kaleidoscope of colours pulsing into his beloveds' hearts across the snow. For, the steadfast love of the King never ceases, his mercies never end. They are new each morning.

Inward, he looked, listening to the cries and praises and curses and pleas of the whispered prayers gallivanting in the streams of the air.

One soul called above the others, one heartbeat thudding like a breathing clock. How she ached beneath the spirits feasting on her last spark of trust.

The Carrier. *His* Carrier.

If only she might remember that when the days turn dark, one must trust in the lullaby that comes before the night. For, enclosed within an utter of praise arises a tool or three. A mere squeak of song transforms into the bellow of a thousand angels, a thing sufficient to send the darkness fleeing, should one choose to use it.

Helen Bell was not alone. A lullaby was offered—one that did not take its chore lightly. The melody wrestled to change the stars, to part the snow, and to steal back a soul destined for the grave. All things are possible, you see.

Furthermore, in an old Volume buried in a cave of ice, it is written: *Worthy is He who sits upon the throne of Winter.* And when the saints cry it o'er the mountains, it changes the spirit in one's very soul. The passage goes on to urge: *Sing, if you will, this column in your darkest hour, and see how it blooms a path: Worthy is He, the King of Kings and Lord of Lords.*

Test such words on your lips.

Hush now.
And wait...
Do you feel it?

Chapter,
The Thirty-Third

O nce, a witch in red had persuaded me to drink poison.
Not even twelve steps.

I was still the same fool. A peg out of its shell after all.

The Timepiece released his hold on the room, and the Red Prince forced me to dance with him late into the night, until my heels bled in my shoes.

Right until the low gong of the clock signalled midnight, all I thought about was Zane and Eliot in the hands of the Reds, and Apple and Fred whose whereabouts were still unknown.

In the future, you are wedded to the third Red Prince.

Zane Cohen-Margus-Bowswither has no part in your future.

She can't lie, Zane had said.

I'd brought this terrible future upon myself.

The morning came with an illness like no other. Even though I'd stayed by Quinten's side—sleeping on the hardwood outside his bedroom door—the crawling poison in my belly didn't care.

My stomach roiled as I unloaded its contents into the bathing room trough. I wouldn't eat breakfast—I *couldn't*. But Quinten dragged me there anyway, in the same dress I'd worn to the Alabaster Ball, now cloaked in the sharp scent of vomit.

I hadn't heard a peep about the Chocolatiers. I didn't know if they were still in my chambers wondering why I never returned, or if they'd fled when they discovered Zane and Eliot had been taken by the Ruby Legion.

I stifled a gag when the smell of eggs hit me. The king wasn't at breakfast; he was too sick to attend. I refused to look across at Quinten when the palace attendant informed us. I didn't want to see the Red Prince's reaction now, to share subtle glances as we had before. I wanted to scream to this family that their own brother was moving in to steal their kingdom, that he sat among them now; a deadly black heart, ready to take his place above them all.

When Quinten took my hand after to escort me away, I wasn't paying attention to where we were going until the low rumble of a roaring crowd brought my stinging eyes up from the polished floor.

Two large doors were heaved opened by Ruby Legion-naires, and the cheering became deafening. Tension locked my legs in place as years of history spilled out from the massive oval auditorium, packed with people in rich gilded seats and silk crimson threads.

Quinten tried to tug me in, but I was paralyzed.

This was not where *any* Carrier wanted to be.

The screaming, bloodthirsty crowd put the witnesses of the Quarrel of Sword and Bone to shame. Ruby-red banners and flags rippled over the domed space, staged for a competition.

Mara Rouge had faced off with Carriers of Truth on this floor.

This was the arena.

"Kingsblood, *move*, or I'll chain you to me like a snow pup." Quinten's quiet, cold words brushed my neck. "You *said* you wanted to see your Patrolmen," he added with a grin.

My breathing wasn't right, but I followed the prince into the wild coliseum to a booth twinkling with ruby garland. The rest of the Red Princes sat, waiting.

Trumpets blasted over the arena and I jumped, clasping my fingers in front of me. The crowd hushed as a man with glittering peach skin emerged and moved to centre-stage.

"Feast your eyes, drink the chaos, and revel in the savagery!" The man spat saliva as he spoke.

Prisoners were yanked from doorways below and shoved onto pedestals with golden numbers. I searched the faces of young men with bound wrists, some in torn, green clothing and wooden armour. I spotted Eliot first. His messy curls covered his eyes; his shoulders were slouched. He wasn't wearing his red coat anymore.

I whimpered at the raven-black uniform that was dragged out next. Zane was shoved onto pedestal number seven; jaw set, electric blue eyes lifting to search the crowd. He found me at Quinten's side, and I bit my lips together to stifle the temptation to scream to him.

The peach man faced the royals. "Take your pick, Your Highnesses!"

"Number two," Prince Tegan called from the end of our booth.

"Prince Forrester?"

The pale-lashed prince waved a hand like he didn't care. "Number eight may bring good tidings."

"Prince Quinten?" His name was fire in my ears.

I looked at Quinten, pleading, offering whatever I could with my stare alone, but he ignored me and stood. "Well. This is easy," he said. "I choose number seven."

My hands fell limp on my lap.

Zane's eyes were steady on Quinten as the other princes made their selections. Eliot wasn't chosen; he and Zane were led through different doors.

It was a mockery of champions that came back—claret feather headdresses and shimmering gold breastplates, long swords and silver spears. Some wore full helmets, but not Zane.

Everything was splashed in red paint; it dripped down

the surface of Zane's bronze armour. But even though the spoiled, jeweled outfits were meant to be a joke, he looked fierce to me. He studied the crowds, eyeing their red flags, and twisted the curved sword in his grip; a despicable replacement for the weapon meant to be there.

"This fight's objective is to be the last soul whose blood drips to the floor! Nine competitors, one chance at freedom," the peach man called. "Good tidings, Princes!"

Bells rang over the arena and the spectators roared, every one of them jumping to their feet, yelling, pushing, screaming, laughing. The youngest Red Princes raced to the rail.

Prisoners sprang for each other, slashing their weapons wildly, but Zane didn't move. He watched the drooling Reds in gilded chairs, and I realized I had no idea if he knew how to use a weapon other than his Patrol staff.

When a prisoner charged for him, he sidestepped, dragging his foot so his opponent tripped and rolled over the arena floor. A ripple of laughter rose from the crowd, but Zane didn't look flattered by the praise.

He slid behind a Green prisoner and hammered the hilt of his cutlass against the man's helmet. The prisoner tumbled to the ground, blacked out.

When a blade swung for Zane's back, he twisted and thrust his hilt into the man's forehead, turning one lifeless body sprawled on the arena floor into two: neither dead, neither bleeding.

I realized what he was doing at the same time as everyone else; booing erupted from the spectators. Zane ignored them and kept striking: one more prisoner fell, then another, and I watched in amazement as Zane forced down opponents without a single cut to their flesh deep enough to drip.

I wanted to cry and laugh. I should have known he'd ruin their show.

Snarls of disapproval boomed; onlookers hurtled plums down to try and hit him, but Zane's bronze armour clattered as he dropped two more prisoners and danced on his toes to evade oncoming blows.

When my Patrolman turned to face the last prisoner, the young man cowered and raised his spear. Zane grabbed the end of the wobbling weapon and yanked it toward him, thumping the heel of his blade along the prisoner's temple. The sound of the last competitor hitting the floor seemed to echo through the coliseum.

Zane alone stood on a stage unblemished by a drop of blood, left to catch his breath and hold the stares of the crowd.

The peach-skinned man slinked back out as Ruby Legionnaires rushed to surround my Patrolman, spears tipped toward his chest and throat. The cutlass slipped from his fingers, and he didn't try for it again.

"He won," I said to Quinten, even though I knew Quinten would never let this count. "He's free."

But Quinten's smile spread. "He's insulted the Crown. I can't wait to see what *the king* will do about it." His amethyst eyes flickered, and I glared at him as Zane was led away. The speckles of worry in my chest began heating to coals of anger as the sour scent of all the tossed plums in the arena filled my nose. My toes curled in my blood-stained heels.

Quinten might have had me on a leash, but I was going to prove I wasn't a peg out of its shell.

Apple's scissors felt heavy in my pocket.

Chapter,
The Thirty-Fourth

y determination didn't waver. Watching Quinten stuff himself with fruit cake and olives at lunch made me want to stick my finger down my throat. That once-handsome dimple on his chin became a target for invisible darts I conjured with my mind.

I followed closely when he led me to his rooms. My hand slid into the pocket of my dress as Quinten opened the chambers' door.

I drew out Apple's scissors, palm damp, and raised them.

Someone grabbed me from behind—Quinten whirled—and I was dragged backward by a set of gloved hands. The prince stalked after me and pried the metal slicers from my grip as the smell of Jolly Cheat's bitter sage and lavender engulfed me.

"Lovely shot, Trite, I dare say," the madman kicked the door shut behind him.

Quinten raised Apple's gold scissors and blinked at them. "Kingsblood, a lovely shot, indeed," he cursed, but his eyes narrowed on the block-letter inscription. "I wonder where you got these? I might have a guess or three."

The threat turned me slack in Jolly's grip. Quinten dropped the scissors and grabbed my arms tight, nails cutting into flesh. "You might think things can't get any more scotchy for you, *my love*, but I assure you, they can."

Jolly released me, and I heard the clatter of chains. My chest deflated as the madman came around, dangling a cuff for me to see.

I'll chain you to me like a snow pup, was Quinten's threat outside the arena.

The cold metal slapped my wrist, and Jolly handed the other cuff to Quinten.

I was dragged along for a walk through the Scarlet City, chained to the snake-prince like an animal. We wandered the obsidian streets for hours on *foot*, as Quinten clasped my hand tightly in his, our fur coats concealing the frigid chain that held us together. Sticky moisture had built up in my heels again.

Quinten showed me candy shops, sleigh parades, reindeer stables, and a lung-torturing smoke room scented of walnuts, spice, and sugar, where I couldn't see my free hand lifted in front of my face.

I was still coughing twenty minutes after we left; the Ruby Legionnaires snickered from where they trailed us.

A shadow moved at my left, too far away to reach, but keeping pace well enough that I tried to glance over. Only glittering storefronts, and hollow alleys looked back.

Quinten stared ahead. The prince was growing tired of walking; I could see it by the sluggish stomping of his boots. I wondered if he would take me back to the palace soon.

I stole another glance to where I thought I'd seen a shadow, wondering if the toxic smokes were teasing my vision. But warm breath brushed the back of my neck and I stiffened, forcing myself to keep walking.

"I'd ask but, ragnashuck, I think I'd rather *not* know," Lucas Leutenski's voice wasn't quiet enough.

The chain at my wrist tightened—I opened my mouth to yell a warning but Lucas spoke first, "Season's greetings, Your Highness!"

A blade was drawn, and I whirled.

"Move your scotcher, Trite!" Lucas's long-knife came down and I shrieked as the silver blade hacked—once, then twice—bending a weak chain loop, and slicing clean through the flesh at Quinten's wrist.

The Red Prince's cry filled the street, turning every eye to the black blood plunging from his skin. The chain snapped and Lucas's topaz eyes flashed up to mine.

"I can't go!" I shouted—he ducked a Ruby Legion sword.

"Well...*frostbite*, that might have been merry to know before I cut his—"

"*Run*, Lucas!" I jumped to avoid a hurtling spear, but the Patrolman grinned.

He slashed at a Legionnaire and scurried off, shouting, "Fine. But I heard—" Metal struck metal, "—and your beloveds...*trouble*...Trite!" He trotted up a pile of crates and across the roof of a building. "...I'll fetch them!" Lucas's shouting grew more undecipherable the further away he got.

Quinten tore me back by a fistful of my coat, eyes wild. "I'll find that sputtlepun!" he seethed. "And I'll punish his brothers in my dungeons for what he's done to a Red Prince!"

My stomach dropped. "Wait, just—"

"Get us back to the palace!" Quinten snapped at the remaining Legionnaires, keeping a tight fist on my coat.

I gasped at the ferocity he dragged me with by his one free hand.

One hand...

My eyes darted to my wrist where the chain that had held me to the snake-prince now dragged through the snow. Quinten hugged his black-stained fingers to his chest, moisture leaking into the sleeve of his otherwise pristine jacket.

Chapter,
The Thirty-Fifth

Quinten was rushed to the healers and magicians. Potions were brewed and poured and chanted over. Candlelight flickered through a long room beneath the palace where sick patients rested on luxurious cots with silk bedding. Bubbling tubes and jars of pastel paste sat neatly on their bedside tables.

A man in a long navy garment with star constellations uttered spells to try and fix Quinten's hand, especially his dangling thumb, which simple Trite science told me was too maimed to be reattached without *real* tools.

I watched for a few minutes, taking in the richest hospital I'd ever seen. Watching more and more lavishly robed healers assemble around the prince like a shimmering curtain.

Quinten assumed I would stay by his side to survive. But if the prince really knew what I'd done last year, he would have known that the poison wouldn't stop me from getting to my Patrolman.

I waited until he was growling at the spellcaster before I slipped into the darkness of the hallway, kicking off my wretched heels to run on numb toes. Thankfully, I'd been in this basement enough to recognize my way around it.

I could almost *feel* Zane's presence beckoning me through the stone floors, his heart-song whispering in the air as I broke into a run. The Red Prince would know exactly where I was headed once he realized I was missing; I had mere seconds for a head start.

The hallways grew cold. I stopped to listen when I heard pouring water, creeping closer. I nearly screamed when a guard in crimson marched around the corner—he stopped short at the sight of me.

"I'm Scarlet Strange," I blurted through a raspy throat. "I'm here to see two prisoners—one was dressed in black…"

The guard studied me for a moment, then nodded and tipped into a shallow bow. "The prisoner you seek is being punished. You may watch if it would bring you cheer." He extended a hand back in the direction of the splashing water.

"He's…in there?" I asked.

"In paint chamber, the third. I can take you there, Lady Strange?"

I nodded, probably too quickly. "Please."

The guard ducked back the way he'd come. We came

into a room where cells lined both walls. Half a dozen prisoners eyed me as we passed, some drifting to the bars to get a better look. But it was the sounds beyond the next hallway that made me drag my feet and abandon my coat to the floor; gritty coughing, splashing, and laughter. The guard stopped walking when he realized. "Would you prefer a closer look, or the spectators' lounge, Lady Strange?"

I tried not to show my revulsion as I nodded my head. "I'd like to get close."

The guard nodded and opened a door but didn't go in himself. "Keep back a measure. I'd hate for your dress to be spoiled."

I swallowed and went into the room where the sounds were magnified, echoing off the rock walls. Chains rattled as liquid was dumped, and I heard his moist coughs before I came around and saw what they were doing to him.

The stars seemed to fall out of the sky.

Zane's wrists were bound in front of him, clipped to a tight rope. He stood, red-soaked in the centre of a ring. A man in a polished coat cackled as he pulled levers, tipping a vat of thick red paint overhead.

The paint came in a flood, encompassing all of Zane except his fingers—only a split-second after he managed to take in a breath and hold it, and a sound escaped my throat. They were *drowning* him.

But Zane stayed solid beneath the current, not collapsing or shuddering. Not running out of air. I couldn't believe how long he could hold his breath.

My eyes followed a splatter of paint to an axe on the wall. I didn't waste another moment before marching through the pool of paint in my bare feet and snatching it off its hook. I took it to the middle of the room just as the vat closed overhead, revealing a dripping, saturated Zane who finally spat to catch his breath around the remaining paint running into his mouth. Every inch of his once-black clothes dripped scarlet.

The well-dressed man objected as I brought the axe down on Zane's ropes and sliced them off.

"Zane," I whispered, but Zane didn't look at me. He stormed across the room, tossing his ropes on the ground, and grabbed the collar of the man with his moist fingers. The scoffer's eyes were so wide, I thought they'd fall out.

"I've always wanted to quarrel with a *Director of Tournaments*," Zane said through his torn voice, the paint from his fingers ruining the man's shirt.

The man, to his credit, kept his face from blanching. He opened his mouth to shout for the guards, but Zane kicked him in his knees, crumpling the man to the messy floor where the man raised his hands in defeat and went quiet.

My Patrolman wiped paint from his face as he rushed back to me.

"Ragnashuck, Helen, how did you even…" But he shook his head like it didn't matter. "Let's go. And let's *never* come back here." Zane took my hand, ready to lead me out, ready to run from this place forever.

"I can't go," I said; the same apology I'd given Lucas.

Zane stopped, blinking away scarlet tears leaking into his eyes. "You bloody what?"

"I wish I had time to tell you…Quinten is the black heart we were looking for. He poisoned me. I can't leave or—"

"Come anyway, Trite." Zane's moist hand tightened on mine. He looked like he'd been pulled from a bloody sea.

"Helen, I'm not leaving you here."

"I *can't* go," I articulated, frustrated he was wasting precious seconds when he should have been running. I wouldn't get another chance to help him if he didn't make it out. "I'll look for Eliot. Just go."

Zane searched my face. "I'm not leaving without you. I'd rather go back under the paint," he said. "We saved you before when you were poisoned. We can do it again."

"No, *Mikal* saved me last time."

But his electric eyes narrowed. "No, Helen," he squished the paint between our palms, "*Elowin* saved you last time. Mikal commissioned a prayer, but the spirit of Elowin brought you back."

"I don't think Elowin is coming this time." I didn't mean to spit on his hope, but Quinten was going to march in with a hundred guards any moment, fuming and ready to toss me to the red floor next.

Zane shut his mouth, jaw set.

"I'm sorry," I added. It was all I could say—not just for now, but for everything. He'd been right all along, and I'd ignored his instincts. But he didn't seem to care about that now.

My Patrolman dropped my hand to slide his fingers into my hair. "I told you I would do whatever it took to keep us together. And I meant it. I'm coming back for you, Helen Bell."

He left me no time to object. Zane's hands slid from my hair as he backed over the spoiled floor, leaving footprints with his curled-toe boots. With one last flicker of hard, starlight eyes, my Patrolman fled, disappearing into a dark hall where I knew he'd have no trouble navigating his way out.

I didn't have time to take another breath before doors began slamming open in the dungeon behind me, and a dozen Ruby Legionnaires shuffled in, followed by a Red Prince's furious shouting.

"There you are!" he said through gritted teeth.

One hand grabbed me.

With a tight grip, Quinten yanked me to him. His crow-black hair was wildly ruffled, his mouth a thin line. I looked back to see a triad of Legionnaires standing at attention, waiting for Quinten's orders.

"You don't know who you're muddling with, Trite," he spat as he yanked me through the hall to a dingy row of cells with rusted metal locks. He tossed me in one with a growl.

I tripped over loose pebbles on the floor and landed on my stomach, my elbows skidding over rock. "Since I *missed* you so much, I thought I'd gift you an early wedding present. After all, the Red Holiday is about getting *gifts*."

Something bounced over the floor, sliding until it touched my fingertips. I blinked at it, trying to register the tool before me—a pair of gunmetal-black scissors.

I snatched them and sprang to my feet just as Quinten slammed the cell door closed and the drop of the lock echoed through the chamber.

"What did you do?!" I swung the tool at him even though he'd backed far away. The metal was ice-cold in my fingers, all traces of Apple's warmth were gone.

"She's a Chocolatier of the Red Kingdom! The best you'll find! She's been serving in this palace her whole life!" I reminded the prince. "Don't hurt her…"

But the prince stared at my neck where a smear of red paint left by Zane was still damp.

"I'm rather tempted to leave you here alone and let my venom take you slowly. But the Timepiece would be livid if I ruined his offering to the Midnight Forest," his voice was monotone. "He still owes another one thousand seasons. I suppose he wants to toss in his replacement soon, lest the forest sucks him back in to pay his dues."

I watched his irises flicker to slits like I'd seen at the ball.

Quinten turned and marched from the rows of cells, leaving me there to stare at the far wall.

AN INTERRUPTION

*D*eep in a glittering grave of ice crystals, Cane Endovan Crimson-Augustus spotted Porethius marching
down the stairs, her sugared tattoos burning bright
against the dimness underground.

"That doesn't look merry," Edward Haid eyed the fairy
as he rotated the rusted blade in his grip. "You ought to check
on her, Red."

"I see I've intimidated you with my sputtlepun sparring.
Very well, you aged snow cat," Cane tossed his sword into a
heap of ancient armour.

Edward snorted and added his blade to the pile with a

clatter. "I must go find Gathadriel anyway. The fairy-folk tend to muddle their buttons when they're separated from their assignments."

"Don't travel far from us, Green. Plum will miss you." Cane grinned wickedly, and Edward offered a deep laugh.

"I'm certain she will," the older man shook his head.

Porethius Plum emitted a certain warmth; Cane felt it at his shoulder as he watched his seasoned friend stroll off to collect his belongings. Edward Haid—the *other* once-prince—different from Cane in age and kingdom, but similar in spirit and circumstance.

"You were looking for me?" Porethius said, the glow of her floral markings casting moving lights upon the rock like the moon's reflection off the snowseas.

"Has Elowin shown himself?" Cane asked, and when Porethius did not utter a response, the once-prince scuffed his wild rosebud hair. "Or have my brothers truly scared him off?"

The new question was posed in jest, but the fairy still bristled at the suggestion; her thin, violet wings giving a flutter.

"Come now, Plum. Do you truly expect Elowin to go face the Beast before his time? To break the true end? He cannot show himself in Winter. Not yet."

The fairy glanced off to a nearby candle, thick as a tree stump and ivory as bone.

"I understand the patient endurance necessary for times such as these," Porethius finally spoke. "I only fear what Nightflesh will do to the Trite if she breaks. I fear what he will do to her if she does *not* break, too."

Being the fairy's assignment for six full seasons, Cane

319

had heard a great measure of Porethius's thoughts. But he rarely saw her as muddled as she was now—a glowing vessel on stormy dunes.

The once-prince glanced to his reflection in the ice wall. He had the reddest features of all his brothers—distinctive mahogany locks and liquid burgundy eyes. Funny, how those pretty features had only worked against him in the end.

He set to tidying himself up from his recent spar. A flick of snow off a shoulder. A shake of his leather boots. A stolen glance back at Porethius.

These were certainly troubling times.

"I'm afraid we have another problem," he finally spat it out when he could hold it in no longer. "I can't recall a great measure of what I've read, Plum." Forgetting his despicably lovely reflection, Cane turned to face his guardian. "In all my seasons studying the sacred truths, I've never felt like such a spinbug. I can't remember right from left when I try to recall the precise wording, and some words shouldn't be rephrased from how they're written."

A spear of ice detached from its perch nearby and smashed over the floor, but Porethius did not move a pinch at the jangle. "What of Edward?" she asked, her tattoos dimming as she looked upon the shelves tucked into the crevices of the cave, where a thousand plus a thousand more slender book spines hosted titles scribed in ages past—the Volume of Truth originals.

"He too has struggled, I think. Though, he wouldn't admit it," Cane sighed. "Of course, he *is* old. Perhaps his mind is turning scotchy." A clever smile.

Porethius shot him a look. "He is only twenty full seasons your elder," she returned. "And I am older than he."

Cane bit his bottom lip. "Right." He moved for the candle to blow it out, certain Porethius's glow would light the way through the tunnels well enough. "I do think we ought to consider an alternative mind to store our Volumes in. Besides, the Beast will find me, eventually. He's been hunting for me all these seasons."

The fairy sighed. "We don't have time for another mind to learn all you've studied. You've been at this for six full seasons."

But a smile pressed into the once-prince's mouth.

"Perhaps. But time is a funny thing."

Chapter,
The Thirty-Sixth

Shadows shifted along the back walls through the night, but nothing really lived this far below the palace. I could tell I was alone by how still the air was; how there was no sound, or warmth. But I knew Quinten had to be nearby because I was still alive.

Through the hours, I'd clutched Apple's scissors to my chest, driven to tears by the thought of the Red Kingdom turning on their Chocolatiers because of me. Apple had been so careful to remind me that this could not fail—that she and Fred would pay for it if it did.

The heat in my stomach had intensified every hour and I'd rolled back and forth in agony. This wasn't the same feeling I'd gotten after drinking Mara Rouge's poison, this was something entirely different—slow and creeping.

"You have visitors." Quinten's voice came through the dark to alert me it was morning. No torches had been lit yet, so I couldn't see his shifting eyes.

Armour clanged through the space as Ruby Legion soldiers moved from one post to the next, setting the torches ablaze.

When the Red Prince became visible, he was glaring. A white glove covered his useless hand where he cradled it to his chest.

"Is it Apple and Fred?" I rasped, pulling my stiff body off the floor. The seat of my dress was damp and cold.

But Quinten's dead-eyed smirk told me I wouldn't be seeing the Chocolatiers.

He leaned in to murmur, "The Winter winds have shifted, my love. That means your intersects are closing." His crow-black hair was darker in the dungeon, even up close. "No going home now."

"What...?" It was barely a whisper.

But Quinten turned and left me alone as distant doors squeaked open and slammed shut.

I'd never figured out how to predict when the intersects would open and close, or if they simply arrived on their own schedule. The timing this year had been different than last. It seemed Winter had finally stolen me once and for all.

I tucked Apple's scissors into my pocket, and my fingers brushed my orb and Shammah necklace. I pulled them out to look at my treasures. Treasures I'd hidden and replaced with the glittering jewels of a false noble's life.

I couldn't wear my orb necklace since I'd damaged the chain, so I slid it back into my skirts. I was halfway through fastening Zane's necklace to my throat when someone appeared past the bars of my cell—beautiful honey-blonde hair, bright gold eyes, less than an inch shorter than me. Holly Kissing was wrapped in one of her finest gowns.

I snorted. "Come to gloat?" I guessed, tossing my Winter accent to the wind. I no longer cared if this noblewoman suspected I wasn't who I said I was.

But she just stared at me like she always did, happy to take her time until all sounds of Quinten and the guards vanished. "You and I have something in common," she finally said. "We're both actors. I'm just a pinch more convincing than you."

I raised a brow and flung a hand through the air. "Well, I didn't realize it was a contest."

"Didn't you?" she asked, and I glanced back. "Isn't that exactly what this was?"

"If you want Quinten, you can have him."

Her sweet eyes narrowed. "Prince Quinten, I don't care for. My reputation, however, that is a thing where my scars run deep." She stared. Stared, and stared. "I had a different name once. I left it behind and hoped to never hear it again. But you brought it back."

I blinked as it dawned on me, and I nearly choked on my own spit. "*You're* Scarlet Strange?"

Her candied eyes flickered down to my patchy dress.

"Naturally, I was aware you were fibbing when you arrived. I had to watch you make a mockery of my name, and I had to endure it, rather than expose myself to stop you." Her pink mouth twitched. "But I don't want revenge. Not on you, and not on *them*," she nodded to the floors above. "I only came here to ask you a thing."

I slid my jaw back and forth. "What do you want to know?"

"I want to know where Cane is. I'll do everything in my power to salvage your reputation if you tell me."

"Prince Cane?" I made a face. For the life of me, I couldn't figure out why everyone wanted to find this estranged prince. Or why they all thought I knew him.

"Not *Prince* Cane," her cheeks turned rosy.

"Right... Well, I don't know where he is. I've never even met him," I said. "And if you all want to find him so badly, maybe you shouldn't have cast him out."

Holly Kissing, or, *Scarlet Strange*, settled her stare on me one last time. It was impossible to tell if she disliked my answer.

"I was trying to warn you, you know. At the Alabaster Ball, I saw them coming for you. I tried to stop you from walking into the ballroom."

My snarky attitude drained. "Why?"

A pause. "I know what it's like to be snared by this kingdom's wolves. We may be standing on different sides, but I wish you good tidings with all of this, Lady Strange."

Without another word, the honey-haired girl made her heel-tapping exit, and I was abandoned to the silent hall and crackling torches again. I gazed at the sweeps of amber on the walls, moving from the live flames, and I thought about the girl with the scars who'd run away.

When I dropped my hand from where I'd dug it into my hair, dried, red paint chips littered my palm. I thought of my Patrolman who'd promised to come back for me. I hoped Zane had made it out of the Red Kingdom.

"Helen."

When I looked up, I blinked at the sapphire eyes before me—almost the same blue I'd just been dreaming about.

The unforgettable fragrance of lavender and roses rushed in along with the sight of Eliot.

"What are you...Wait..." I looked down the empty halls. I took note of his unbound wrists, the untorn clothes, the absence of drying red paint on his body.

Eliot wore a clean white shirt and black hose fit for a nobleman. His usually tossed curls rested calm atop his head without a single bruise, apart from the yellowing speckles on his cheek where I'd hit him the day we met.

He wouldn't have had bruises from the arena—he hadn't been selected to fight. Suddenly, it made sense why.

"Are you kidding me?" I whispered it, but it was flame on my tongue.

Eliot lacked expression. "Come on, Trite. You never even tried to figure out who the green heart was."

The emerald. *The heart green with envy.*

The most deceiving one.

I shook my head in disgust. We'd become friends. Eliot and I had become *real* friends—it hadn't been part of the role I'd been playing.

"I told you I had met Asteroth. You didn't even bat an eye when I said it." Eliot slinked a hand through the bars for me to take. "Let me show you the rest of the vision from that night. The part I kept to myself."

I stared at his hand, covered in tiny, pale scars.

"Is this why you were trying to steal me from Zane?" I slapped his hand away. I didn't want to watch Mikal die again. I didn't want to see Lucas crumple to the floor.

Eliot scowled and tugged his hand back. "I was forced

to make a deal," he said.

"No one is *forced* to make a deal," my hollering echoed down the hall. "I wouldn't have taken their deal. Zane wouldn't have taken their deal! You *chose* them."

Eliot set his jaw and grabbed the bars on either side of his face. "Ragnashuck, Trite! Fine, you're right! They turned me. They said all I had to do was persuade you to come to the Red Kingdom, but it seems like you were already prepared to do that yourself."

"Because of the Timepiece," I assured. "*You* didn't convince me of anything."

"Yes. Well. There were a generous measure of forces at work to get you here, in case you haven't noticed that yet."

I couldn't believe it. I could barely look at Eliot in his clean clothes. "What did Quinten do to the Chocolatiers?" I asked to remind Eliot that he hadn't only betrayed me, he'd betrayed Apple and Fred too—good, thoughtful people who had never done anything to him.

"Apple is making your wedding dress," he said, dropping his blue eyes to the dungeon floor. "Every fashionista's dream—to design the dress of the next Crimson Queen."

I jumped to smack him, but he saw it coming and sprang back, messing up his perfect curls.

"I always knew there was something off about you, Eliot Gray," I said. "What in the world could have persuaded you to betray the Patrol? And me? And *Elowin*? Why, Eliot?"

"Because everyone's forgotten who I frostbitten was!" His fist pounded the metal bar above my hand. "No one even *told* you who I was, Trite, did they?!"

I stared at this person I thought I understood, who had confessed his own tragedies to me, and I'd felt something for him because of it. He was a hard person to get along with, but I figured it was because of his past. I had no idea who he really was—that he was *this*.

"Who are you? What did they forget?"

Air filled his chest and he huffed it out his nose. "My Carrier's name was Harmony Hucklebunk-Reyes. I spent my finest seasons guarding her from the dark forces of Winter, keeping her out of the witch's grip when other Patrols couldn't save their own Carriers and started giving up. I was loyal to a fault, until the day I shoved her ahead of me onto the train and stayed behind in the blue wasp fields to fool the gnomes into going another way."

Harmony Hucklebunk-Reyes.

I closed my eyes in disbelief as the familiar name rang like a bell. No one had told me—that while I was gallivant- ing across the Winter snow last year, the scarf-girl's Patrol- man had still been alive. Suffering his loss.

I knew I'd never seen Eliot before the day he came to my school. He hadn't shown up to fight the Red army outside the key room in Wentchester Cove with the other Patrols. He hadn't come to find me and Zane, even after he knew the orb had been passed on to someone else, that his Carrier had fallen. The longest active Patrolman of his time hadn't shown himself once.

"But the train was pursued by the witch's spies, no thanks to Cornelius Britley's sky-high steam show making it so frostbit easy to follow. And when Harmony tried to slip off without the spies noticing, she ran right into *you*." Eliot's nostrils flared. "By the time I finished leading the gnomes to the dunes, I already knew she was gone. My bond split like an ice dagger through my heart." He swallowed. "It took me a full quarter to drag myself to that spot to see where she'd turned back to snow."

Eliot's irises were storm-gray. I could see that he cared, *too* much.

"So, you're angry with me for taking her place?" Moisture stung my eyes.

"I'm angry because she was *mine* to protect, and you should have been mine, too. I kept my Carrier alive longer than any Patrolman. I proved I was the finest of the Patrol!" He spoke through his teeth now, words rasped, "And, I'm angry that the Patrolman who took my place, who *stole* my responsibility, was a frostbitten snow pirate who gave up hope *seasons* before I did," he growled.

I looked back and forth between those beautiful blue eyes, mouth parting. "This was about *Zane*?"

"This was about me being given the responsibility I was owed! There are rules, Trite. My Carrier's orb was passed to you, so I should have been passed to you, too. But the Elders didn't feel it was fair to grant me the last charge after you'd formed such a strong bond with Cohen, so they refused," he snarled.

"So you threw away your beliefs and sided with *Asteroth Ryuu*, instead of accepting the decision of the Patrol Elders?" I had half a mind to try and slap him again. "Asteroth killed Mikal!" I shrieked, tears dripping down my cheeks.

"Helen..." he shook his head and apology cracked through his mask. "I was never going to be recognized as anything among the Patrols after I witnessed Mikal's murder and didn't intervene. That's why I gave false information to the Elders and sent Cohen into Asteroth's trap on the Eastern Plains. Because a line was drawn in the snow, and after all I did to keep Harmony alive in her seasons, the Patrol still saw me as being on the wrong side of it."

"Eliot Gray, you're out of your mind."

"Digging in your heels to resist Nightflesh will only break your legs. He's planning to make you *queen* of this kingdom. Take this life, Helen. You're going to wed Quinten either way. Be on my side of this, for once, and let me be the guardsman of someone I can call a friend, instead of a prisoner. You love this Red life already! I know you do."

I was too amazed and appalled to reply.

"Why do you even care what happens to me?" I whispered, clasping my shaking fingers to the bars for support.

Eliot huffed. "Because I've already started to bond to you, Trite," he murmured it, like he was afraid the insects on the walls would hear. "I didn't mean to; I was never *supposed* to. But I said the frostbitten words out loud and then they became real. I am your Patrolman, in part. Cohen and I are both tied to you that way."

I pushed a hand through the bars, palm up. "Then help me get out of here. You can still change everything. Zane will convince the Patrol to forgive you if you fix this."

But his irises steeled over. "I don't want Cohen's forgiveness!" He leaned in with a growl, ignoring my hand, cheeks pink, and I knew whatever bridge we'd just built had shattered.

My hand balled into a fist when I tore it back. "Well you're going to need it, because when Zane gets his hands on you, you're dead meat, Eliot!"

He stared, unblinking. Unmoved by my threat.

"You know what, Trite? You made an even bigger mistake than falling into the traps," he said. "Your biggest mistake of all was letting me see what your beloved sister looked like the day I came for you."

The world tipped inward, the floor falling beneath my feet.

"Wait...Eliot..." I croaked. "You didn't..."

New noises filled the dungeon hallway. My fingers tightened around the bars between us. "Eliot, *please* tell me you didn't...You didn't *actually*..."

But it was Kaley's shriek that dug my paint-red-heart from my chest where I imagined it splattering on the dungeon floor at Eliot's feet.

"Just do what they want, Helen," Eliot pleaded. "Pay your dues to the Midnight Forest, marry the frostbit Red Prince, and bow to Nightflesh. Or this nightmare will just keep getting worse." Eliot stepped back as six Ruby Legionnaires escorted two prisoners past my cell—prisoners in Trite clothing.

My lungs constricted; I couldn't *breathe*.

Kaley's forest-green eyes were big with questions, Winston walked like a robot—staring ahead with a waxen face.

"Stop!" I shouted, drawing the attention of my siblings. "Put them in this cell with me!" I begged in a voice that didn't sound like my own, but the guards ignored me.

Relief mixed with the pink heating Kaley's eyes when she saw me. Her cardigan was stretched, but she stood tall and gambled a message, "Grandma was gone when they came."

A Legionnaire clasped a hand over her mouth, but she'd gotten her words out.

"Wait!" I tried again, but my brother and sister were ushered around a bend, swallowed into the maze of cold prison cages.

My gaze fired back to find that Eliot had disappeared during the commotion.

I had to get out.

I *had* to get out.

I dove into my dress pocket for my orb. "Please," I begged to whatever markings of Truth had twice now blazed over my skin and given me an extraordinary gift in the face of death. I stared at my arms, my shoulders, my fingers.

But there was no trace of light.

The Truth was silent.

I was alone down here.

My family was alone down here.

I was supposed to protect them, to hold us together with my mother gone.

"Elowin," my whisper hitched. "Why didn't you come for us?"

THE
STORYTELLER

YET ANOTHER INTERRUPTION

"'Twas on a cold morning that Wendy Wilthsmurther arrived at her modest home with a troubled spec on her brow. A spec left there after a long meeting with the officials who claimed that this little home she had nurtured for a great measure was no longer safe to occupy— a thing she had been fearing for quite some time but had kept to herself.

There's mould in the walls.
The chimney is half-blocked! It's a fire hazard.
And now you're having issues with the plumbing, too?

The spec of trouble only grew as the aged woman considered where she and her dearests would go, who might be willing to help, and how she would tell the children. Her brow was beginning to feel quite heavy from it all.

Condemned.

She could not stand to speak the dreadful word aloud in fear that the home itself might hear it.

But as Wendy set her purse atop the kitchen table where a half-eaten bowl of oats had begun to sodden, a strange feeling crept in regarding the duo of backpacks clinging to their hooks by the door.

How were the Bell children supposed to survive at school without their bags, she wondered? And how unusual, that *both* Kaley and Winston might forget. Her eyes travelled back to the bowl of cereal.

It was then that Wendy Wilthsmurther knew a thing was not right.

The copper-cotton contents of her purse spilled off the table into a waterfall of pennies and tissues as she sank her old bones to the kitchen floor, a flood of whispered pleas tumbling into the air of her condemned home, putting life in its belly one last time.

The prayer did a flip and flop as it came out, before rolling into flight, embracing the bubbles of power lifting in its breast. It was a measure too much excitement all at once, and it sneezed, silencing the old woman on the floor, who thought she had heard a thing.

Though the blessed woman of age and invaluable wisdom could not see it, the prayer waved goodbye to Wendy Wilthsmurther before slipping out the keyhole and into the frosty air to chase a squall.

Wendy clasped her hands and closed her eyes, for there was a thing or three to be done still. She lifted her voice, raspy with seasons of use, and cried out a psalm, bellowing into the atmosphere a tune she recalled from the early seasons of her timestring when she had sat in a pew beneath a steeple. The praises filled the kitchen—right into the corners where the wallpaper peeled—and soared into every crevice of brittle wood and beam that held her home together.

The hymn slipped out the windows, seeped from the cracks, and lifted into the air outside like a crystal wildfire of cerulean stars and glittering lilacs sprouting golden crowns. And though her eyes could not witness the burning in the skies, it was a rather marvellous painting—a symbol in the heavens that sent evil spirits throughout the city rushing away.

One such spirit lunged out of a head.

Another fled from a heart.

And a third raced out of a home nearby.

For worship is a cry of war, you see.

From there, the lullaby of intercession channelled backward in time and space, past the gateways of realms, where it found a young Patrolman on the verge of his death. The hymn's extremity reached into his chest to hand him one last push, and a promise to go before him, stand behind him, and stay always by his side.

Ah, yes. Time is a funny thing.

Chapter,
The Thirty-Seventh

I was certain I could hear the wild, howling cackle of Mara Rouge trickling up like steam from below the snow, and the grunts and clashing instruments of her gnomes crying out for revenge. It filtered into my sanity as the hours passed. After a while, the laughter turned to rattling bells. They mocked what would become of me. They cheered for the cold and lonely end I faced.

A dull echo of footsteps told me the Ruby Legion was coming back. I kept my stare on the floor as they flung open the rusted bars of my cell and dragged me out.

I didn't object. I needed to learn something—*anything*—about my siblings. I strained to hear whispers of gossip as the Legionnaires led me up to the palace.

We passed by a mirror on the wall, and I glanced at my reflection—eyes dulled to milky brown, hair fading to unremarkable tan. A few days ago, I would have been bothered by the sight of my true self, but now it was a strange relief.

We came into a large room with descending theatre seating full of Rime Folk dressed in red—scarlet-berry headdresses and rosette-bouquet hats, claret bird feathers and silk bows with ribbon tassels, and the widespread odour of potent perfumes and power-hungry nobles.

The Crimson Court.

Their stares were dead, cold, and empty. They sipped on bubbling drinks and puffed trails of vapour from their red-stained lips. Greedy smiles prospered among the spearmint-steam.

A thick podium adorned a stage, behind which the Crimson King stood, and beside him, Prince Quinten. The prince's mouth quirked into a smile at the sight of me being hauled in like a chained bull.

My temper flared when I saw the rest of them—the Timepiece to Quinten's right, Asteroth Ryuu on the king's left. Prince Tegan and Prince Forrester stood at their former-prophet's side.

And, of course, the infamous palace magician leaned against a pillar in his white mask, far enough to the side to not draw attention, but when he saw my glance, he waved flirtatiously.

Holly Kissing sat in the front row. She twisted in her chair to glance at me—her face blank, her acting flawless, and her naturally golden eyes giving me no hope. Beside her, Eliot sat in his clean tunic, facing forward. He wouldn't look at me.

Past them, someone else was guided to the front of the room, and I faltered.

Apple.

She hadn't worn her cocoa lipstick or glistening chandelier earrings this morning. Her brunette locks were messy, her deep eyes sorrowful, and below them, crescents of shadow dipped toward her cheeks like she hadn't slept all night. As though she'd been up all night working like she'd done to create my gown for the Silver Masquerade Festival.

Apple is making your wedding dress, Eliot had said.

My heart rate galloped as I looked around at the guests, at the Crimson King who stood silently at the front, at Quinten waiting for me—but why the podium?

No, this wasn't my wedding…

Sure enough, the Crimson King smashed a silver gavel against the dais to silence the mutterings in the room, and I realized, as everybody turned to face the front and give the king their attention, that this was my *trial*.

"Furthermore, our next matter is to address Lady Scarlet Strange of the Crimson Court, who has made an official trade for a measure of her time, gifted to Ebenezer of the time overseers in exchange for information which he has supplied in full." The king went on with whatever he'd been saying before I arrived.

The Timepiece's cinder-scent reached where I stood, and I coughed.

I noticed he stood a foot ahead of the others. The other Timepieces lined the front, waiting with coiling mist brushing the walls at their backs.

No, this wasn't my trial. This was the *Timepiece's* trial.

The glare I'd been saving specially for Eliot rose to the

surface. The Timepiece had tricked me thrice over. Even standing beside Quinten and Asteroth, he was the cleverest villain in the room.

"A *short* measure of my time," I corrected, loud enough for the closest rows of the court to hear. The king paused, plum-rot eyes finding me.

"It shall be a short measure of time," the Timepiece's airy whisper flitted over my flesh, "for the rest of us."

But one thousand years for me.

I set my jaw, stifling my response as cold Legionnaire fingers tightened around my arms.

Apple wasn't far now—I might have been able to touch her if I lunged.

The Chocolatier stood silent and still; a soul normally bursting with life. I wanted to tell her I was sorry for putting her before the nobles she loved to learn about and study, as a criminal who would never work for the Red Kingdom again.

I worried about where Fred was.

Apple glanced at me; her hands clasped tight before of her. A lick of hair was stuck to her neck, either from past tears or current sweat, I wasn't sure. But her gaze flickered down to the Shammah necklace at my throat. Then to the dress pocket where she knew I kept my orb. And through the gruelling tension filling the room as the king spoke, Apple Dough smiled.

It was so brief, and small. And hopeful.

She knew what would become of us, but I felt she was reminding me that I wasn't alone.

The air sifted from my lungs. I braced myself for the king's judgement.

"...and so, Lady Strange shall be shackled to the Midnight Forest for the measure of one thousand full seasons. At which time, she will be granted the opportunity to return to us and fulfill her vows to my third son, Prince Quinten Barsavian Crimson-Choal, to whom she has been secretly, merrily betrothed."

For a split-second, a troubled look crossed the king's face. But he continued, "The Court recognizes Lady Strange's sacrifice as honour-worthy, even though she takes the punishment for actions *not* honour-worthy," he scowled at the Timepiece.

Applause erupted behind me, but my stare was still interlocked with Apple's.

The guards guided me toward a side-door, and Apple's head dipped into a nod as I passed, every trace of the smile she'd had to offer a moment ago, vanished. "Don't forget," she whispered, the first real trace of fear paling her face.

You're not alone.

There was only one reason Quinten would have brought Apple to this trial. She was the cost if I refused to go into the Midnight Forest. I trudged over the tile floor in bare feet, keeping my eyes on my friend until I was led around a bend in the hall.

Quinten beat us there; he waited in a small, windowless room. In the wall, an iron gate was clamped over an arch, beyond which was only hollow black.

Atop the doorway, a plate of stone held a message:

HERE LIES THE GATE
THROUGH WHICH DUES ARE TO BE PAID

Asteroth appeared, along with the Timepiece, and the palace magician. As if given a silent command, the Ruby Legion guards left me alone with them.

I expected Quinten to gloat, but he remained silent, as if waiting for someone else to speak first. I had a feeling I knew who he was waiting for.

Asteroth's smile grew to that disturbingly wide, feral thing—the same smile I'd seen on *her*, in the ice dome. The dark rings around his silver irises hollowed, and when he spoke, shudders erupted down my spine. "Pity," he said, two voices in one.

I turned my face, unable to look at him, to see that *thing* again.

"I thought he would come for you."

"He didn't fall for your tricks," my voice was unsteady.

Asteroth angled his head and drifted closer, his thin, pale nose dipping toward me. He wanted me to look, to see the creature. I glanced up, guarded. "But you did," it whispered.

I swallowed, fear knotting in my gut. "He might still come for me," I tried, not because I wanted Elowin to fall into this trap, but because part of me still hoped he might come spare me from the forest.

"I am a generous god, Trite," the low dip of Asteroth's voice forced me a step back. "I'll offer one time more, but I will not offer a third time."

"No," I rasped before he said it. I remembered Mara Rouge's offer. "I'm not going to side with you. I'm not going to toss away the Truth, or help you squander the hope of the believers." My throat was dry.

Asteroth's stare flickered.

But he straightened. "I shall show no mercy to the off-spring of Mikal Migraithe who wait outside the palace walls at present. A penalty for your choice."

The words slammed into me—I stepped after the diamond-haired prophet who turned for the hall, his staff clinking against the tiles. "Bind the Carrier to the darkness."

Jolly Cheat snatched my shoulders and dragged me toward the hollow arch where Quinten turned a key to unlock the gate. I gasped as the Timepiece's wind hit my back, rippling the hem of my dress.

I met the boundary of the arch's mouth, chest pounding, toes curling over the edge.

Quinten's gloved hand came against my shoulder and thrust me in.

"Good tidings, *my love!*"

Every inch of me was encompassed in blackness.

TICKET NOTICE

YOU HAVE PASSED
INTO THE
MIDNIGHT FOREST

YOUR DUES:
ONE THOUSAND
SEASONS

PART 5

THE TENTH INTERRUPTION

Folly is indeed how it all began. A trick and a twiddle, a snake and a slide. A thing that set the winds in motion. A tale starting even before time, between ancient powers of darkness and daylight.

But, and furthermore, a lullaby is how this story first began. A hum that now lived in the beating chest of a Rime Folk raised for a moment such as this.

Zane Cohen-Margus-Bowswither was his name in full.

The Patrolman's hand tightened around a weapon salvaged from the library's ruins, and he gasped as a flood of cold erupted in his chest.

But what did it mean? A pebble of warmth remained there still. Surely, Helen Bell was not...

"Lucas," Zane whispered, rubbing over his heart. "I feel...*cold*."

Lucas released a heavy breath and looked upon the palace before them. "Well. Frostbite."

Red cloaks littered the snow like pools of blood at their ankles; cloaks Zane and his brothers had donned to sneak through the iron kingdom gates.

Before the mighty palace walls, they had cast off their cloaks to reveal their true colours; those of a host of blackbirds.

At Zane's side, Lucas stood with Mirkra, Timblewon, Wanda, Oden, Silas, and thirty more plus nine—all the seasoned Patrols who had not been scattered in the wake of the library's fall.

Concealed in the ice gardens, two hundred plus four of the youngest Patrolmen waited, tucked into the cracks, awaiting an order, eager and itchy and untrained, still rosy with burns from the fire. Many were missing their mentors. All were missing their librarians and their Elders.

To the palace residents, the Patrols' arrival had been considered an act of war. That, and the simple fact that Zane had shouted, "We've come as an act of war! We will not hesitate to take aim at your princes unless our Carrier is sent out!"

So, that had added to the hostility in the air as well.

But as the Ruby Legion assembled at the palace's base in great numbers, Zane adjusted his grip on his weapon, counting the swell of red capes. His fingers could not still their fidgeting.

The Crimson King and the Red Princes made their appearance—only three princes, coated in gleaming copper armour and matching purple eyes. But it was not the eldest prince or the king who stepped forward to lead the armies; it was the third prince. Zane's eyes narrowed on the thin, silver crown that wrapped the young man's crow-black hair, and the one hand he held tightly to his chest.

Asteroth Ryuu's long, velvet cape swept out like a flag over his army when he appeared on a balcony. A beastly reindeer snarled at his side, and the white-cloaked palace magician stepped around the animal and took his place at the rail.

A storm of wind and smoke rushed from the palace, rippling the fabric at Zane's shoulders. A faceless cloaked figure hovered above them all.

"Let me swing at Asteroth first," Lucas said, and Zane should have stopped him right there.

Instead, he claimed, "That bloody Timepiece is mine."

"What about *him*?" Mirkra's uneven voice drew them to the third Red Prince at the head of the army, whose face twitched and shuddered, his purple eyes rolling back.

"Ragnashuck," Lucas muttered. "That's the grossest thing I've ever—"

The beautiful Red Prince collapsed in the snow, leaving the Patrolmen blinking.

Only a pinch passed, and then he rose again.

The prince's body stretched this way and that, tugging upward, downward, around and out, inking to leathery onyx flesh and widened eyes until the row of Patrolmen broke, forced back a step or three.

'Twas not quite a snake, rather, it was a glittering mass of smoke and liquid whose serpentine body stretched half the courtyard, and Zane's heart pounded, his bright tones flickering.

Behind the convulsing serpent, Prince Forrester drew a long, steel sword, the Ruby Legion imitating his motion until five hundred plus a measure more cold blades filled the space like silver stitching in a red and copper tapestry.

Zane's colours erupted as he spun to shout to the young ones in the ice garden to run, but a thick wall of wind and smoke fell from the sky, dimming the sunlight and smacking down behind the seasoned Patrolmen to split them from the ice sculptures where the youngsters hid. Everything beyond the misty barrier became as still as stone.

Zane looked upon the remaining stretch of Patrolmen who stood at his side, now a dreadfully modest number against the hundreds in crimson.

"A time pocket," Mirkra muttered down the line. "We're frostbitten trapped."

Sure enough, the Timepiece's hands were outstretched to the shadow-dome, trapping them in with the Ruby Legion, the Red Princes, Asteroth Ryuu, and the rising serpent.

Chapter,
The Thirty-Eighth

I felt like I was under water. The thick darkness warmed my blood, conquering my head, spinning my every thought into a liquid wheel.

I heard *her*. Over and over. Laughing.

The scrape of her sabatons over the ice, the pounding of her gauntlet against her breastplate. She whispered in my ears.

The Queen of the Snow made so much noise, I could hardly think. The iron nails dug deep into my mind with every taunt: *You should have joined me, Trite*, she uttered. *You could have been powerful. I would have made you beautiful, too. And now, you're nothing. Even the King you fight for does not want you.*

After an incalculable number of hours, her presence finally wisped away, and the forest turned quiet. I stopped walking, not consoled by the silence. I was afraid she would come back.

Some time ago, I'd landed on a moist, dirt path. Murk ground beneath my toenails as I dragged one bare foot in front of the other. The trees mocked me; their bent branches were crooked, pointing fingers, and deep rumbling laughter ruffled the leaves overhead with a stale breeze.

I had no idea how long I'd been wandering in circles. *If* I was wandering in circles. The silence made me jump at every stir of breeze, potent with the stench of wet earth, and vast emptiness. As time passed, my pebble of hope eroded beneath this dark sea.

I thought of Kaley and Winston in the palace dungeon. And I thought of Grandma, all those worlds away, childless and alone. My family had fallen apart.

Other thoughts planted their seeds into the soil of my agony, sprouting wings and taking flight until all I saw, felt, and *breathed* were phantom butterflies of resentment. My logic slipped into different cracks of the forest, where it tucked itself into tree roots, gaps in the bark, and into folds of the leaves.

You're not alone. Apple's glance before I'd been dragged away.

But Apple wasn't here now I had realized, again and again. No one was.

So I walked, and walked, and walked.

You're not alone.

You're not alone.

You're not alone.

I couldn't remember how long I'd been walking.

THE ELEVENTH INTERRUPTION

The thudding of staff heels thundered through the time pocket. Patrolmen thrust up a wall of snow to split the courtyard and mask their enemies; it was all they had—a cheap trick.

The Patrolmen burst through the rippling barrier of snow at rapid intervals, descending upon the crimson army in giant leaps like birds in flight.

Zane punched through, hoisting his weapon as he collided with swinging metal swords on the other side. Across the courtyard, wood and ice struck steel and strong wills.

The Timepiece glided over the rail, descending toward

the chaos; Asteroth drifting at his side.

Wanda raged upon Prince Forrester, Mirkra at her back, pinning a Ruby Legionnaire to the snow. Past them, the viper hissed, liquid and smoke solidifying into a sleek body, slit eyes narrowing on the pair. Zane's throat thickened to yell, but the snake launched.

Wanda saw and thrust Mirkra aside, but the serpent's pin-sharp teeth sliced her shoulder and Mirkra's legs in the same snap.

Mouth tight, Zane leapt onto the shoulders of the closest Legionnaire, springing his way over the soldiers and kicking faces on his way.

The viper returned to smoke and liquid, swerving to where it hardened back to leathery skin and poised to aim for another.

Wanda and Mirkra both lay unmoving in the snow.

The song of Winter that fed the sparrows and beckoned the frostlillies to open, soothed the air where Porethius stood upon snowy fields. Her lashes fluttered, but she otherwise remained still. Listening.

For, there had been a great, deafening shift in the Winter winds.

"Are we meant to wait, even now?" Her heart sent the whisper adrift. "I sensed the Carrier leave Winter at dawn."

Porethius's spirit buzzed; nothing felt as it should, and calling wickets swarmed the air. She came to petition the One who listens, her lavender eyes taking in the rolls of white that transformed into dunes a pinch and a dip away.

A measure behind her, Cane leaned against the ice tunnel entrance, whistling to himself to pass the seconds.

Porethius nearly faltered when a voice returned, the voice of the sun with the fragrance of sweet rain and new buds.

It is as you say. At last, my Carrier is not in Winter.

A pinch of silence crossed the fields as revelation dawned on the fairy. For, indeed, the King could not show himself in the flesh before the time was right, in *Winter*.

Snare the serpent.

The doubled-bladed sword at her back grew in weight. Porethius's chin lifted to glimpse o'er the peaks of the dunes, past the mountains, and into the heart of a kingdom painted red.

A brilliant white light appeared in the sky. At the familiar and dearly missed presence, the fairy's lavender eyes blazed to flame, her symbols sweeping into a glide over her skin. The light brushed across the sky like a great winged bird.

Elowin's spirit.

The King was going after his Carrier.

Zane slid on his knees to Mirkra and Wanda, shaking them a time or three, certain he would burst into a puddle of colours.

"Ragnashuck," he croaked, his fist slamming over his lips, a salted tear stinging his eye.

But the Patrolman stood; vision stinging with blush and veins, chest writhing. He lifted his fire-rimmed gaze to the serpent swerving around Timblewon's languid slashing. The boy's fuchsia hair was scuffed to a nest, his legs wobbling.

Zane rotated the staff in his grip as he strutted to feed his furies on the Red Prince.

Timblewon croaked a scream as the serpent's fangs sliced his thigh, and Zane broke into a sprint. The fuchsia-haired boy shuddered and stumbled—he did not make it another two steps before rolling into the snow like Mirkra and Wanda.

By some unholy warning, the snake saw the Patrolman coming. Its ashen skin glided over the snow with a flick of its body, and it gazed at Zane, amethyst slit-eyes thinning.

With his staff, Zane thrust ice into those eyes and the serpent recoiled, hissing tongue slashing the air as it shook glassy scraps from its skull, its body rolling over on itself and shifting back to fluid and fume. Zane lunged to the skies of the time pocket, dragging his staff behind through the smoke so the ice might slice into the obsidian snake-flesh as it changed back. But the creature arched and solidified, opening its mouth wide beneath Zane's legs, ready to snap shut and swallow him in full.

With a growl, Zane tore up a lap of snow from the court-yard to catch himself, but the snake's tail smashed it to grains, sending him tumbling into the slush.

Cold flakes clung to Zane's mouth, but he gasped and forced himself to lift before he might be pierced in his back. "Bloody, frostbitten, ashworm *prince*—" he muttered. But as he spun, the skies of the time pocket rattled, catching the attention of Zane and the snake-prince alike.

Even with everything beyond the time pocket lifeless, Zane was certain he saw something *coming*.

A light—indecipherable in shape. Like a star moving at a tremendous speed.

The snake hissed, and the Timepiece bellowed an objection as the star punctured the wall of the pocket, flew past overhead, and punched through the other side.

It fired over the sky and disappeared into the horizon.

But a second being flew in through the opening the shooting star had made, on violet, tulip-like wings. She rattled the yard stones when she landed, her dark hair sailing in the Timepiece's windstorm as she reached and dislodged a double-bladed sword from her back. Her sights fell on the arching snake-prince.

Beyond them, Asteroth stared at where the light had burned past in the skies. The once-prophet shuddered, skin morphing gray, silver eyes liquifying to black, and a sinister growl shook the courtyard.

"Kill the sons of Mikal Migraithe!" A deep, beastly voice filled the pocket, stiffening Zane's spine.

At the courtyard's opposite end, Lucas had gone still at the sound of the voice.

Zane's bright eyes slid to the palace, where he hoped beyond all measure Helen was still inside, alive.

He had wanted her to stay in Winter.

He had promised he would keep them together.

All over the time pocket, the remaining Patrols were thrust to their knees.

Chapter,
The Thirty-Ninth

A pool of still water blocked the path. I watched it seep into the air in response to my nearness, drip by drip, to form a dark, oval mirror before me.

Up until that point, I'd stayed on the dirt path that never led anywhere. Always traveling in the same circles, never finding an end destination. It reminded me of the life I'd lived before I found Winter. Before I found purpose.

The girl in the mirror's reflection appeared defeated. My hair was leaked of its golden sheen, my skin was pale, my lips dry, and my eyes…good grief, my eyes were shadowed by the tiredness of my soul.

The same black dress with the same metallic shoulders

hugged my body, the same gold necklace clung to my throat. My fingers idly traced over the snowflake pendant as I stared at myself.

Perhaps this pool was meant for reflection, not only literally, but also to go back over one's mistakes. It seemed appropriate for a prison.

But then *she* came back.

I shook my head at the sight of her lapping tendrils of wild hair, her wide-smiling red lips, and her black helmet from which the antlers grew.

Season's greetings...Trite. Her voice was in my head, but I could feel her words against my spine from where she stood behind me.

I spun, dead chest pounding to life, but was met with only an empty path shaded by crooked trees.

When I turned back to the mirror, she was still at my shoulder. Still smiling too wide.

"You're not real," I breathed, but I was afraid I was wrong. Afraid I was trapped in this woodland with *her*.

You chose this. Don't you remember? At her words, I recalled facing her in that dome of ice in Wentchester Cove, how I'd conjured a wall between us, and she'd banged her way through with a cackle. A cackle she mimicked now— throwing her head back and howling into the darkness above, the black scales of her armour quivering in echo. Suddenly her gauntlet swung around me and her metal fingers grabbed my chin.

I *felt* it; my blood froze.

She grinned as it dawned on me that this wasn't a figment of my imagination. Mara Rouge was here; the cold steel of her armour chilled my back. "You're not real," I stifled a gasp, begging it to be true. "You were beaten in the duel…"

Don't you see, Carrier? she whispered. *All of this* is *about my duel with you.* The two-tone hiss of her voice dove into my soul.

I wasn't speaking to *her*. Just like when I'd looked into her swimming eyes during the Quarrel of Sword and Bone, I was speaking to the *creature*.

"Nightflesh…" I whispered the name, my dry lips cracking with my heart.

As if I'd shouted it from the top of a mountain, the name echoed down the path both ways, tumbling through the humid trunks and coming back to hit me like a boomerang.

Mara Rouge's eyes warped black as she triumphed, voice changing to nothing but a deep growl, *You're the last Carrier of Falsehoods.* The scent of sour wine and hot toxins filled my nose and I tried not to breathe. *You don't deserve forgiveness; your false king knows that. It's why he did not save you. It's why you were always destined to fall like the Carriers before you that I slaughtered as martyrs. It's why I shall destroy you in the end.*

"They'll make more Carriers," I tried, voice hitching.

The Beast's low snarl shook the pebbles at my feet. *If such a thing were possible, wouldn't the believers have done so already?*

I looked back at the witch's face in the mirror, into the pupils through which he watched me. What did he mean *If such a thing were possible?*

"The Truth wouldn't leave Winter without a way."

There was a way, in an age of the past. But I destroyed

it, he growled. *The end is near, Trite. And you have been abandoned. You…*

Mara's reflection stilled. I blinked.

Then I heard it; the quiet, feminine words of someone else. A voice I knew—from old memories and a stolen childhood.

Have faith, Helen, the female voice said, and my skin pulled tight.

Mara Rouge's hair whipped as she turned, eyes darting.

A woman stepped into the pool's reflection at my other shoulder, and my chest writhed with heartache. Her hair was dark and wavy like Kaley's, her eyes tilted and brown like mine, her jaw square like Winston's. *Have faith, Helen. They cannot defeat you if you still believe,* she said.

"Mom…?" The moisture escaped my eyes and rolled down my cheeks, splashing on my bare feet.

My mother cast me a knowing smile I'd seen a hundred times as a child but hadn't witnessed since the day Grandma had knelt on one knee and told me she was never coming home.

I knew if I turned around, she wouldn't be there. But looking at my mother's reflection, I wanted to tell her how lonely it had been without her. How I'd prayed for her to come back from the dead, how our family had crumbled.

"I miss you," was what came out instead. A slight smile cracked my face.

She smiled back.

Mara Rouge snarled at my mother; beastly, inhuman.

A spot of orange flickered in the sky. My watery gaze lifted as a ripple of dull thuds descended upon the forest. When I looked back to the mirror, my mother and Mara

Rouge had disappeared. I tried to grab it—the window to my mother—but the mirror melted, draining back down into the puddle on the path.

Filtered light glimmered above, and warmth cascaded over my numb face as I tried to figure out what was happening.

A tearing sound filled the forest. The black sky peeled open like the curtain of a starless heaven was being pulled back, revealing a white glow that made me sink to my knees and shield my eyes.

An oval of colours burst through, swarming like a hive of jewel-toned bees. The fire in the sky lit up the forest, a familiar song accompanying it like the quiet strings of cellos:

*D, D, down to C, down to B flat, down to G,
down to F, back up to A#...*

The descending glow faded to reveal a person. His warmth encompassed me, and I nearly buckled at the first taste of relief from the cold.

The light and colour swam like a current, travelling up his arms and around his body—some in the shapes of foreign words and symbols like my tattoos had been. He had a strangely familiar face; eyes with dancing rainbows I'd seen on a bird once, from what felt like a lifetime ago.

His hand came out in invitation. "Get up, Trite," he said, a smile tugging on his face where words brushed over his skin in gold and silver. "You're almost there."

I stared like a deer in headlights, feeling the rhythm of my heartbeat change. It lifted into a chorus of hope as I grabbed his hand.

My soul sang, sewing itself back together with ribbons

of courage as colours seeped from his chest like paint in water, rippling over my skin. I was lifted from the dirty forest floor, up into the sky above the tricks of the laughing trees and reflective waters. He aimed for the tear in the fabric of the atmosphere.

You're not alone.

A NECESSARY INTERRUPTION

The violet-winged woman sliced faster than the wind with her dual-bladed sword, her acrobatic wonders forcing the viper's body of fog to swivel and snap its dripping jaws at random.

Lucas Leutenski stole a glance at them as he grabbed a Ruby Legionnaire's shoulder and tore him off Brady Chorus who had fallen to his knees, the boy's orange beard dripping with sweat and snow.

Lucas extended a hand to Brady, but a deafening crack splintered up the side of the time pocket's dome, and they

364

both started.

The Timepiece shuddered his ashes, his dark cloak tugging this way and that.

"*Noooo*!" His hollow scream bounced off the flaking walls. The Timepiece folded into himself, his cloak lurching like he had been yanked by a terrible force, gray fumes curling into nothingness as he disappeared into the air; vanished entirely.

Perhaps, taken by another place.

The dome shattered like glass in its master's absence, pellets dropping over the yard like brittle ash.

A roar erupted from the ice gardens. Young sputtlepuns in raven-black swept in, springing upon the crimson soldiers with primed spears and a war cry.

The white magician leapt from the balcony and strode through the chaos to get his fill of young foes, joining the two eldest Red Princes in their swordplay.

Lucas charged for him—the man in white—but was cut off by a blast of red fire that spiralled across the yard and struck the chest of Zane Cohen.

Asteroth glided over the snow after Zane, who clutched his chest and crawled back on the heels of his bloodied hands, staff nowhere in sight.

"Asteroth!" Lucas beckoned, striding that way, summoning snow from the crushed remains in the yard.

But as Lucas moved to intervene, a great host of silver birds soared from the Scarlet City mist. They swarmed Asteroth in a blizzard of wings. One broke away and landed on Zane's shoulder, bending its beak to whisper into his ear.

Zane's eyes ignited, and though the boy was wilted, he

sprang from the courtyard to the nearest building top, sprinting from one roof to the next.

Lucas dug his heels in to stop as Zane disappeared into the city's haze.

Asteroth slashed, sending silver creatures rolling and feathers floating to the snow.

His scepter burned red as he spun toward the Timepiece's vacant place in the sky, hoary eyes then flickering to the snake, where the violet-winged warrior's elbow hooked its neck.

The thrashing serpent's jaws snapped at her chin; fog, liquid, and flesh all fighting back. With a tattooed arm, she raised her weapon and Lucas squeezed his eyes shut like a wibbly peg out of its shell.

A moist slash reverberated across the yard.

Lucas peeked an eye open.

A gush of glittering black liquid stained the snow. And just like that, the head of the snake was no longer the head of the snake. But just a snakey head.

Lucas huffed and leaned forward with his palms on his knees, stifling the urge to wretch.

Asteroth's features morphed grey; his body lifting from the snow to vanish into the Winter skies. But Lucas glanced to the balcony where Asteroth had left his perfectly good reindeer unattended.

A bright red nose, the creature had. And shiny.

As Lucas admired the snorting, fur-skinned creature, he recalled a promise he had made to Helen Bell when he had spotted her in chains in the Scarlet City. And he wondered if he might do a noble thing, while also doing a pesky thing at Asteroth Ryuu's expense.

Chapter,
The Fortieth

I 'd heard the song of Winter last year, but it wasn't until I awoke in a bright woodland, famished and disoriented, that I realized I'd been hearing that song since I was a little girl. An old Sunday school teacher appeared in my mind, from a time when my mother was alive.

It was a song about a mountain.

Emerald grass surrounded me in a capsule of warmth the scent of maple. Everything beyond was sprinkled with fresh flakes and smooth, icy surfaces; white and glowing, with sounds of life trickling through the tranquil trees that didn't laugh or scoff or clap their leaves.

There was another sound in the distance—one of shouts and clanging metal. I didn't know which direction it was coming from.

Warmth lingered on my fingertips.

You're not alone. A quiet hum in my ears, barely a sound over the living forest. And then my mother's voice: *Have faith, Helen.*

A single hot tear rolled down my cheek and into the grass.

My body was flat on the ground, my skirts sweeping out like a blanket. But a new voice hurtled me to a sitting position.

"Helen?! Ragnashuck, Trite, *where are you*?!" I heard him before I saw him—snapping branches and crunching ice.

"I'm here!"

Zane kicked through an ice berry bush, flinging celadon beads aside as he broke through and tripped into a crawl, coming to meet me with dragging boots. It was the clumsiest, *bloodiest* I'd ever seen him.

A silver-winged bird soared past, arching up and fluttering away as my Patrolman clambered over; a blood-soaked arm outstretched to drag me to him. I came against Zane's pounding chest, the thundering of his heart a sweet sound against my ears, until he suddenly laughed, and that sound was even better.

"Ragnashuck..." he whispered against my tossed mane of hair. "You're alright."

"What happened to you?"

"Me? What happened to *you*, Helen? I thought you were dead. If that bird hadn't shown up, I might have just let Asteroth have me."

"They sent me to the Midnight Forest."

He drew back to look at my face. "They bloody what?" A cut glimmered on his bottom lip; his brows tilted in. "How long were you...*inside*?"

"I don't know. Elowin pulled me out," I said. "I *saw* him, as a person. He lifted me from the dirt and *carried* me out."

The deep tones leaked from his stare. "I led the Patrol to the Red palace doors to get you back. The young ones aren't trained. I could hardly keep on my feet against Asteroth; they won't stand a chance," he swallowed. "And Wanda, Mirkra, Timblewon..." he glanced off, face paling. "Dentone, and Silas..."

"Zane, there's something else. Quinten has my brother and sister in the palace," I climbed to my feet.

Zane dragged himself up, too. "Lucas told me Asteroth was planning to snatch them. Lucas *also* said he planned to get them back. He's still in the courtyard and he's feeling as bloody reckless as a spinbug, so maybe he'll surprise us." His hand found mine again. "I need to go back and protect the young ones. It's not far—just past these trees."

"Let's go." I moved in the direction he'd come from, but he took my shoulder to stop me.

"Helen, you're staying here. And...I know this isn't the right time to bring this up, but I have to tell you a story, Trite. Later," he said out of the blue. He chewed on his bottom lip. "There's a reason we haven't started training new Carriers. I need to explain a thing or three."

"Ah, yes. The Triad of Signs. That tricky thing." A smooth voice filled the clearing and Zane caught my arm.

The boy leaning against a tree trunk—who'd been watching us for who *knew* how long—was as tall as Zane, with deep red hair and wild purple eyes that drove a shudder up my spine. He looked like...

"You're a Red Prince," Zane said before I could, edging himself between me and the stranger.

"Oh, few would still call me that, I think." A smile twinkled at the edge of his mouth. "I knew there was a reason Porethius brought me along," he added with a sigh. "Alright then, Carrier. I'll keep an eye on you while your Patrolman settles his matters. But only until the quarrel at the palace is over. I have a pinch of sneaking around to do after that."

Zane and I exchanged a look. "Who are you?" Zane loosened his grip.

But I already knew who this boy was. I knew because of his eyes. Because of his beauty. Because of his natural, princely confidence.

"I suppose we were bound to meet, eventually." He came over and extended a hand adorned with half a dozen gold and copper rings. "I'm Cane."

THE
STORYTELLER

AN INTERRUPTION

The high leap Lucas Leutenski had taken to the balcony may have broken records, and 'twas a shame no one had been looking to see it. The Patrolman snatched the reins of the creature as he soared, ducking beneath its prickly bush of antlers. He swept over the icy balcony and hopped upon the reindeer's back.

A truly wicked smile found his face, unrelated to the fact that this was his first ever deer-ride.

He managed to turn the beast and charged into the halls of the palace, startling crowds of nobles gathered by stained-glass windows to watch the bloodshed outside. They raised

371

shrieks that mixed with Lucas's bellowing cackle as he kicked aside vases and knocked over end tables.

It was not a long journey to the palace's dingy bowels, and once Lucas had travelled over numerous paint-splattered floors, he sniffed the air for common blood, finally discovering the prisoners in the furthest cage.

Helen Bell's beloveds gaped up at him. And Lucas meant to say a charming thing or three, but...

"Season's greetings," was all he muttered, his gaze locked on the she-Trite's deep green eyes. Her dark lashes made him look twice, and then thrice, and then a time or three more. "Trites," he added at the end.

The girl was on her feet and at the cell door before Lucas could find the words to admit he was there to rescue them. Also, he forgot why he had come, so, that hindered his words too.

"I've come to fetch you on behalf of my Carrier," he finally spit out, sliding off the reindeer and tugging a blade from his belt—one he had used to do a naughty thing to a naughty prince—and slashed at the lock. But the lock was stubborn.

So, Lucas switched to the staff which he unhooked from his back to try another thing. He eyed the lock. The door. "You may wish to step aside, Trites."

Lucas rounded behind the reindeer and stuffed his icy staff against the great creature's rear.

With a dreadful screech, the beast charged forward, snapping the cage's bars like blossom stems. The reindeer found itself inside the cage with the Trites. "Not so fast, Rudy," Lucas named him on a whim. "We still need a ride out of here, you brute."

Two startled Trites blinked at him through the bars. The boy especially, with his light hair and distrusting, tugged brow, looked a thing like Helen Bell.

The girl darted out first, keeping a sweet eye on that reindeer as she did.

Lucas snapped lofty fingers at the scarlet-nosed creature to call it back, but it did not move a pinch from where it snarled in the corner.

"Are you Zane?" the girl asked, bringing Lucas's full attention back to the hint of hope in her eyes that transformed her into a lovely, dreamy, young snow fawn.

So, Lucas placed a confident hand on his hip. "Absolutely." And he winked.

Cane watched the quarrel's conclusion from the shadows of the orchard—a collection of white-appled trees he had once played in as a boy, throwing its fruits at passersby in the streets simply to be cruel. 'Twas a thing he felt a flit of shame about now.

Asteroth rose to the skies a gray monster, swallowed by a sweeping cloud. The palace magician slithered to the hills beyond, disappearing against the white snow. Only Cane's brothers were left to the merry band of children-boys who fought like blue wasps after sipping syrup. Those in red were forced to retreat when Porethius Plum locked gazes with the Crimson King, who perhaps finally saw with true eyes, clear of Quinten's mindsweeping, that he might be at a disadvantage.

The king raised an arm to quit his army, and the Ruby Legion dragged back to the palace's heel.

With the Carrier returned to her Patrolman's care in the woods, Cane drifted to stand by Porethius Plum. The shade of his hood hid his remarkably rosy hair, transforming him into a nameless, faceless companion, as his once-father approached the fairy now that the quarrel had hushed.

"A good warrior knows when to make an ally instead of an enemy." The king eyed the lavender wings at Porethius's back as he spoke, and the sword stained with obsidian blood in her grip.

"An ally, perhaps. But I cannot fight *for* you, King. I fight for another."

Another, indeed. Cane smiled beneath his hood.

"But I will strike an alliance with you. I will not raise my weapon against you, or your sons, permitting they do not raise their blades against the sons of Mikal Migraithe in the days ahead. Should this alliance be broken by you or your offspring, you will see me again," the fairy said. "And I ask for one thing more; when the right day of Winter future comes that I should return here to this palace, you will grant me an audience without question."

When the king's copper gauntlet came out, Cane felt a flinch in his spirit. An alliance between the father that had disowned him, and the guardian that had taken him on as her assignment to see that he survived the hunt that came afterwards.

"Your deal seems to carry a measure of reason." The scraping wind of the king's voice travelled over the yard.

Porethius and the Crimson King shook, and it was settled.

The Patrolmen began to gather their wounded and poisoned, the fairy moving to help until her seconds would run out and she would be beckoned back to her post.

But Cane turned to the steaming, serpentine body coiled at the yard's edge, shiny onyx skin dulling beneath the creeping sun. A dark river leaked its way into the ice garden; a testament to Elowin's ability.

That was what a single instruction from the Truth himself could do to a serpent, lest the world forget.

The once-prince headed that way by the dragging of his boots, his mahogany brows tilting as he looked upon the snake. Though he had abandoned his heritage, Cane whispered a prayer of remembrance for the brother he once had. The brother who took up his mantle as the third prince. The most beloved prince in the Red Kingdom since the eve Cane left.

These thoughts vanished as Cane felt the cold point of a dagger dip into the flesh between his shoulder blades. Though the attacker did not reveal herself with words or threats, he guessed who held the weapon as he turned, risking the thrust of that dagger.

There she stood: a young woman now, with golden hair and bright bronze eyes. Everything as lovely as she had always been, even when she had carried her scars on the outside. And this close, Cane was certain his hood would not hide much.

"I know who you are," she whispered in a voice that had haunted his dreams for many seasons.

Holly Kissing, they called her now. But, Holly Kissing, she was not. And the Crimson Court was a flock of fools for not realizing it.

"And I know who *you* are," Cane countered in the softest voice he might try with her—the girl he had loved to torment. Who he had perhaps grown to love in other ways, too.

He took her in, her guarded expression, the anger in those brassy eyes. There because of him, and possibly his brothers also, but mostly because of him. He wished he could undo it all and make her understand that a young, entitled boy with a shallow heart could be the most cruel of all the monsters in Winter, if given the proper setting.

"You don't need to listen to my nattering. But you should know that I left because of what I did to you. I meant to make it right. I still do."

Scarlet did not flinch or seem convinced. But she also did not slash him with the dagger stationed provocatively close to the dip below his throat. "Come with me now, Scarlet. And I will tell you everything."

For a pinch, her golden gaze flickered to the Crimson dynasty at her back.

"I'll show you a better way to live. A way I think you already discovered when you first tried to look for me," he added. "That's why you didn't expose the Carrier of Truth, I think. When you discovered who exactly she was."

"I kept her secret to keep mine," Scarlet countered. But the twitch in her mouth did not say as much.

Cane held out his palms. "Try it my way for the measure of one season, and see what your heart thinks of it," he said. "And don't look back at this kingdom as you leave it. They don't bring you true cheer."

Though she didn't take his hands, Scarlet lowered the dagger from his chest.

A roguish smile found the once-prince's face. "Besides.

I heard a rumour that the new Red prophetess has been muttering insights that Scarlet Strange will marry the third Red Prince." A tug wider grew that smile. "And I hear she can't lie."

'Twas the first real reaction Cane got from Scarlet when her creamy skin bloomed pink.

The dagger slid from her grip and clattered to the courtyard stones. But still, Scarlet was not convinced by him, and he could not blame her for it.

"Not on this afternoon, Cane. And not tomorrow, either," was what she said. "Leave this kingdom. You do not belong here anymore."

He nodded at that. "You're right. This is not my home. That is not my family. Those are not my people."

With that, the once-prince adjusted his hood and moved for the ice garden where Porethius waited by a statue of the Crimson King himself. A statue that aimed to reach the clouds, visible across the Scarlet City.

A statue of a false king. A greedy king. A king in need of Truth.

Chapter,
The Forty-First

The Pebble Paper
NEWS FROM THE CRIMSON COURT

A MEASURE OF QUESTIONS HAVE BEEN ASKED
OF THE COURT THIS DAY REGARDING THE
SCUTTLE IN THE COURTYARD AT SUNRISE.

THE COURT WISHES TO INFORM THE POPULACE
THAT A BAND OF BELIEVERS OF THE OLD
TRUTHS ASSAULTED THE PALACE THIS
MORNING, BRINGING WITH THEM A MYSTICAL
SERPENT TO REBEL AGAINST THE LAWS OF THE

LAND. THESE BELIEVERS ARE NOT TO BE
TRUSTED AND ARE CONSIDERED DANGEROUS.
THOSE WHO BELIEVE IN THE OLD TRUTHS HAVE
BEEN PROVEN VIOLENT, MISLED, AND SMALL
MINDED. BUT HAVE CHEER, FOR ALL FOES WHO
RIOTED AT SUNRISE WERE EASILY OUTMATCHED
BY THE TWO ELDEST RED PRINCES, WHO
HANDLED THE SITUATION RESPECTABLY.

NO MORE QUESTIONS ARE NEEDED, THIS MATTER
HAS BEEN SORTED OUT.
WE THANK YOU FOR YOUR CONCERNS.

IN UNRELATED NEWS, LADY SCARLET STRANGE
WAS ADMITTED TO THE UNREACHABLE PRISON
AT SUNRISE TO PAY A MEASURE OF COMPILED
DUES.

HER BETROTHED, OUR THIRD PRINCE, PRINCE
QUINTEN, HAS BEEN MISSING SINCE THE TRIAL,
PRESUMABLY DUE TO GRIEF.

STAY SAFE.
STAY UNITED.

YOUR EDITOR IN CHIEF,
Sullen Sprit-Spellborrow

Apple read the news aloud as the young Patrols carried their injured mentors into the factory on their backs and in their arms: Wanda, the fuchsia-haired competition host, a handful of others, and Mirkra—whose large frame was dragged in by half a dozen boys—all of whom had suffered venomous bites from a viper.

I'd nearly retched when I saw the smoking body of that snake sprawled by the palace. And to think, that *thing* had kissed me.

I watched the chocolate river bubbling along in the moat. It felt like I'd been staring at it for hours.

There was no sign of Kaley or Winston. Or Lucas. Everyone had a different story of what they'd seen during the last moments of the battle—one boy swore he saw Lucas go into the palace. But no one saw him come out.

The factory had been transformed into a makeshift Patrol base after a hundred messages had been passed along in a somewhat disorganized fashion. It seemed the Patrolmen we'd left behind in the Chocolatiers' home had spent their days sending word across Winter, alerting the Patrol Elders who'd been dispersed among their allies. And the dwarves, who had retreated to their cottage after the attack, had then gone back to try and salvage what they could from the library's remains. The dwarves were at the factory when I arrived.

But there was no Eliot. He never came back.

The russet river lifted the warm scent of sugar into the air, and though Apple had made such a thing of it before, I caught at least four Patrolmen sneaking over to stick their fingers in and lick them off.

The Chocolatier fashioned a glamorous white robe,

somehow unblemished by cocoa stains. She didn't scold the boys creeping past to taste the chocolate. After she finished reading *The Pebble Paper*, she was quiet like me for a while.

"Everything will change now, friend," she finally said. "The Crimson Court didn't charge me and my father after the king tried to sweep all that had happened under the rug. His own arrogance saved us. The brute was unwilling to admit he'd been duped by his own son," she said. "And since Prince Quinten never told anyone you weren't the real Scarlet Strange, it seems your false name still holds. The court believes you're currently wandering the Midnight Forest, even though Ebenezer disappeared. Truly, I don't think they know *what* to make of it all."

"They're a bunch of heartless creeps." I thought of their hollow stares and lack of conviction at the trial. "They let me go in there."

Annabelle grunted from where she was perched atop a stool, braiding my hair.

"Needless to say…" Apple's dark lips quirked when she faced me. "They don't trust us now, even if they can't exactly figure out what we were up to. So, it seems my father and I are out of work for the time being. I wish them well, though. I'll enjoy watching the Reds try to find new Chocolatiers as excellent as us."

"They never will," I swore, giving her all the flattery she was fishing for.

But she smirked. "Perhaps someday, when we sort out a thing or three, we can serve our decadent chocolates to the Trites."

My face changed. She couldn't be serious—Apple in the Trite world? The thought of all her outlandish Rime habits among my people almost made me laugh. But I had to admit, she did a persuasive job at dimming her eyes to brunette.

And it would be nice to finally have a friend at home.

"Anyway, I imagine you'll never touch another plum again," she went on with a chuckle. "It's a sign of affection, you know. I realized you weren't aware of its significance when Quinten handed you one outside your chambers and you took it so fast."

"What's a sign of affection?"

Annabelle laughed. "The *plum*," the dwarf woman snorted. "When a boy likes a girl, he fetches her a sweet piece of fruit. It's a symbol in Winter—a boy passing a single fruit to a girl. Sometimes it's subtle. Sometimes it means nothing, of course, because it happens naturally every now and again. But sometimes... *sometimes* it means a thing." Annabelle poked her head around so I could see her wink.

To my surprise, Apple dunked her finger into the river and lifted it to her brown lips. It dripped down her wrist into her bangle bracelets.

"Huh..." But I wasn't thinking about Prince Quinten, or the plum he'd offered me. My mind went to the orchard at the prince's birthday celebration when the magician had handed me the white apple.

Startled shouts filled the factory's main room when the front doors swung open.

Apple's hand sprang to my wrist as a heavy, dark creature trotted in, fumes from its nostrils filling the entrance with haze.

Patrolmen drew their staffs until the antlered beast turned, revealing Lucas on its back with his impossibly wide grin.

"Kaley! *Winston!*" Their names scratched from my throat as I raced over.

Kaley slid off the reindeer's back, her light-footed dexterity rivalling the boys in raven-black. My sister caught me, but Winston didn't leave his perch. His blond brows furrowed as he looked around at everything—the Patrols sleeping on cots while the snake poison leaked from their blood, the chocolate towers stacked like trees, the gears grinding through the ceiling heights with the butterflies, the machines all humming in unison.

His stare found Zane, somehow, among the crowd.

Then me.

Kaley.

Finally, he lifted his leg and slid off less gracefully than Kaley had, scuffing his jersey. My brother didn't rush to hug me. "How do we get back?" he asked from where he stood half a metre away.

"*Winston,*" Kaley scolded.

Zane appeared, extending a gloved hand to my brother. "Season's greetings."

Winston lifted his chin, flashing his absurd neck tattoo to the room. To my surprise, he shook Zane's hand; a simple, hard shake, then dropped it. "Are you the one she rattled on about last January?" My brother's question was cold.

I might have blushed, but Zane smiled. "I certainly hope so."

Kaley stole a look at Lucas as he tried to sneak past. He shrugged to her in response, and I wondered what nonsense he'd told my siblings about Zane. Nothing good, I imagined, judging by the scowl on my sister's face.

A clock alarm clamoured through the factory as Apple

arrived. "Time to chase the train, friends. Cornelius Britley has a schedule to keep." She held up three brown paper packages tied carefully with ivory string. "Trifles! Gifts to put beneath your Trite tree," she said, and then dug a hand into her robe pocket. "And this. For you, my dear friend. So you remember."

I looked down and blinked at the golden scissors she'd given me once before, with the block letter inscription in the metal. She must have doubled back into the palace to find them after all that had happened. A thin, scarlet bow wrapped the scissors now. A new and old gift at the same time.

"We have gifts to send, too!" Theresa pushed her way into the circle with armfuls of rolled knit blankets in sage ribbons—one for each of us, and an extra for Grandma.

"Not so fast, Leutenski," Zane halted Lucas before he could disappear. Lucas's sheepish, caramel eyes crept back. "I want you to get Helen's beloveds home when we reach the intersect. I have a gift for Helen, too."

My gaze shot up to him, but Zane's mouth only curled.

Lucas snorted a laugh. "Well, ragnashuck, *this* will be awkward."

Kaley folded her arms and looked off when he returned to stand beside her.

"Come on." Zane took my hand in his. "Unless you want to be here when Wanda wakes up. Trust me, she doesn't take goodbyes well," he said.

Theresa was the first to hug me in farewell, followed by a long line of dwarves. And then came Patrolmen I hadn't even learned the names of, some with real tears moistening their eyes as they said goodbye, like we'd known each other forever.

It made me think of what Eliot had said in the palace dungeon about starting to bond to me as my Patrolman, and I wondered if *all* the Patrols had begun to attach themselves to me that way. Zane had said I was in the care of all the Patrols now. Maybe I was.

Young Kilen waved from where he sat at Wanda's bedside, and that triggered wild farewells from the rest of the room.

A heavy weight sank through my chest. These people had fought for me and what I represented, some more than once.

"I want to know their names. They all know mine," I said to Zane. "Who's the boy with pink hair?"

"Timblewon. Mikal helped him escape from under the thumb of a cruel ringmaster. He trained white lions in the circus." Zane pointed to a sleeping, tanned-skinned Patrolman. "That's Silas. He was a beggar in Fogworn when Mikal found him. And that—" he pointed to another broad-chested Patrolman sleeping on his side, his curly, cocoa hair draping over his eyes. He reminded me of Eliot and a pang wedged into my chest. "—that's Stephor. He was training alongside Mirkra to join the Ruby Legion—not by choice—but Mikal made a deal with a Legion Commander for them."

It seemed Mikal had done a lot of work to save a lot of boys. The evidence of his fervour was this room full of beating hearts. I wished I had more time for Zane to tell me their stories.

Oh, the stories. I stole a glance at my Patrolman, imagining listening to his smooth voice recite them. But, another day, perhaps. Another year.

Kaley and Winston waited to my left, eager to get home. Yes, it was time to go.

Only Zane's hand in mine gave me the guts to turn away from this factory, from Apple, from the dwarves, and from the Patrolmen who hadn't woken up yet, and to begin the journey home alongside Lucas and his preposterous reindeer.

Chapter,
The Forty-Second

Lucas hadn't been kidding about the train ride. It *was* awkward in our cabin, until Kaley finally said, "You don't even have blue eyes."

Lucas grinned.

Kaley and miserable Winston sat across from Zane and I, while Lucas was lodged into the corner.

"It's a two-way street, you know," I whispered. Zane turned his head, the grinding of the train's gears hiding my words from the others. "You could come to the Trite world, keep an eye on me there."

I expected him to at least consider it, but he laughed. "Trite, you and I both know I don't belong in the dead world with you dreary, lazy, boring folk."

I shot him a look. "We're not dreary and boring. Or lazy."

"Yes, you are. And I'm none of those things."

It took all my self-control not to roll my eyes.

"You still owe me a story," I reminded him of what he'd said in the woods.

"Ragnashuck, you're right," he seemed to realize.

I wondered how he planned to tell it when time was chasing us home.

Cornelius Britley appeared in the doorway and slouched against the frame. His turquoise coat hung open at the collar where he hadn't fastened the silver buttons, his top hat tucked beneath his arm.

"Peg," he greeted. "Seems you figured out a thing or three." The train conductor didn't elaborate, but his small mouth pinched back a smirk. "Just came to say, 'safe travels.'"

He glanced over at Winston and Kaley, noting all they wore and every feature. "Lots of pegs, then," he realized, nodding as he lifted from the frame. Though, his turquoise eyes lingered on Kaley like he wasn't sure he could call her such a thing.

"Hello," Kaley flashed a pretty smile.

Cornelius replaced his hat and tipped it in return, "Season's greetings, Miss Bell."

Her face changed when he said her name, but Cornelius was already heading away.

When he was gone, Lucas yawned and tousled his dark hair. "He's so stuffy."

All the gifts were tucked beneath Lucas's arms as he skated alongside Kaley and Winston through the busy Waterloo street.

"Tell me," I said as the train pulled away from the platform. "Why hasn't the Patrol trained new Carriers?"

Zane didn't know that I'd talked with the Beast of Nightflesh. That the Beast had told me he'd destroyed the *way*. That he'd vowed to destroy *me*.

"Well," Zane sighed, yanking up his pointed hood. "Because it might require something from you that I don't think you're ready to give, for bloody starters." He tugged his hood back down again, fiddling with the brim.

To stay, I realized. It might require me to stay in Winter.

I closed my eyes in disbelief, grasping why he'd really been trying to convince me since I arrived. It hadn't only been about him wanting me at his side. He'd been testing me to see what I would be willing to do.

"I'll tell you the story, Trite. At least, the start of it." He tugged me to the platform's edge and plopped down to let his feet dangle.

"We don't have time—"

"I'll be done in a pinch."

He pulled a handful of snow from his pocket and tossed it into the air where it formed rolling hills, bright and white.

"In the beginning, Elowin painted Winter. He raised the ice mountains and formed the Rime Folk from the snow. But one rose from among Elowin's greatest guardians, even more powerful than Porethius Plum, if you can imagine that, and challenged Elowin for command of Winter. His name was *Night*."

The snow morphed into two shapes: one a bright torch, the other a shifting, dark moon.

"Night..." I whispered. It felt like ages ago when I'd read that name in a book at the library. Something had been calling me to that story, but I'd lost my chance to finish it.

"Night tried to change the ending that Elowin had set in motion to come. He meant to steal the True King's crown of authority and take Winter under his own wings to control it. But his first plot was overthrown, and Elowin cast him out of the White Kingdom. Night landed on his feet in Winter, where his spirit took on flesh and he turned into a beast. He wandered the snow globe for an age or three, keeping out of sight, trying time and time again to change the approaching end," he said.

The snow before me took on the shape of a young man, as bright as the stars.

"As is written in the Volumes of Wisdom, the ancient prophets of the Truth foresaw three signs that would prove that the painter of Winter—Elowin—would take on Rime flesh and tread upon the snow among us. It was written that he'd raise an army to stand against the Night Beast, who had tempted all creatures since the day he fell to the globe. When Elowin arrived in Winter, these three signs always turned up wherever he went to confirm that he was who he said he was—the True King the prophets foretold was coming," Zane was nearly whispering now.

"Elowin raised the Carriers of Truth to travel across the Winter globe and grow an army of believers. He gave them orbs as tools to teach, filled with the knowledge written in the Volumes of Wisdom. By combining the three signs that followed him, he created the *Triad of Signs*, an instrument which gave us the ability to create more orbs, and thus, more Carriers, so the mission could grow and spread. Seasoned Carriers would take on apprentices and train new Carriers, and so on. But even though they took the Truth across Winter, most of the Rime Folk in power were stubborn and refused to believe. It's why the Folk killed Elowin, even after he'd demonstrated miracles and was proven true by the signs," he huffed. "There isn't time to tell you everything, Helen, but you need to know—"

"Nightflesh destroyed the Triad of Signs," I guessed, remembering the Beast's deep voice coming through Mara Rouge's mouth in that mirror.

"Well, there's a pinch more to it," Zane said. "But yes, Nightflesh scattered the signs across the snow globe and tucked them into places they would never be found."

"I should pass my orb on to someone else," I realized. "The same way Harmony Hucklebunk-Reyes did with me. To someone who will be *in* Winter and can train new Carriers if you find another way to revive the orbs—"

"*You* were called to be this, Helen. I doubted it when I first met you, but I don't doubt it now," Zane said.

I sighed and scrubbed my eyes.

"Besides, the Triad of Signs was the only way to do it, so we can't create new orbs either way," he huffed. "But I wish you could have seen what it was like when we had hundreds of orbs lighting up the dark places in Winter. You saw what happened when you placed your orb in the key room in the season past. And that was just *one* orb," he said. "There used to be enough to make a valley glow."

"But then Mara Rouge hunted them all down and destroyed them." I hugged my arms to myself.

I shall destroy you in the end. Nightflesh's words to me in the mirror. I wanted to tell Zane that I'd spoken to Nightflesh, and that this *Beast* had a plan in place to destroy me. But I couldn't bring myself to spill about it when it would ruin our goodbye. Telling Zane would have to wait until next year, because he'd never let me return to the Trite world if he knew.

The wind changed direction and Zane sprang to his feet. "Anyway, the rest can wait. I can feel ripples growing in the intersect."

He tugged me off the platform and glided us to the field beyond before I could gather my thoughts about his story.

"What are we doing?" I asked, and he bit his bottom lip through a grin.

"Ice dancing."

He stomped his staff in the snow and a garden of hills and icy flowers grew, bending and twisting into a city of frost and petals. Half a dozen snow rabbits rolled out, stirred awake from their naps.

I laughed as Zane's arm came around my waist. I'd missed this—we hadn't had many opportunities to skate over the snow this time around, as opposed to last year when it was almost all we'd done. I wound my arms around his neck to hold on as we took off up a ramp and spiralled off the end.

"You're still a show-off," I called against the wind.

We soared off another incline and I squealed. He slowed us to an easy glide, dimples threatening to show. "It comes easier when I have someone I *want* to show off for," he said.

My laughter subsided as we drifted to a stop. All the

jokes we'd made about it, and the moment he'd confessed his feelings at the Red Kingdom palace came flooding back.

"Zane," I scolded quietly. "You can't say things like that when we're about to be," my hand waved toward Waterloo, "split up."

His jaw flexed, dampening the smile there. "You wanted my truths."

"I drank truthspire before I said that."

"Truthspire makes you tell the truth," he said. "But stop worrying. Trust me, if I wanted to make you *feel* a certain way, Helen, you'd know it."

Behind him, the skies began to pale, the snow sweeping over the fields like a curtain.

It had come too fast—the closing. The thing that would seal off Winter, and Zane along with it. I swallowed as hills in the distance disappeared. I wasn't sure I could let go. Zane held me tighter than he ever had.

"Maybe you can spend this year practicing to be *less* confident," I jabbed.

He leaned his forehead against mine.

"You're bossy, Trite," he whispered. "Perhaps you should spend this season practicing to be less bossy."

I smirked.

He stepped back and pulled something from his jacket. A light pink fruit appeared, outstretched on his palm.

"Until next year," he said, unlatching his staff and holding it at his side like a shepherd. "Merry Christmas, Helen. Or whatever you Trites call your season-end these days."

The wind swept in, tearing up the hills of the field, and the Rime stores tucked within the cracks of the city nearby. Zane's snowy garden began to fizzle away around us.

393

"Merry Christmas!" It barely had time to leave my lips. He tossed the fruit and I miraculously caught it.

Zane smiled and shouted as the snowy hand of the closing intersect began to turn him to dust, "In the season next, I'm going to convince you to stay!"

Then he was gone, swept away with the gale.

A drift of snow trickled over the place where he'd been standing. I ran a hand though the air in front of me but there was nothing left.

Winter felt far away as a river of cold began to trickle into my heart where warmth had just been. I wondered if I'd made a mistake in coming home.

Chapter,
The Forty-Third

C hristmas arrived with the smell of buttery pancakes
and eggnog, mixing with the scent of the fruit Zane
had tossed at me before the intersect closed. I'd
placed it on the kitchen table where it had unpeeled on its
own overnight, transforming into a pink flower with a bulb
centre, and filling the house with a citrusy syrup smell. I'd
laughed when I realized it was a sugarmelon.

I yawned, giving a moan of gratitude when I came into
the living room and Grandma passed me a steaming mug of
coffee. I flashed a smile to my siblings, but it fell when I
realized only Kaley was there.

I scanned the staircase and the hall, but there was no
movement beyond the kitchen and living room. I swallowed

my disappointment and forced another smile.

Grandma pushed her glasses up her nose, making me think of Fred Dough. "So, you're telling me, all these gifts came from *Winter*?" she asked as she hobbled to her rocking chair.

Even though Grandma had always been my biggest advocate, there was still a trace of doubt in her voice. I couldn't blame her—how was she supposed to react to the stories I came home with about a snake-prince, a chocolate factory, and a dark, mocking forest?

Kaley darted to the tree and pulled out one of the dwarves' rolled knits to give to Grandma, who would no doubt use it to keep warm in that old chair. But my sister blinked at the small collection of gifts.

"Helen, there's a new one for you," she said, sliding over a thick rectangle package tied with a ribbon.

I set my coffee on the end table to take the parcel. A small note was stuck to the corner with an address:

MISS HELEN BELL

211 BRINK COURT,
WATERLOO, ONTARIO
(IN THE DEAD WORLD,
MIND YOU)
UNDER THE TREE PLEASE,
IF YOU WOULDN'T MIND

I brushed the ribbon aside to see the return address, but there was only a stamped name: THE LIBRARY.

"Open it!" Kaley ordered, drawing a closed-mouth chuckle from Grandma.

I blinked at the package. Finally, I tore the brown paper away.

A familiar violet tome was inside, one I was sure I'd left on my bedside table in Wanda's room before the library had burned...

I tucked it under my arm sheepishly.

"Who's next?" I asked, even though Kaley and Grandma were waiting for an explanation.

Kaley grunted and dragged the next gift from beneath the tree to read the card. But she paused. "Winston." Her green eyes flickered up to mine. Grandma's did, too. And their faces said all the things none of us had admitted to each other yet.

I moved for my grandmother and sister, taking their hands. It didn't need to be said aloud that Winston wouldn't survive if he broke off from our family.

Gripping each other on Christmas morning, we made a silent commitment in that cold, creaking home, to not give up on Winston. To be three souls who'd fight against the blackness trying to take his.

I didn't pull the violet book out until school started up again. I wasn't sure why I waited so long, but I was sitting in the school library during my lunch hour when the snarling, high voice of Mia Fillard blessed my ears. She appeared past the pages, along with David Boram, who smelled of a sour vaping flavour and an unsustainably large ego.

"I can always count on finding you in the *library*." Along with her acute observation, Mia graced me with a particularly derogatory name she'd crafted up all on her own.

High school.

I took in a deep breath to form a response when hot liquid splashed over my lap and *soaked* the pages of the book beneath my fingers. My gasp was almost silent.

No. She hadn't just…

I blinked.

Brown coffee leaked through the sheets, the treasured paper drinking every drop. My hands trembled as I stared at it.

Mia snorted a laugh, "*Oops.*" She slammed her empty coffee cup on the table in front of me, but all I could see was the soaking Volume of Wisdom in my hands. "Why are you staring at a book without words anyway?"

"What's the matter, Mia? After all this time, you *still* don't know how to read?"

At the sound of the new voice behind me, I stilled.

I'd imagined it. That voice. A voice I didn't expect to ever hear again. I'd blabbed about everything, *everything*, to a body with that voice.

Sweet mother of pearl, I should have stayed in Winter.

Emily Parker rounded the table and sized up her best friend. Then David. Her dark hair was brushed for the first time in well over a year, and she was wearing makeup, transforming her back into the cannibalistic butterfly I remembered from before the day she cracked her head open by the swamp where I'd found her.

Mia's face paled, and David was a statue, telling me this

was the first time they'd seen the once-unconscious girl awake, too.

"Em?" Mia sputtered.

"Oh, I'm sorry. Do you think you still get to call me a cute little nickname after—"

Suddenly, the book in my hands jolted out of my grip. The cover slapped shut, then open again, and all the pages began to flutter as it lifted into the air before us like a bird. The tome paused, leaving even the tyrants before me speechless.

This. Could *not*. Be happening.

The book jerked into a wild shake like a wet dog, spraying flecks of coffee all over Mia, David, Emily, and myself.

Mia screamed first—a high, piercing pitch—then Emily screamed, and then David in his shocking falsetto. So, for the heck of it, I screamed too, fumbling for the book and slamming it down on the table as the whole nerd herd of the student body lifted their noses from their textbooks to see what in the world was going on.

THE
STORYTELLER

EPILOGUE

"'Twas a chilly day in Wentchester Cove, even with the walls of stone countering the roaring winds rushing to seek them out, to kill, to destroy. Within the cove's labyrinth of tunnels, around rows of desks encircling the illuminated sun, sat the court Porethius had commissioned in these last quarters. For, the end was near.

The tunnel curtains ruffled as one ally more entered the congregation, and Porethius caught the eye of Cane Endovan Crimson-Augustus.

Cane's burgundy gaze shot her a knowing look, and the

fairy bristled her wings in response to his tardiness.

The Patrol Elders sat quietly at the back by the Chocolatiers and the Gingerbaker, and the ten plus two dwarves that had come to stand in for the librarians.

By them sat gray-haired Cora Thimble herself—master of keys—alongside Charlie Little, the Choir Director of the underground cathedral. Past the cathedral ministers was another once-prince, Edward Haid—his guardian fairy at his side.

Hidden away in this cove were faces never shown to the other believers until now; flits and gasps of surprise lifted as they realized who had been on their side since the beginning, all working toward the same thing. There were blacksmiths, circus dancers, jelly-legged ice maids, and a quiet, old white bear sitting at the back. There were bird breeders and bookkeepers, tentmakers, shipbuilders, luminaries, and others.

Porethius whistled a tune to call the room to notice.

Cane hopped upon a desk nearby, always just a pinch away. He sent a subtle smirk to the back of the room where Edward Haid seemed to catch it.

When all was quiet, the fairy began, "Nightflesh is building his throne and forming his court—"

"Did you see what the Crimson Court said about us in their publication?!" The tentmaker sprang to his feet, fist clenched around a leaflet of paper. "Are we to sit by and allow them to say such things about us?"

Porethius raised a gentle hand. "In the times to come, they *will* slander us with their publications. They will turn all of Winter against us, for what we believe. But we are not to argue to try to prove them wrong." Porethius lifted her chin. "Nightflesh aims to distract and anger us with these things so that we might rise to defend ourselves. But we cannot get drawn into the fights and opinions of the papers. We are not made for wars of flesh and blood, but for wars in the quiet, fought on our knees in prayer and warsong. We must not turn into giants shouting in the daylight."

"What of an army?" Trevor South also stood from his chair to speak on behalf of the Patrol. "I thought Elowin would have formed one by now, but there's no army outside of this small group."

"I've gathered you for a different reason than to speak of armies," Porethius said.

Cane finally tugged his hood down where he sat, revealing his deep mahogany hair to the gathering. A head or three turned—more than one recognizing the once-prince from his seasons as a Red Prince. A secret kept from most until this moment.

"Nightflesh means to burn the underground libraries, like he burned the Patrol's home," Porethius said, and gasps fluttered about the dome. "We must be wise. Because he will succeed."

"He will *not*," Bertra objected. The dark-skinned dwarf's cheeks blossomed as she looked to those around her. "By the sharpest wind, we are warriors! We will protect the remaining Volumes of Wisdom at any cost!" A roar of agreement and applause came from the dwarves, until a small hand lifted to Bertra's shoulder.

"I do not think the True King's messenger was merely *guessing* at this thing of the future, love." Theresa's soft voice quieted the passion. The woman's knitting rested idly on her lap.

All eyes reverted to Porethius Plum.

"The Beast will act soon. He will aim to destroy every record of Truth, as we have always feared. And he will begin his reign."

"This is blasphemy!" a fisherman cried, thumping his fist upon the desk.

"This is what the ancient prophets of the King of Truth foretold," Porethius corrected. "The Beast will turn some of us, and crush others. Fear will be contagious and will scuttle through the great cities faster than we can squash it."

"Our only hope at preserving the sacred truths—" Cane spoke for the first time, "—is to find a Folk who can keep the Volumes recorded even once the hidden libraries are burned."

He lifted from his desk to face them, drifting to the middle by the glorious golden sphere spinning on its axis. "Edward Haid and I have been studying the Volumes of Wisdom for a measure of seasons, but we've learned we don't have the right minds for it. And even if we send *many* into the hidden libraries to study the verses, Nightflesh will hunt us down here in Winter. His greatest weakness is Elowin's Truth. So, we must keep it where he can't reach it."

"What are you proposing, *prince*?" the fisherman's question was not uttered kindly and the markings on Porethius's skin flared before she could cool them.

Though he was reminded of his past, Cane did not take offense at the fisherman's tone. "I propose we store the Volumes in a mind greater than mine, in one *beyond* Winter's winds. If we know Nightflesh will burn our remaining books, then perhaps we ought to not fight him. Perhaps we ought to use our last measure of time to make a move first."

"You're uttering nonsense." Even Trevor could not see it. "How could we even do such a thing? We're better off to move the Volumes someplace else."

"No, Patrolman," Porethius said. "The Beast *will* burn the records—this does not change if we move them." The fairy's stare darted back to Cane, since this was, after all, his notion.

"A young, common-blooded girl was pulled into the wintersphere this quarter by Nightflesh's current vessel, Asteroth Ryuu. She has a rather unique mind. And somehow, her eyes were opened to our realm this quarter on their own. I've taken that as a sign."

"A Trite?" 'Twas the fisherman, again.

"Yes."

"You want to put the future of our libraries in the hands of a young, common girl?"

Cane nodded, gliding a hand through his rosebud hair. "Our next move *must* be wise, for we will only have time for one move more. I think we ought to hide the Volumes in the dead world, in that unique Trite mind of hers, while we keep Nightflesh distracted here."

"There's just not time," Trevor said, and Porethius's heart sank to find the man's inner spark wrestling to stay lit.

But Cane smiled. "Perhaps. But even so, time is a funny thing."

ACKNOWLEDGEMENTS

First and foremost, this book is dedicated to my daughter, Ellie Lynn; a girl who chases butterflies, picks wildflowers, and who dreams of riding unicorns into the sunset. Before she was born, I prayed that she would be a prayer warrior with mountain-moving faith. So far, I have not been disappointed by those prayers.

God is good. Let's all just take a minute to acknowledge that. Even on the hard days, He knows your heart and your struggles. He hears you when you pray. And He's got a plan even if you can't see it in front of you. So, my next thank you goes to Him. Being an author has been my dream since I was fifteen years old, and He had a plan for me to live that dream.

Frankly, I'd probably still be dreaming about being an author and not actually doing it if it wasn't for my incredibly supportive husband, Phil. Thank you for believing that this was worth it and for moving mountains to make sure this happened for me even when the Covid 19 pandemic threw our lives into a tailspin. These haven't been easy years to step out and publish books, but you made sure it happened anyway. I dig that in a man.

Thank you to my editor, Melissa Cole, for catching all my absurd writing habits, and for being excited about my stories since we were little girls whispering about my top-secret novels at night until we fell asleep. (Well, until *you* fell asleep, and I would just keep talking for another hour before I realized.)

Thank you to all my beta readers: Jennifer Sargent (aka: Author Havana Wilder), Kelly Port, Xantina (aka: Author Hananya Le Clercq), and last but not least, the brutally honest and mind-blowingly brilliant Jesse Calder, who has been reading my books since the days of Dusty O'Lantern. (Do you remember that first book I wrote about pirates when we were little?)

Thank you to my mother, Sandy, and my mother-in-law, Donna, and to all my family and friends who helped me out in some way this year and therefore allowed this book to exist.

Thank you to my dad, Jay, for reading me books when I was Ellie's age. Thank you to my two sons, Chase and Austin, for possessing the biggest smiles I've ever seen in my life.

Thank you to my church family at Wilmot Centre, and my amazing author friends from all around the world that have been so encouraging since the start of this, and to everyone who's ever left me a review, read my books, or said a kind word. Your encouragement goes so much further than you know!

ABOUT THE AUTHOR

Jennifer Kropf is the Canadian author of *The Winter Souls Series*, and *ICE CREAM: You Scream. We All Scream.* She's the founder of Winter Publishing House, has a mildly unhealthy obsession with books, and hoards a preposterously large mug collection.

Find her on Instagram at @authorjenniferkropf or visit her website at www.JenniferKropf.com to subscribe to her newsletter.